PRAISE FOR

Donut Fall in Love

"The book is a perfect example of how realistic personal stakes—say, your disappointed dad starting a dry but hilarious Twitter account to roast you in public—can feel world-shiftingly large in the right hands." —*The New York Times Book Review*

"Anyone who loves baking and rom-coms will breeze through this flavorful read." —*USA Today*

"A warmhearted romance." —PopSugar

"Jackie Lau's *Donut Fall in Love* has the perfect proportions of emotion, heat, family ties, and romance to make one absolutely delicious treat." —*New York Times* bestselling author Courtney Milan

"Jackie Lau's *Donut Fall in Love* is a quintessential comfort read, full of good, well-intentioned people attempting to navigate complicated family relationships, careers, friendships, and grief. This sexy, thoughtful story will also leave you very (VERY) hungry for donuts, so prepare your baked goods supply accordingly before reading." —Olivia Dade, national bestselling author of *Spoiler Alert*

"Full of delicious food, relatable emotions, and a satisfying happily ever after, *Donut Fall in Love* is a real treat." —*New York Times* bestselling author Vivian Arend

"You'll be rooting for Ryan and Lindsay. Their romance is like the best donut: a sweet, light confection wrapped around a rich, complex center." —*USA Today* bestselling author Jenny Holiday

The Stand-Up Groomsman

JACKIE LAU

BERKLEY ROMANCE
NEW YORK

BERKLEY ROMANCE
Published by Berkley
An imprint of Penguin Random House LLC
penguinrandomhouse.com

Library of Congress Cataloging-in-Publication Data

Names: Lau, Jackie, author.
Title: The stand-up groomsman / Jackie Lau.
Description: First edition. | New York: Berkley Romance, 2022. |
Identifiers: LCCN 2022014621 (print) | LCCN 2022014622 (ebook) |
ISBN 9780593334324 (trade paperback) | ISBN 9780593334331 (ebook)
Subjects: LCGFT: Romance fiction. | Humorous fiction.
Classification: LCC PR9199.4.L3825 S73 2022 (print) | LCC PR9199.4.L3825
(ebook) | DDC 813/.6—dc23/eng/20220401
LC record available at https://lccn.loc.gov/2022014621
LC ebook record available at https://lccn.loc.gov/2022014622

First Edition: October 2022

Printed in the United States of America
1st Printing

Book design by Kristin del Rosario
Interior art: Wedding cake and flowers by Vi-An Nguyen

The
Stand-Up
Groomsman

Prologue

Vivian Liao hated meeting new people.

She wasn't at ease around an unfamiliar face, but over the years, she'd become adept at hiding her anxiety. She didn't hide it behind a friendly smile, though.

Instead, she was cool. Guarded. Deliberate in her words.

It was best to be careful with someone new.

This was a little different, however. The man she was meeting, Melvin Lee—well, she felt like she already knew him. She'd watched every episode of *Just Another New York Sitcom* an embarrassing number of times, plus comedy specials and YouTube videos. He had a certain je ne sais quoi that made him her favorite comedian.

Still, she only knew who he was when he performed, and that was probably very different from who he was in real life. In fact, when Lindsay had suggested this, Vivian hadn't been enthusiastic. Rather, she'd been afraid of shattering the illusion.

But even though she'd done her best to adjust her expectations downward, after watching his hour-long set—and laughing during much of it—she now felt a buzz of excitement. Not that she showed it, of course.

Melvin Lee walked toward the table where she was seated with Ryan Kwok and Lindsay. The two men, who'd been co-stars in

JANYS, gave each other a hearty slap on the back, and then Ryan introduced them to Melvin.

"This is Lindsay McLeod, my baking instructor. And Vivian Liao, her roommate. Ladies, the man who talked your ears off for the last hour is Melvin Lee, as I'm sure you know."

Vivian shook his hand, hoping hers wasn't sweaty, and he smiled at her. He was wearing a brightly colored flowered shirt, which was his thing.

"Pleased to meet you," she murmured.

Ryan Kwok was the classically handsome one. The guy that women—including her roommate—swooned over, though Vivian had always preferred Melvin Lee. And when she'd seen Ryan's latest movie, she'd been more attracted to his co-star, Irene Lai. Pity Melvin hadn't been in that movie.

But today, he was in front of her. In the flesh.

The four of them headed to a quieter table upstairs at the comedy club. Vivian sat at the round table between Lindsay and Melvin. She wondered if Ryan and Lindsay would play footsie under the table. Lindsay might claim there was nothing happening between the two of them, but Vivian suspected that would change soon. She'd seen the way Ryan looked at Lindsay.

"How'd you like the show?" Melvin Lee asked the table.

"You can tell him that he sucked," Ryan said. "It's fine. He can take it."

"I don't know about that, man. My ego is like a fragile glass flower."

Vivian couldn't help chuckling.

"I enjoyed it," Lindsay said. "I'm glad I got the chance to go. Thank you."

"Hey, you've had to put up with this guy here." Melvin gave Ryan a light smack. "You deserve a little high-class comedy in return for your sacrifice, though I'm sure you enjoyed watching him dump those egg whites on his head."

"He told you about that?"

Lindsay and Ryan had met at her bakery, and she was now helping him prepare for his appearance on a celebrity baking show. It sounded like he had more than a few things to learn, but fortunately, amazing baking prowess wasn't required for something called *Baking Fail*.

Melvin put his hands together and looked upward. "Please tell me you have pictures of this. Please."

Lindsay laughed. "Sorry to disappoint you."

"Thank God," Ryan said. "You give anything like that to Mel, and it'll be all over social media in two minutes flat."

So, his friends called him Mel, not Melvin.

"Nah, man," Mel said, "I know you want to keep the whole learning-to-bake thing on the down low for now. I'd just keep them for my own private amusement. Or blackmail purposes. You know, normal shit like that."

"So normal," Ryan said.

Mel laughed before turning his smile to Vivian. "And what about you?"

"It was good." Vivian sipped her drink. "I'd seen most of it before, aside from the part where you pointed out Ryan Kwok in the audience."

"But I'm more charming in person, aren't I? Not sure the Netflix special shows the full extent of my animal magnetism."

"What kind of animal?" Ryan asked. "A skunk? Or will you chirp like a penguin again?"

It was entertaining to watch them interact, unscripted.

"I've seen you in person before, actually," Vivian said. "When you were in Toronto a year ago."

"So you really are a fan." Mel paused. "Wait a second. Vivian Liao. Your name sounds familiar."

"Really?" Vivian couldn't help feeling a little alarmed.

Calm down. He probably just knows someone else with the same name.

He snapped his fingers. "I've got it. You did this, didn't you?"

He showed them all a picture on his phone. A very familiar picture: it was the illustration she'd done of Melvin Lee's character puzzling over his Rube Goldberg machine in *Just Another New York Sitcom.*

He read the signature in the bottom right. "Vivian Liao."

Oh God. Melvin Lee had seen her fan art.

This wasn't something she'd anticipated. Vivian wanted the earth to swallow her up. Or a dragon. Maybe a kraken. Godzilla. Whatever could get her out of this situation the fastest; she was flexible.

"That's pretty cool," Ryan said.

"Where did you get that?" Vivian asked Mel, hoping her voice didn't waver.

"A friend sent it to me. Don't be embarrassed! The show has lots of fans, and you're hardly the only person who's created fan art. Are you an artist? Is that what you do for a living?"

"No, I work in finance."

He made a face. "You're, like, one of those people who make the stock market run? Working for the man and everything?"

This was just getting worse. Embarrassing enough that he'd seen her art—he'd told her not to be embarrassed, but that was impossible. And now he was criticizing her job? He was definitely different up close and personal than he was on TV.

If there was one thing Vivian hated—other than meeting new people—it was being told what to do with her life. She'd spent many years not really living for herself, but those days were gone. Now she lived on her own terms.

"That's not quite how I would describe my job," she said, "but—"

"Why work in finance when you're such a talented artist? Unless finance is your true passion." He grimaced.

"Hey, do you guys want to stay here, or should we head out?" Ryan asked, clearly trying to break the tension. "Bubble tea? Late-night dumplings?"

Mel ignored his friend. "So, what is it, Vivian?"

"I prefer art," she began, "but—"

"You had strict parents who stuck up their noses at something like that? They would have preferred you be a neurosurgeon, but finance or law would be okay, too?"

"Mel," Ryan hissed.

"Or maybe I'm wrong," Mel said. "Maybe you're working toward a different career, just keeping your finance job to pay the bills for now."

"I like my life the way it is," Vivian said, "and I shouldn't have to justify it to you."

"I'm not trying to be an ass—"

"Then you've grossly misjudged your words."

She couldn't believe she was saying this to Melvin Lee, but when he'd criticized her, mere minutes after meeting her for the first time, something in her had cracked. She couldn't remain as cool and collected as usual.

Ryan grabbed Mel's arm. "Mel, she's right, you *are* being an ass. Let's head to the bar and get you another drink or some water."

"No, let me finish. I'm trying to be encouraging."

Vivian practically sputtered. This was Melvin Lee being *encouraging*?

"I made it." Mel pointed at Ryan. "He pissed off his dad and spent a few years working as a barista with only the occasional acting job, but he made it. Why can't you do it, too?"

"Why should art be my dream?" she asked.

"Well, you already said finance isn't your passion . . ."

Ryan hauled Mel out of his chair. "We'll be back in ten minutes, Lindsay." The two of them started walking away.

For a split second, Vivian wondered if Mel was usually like this. Perhaps their conversation had hit on a sore point of sorts for him, although she couldn't see how it would have, and it had gotten him worked up. She knew what it was like for a particular topic to make you act differently from normal.

She quickly dismissed the thought; she wouldn't give him the benefit of the doubt. Melvin Lee was a judgmental ass, and she should have known better than to meet a minor celebrity she'd admired. Now it felt like all the episodes of *Just Another New York Sitcom* had been tarnished. This was why you weren't supposed to meet your heroes.

"Let's leave," Vivian said to Lindsay.

Chapter 1

"I have a great plan for the rest of the afternoon." Mel adjusted his position on the barstool and reached for a piece of marinated tofu with his chopsticks.

Chu's was his favorite bar in Manhattan. Located on a small street in Chinatown, it lacked a proper sign and was never very busy, but somehow, it managed to stay in business. Mr. Chu made great lychee cocktails, which were infinitely better than the nonalcoholic sour plum shit that Ryan was drinking, and the food was good, too. Though Mel came here all the time, he hadn't been here with Ryan in almost a year.

"A great plan?" Ryan said. "Okay, let's hear it."

Mel couldn't help laughing at the skepticism in his friend's voice.

He was right to be skeptical, of course.

"I'm telling you," Mel said, "you're really going to like it."

"Is that so?" Ryan's voice continued to drip with skepticism.

"You know those threads on Twitter that match pictures of you in various outfits to pictures of other things? Like 'Ryan Kwok as Bubble Tea' or 'Ryan Kwok as Cupcakes.' Or 'Ryan Kwok as Vases from the Qing Dynasty.' Maybe 'Ryan Kwok as Poisonous Frogs.'"

"I recall you making one of those threads before. 'Ryan Kwok as Baby Pandas.'"

"There was also one I did of you as raccoons stealing from trash bins."

"How could I forget?" Ryan said dryly. "Okay, what's your brilliant plan?"

"I didn't actually call it *brilliant*."

"But you think all your plans are brilliant."

Mel shrugged casually. "What can I say? I'm a genius."

Behind the bar, Mr. Chu's lips twitched.

"I told your father about this plan," Mel said.

Ryan shook his head. "Of course you did."

"He approved."

"Unlikely. Or if he did, it was just so you'd stop bothering him. You're really talking this up, Mel. Expectations are high."

"Well, it's a 'Ryan Kwok as Donuts' thread. Lindsay will appreciate it."

"That sounds relatively benign for you. I'm disappointed. And relieved, to be honest."

"Ah." Mel held up a finger. "But I'm going to take these pictures myself. I've brought a bunch of different outfits for you"—he held up his knapsack—"and I'm going to make you eat all the donuts. Eight donuts in three hours before you go to the airport."

"You want me to spend the entire flight in the tiny airplane toilet?" But Ryan was chuckling.

"I've planned our route carefully. First up, there's a place in Brooklyn that makes herb-and-bone-marrow donuts."

"Did you say *bone marrow*? In donuts?"

"Then, I hear you like matcha donuts, and these ones are a scary green color. Oh, and they have a wasabi filling. I've brought a lovely shirt for you to wear, and it complements the donuts: a green Hawaiian shirt with palm fronds."

"Are all your donuts savory?" Ryan asked.

"Glad you asked." Mel picked up his phone and flipped through a few pictures. "Behold, the quintuple chocolate donut."

"That doesn't look too bad. I'll eat that one and skip everything else."

"You sure you can manage?" Mel flipped to the next picture, which showed someone's hand next to the donut for comparison—it was about ten times the size of a normal donut. "I've also found a bakery that sells donut sundaes. Pretty excited about those."

"Look, Mel." Ryan scratched the back of his neck. "Much as I'd love to run around New York stuffing my face with donuts, I have something serious to tell you." He pulled a small box out of his pocket and opened it up, revealing an engagement ring.

Mel's instinct was to make a joke and pretend Ryan was proposing to him, but this didn't seem the time for such theatrics.

"You're going to ask Lindsay to marry you?" he asked instead.

Ryan nodded solemnly.

"Congratulations." Mel slapped Ryan's shoulder and ignored the twinge of envy in his chest. He was genuinely happy for his friend.

"Don't congratulate me yet. She has to say yes first."

"But she will. You know that."

"Well, I think she'll say yes, but . . ."

"When are you going to pop the question?"

"Tomorrow." Ryan slipped the ring box back into his pocket.

"I assume you're going to do it in private, just the two of you, rather than live-streaming it from the top of the CN Tower or similar."

"Of course."

Mel slapped Ryan's shoulder again, then caught Mr. Chu's eye. "Hey, could you get us each a glass of sour plum drink? Thanks."

Ryan's eyebrows shot up. "You're going to drink that?"

"To show my support for you," Mel said.

"A great sacrifice on your part."

"Indeed. Unless I end up spitting it all over your clothes."

"I'll be sure to keep my distance."

Ryan walked over to the slightly grimy windows of the bar as though looking for something, which was odd, but Mel didn't make much of it. Perhaps his friend was just lost in thought about his fiancée-to-be.

Mel liked Lindsay. She and Ryan were a good couple.

But why did a sweet, friendly woman like Lindsay have a roommate like Vivian Liao?

It annoyed Mel that he thought of Vivian whenever Ryan mentioned Lindsay. And it didn't make sense. They'd only met twice, and the second time, they'd been polite and distant.

The first time, on the other hand . . .

He'd probably see Vivian again at the wedding. Ah, well. His mouth had a tendency to run away from him, but he supposed he could manage to keep it shut.

As Mr. Chu slid two glasses across the bar, Ryan returned to his seat. Mel lifted his glass and clinked it against Ryan's . . . and then he had a too-big sip of his sour plum drink and almost gagged.

"Jesus," he muttered. "That really is disgusting."

Ryan laughed at his misery, which Mel supposed he deserved.

"Oh, by the way," Ryan said nonchalantly, as Mel was still coughing, "if she says yes, will you be my best man?"

Mel recovered and grinned at his friend. "Of course."

"I have a feeling I might regret this—"

"Don't worry, I'll plan the wildest bachelor party ever."

"That's what I was afraid of."

"Nah, you know I won't make it too over the top. Just a little over the top."

"I know." Ryan leaned forward, and they embraced.

Mel was pulling back when he saw something strange over Ryan's shoulder: a bright pink limo parked in front of the dingy bar.

"Right on time," Ryan said.

"Didn't think that was your style, but . . ." Mel trailed off as a familiar figure stepped out of the limo. Was that Po Po?

Strangely, Ryan didn't seem shocked by this development.

Mel's grandma shuffled into the bar, and Mel rushed over to meet her. "What are you doing here?"

"Why are you greeting me like that? You should say, 'Hello, Po Po, so nice of you to visit me.'" She turned to Ryan. "Everything is going as planned."

Were his grandmother and Ryan up to something? He shot his friend a questioning look.

Ryan shrugged. "This is payback."

Those were some terrifying words.

"Payback for all the times you stole my phone," Ryan clarified, "and posted weird polls on my Twitter account and called my father. Payback for—"

"Okay, okay," Mel said. "I get it."

"You will *love* this surprise," Po Po said with an enthusiasm she usually saved for karaoke and reusing Ziploc bags. She grasped Mel's arm and led him toward the door. "Have a good flight to Toronto, Ryan."

"Thank you. Remember to send me the video."

The video?

Mel helped Po Po into the limo and climbed in after her. He wouldn't mind being chauffeured around the city in a pink limo— after all, attention and bright colors were kind of his thing. But the surprise was clearly about more than the vehicle.

Indeed, inside the car were three people he'd never seen before, plus his little sister, Joy.

Despite her name, Joy wasn't really, well, joyful. As usual, she was clad entirely in black; unlike usual, she was sporting a smile. Though perhaps that smile was a bit . . . evil?

She held up her phone.

"What is this?" he asked. "Some kind of *Just for Laughs* gag?"

Po Po sat down and lifted up a sign that said: "Po Po's Speed Dating."

The limo started moving. Mel was trapped.

"Meet your prospective dates," Joy said in her signature bored voice. She gestured at the three strangers—two women and one man.

Two of them looked just as unhappy to be here as Mel was, but one of the women was smiling as though she were looking forward to this.

It wasn't that Mel objected to dating. He had a somewhat active dating life, and not just because it provided good inspiration for his comedy. He enjoyed going out and meeting people. Though for whatever reason, his relationships tended not to last long or be too serious.

He did, however, object to dating people his grandmother had picked out for him.

Five years ago, Po Po had set up Mel's older sister with the grandson of one of her mahjong buddies, and against all odds, they'd hit it off and gotten married.

A very unfortunate development.

Sure, Mel was happy for his sister, but Po Po still bragged about that as though it had happened yesterday, and she fancied herself a good matchmaker.

And now Po Po was turning her focus to Mel. That wasn't a surprise; if anything, he was shocked it had taken this long.

Po Po gestured at the three East Asian strangers seated across from Mel. "The woman on the left is Cindy."

Cindy briefly nodded in his direction. "Hi."

Undeterred by the lack of enthusiasm, Po Po continued, "Cindy

works as a pharmacist. Also a brilliant pianist and tennis player."
She turned her attention to the man in the middle. "Next is Felix.
I hear he has many tattoos. Maybe he can show you later."

Felix didn't even blink at Mel's octogenarian grandmother talking about his tattoos, but Mel wasn't as calm. "Po Po!"

Po Po ignored his outrage. "Felix is a banker. Respectable job,
yes?"

A banker. Annoyingly, that reminded Mel of a certain woman
who worked for a bank. It also reminded him of his first couple of
years after college, when he'd had a job that required him to be
somewhat respectable—not really his thing.

"His grandma says he makes excellent dumplings," Po Po added.

That made Felix a little tempting, but . . .

No.

Po Po gestured to the last woman, the only one who seemed
excited about this. "This is Aubrey."

"Hi, Melvin!" she said, holding out her hand, which he shook
rather limply.

"Aubrey is a researcher in Joy's lab," Po Po said.

Oh God. That meant she liked creepy-crawlies.

"But I found Cindy and Felix myself." Po Po sounded quite
proud of this accomplishment. "Cindy is the granddaughter of my
friend at the karaoke club. Felix is the grandson of another friend.
See? I even found you a man."

"Yes, I can see that," Mel said.

"You are thirty-four." Po Po shook her finger at him.

"I know how old I am." He didn't usually get this annoyed at
his grandmother, but then again, she didn't usually hold him hos-
tage in a limo of prospective spouses.

Because he knew Po Po's next sentence would involve marriage.

"It's time you get married!" she said. "Way past time. You like all genders, so it should be easy for you to find someone. Do not understand why it's taking so long."

Cindy shot him a sympathetic look. Likely she had to deal with similar comments from her own family, but he hoped for her sake that her friends weren't assisting her family—which sadly didn't appear to be the case for him.

"Ryan was in on the whole thing?" Mel asked.

"Yes," Po Po replied. "Very kind of him, wasn't it?"

"I'm going to hack into his Twitter account," Mel muttered, "and post all sorts of embarrassing stuff."

"He said he would keep you at Mr. Chu's until we arrived in style."

Joy snorted.

"Aiyah!" Po Po shouted. "Pink limo is very stylish. Are you saying you prefer a black limo covered in bugs?"

"Definitely." Joy turned to Mel. "How does it feel to have the tables turned for once? Usually, you're the attention-seeking middle child who's hell-bent—"

"I wouldn't say *hell-bent.*"

"—on playing pranks and getting on everyone's nerves. And now you're having it done to you." Joy was still holding up her phone, presumably filming the whole thing.

"As though you've never done anything to get on my nerves?" he asked. "You released your ant colony in my bedroom!"

"I was six. It was an accident, and I was just as upset about it as you were. I'd put a lot of work into that colony."

"And now you've moved on from ants to—"

"Stop arguing!" Po Po said. "Not much time. Mel needs to talk to Cindy, Felix, and Aubrey. Not to you, Joy. The trip to Queens shouldn't be too bad right now, so ten minutes for each date, yes? I supply the drinks." She pulled out a bottle of champagne.

"Here, let me open that for you," Felix said.

She handed it over then winked at Mel. "You see? He's so thoughtful!"

Well, Felix was probably just concerned about what disaster might occur if Po Po attempted to open the bottle.

But as aggravating as this whole situation was, Mel did feel a moment of gratitude for the fact that Po Po had been so accepting when he'd come out. He'd expected his father to handle it better than his maternal grandmother, but he'd been very much mistaken. (To be fair, he'd been mistaken about a lot of things as a teenager.)

"Ooh, I'll go first!" Aubrey said, shifting toward Mel. "I've watched every episode of *Just Another New York Sitcom*, plus your Netflix special!"

Oh no. She'd probably expect him to be *funny*.

Yes, his Netflix special was good, but he hadn't just gone up there and spewed out any old thing that came to mind. No, it had taken lots of careful preparation.

And he might generally be a funny dude, but he just wasn't feeling it now. Seriously, who wanted to do speed dating under the watchful eyes of their grandmother and little sister? His donut plan with Ryan had been much better than this—and nowhere near as cruel.

"Uh, thanks," Mel said, not bothering to attempt a joke now.

Cindy interrupted his so-called date with Aubrey. "Was that Ryan Kwok in the bar with you?" she asked, leaning forward.

"Yeah, he's in New York for a few days," Mel replied.

Cindy looked like she was drooling at the thought of Ryan, which wasn't surprising. After all, there had been a hashtag about his abs on social media. Mel, on the other hand, was the shorter, fatter, funnier sidekick. Not that he was jealous. He was pretty happy with things as they were. Well, he waffled between arrogance and insecurity, but that averaged out to something reasonable, didn't it?

Hmm. Perhaps Cindy had only agreed to this speed-dating thing because of his friendship with Ryan.

Or because her own grandmother had strong-armed her into it. Maybe she'd sung Céline Dion off-tune at the top of her lungs until Cindy had agreed.

Mel didn't say that out loud. He didn't want to give his grandma any ideas.

"I made your favorite, Mel! Do you mind if I call you Mel?" Aubrey didn't give him time to answer. "That's what your grandma says everyone calls you." She pulled a bag of cookies out of her purse, just as Felix handed Mel a plastic cup of champagne.

Now this was getting a little better. Cookies and champagne.

But as he reached for a cookie, he noticed it was chockful of—

"Oatmeal raisin cookies with extra raisins!" Aubrey said brightly.

If there was one thing Mel didn't like, other than surprise dates arranged by his grandma, it was raisins in his food. He even had a bit about raisins in potato salad that he performed onstage. Joy must have made a point of claiming he liked such cookies, knowing Aubrey would latch on to it, just to piss him off further.

Not wanting to be too rude to a stranger, Mel grabbed a cookie, took a bite, and managed not to grimace as he inwardly cursed his family. Even if there was no traffic—ha!—it would be a long, long drive to Queens.

Aubrey chattered as he gulped his champagne and tried not to look too unhappy to be talking to her. Their "date" was better than the one with Felix, however. Felix didn't seem inclined to talk much at all, replying to Mel's forced questions with brief answers, and Mel could hardly stand it. This situation was growing more awkward by the second . . . and his final speed date would be with a woman who was clearly more enamored with one of his best friends.

One day, he hoped to have what Ryan and Lindsay had, even if long-term relationships had eluded him up until now, but he certainly wasn't going to find it in this limo.

· · · · · · · ·

The next night, Mel was up late, notebook in hand, when his phone beeped. He looked at his message from Ryan.

> RYAN: She said yes!
>
> MEL: Congrats, man. I'm happy for you.
>
> RYAN: So you'll be my best man?
>
> MEL: Of course
>
> MEL: Even though you were part of Po Po's speed dating.
>
> RYAN: There's just one little problem . . .
>
> RYAN: Lindsay is going to ask Vivian to be a bridesmaid.

Chapter 2

That Monday, after a long day of work, Vivian was sitting in bed and drawing on her iPad. She'd outlined Dean Kobayashi in a cowboy hat and was now working on his trusty horse, but when she heard a key in the lock, she put down her iPad and headed out to greet her roommate.

"Vivian!" Lindsay beamed as she thrust her hand in Vivian's direction.

Why . . . ?

It took Vivian a few seconds to comprehend what she was seeing. Then warmth spread through her chest as she lifted Lindsay's hand and examined the ring.

"Congratulations." Vivian tried to sound excited. She truly was pleased for her roommate.

The problem was that she'd never been the sort of person who naturally expressed excitement, who was prone to anything but mild reactions, and sometimes that got her in trouble. She heard her sister's voice in her head, after Amanda had gotten into her university of choice. *You're not happy for me?*

But Lindsay didn't seem bothered by Vivian's mild reaction and lack of squeeing. She slipped off her shoes and admired her ring. It was classy and understated, probably different from what some movie stars would buy for their partners.

"How did he propose?" Vivian asked.

"He made me a nice dinner last night. For dessert, he brought out a cake that said 'Will you marry me?' on top, and he dropped down on one knee . . ." Lindsay covered her mouth with her hand and giggled.

"And then you spent the next twenty-four hours in bed?"

"Stop it! We . . . well . . . Yeah, maybe we did."

"Did he make the cake himself?"

"Yes! Let me show you." Lindsay took out her phone and pulled up a picture of a chocolate cake. It wasn't as fancy as some of the things Lindsay made at Kensington Bake Shop, but it was a solid effort.

"Did it taste good? Or were you too busy kissing him to try it?"

"We ate it, of course. I mean . . . not for a few hours. But we did."

When Vivian had first discovered *Just Another New York Sitcom*—unfortunately, after the show had already been canceled—she'd immediately become a big fan. She'd certainly never imagined that she'd ever meet Ryan Kwok and Melvin Lee, and that her roommate would marry one of them.

"I have something to ask you," Lindsay said, a little more serious now. "Will you be one of my bridesmaids?"

Vivian's lips parted slightly in surprise. She didn't have a lot of friends, and in her thirty-four years, it had never occurred to her that anyone would want her to be a bridesmaid. Some people were always the bridesmaid and never the bride, but she'd never been either.

If someone had asked for Vivian's hand in marriage, she would have broken out in a cold sweat; in contrast, now that she'd gotten her head around the idea, she liked the thought of being in her roommate's wedding party.

Lindsay seemed to take Vivian's slow response as uncertainty, however. "I won't be a bridezilla, I promise, and you won't have to wear a horrid dress—wait, are you comfortable wearing a dress? I've never seen you wear one before."

"I'll wear a dress, and I'd be happy to be your bridesmaid."

"There's something I should you warn you about, though." Lindsay paused. "Mel will be Ryan's best man."

Right. Vivian hadn't considered that—she'd only known Lindsay was engaged for five minutes, after all—but it wasn't a shock.

"I know you two don't get along," Lindsay said, "and it's not like you'll be forced to spend tons of time together, but you'll see him a bunch. Is that okay? He's always been nice to me. I don't know why he was such a jerk to you."

"I think I can manage, as long as he behaves himself."

"Thank you! I'm sure Ryan will give him a stern talking-to. By the way, Ryan saw Mel in New York, and Mel's grandmother surprised him by arriving in a pink limo full of prospective dates."

Vivian couldn't help chuckling at the thought of Mel being forced to endure setups from his grandmother. Served him right for being judgmental.

"I've got to make some calls," Lindsay said.

"Have you told your mom yet?"

"Yep, she's already sending me pictures of wedding dresses. Noreen knows, too, but nobody else. Got a bunch more people to tell before we make the news public, and then I'll avoid the internet so I don't see any terrible comments."

Lindsay skipped off to her room, and Vivian made herself some tea before returning to her own room. She picked up her iPad, but for some reason, she wasn't in the mood to draw pictures of *Only the Best*, which had become her obsession after Melvin Lee had ruined *Just Another New York Sitcom* for her.

Instead, she found herself googling him, something she did every few months. She watched a video from a comedy festival and hated herself for laughing. Why did she still find him funny?

She returned to the search results and discovered he was doing a couple of shows in Toronto next month, and against her better judgment, she ordered a ticket.

What was wrong with her? She didn't like the man.

And what if he saw her in the audience?

No, she'd sit at the back, and surely the venue would be big enough that she'd escape his notice.

She'd just cleared her browser of all evidence of Melvin Lee—though that wouldn't erase the ticket she'd bought—when her phone buzzed.

> Hey, can you lend me a hundred bucks?
> I'll pay you back.

She rolled her eyes at the text from Andy. Her brother was terrible with finances and had recently gotten another tattoo. Not that Vivian had anything against tattoos, though she'd never get one herself, but if you were regularly running out of money to pay your bills, perhaps it wasn't the smartest decision. Also, his tattoos were hideous and offended her artistic sensibilities.

And he always said he'd pay her back, but he never did.

She felt responsible for the fact that Andy seemed to be bad at adulting. He was only a year and a half younger than her, but she still felt like she should have done a better job of parenting him, as she'd done for her younger siblings.

Vivian was the good daughter. The one who could always be counted on, who'd never really been allowed to be a child.

But now she could spend her free time doing frivolous things like shopping for clothes she didn't need, binge-watching TV shows about Japanese cowboys, and drawing fan art. Even attending comedy shows featuring asshole comedians.

She had the freedom to do that shit because she'd worked hard to get where she was, though she wouldn't deny there had been some luck as well.

She had a good job at one of the banks on Bay Street. Not the best she could get, but she was fortunate that this one allowed her a decent work-life balance. She had money to spend on fabulous clothes . . . and to occasionally give her brother a hundred bucks without it hurting her.

I'll send it to you tomorrow, she texted.

Thanks, Viv, you're the best.

She made a face. Andy was the only one who called her "Viv," and he only said nice things to her when he wanted something.

She set a reminder on her phone to send him the money, then went to her closet to pick out her work outfit for tomorrow. Slim gray pantsuit, white blouse, stilettos, pearl drop earrings. She enjoyed getting dressed up for work every day.

Her phone buzzed again.

Let's go shopping this weekend!

Vivian sighed. Somehow, it was easier to deal with Andy's requests for money than Amanda's requests to hang out. Amanda made Vivian irrational and unable to control her bitterness, even if Amanda had merely sent her an innocent text.

The two of them didn't have a sisterly relationship. Amanda, the youngest child, was more than ten years younger than Vivian.

Vivian had always felt more like a third parent; this was even more true with Amanda than with Andy and Stephen. It wasn't because her parents had needed to work so hard to put food on the table; they'd lived fairly comfortably. Rather, Ma and Ba had been committed to being the perfect employees, hoping for raises and promotions at their office jobs.

As a result, there were many things that had been delegated to Vivian. So many things that she'd been forced to deal with because otherwise nobody would have done it, and she'd often felt resentful.

And little Amanda had been great at pushing her to the end of her rope.

Vivian remembered cutting up Amanda's bananas into circular slices, at Amanda's request . . . and then her little sister had thrown an absolute fit because she'd decided she wanted something else. Vivian also remembered hopelessly explaining to Amanda that she couldn't swim in the lobster tank at a restaurant. In frustration, fourteen-year-old Vivian had said the lobsters would bite off Amanda's toes, and Amanda had had nightmares for a week.

The toddler years had been the worst, especially since they'd had to share a room.

But now, Amanda was grown up. She'd moved back to Toronto a few weeks ago for grad school, and this wasn't the first time she'd texted Vivian about hanging out. Vivian shouldn't keep dodging her sister's attempts to connect, but she couldn't seem to help it. Hearing from Amanda brought up so many things she'd prefer not to think about.

After setting her phone on silent, Vivian changed into her pajamas. Gray with pink piping—yes, she liked the color gray. Then she picked up her e-reader. She was reading a fantasy novel inspired by Chinese mythology, and she'd been quite enjoying it.

Except tonight, she couldn't concentrate.

Her roommate was getting married! She was going to be a bridesmaid for the first time! Her little sister wanted to go shopping with her! She had tickets to see a comedy show! Her picture of Dean Kobayashi was her best yet!

Ugh, just putting exclamation marks in her thoughts—let alone sounding excited when she spoke—was exhausting.

She should be in a good mood, even if Andy needed more money. Lots of great things were happening, and it frustrated her that her feelings weren't quite logical.

Maybe you're jealous of Lindsay.

Nah, it wasn't like she wanted Ryan Kwok for herself, and it wasn't like she ever wanted to get married—Jared Barnes had cured her of the desire for a long-term relationship. Better to simply admire beautiful people like Dean Kobayashi from afar rather than meet them and have them judge her life.

She willed Melvin Lee to stop taking up so much space in her brain, but he never seemed to listen. Just as he hadn't listened when she'd met him in person.

Fortunately, when she finally fell asleep that night, she didn't dream of Melvin Lee.

Instead, she dreamed of a lobster who was wearing a sunshine-yellow (the absolute worst color, in Vivian's opinion) bridesmaid dress and eating twenty-three-year-old Amanda. Amanda was clutching a banana plushie and, bizarrely, yelling about the fact that the banana plushie wasn't sliced up, not the fact that she was being eaten by a giant lobster in a dress.

· · · · · · · ·

"Bye, Lindsay. I'm heading out," Vivian said in an unnaturally cheerful voice.

Lindsay waved from her position in front of the TV. "Okay, have fun!"

Yesterday, Vivian had told Lindsay that she was having drinks with a friend from high school tonight. Somehow, Lindsay hadn't been at all suspicious, even though Vivian rarely went out for drinks with anyone.

But she felt weird about telling her roommate the truth.

Yeah, I kind of hate the man, but for some reason, I got tickets to his show . . . Lindsay would probably tease her.

Vivian hadn't wanted a roommate, but it would be tough to afford her mortgage without one. This hadn't been the plan when she'd bought the place, of course. She and Jared were supposed to be living together, but after he'd gotten mad at her for "nagging" him to empty the dishwasher—when she'd done all the cooking for weeks!—she'd snapped.

That hadn't been the deeper reason they'd broken up, just the last straw. Really, it was more because he'd assumed she'd change her mind about not wanting children, and he'd been perturbed when she'd started questioning her sexuality.

Vivian had been a little cold and guarded with Lindsay at first, as was her nature, but they'd gradually become friends.

As she walked to the subway, something occurred to her. Lindsay would live with Ryan once they were married, wouldn't she? They were looking at getting married in the winter—because it fit in Ryan's schedule, and they didn't want to wait more than a year—so there were still more than six months. But perhaps Lindsay would move in with him before then, though surely she would have told Vivian if that were the case.

Damn. Vivian hated the idea of having to find a new roommate. It was stressful. Perhaps she'd sell the place instead and get something smaller.

She obsessed about it on the subway ride to Eglinton, but when she got off the train, she told herself to forget about the issue until tomorrow.

The show wasn't until ten, and it was only eight now. She was right on schedule.

Vivian headed to a Japanese soufflé pancake shop that she'd been meaning to try and managed to grab the last table. If people wanted to judge her for eating alone, let them. Unlike Melvin Lee, she was sure they wouldn't be rude enough to say anything to her face. She knew she looked fabulous, and it was actually quite nice to be alone as she waited for her food. She didn't have to listen to, say, Jared complaining there was nothing he wanted to eat.

Vivian had looked at the menu numerous times before coming here, so she knew she was getting the soufflé pancakes with blueberry sauce and cream. She'd always been a sucker for anything with blueberries. Blueberry cheesecake, for example.

The fluffy pancakes were as delicious as the online reviews had suggested. She savored them and drank her tea. After wandering around the area and taking a few random pictures, she headed to the comedy club, her heart beating a little fast, as though *she* were the one who'd be performing.

Maybe she'd just head home . . .

No. As ridiculous as it was, she'd bought a ticket. She wasn't going to waste money by not going, and although she was nervous, she was also looking forward to this. It had been a while since she'd seen any kind of live performance, and she wouldn't actually have to interact with Melvin Lee. She'd just enjoy his set and see him as a comedian, rather than someone who was critical of her life choices.

The venue was smaller than expected. She ordered a glass of wine and sat at a table near the back with another single woman. They smiled at each other before returning to their phones.

There were three comedians performing today, all Asian. The first guy, the emcee, did a short set before introducing the second comedian, a guy with deadpan delivery. They were both decent, but they weren't the reason Vivian was here.

Finally, it was time for the headliner.

Melvin Lee, wearing an utterly ridiculous dress shirt with sunshine-yellow flowers—why did Vivian find his awful fashion sense charming?—stepped onstage.

Chapter 3

"The problem with being a comedian," Mel said, "is that people expect you to be funny."

He paused. There were some laughs.

"If you're an actuary, people don't expect you to talk about actuarial shit in your free time, right? In fact, they really, really don't want you to. And if you're a plumber, nobody wants you to talk about literal shit and sewage at a party. At least I hope not. If they do, you know some pretty weird people. Maybe your friends expect you to fix their toilet for free—that could be annoying, I admit—but they don't want you to actually *talk* about it."

He walked to the other end of the small stage. He had a soft spot for this place. It was where he'd done his first international show, and little had changed here in the past eight years.

It was reassuring when certain things didn't change.

"My little sister is an entomologist," he said. "Let me tell you, that's another thing people prefer you don't talk about. En-to-mol-o-gist." He exaggerated each syllable. "If you're nodding along, pretending to know what the fuck I'm talking about, she studies bugs. And unfortunately for me, she likes talking about bugs. Specifically, beetles. I've heard more about insects in the past twenty-five years than I ever needed to know. This girl has been hooked on bugs since she was a fucking toddler.

"Most kids go through phases. They might be obsessed with princesses or unicorns. Maybe wrestling—I admit I was one of those kids. Unicorns, princesses, wrestling, firefighters, LEGO. Wearing your underwear on your head in public. You know, normal shit like that. I did it, and I bet you did, too.

"Anyway, my sister was obsessed with bugs, and it wasn't just a phase. She's now twenty-seven, and she's doing a PhD."

One person clapped.

"Yeah, that's right! Give her a round of applause. I'm proud of her. I just wish she didn't talk about beetles all the time while we suffer in silence. By which I mean, we do not suffer in silence, not one bit. We tell her that beetles aren't appropriate conversation for dim sum. Last week, she started talking about redheaded cockchafers—yes, that's a type of beetle—and my mom choked on her har gow.

"Me, however? I'm a comedian, and people expect me to be funny all the time, even when I'm not working. It's especially bad when I'm meeting someone new. I feel the pressure of a thousand cockchafers on my . . . Well, let's change it to a hippo on my chest instead. Cockchafers sound pretty painful. Though hippos are quite deadly—did you know that? They may be cute and chonky but they're fucking dangerous.

"Anyway. I feel this hippo-size pressure to be funny." Mel then changed his voice to what he imagined the burly white dude at the front, who was drinking crappy Canadian beer, sounded like. "'But, Melvin!' you cry. 'That's just what comedians do. They're supposed to make people laugh. What the fuck am I doing at your show? Learning about the dangers of hippos?'" He walked across the stage. "I actually do like trying to be funny. Most of the time. People's laughter is like a drug to me. Like meth or cocaine . . . or

an antacid. Or those brownies your auntie made that definitely
didn't have anything special in them." He made a show of winking.
"Seriously, ever heard about how comedians are depressed? It's a
thing. Funny people are fucking depressed. Getting up here and
making people laugh is the only thing that's preventing me from
holing up in my bedroom for a month, eating nothing but wasabi
peas and binge-watching some terrible sitcom about three dudes
sharing a tiny apartment in Brooklyn." He paused. "Okay, you were
supposed to laugh there, not think about your own miserable lives.

"But like I said, comedians, we're not always the happiest people.
And sometimes, when I'm not onstage, I don't want to be funny, you
know? I'm a person, too, just like all of you in the audience. Except
you." He pointed to the club owner in the back corner. "I think
you're an alien disguising yourself in human form. Maybe somebody
can check that out later. Anyway, my point is, there are times I feel
like shit and I'm not in the mood to make the effort to be funny. Like
after a breakup, I just want to cry, eat chocolate, and tenderly stroke
my human-size Pokémon plushie. You know how it is." He had a sip
of his water. "I'm bi, which is *great*, let me tell you. I've got, like, twice
as many people to screw up with. What could be better?"

The next bit was about dating, and he'd done it a zillion times
before. He had the timing down to the millisecond. But today,
something was different. There was a weird prickling sensation on
the back of his neck. The crowd didn't energize him the way it usually did, and his mind briefly wandered to the time he'd been in
Toronto last summer. To a particular woman. What would she find
funny? And why did he care?

"You know what I want to do one day?" he said, pushing aside
those thoughts. "Write a book. I know, I know, it's not very origi-
nal. Lots of comedians write books. But I don't want to write a
collection of humorous essays about online dating, being Asian, or

the year I spent running around with underwear on my head. No, I want to write a novel about time travel.

"Yes, that's right. Time travel. In part because I loved *Back to the Future* when I was a kid. I had a phase where I watched that movie every day and would recite scenes at the dinner table, which my parents didn't mind because it was better than my act-like-a-Teletubby phase. That might have been cute if I was four, but the show didn't air until I was . . . sixteen. Just kidding. I was ten.

"But back to time travel. It's fucking hilarious, don't you think? Just imagine Einstein using a smartphone, maybe ordering curly fries on Grubhub at three in the morning. Or Abraham Lincoln on Instagram. Cleopatra on TikTok. When I get bored, I think about famous people throughout history discovering we have these powerful, handheld devices that we use to watch cute videos of baby goats and pandas. Or videos of people cutting into random objects and discovering they're actually cake.

"Now imagine, I don't know, a Viking. A big Scandinavian dude wearing a helmet with horns, who spends his life pillaging and sailing the high seas, walking around New York. What would he think of the tall buildings? Would he ram his helmet into them?" Mel did an act-out in which the Viking tried to commandeer the Staten Island Ferry and was absolutely blown away by giant pretzels.

"Maybe the Viking isn't drawing all that much attention because in New York, people are used to some weird shit. But let's say there's another dude from the past wandering around, and he notices the Viking. Let's call him, I don't know, Shakespeare." Mel performed his imitation of the Bard, totally perplexed by movie theaters and taxis.

"Would Shakespeare have been a great writer if he'd lived in the modern age? Or would he have wasted all his time trolling people on Twitter and playing *Stardew Valley*? And yes, you may have noticed that the Viking and Shakespeare have the same accent. I tend to imagine all old people had British accents." He paused. "This is just my way of saying I'm absolute shit at accents. So, let's say we've got a Viking and Shakespeare wandering the streets of New York together. For fun, let's also add a Samurai." He transitioned to another act-out, this one of the Samurai wielding his sword, trying to fight a double-decker tourist bus, then nearly chopping off Shakespeare's head. Naturally, the Samurai also had a British accent.

Mel had just finished swinging his imaginary sword when someone caught his eye at the far end of the room. That figure was remarkably familiar, even though he didn't know her well.

Vivian Liao.

Vivian had come to his show?

Convinced he must be seeing things, he mentally shook his head—it wouldn't do any good to actually shake his head, as it didn't fit with his performance. Vivian had supposedly been a fan of his, once upon a time, but she wasn't anymore. It made no sense for her to be here. He must have just imagined it because he'd been thinking about her a few minutes ago.

Mel wouldn't let himself be rattled. He continued with his set. "So, a Viking, a Samurai, and Shakespeare walk into a bar in twenty-first-century New York. You see what I'm saying about time travel? It's hilarious. I don't even have to say much. Just imagine a Viking, a Samurai, and Shakespeare sitting at the bar, all on their smartphones. Maybe the Samurai is jealous that Shakespeare has more Twitter followers than he does. Or maybe they see a football game on TV, and they're trying to figure out what on earth American football is. And what on earth a TV is, too. One of them orders a giant strawberry daiquiri—that's just what this scene needs, right?"

He glanced at the back of the room. It couldn't be Vivian, right?

But it sure looked an awful lot like her. Perhaps it wasn't his imagination after all.

"You know what else this scene needs? A Chinese grandmother. A Chinese grandmother walks into the bar with her thirty-four-year-old bisexual comedian grandson—no idea who that could possibly be, I just made him up—and she senses an opportunity. There's a funny-looking white guy with a big lacy collar drinking a strawberry daiquiri. Surely, she thinks, this man couldn't possibly be straight. Why doesn't she set him up with her grandson? So, she walks over and taps him on the shoulder, and when he turns around, she recognizes him. It's Shakespeare! She knows he wrote some famous plays, and she knows he died a long time ago, but she doesn't question what he's doing here. She just continues on with her plan.

"Her first choice for her grandson might be a proper Chinese girl, but he's getting old and she's desperate now. After all, she still has to find a match for his sister, who studies redheaded cockchafers. A white writer dude will do. She taps him on the shoulder again and says . . ." Mel adopted the posture and voice of his grandmother. "'You like to marry my grandson?'"

As he said that, he looked to the back of the room again, and he recognized the way the woman's body shook when she laughed.

It was definitely Vivian Liao.

• • • • • • •

Vivian was laughing in spite of herself. A part of her had wanted to glare at Mel from the corner, but he hadn't been her favorite comedian for no reason.

A lot of it was the delivery. If she saw some of his jokes written down, maybe she wouldn't even think they were funny, and if she said exactly the same words as Mel did, nobody would laugh—or they'd just laugh at how awkward and stuck-up she sounded. But there was something about his charisma, his timing, his energy . . .

She wanted to draw him performing like this.

Annoyed at the impulse, she clenched her hands. In the past, she'd only drawn Mel as his character in *JANYS*, and she'd stopped making fan art of that show after their infamous meeting.

"White people are weird." He walked across the stage. "Like, white people think Asian people are weird, because some of us enjoy stinky tofu—or just tofu in general—and we actually season our food. But do you know how many times white people have asked if I eat dogs? How many times people have greeted me with 'konichiwa' after hearing me speak English with an American accent? How many times, after saying I was born and raised in Queens, people have asked where I was *really* from? Or asked where my parents were from and argued—yes, fucking *argued* with me—when I told them my parents were born in the US? Asian people didn't magically appear for the first time in North America in 1970. It's not like, I don't know, Shakespeare, a Viking, and a Samurai suddenly appearing in a New York bar in the twenty-first century."

Not for the first time, Mel looked in Vivian's direction.

She had a foolish urge to cover her face.

"I'm telling you," he said, "white people are fucking weird. They complain that a single sprinkle of black pepper makes food too spicy. Or they cook tofu in the most unappetizing way possible, so it's like cardboard, then complain it doesn't taste good." He made a face. "That was my surprised Pikachu face, in case you couldn't tell from way at the back."

When he pointed at the back of the room, Vivian felt like he was pointing right at her and everyone in the room must be staring. They weren't, but she couldn't help feeling unsettled. She hated being the center of attention. If she had the ability to time travel, she'd transport herself back five hundred years to get away from this moment.

People who loved the spotlight, like Melvin Lee, were the strange ones.

"There's also something in the US—I don't know if you have it here in Canada—called Snickers salad. You heard of this?" He glanced around the room before continuing his bit on the ridiculousness of Snickers salad and saying he was a health nut who liked his Snickers plain.

Vivian was sure the pauses in his routine were carefully planned, but the next time he paused—while talking about bizarre food from the seventies—she could swear he was slightly off-kilter and it went on for a beat too long again. Was he unsettled by her presence? Surely not. But he seemed to know she was here, and she continued to feel embarrassed.

Still, she stayed. After all, leaving would draw even more attention to her, wouldn't it?

"So, yeah," Mel continued. "The food white people eat? Fucking weird. And you know what else is weird? The way some of them think Asian women are meek and submissive." He related some anecdotes about the women in his family that had the audience in stitches. "Seriously, if they spent two seconds in the company of my grandma, mother, and sisters, they'd change their minds. Or maybe not—they see what they want to see."

Well, Vivian wasn't seeing and hearing what *she* wanted to see. She wanted to see a guy who was a complete ass, yet she still found him funny. How unfortunate.

At the end of his set, she made her escape. She'd just gotten to the street when she realized she'd left her scarf behind. She considered abandoning it, and if it were any other scarf, she probably would, but this was a pink and gray silk scarf, and it was her favorite.

With a sigh, she hurried back, grabbed her scarf off the chair, and returned to the street.

"Vivian!"

She'd just stepped onto the sidewalk, and she considered running, maybe trying to hide around the corner. But if he saw her hiding from him, that would be more embarrassing, so she turned in the direction of his voice.

Mel stood in front of her, arms crossed over his chest and a smirk on his face.

Never meet your heroes. If only she'd taken that clichéd advice.

"No reason I can't go to your show." Her voice sounded cold and haughty. As it should.

Her armor.

"I assumed you thought I was an arrogant ass," he said, "yet here you are."

"I'm separating the art from the artist."

"Like when I look at one of your illustrations and appreciate the incredible skill, rather than thinking about how the artist is a stuck-up ice princess."

"Ice queen." She angrily wrapped her beautiful scarf around her neck and tossed one end over her shoulder with a flourish.

He chuckled, which irritated her. She didn't like him laughing at her power moves.

"I noticed you've moved on to fan art of *Only the Best*," he said.

"How did you know about that?"

"You have a website. You do realize that, don't you?" He smirked again.

"So, you were googling me."

"You went to my show."

"And *you* followed me onto the sidewalk."

"What can I say? I like getting on your nerves."

She rolled her eyes. "How mature of you."

"I've never claimed to be mature."

"Yeah, you can't make fart jokes onstage if you're supposed to be mature."

"There was only one fart joke. And farts are funny."

This conversation was going nowhere.

"Though I promised to be on my best behavior with you," Mel said, "since you're going to be one of Lindsay's bridesmaids."

"I suspect your best behavior isn't actually very good."

"You think I don't want this wedding to go smoothly?" He seemed to be taking this personally. "Ryan is one of my best friends, and I want everything to go as well as possible for him and Lindsay."

"Me, too. We agree on something. How shocking."

"Not really all that surprising. We both think I'm funny." He shot her a lopsided smile.

"I don't think you're funny."

"Then why did you come tonight? And why did you laugh?"

She couldn't deny that, because he'd been looking at her, however . . .

"Why were you paying so much attention to my reactions?" she asked. "There were lots of other people, yet you kept looking at *me*."

"Contrary to what you think, I don't dislike you, Vivian. To be honest, I'm not sure I know you well enough to dislike you."

"You just don't approve of how I live my life."

She fisted her hand at her side. She shouldn't care what anyone thought. It was *her* life, and besides, she'd always been a bit of a loner. Apart from the crowd. The girl who couldn't do extracurriculars, hang out at the mall, or talk on MSN Messenger because she had to potty train her little sister.

"I'm sorry for what I said." He looked her in the eye. "It was wrong of me."

His unexpected apology caught her off guard, but it didn't make her feel better. "You're only sorry for saying it out loud. It doesn't change how you feel about my decision not to pursue art."

"Like I said, I don't know you very well, but maybe if—"

"No." She held up a hand. "We'll be civil to each other for anything related to the wedding, just like we were civil for the *Baking Fail* viewing party last year. That's all."

"Are you afraid of people getting to know you?"

There was something about his tone that made her skin itch, but she wouldn't deign to give him a response. He was just one of those people who delighted in pissing others off and probably enjoyed playing devil's advocate for funsies, like the white dudes he made fun of.

She straightened her scarf. "Goodbye."

"See you at the engagement party," he called as she walked down the street.

Shit. She'd forgotten about that.

. . . .

When Vivian arrived home, it was almost midnight. Lindsay was in bed. Not surprising since Lindsay had to wake up early for work tomorrow.

Vivian put on her gray pajamas. What would Mel think of these? Did he favor tie-dye pajamas, and would he say hers were boring and prim?

And why was she thinking of him seeing her night clothes? What was wrong with her?

The man didn't deserve her attention and mental energy. She'd stop watching videos of him, and she'd never go to his shows again. She'd put him completely out of her mind, except when he was in her presence for Ryan and Lindsay's wedding. Then she'd be cool and polite, and he'd probably think she was a frigid ice princess, but who the fuck cared what he thought?

There weren't tons of queer Asian people on-screen, and Melvin Lee might make insightful observations and do a hilarious impression of a Samurai with a British accent, but he was a jerk. A jerk who had terrible taste, as evidenced by his wardrobe.

The next time she saw him, she wouldn't let him goad her into anger.

Nope, next time would be different.

Chapter 4

When Mel arrived at the engagement party, Vivian wasn't there yet.

He shouldn't care. He really shouldn't. But for some reason, she'd gotten under his skin.

When he'd met her last year, he'd thought she was attractive, and then he'd discovered she was the creator of his favorite *Just Another New York Sitcom* fan art . . . and they'd had a bit of an argument.

But he hadn't given her much thought afterward, not really.

Except she'd been on his mind since he'd seen her at his show a few days ago. With her cool persona and perfect clothes, she frustrated him, but at the same time, he found himself drawn to her.

Ryan and Lindsay's wedding reception would be held at a Chinese banquet hall, but the engagement party was a small affair, in a private room at a somewhat fancy non-Asian restaurant, where they'd gone for their first date. It wasn't a sit-down meal; just a couple of hours of drinks and finger food, plus treats from Lindsay's bakery.

Ryan was conversing with his future mother-in-law and her boyfriend, so Mel didn't interrupt. He helped himself to a few items on the charcuterie board, then approached Ryan's father.

"Hey, Mr. Kwok! How's it hanging?"

Mr. Kwok looked annoyed that his intense study of the food had been disrupted. In Mel's experience, the older man tended not to look happy about most things, so Mel wasn't put off.

"It's *hanging* okay," Mr. Kwok said.

"How's it going on Twitter?"

Mr. Kwok looked like a deer caught in headlights.

"I do not talk about Twitter in real life," he said at last.

"But *I* do. I noticed you tweeted about someone mixing up Ryan with Ricky Shen."

Mr. Kwok swore under his breath, which made Mel laugh.

"My grandma is inspired by your example," Mel said. "You've got twenty thousand followers on Twitter, just for goofing off as Ryan's father. She's created her Twitter account as Melvin Lee's grandma, but she hasn't tweeted yet. Maybe you could give her some pointers."

"Pointers on how to be a pain in your ass?"

"No, she doesn't need help with that. Just with using Twitter." Mel wasn't actually serious about this, but Po Po had created a Twitter account, it was true. He stuffed some delicious cured meat in his mouth. "She'd be thrilled if I got engaged. She even arranged some speed dates for me."

"Gaga!" A small human toddled over and affixed himself to Mr. Kwok's leg. Presumably this was Mr. Kwok's grandson—Ryan's nephew, Ezra.

Mr. Kwok picked Ezra up, and Ezra shot his grandpa a one-toothed grin before grabbing his beard. Mr. Kwok winced, and Ezra cried when he was prevented from doing any further grabbing.

"Here, let me take him." Ryan's sister reached for her son and started pointing out different foods on the table to him.

Mr. Kwok returned his attention to Mel. "Were any of these

speed dates"—he said the term as though it was some distasteful newfangled thing—"successful?"

"No, they weren't," Mel replied.

"I'm not sure why your grandma feels the need to help you with dating, except for her own amusement. I thought you already dated a lot?"

"Did you watch my Netflix special, Mr. Kwok?"

"I would never do anything like that," Mr. Kwok scoffed.

"Clearly an enormous lie, but I'm not going to call you on it." Mel helped himself to a glass of red wine as a server passed by. Then he caught sight of Vivian, wearing a pinstripe pantsuit and staring at him.

Well, well, well.

· · · · · · · ·

When Mel winked at her, Vivian quickly looked away.

God. She couldn't believe he'd caught her looking. How mortifying.

But he looked smart today in his floral dress shirt, which wasn't as loud as usual, in part because it was covered by a navy suit. He was also wearing a bowtie. His hair—longer on top than on the sides—had a little too much product in it, but somehow, the outfit worked on him.

She was intrigued by his conversation with the man who was presumably Ryan's father. She had a feeling Ryan's dad was the sort who didn't laugh much, but Mel was talking to him easily and making him chuckle.

And Vivian was jealous.

Why couldn't Mel talk like that with her, rather than being infuriating?

That wink, for example. Definitely infuriating.

She made a beeline for the food table and picked up a mini-cheesecake, feeling like she deserved one. At parties where she was surrounded by a dozen or more people, many of whom she didn't know, she often felt a bit anxious and was tempted to spend all her time in two places: by the food or in the washroom.

While she usually favored the latter, she'd try to be more social today. After all, Lindsay had chosen her to be a bridesmaid. But everyone seemed to be involved in their own conversations, and Vivian felt weird about joining in.

She saw a familiar South Asian woman, Noreen, who was the maid of honor and co-owner of Kensington Bake Shop. Noreen was talking to some other women, and Vivian figured she could stand near them and quietly listen.

"Vivian!" Noreen enfolded Vivian in a hug, as though they were long-lost sisters and not people who'd met only a handful of times. "Ooh, you're having one of my lemon cheesecakes. They're really good, aren't they?"

Lindsay walked over. "Is Noreen bragging again?"

"Me?" Noreen said. "I'm as humble as . . . maple bourbon pecan pie. With extra bourbon."

Lindsay laughed. She was wearing an off-the-shoulder burgundy cocktail dress, her hair down, and she looked gorgeous and radiant. Like someone who was happily in love with a movie star.

Ryan came by and whispered something in Lindsay's ear, and she laughed again. She stood on her toes to kiss his cheek and whisper something back.

Much to her annoyance, Vivian was hit with a bolt of longing. She liked being single, but every now and then, she still wished someone would look at her like that. For some reason, she glanced across the room at Mel, which made her more annoyed.

With herself, not with Mel. Why did she keep looking at him?

She turned back to Lindsay and Ryan just as her phone vibrated in her purse. She ignored it, but then she got a second text message.

She headed out to the hallway and leaned against the wall near the washroom as she checked her phone.

I need a root canal ahhhh, Andy said.

Damn, that sucked.

> Could you lend me a couple hundred
> bucks?

He was asking her for money, naturally. Root canals were expensive, and while doctor visits were covered by provincial healthcare, this wouldn't be. The surprise was that he *only* needed a couple hundred, because root canals were almost certainly more than that.

It was tough for people in their generation. Tough to find good jobs, live in an expensive city, and plan for emergencies like root canals. She was lucky; she knew that. And while Andy could live with their parents, she couldn't blame him for not doing so. If she were broke, she'd still be doing everything in her power to avoid living with them.

But she was irritated that he was asking *her* for money, not Ma and Ba, even though their parents would give him what he needed without berating him much. He'd always gotten away with a lot more than she had, and he'd never been given near as many responsibilities.

Okay, she texted him. No problem.

"Avoiding the party?"

Vivian jumped and dropped her phone.

· · · · · · · ·

He shouldn't be doing this. He really shouldn't.

But on his way to the bathroom, Mel had happened upon Vivian. He couldn't help feeling a little bothered that she was out here on her phone rather than inside the party, and he couldn't seem to stop needling her.

He picked up her phone from the floor and handed it to her.

"Family matters," she mumbled. "I'm going back in a moment."

She looked quite handsome and composed today. Her hair—cut in a rather short, asymmetrical bob—was black and shiny, and there wasn't a strand out of place. Along with her sleek pantsuit, she was wearing crystal earrings that were a little showier than her usual accessories. Not that he'd seen her more than four times, including today, and not that he was counting, but . . .

She threw him off balance.

Vivian tucked a lock of hair behind her ear, in a way that looked almost regal.

"You didn't seem terribly excited in there," he said. "Aren't you happy for our friends?"

"Of course. But I have resting bitch face."

"That's not quite how I'd describe it. More like resting ice queen face."

"Thank you for using the proper terminology," she said, deadpan.

He laughed and leaned in closer.

He was five-six, and in her heels, she was a couple of inches taller than him. She was all inviting angles and harsh, beautiful lines—nothing like Mel, in other words. Usually, such perfection wouldn't appeal to him, but for some reason, she was different.

"Don't you have better things to do," she said, "than standing out here, talking to me? Shouldn't you be stealing Ryan's phone and posting Twitter polls about his abs? Writing jokes about the Easter Bunny encountering a Viking on the Brooklyn Bridge?"

"Great idea." He took out an imaginary notepad and wrote it down.

She stuck her phone in her purse. "If you must know why I'm

out here, my brother needs a root canal and can't afford it. That's what I was dealing with."

That sounded more important than the texts he received from his family, which were mostly Joy sending him pictures of beetles and Mom sending him videos of Po Po singing Andy Lau or Shania Twain at karaoke. "That Don't Impress Me Much" was a recent favorite. He'd already seen four videos of it.

"Root canals suck," he said. "My mom needed one recently."

Vivian looked at him strangely. Was she caught off guard because he wasn't antagonizing her? Or was she thinking about insulting his fabulous shirt? He would love to see Vivian in one of his bright floral shirts . . . and nothing else. Preferably with all the buttons undone. It would be quite a contrast to her current look.

He swallowed and put his hand on the wall behind Vivian, and her tongue peeked out of her pale pink lips. Just the tiniest bit, but it was more than the tiniest bit appealing, and his blasted suit pants felt even tighter.

He shot her a lopsided smile, but she seemed unaffected by it. Maybe that was an act, and she was simply used to keeping everything inside her.

He wanted to make her snap.

"Enjoying my animal magnetism?" he asked.

Mel might not have Ryan's conventional good looks, but according to Lindsay, Vivian had said Mel was the more attractive one on *Just Another New York Sitcom*.

She shrugged and looked at her nails. "You mentioned something about animal magnetism the first time I met you. You need to come up with some new lines."

"You remember words I said a year ago. Interesting."

"I have a good memory. Don't think much of it."

"Mm-hmm. You just don't want to admit how much you like me."

Being annoying was one of his special skills. Just ask his sisters.

Vivian glared at him. "I'm not sure I'll be able to separate the art from the artist now."

He twirled his imaginary mustache, picked up an imaginary paintbrush, and started working on a painting. "Zee waterlilies are *magnifique*. How can you not appreciate zem?"

"Your French accent is dreadful."

"I'm aware," he said cheerfully.

Her mouth curved, and there was something about her slight smile that made desire pump through his veins. When he leaned in slightly, she did, too. Just a little farther and her lips would meet his. It would be—

"Is the washroom down here?"

At the unfamiliar voice, Vivian pushed Mel into the middle of the hallway.

The next thing he knew, he was on the floor, and two women were toppling toward him. Vivian managed to grab on to one of them, but the other fell, hitting his stomach rather than the floor, which might have saved her a concussion. Her friend helped her up.

And now there was a volley of *sorry*s around him, everyone apologizing profusely as if they were all at fault—indeed, this was Canada. Vivian reached out to pull him up, and the other women headed to the restroom with one final, "Sorry!"

"I really am sorry," Vivian said to him.

"You were leaning in for a kiss then decided you didn't want it?" He crossed his arms over his chest. "You're welcome to change your mind, of course—"

"I shouldn't have pushed you into the path of those women."

"—though I think you still want to kiss me. But you hate yourself for it. You don't want to want this." He shook his hips.

"You're one infuriating man," she muttered.

"Thank you. You're lots of fun to infuriate."

She rolled her eyes. "I thought we agreed to be civil to one another."

"Well, is anyone here to witness us misbehaving?"

"You're the one who spoke to me first. I was just checking a text. I didn't misbehave."

"Except when you almost kissed me, then pushed me into the line of fire."

She sighed. "Since being civil to each other seems to be a problem—especially for you—why don't we avoid each other as much as possible during the wedding festivities? Keep any words exchanged between us to a minimum."

Mel was a little disappointed—okay, more than a little disappointed. He found her icy prickliness rather intriguing. Plus, she'd almost kissed him *and* had gone to his show.

But he'd respect her wishes. "All right. I can manage that."

She simply nodded.

He made a quick trip to the bathroom before returning to the party.

"Hey, Ryan." Mel walked up to his friend and slapped him on the back. When Ryan turned toward him, Mel said, "Oh, shit. Sorry, man. Ricky Shen, isn't it? I thought you were Ryan Kwok. Funny how all you guys look alike."

Chapter 5

"Have you ever put really hot shit in a blender?" Adrian Morales, Filipino American comedian, asked the audience.

Mel chuckled before helping himself to another nacho. They were at a small comedy club on the Lower East Side, practicing new material. Stuff they hadn't gotten quite right yet. Their friend Dani Yoon—who wasn't a comedian but worked behind the camera—was there, too.

Adrian continued his story about blending hot soup and causing an explosion. Twice. "But I decided to do it one more time, just to be sure." He took a long pause and the audience laughed. "For science."

Doing things "for science" was part of Adrian's schtick. He really was a disaster in the kitchen, and he really had managed to make soup explode in the blender, but only once—the rest had been embellished for the story.

After Adrian, there were a few other comics before it was Mel's turn to head to the stage.

"Straight cis men are really, really afraid of anything feminine," Mel said into the microphone, which he'd picked up from the stand. "The way that, say, a rabbit is afraid of a fox. Or a parent is afraid their two-year-old will become obsessed with the world's. Most. Annoying. Video. And insist on watching it twenty times in a row . . . on a good day. Or the way my grandmother is afraid I'll never get married. That's how afraid some straight men are of anything remotely feminine. Such things, you know, might lead to someone thinking they're gay. They have a specific idea of what being a gay guy means, and that six-foot-two welder I dated, the one who's also a hardcore gamer and baseball fanatic, wouldn't be what they expect.

"These men are afraid of wearing pink. They're afraid of doing chores. They're afraid of watching a rom-com *while on a date with a woman*. They're afraid of doing anything but playing video games while grunting, drinking beer, and chopping wood. All at the same time. In clothes that haven't been washed in weeks because doing laundry is . . . well."

He sipped his water and looked out at the crowd. Well, it wasn't really a *crowd*. It was a Tuesday, not the most popular night of the week at this club.

"It's gotten to the point where some straight men are afraid of having sex with a woman because they fear it might be gay. I'm serious. Have you seen this? I swear, the other day, a man online was saying that a woman being on top during sex was gay. And yes, having sex with a woman isn't proof that a man is straight . . ." He gestured to himself. "But still. Another thing I've heard being called gay? A man *eating pussy*. Now, not every person with a pussy is a wo—"

Mel faltered.

He was a pro. He'd been onstage many, *many* times. Even when he totally forgot what he was supposed to say next, he could pull it off by making jokes about his memory. He was rarely stunned into silence.

But just after he'd said 'eating pussy,' he'd noticed something horrifying.

His grandmother. In the audience.

Because of the lights, he couldn't see very well, but that was definitely Po Po at a table off to the right, and she had a collection of elderly Asian people with her. Why were they at a comedy club in Manhattan rather than doing karaoke in Queens?

Oh God.

Oh God. Oh God.

It wasn't like his grandma had never seen him do stand-up before. Anything she could watch from the comfort of her living room, she'd watched, and she'd seen him live a few times, including at one unfortunate bringer show he'd done early on.

However, she'd never shown up with no notice while he was talking about oral sex.

Until tonight.

This felt like a new low, but he *was* a pro, and so after a longer-than-usual pause, he continued with his bit and tried to focus on his performance rather than wondering how much he was scandalizing his grandmother and her friends.

Po Po had done a great job of making his life nightmarish lately. First, she'd shown up in a limo at Chu's . . .

And *that* was the story he'd planned to tell next. He wouldn't let Po Po get in the way of his plans, so he did the story as intended. Mostly.

"We've got a special guest in the audience today," Mel said. "See my grandma, sitting at that table?" He pointed in her general direction. "If I'd known she was coming, I might not have said, you know, all that sex stuff. Instead, I might have done my joke about Snickers salad. A bit more grandmother-friendly. But coincidentally, the next story is about her . . ."

• • • • • • •

They stood outside the club at midnight. Po Po, three of her elderly friends—one of whom was accompanied by her middle-aged
daughter—Dani, and Mel. Adrian was still inside.

Dani was doing a poor job of containing her laughter.

"How did you know I'd be performing tonight?" Mel asked
Po Po.

"Joy told me. She says you're often here on Tuesday nights,
trying new jokes."

Goddammit. He was going to release a family of raccoons in
Joy's room. Or would Joy like that? It was hard to know with her.

"I told my new friends you're a stand-up comedian," Po Po
said, "and they thought it would be fun to see you perform." She
gestured at her friends. One woman's face was frozen in an expression of horrified surprise, as it probably had been for the past hour.
"But you made mistakes in the story about me. You were wrong
about—"

"It's a performance, Po Po. Not investigative journalism."

"Wah, I wish I could make lots of money just from telling fake
stories about life."

Mel shoved a hand through his hair. While his family was generally supportive, they didn't understand the amount of work that
went into what he did.

He'd asked her earlier if she'd be okay with him telling this story,
and she'd said yes—as she usually did—but he hadn't thought she'd
actually hear it. Certainly not while he was still figuring out his
performance.

Po Po clucked her tongue. "I saw you were sitting with that
other man. Adrian? You shouldn't be friends with him. I don't approve."

"Why not?" Mel asked.

"If you spend too much time with him, I think you will die in a house fire. Or get caught in a gang war. He'll blow something up in your face and you'll lose an eye!"

Mel sighed. "That's just Adrian's stage persona. He's actually quite intelligent."

"Then why does he act so foolish?"

Mel didn't feel like responding, but maybe that was a mistake because Po Po moved on to a worse topic.

"You have to explain some things to me," she said. "What is eating p—"

"No." Mel held up his hands. "Absolutely not."

Po Po turned to Dani. "Hi, Dani. Nice to see you again. Will you—"

"No, she's not explaining anything, either," Mel cut in.

"Okay, you can explain it at dim sum on Sunday. But we should leave. It's past my bedtime. We'll be talking about you on the drive home."

Yeah, Mel bet they would.

Po Po and her friends tottered down the sidewalk.

"I can't believe your grandma stayed for two hours," Dani said to Mel once they were alone. "Some of that stuff was pretty raunchy. My grandmother probably would have fainted the first time someone said 'sex.' Anyway, you're still good for Friday?"

"Yep, wouldn't miss it."

But now Mel planned to go home and have a drink. A strong one.

· · · · · · · ·

"And then," Mel said, "my grandma told me not to be friends with Adrian, in case he blows something up or starts a fire and I get injured."

"What?" Adrian said. "You didn't tell me this."

"I'm telling you now."

Dani and Shannon, who were seated on the other side of the booth, both laughed.

That Friday, they were at an Irish pub, celebrating the fact that Shannon had gotten her first job in set design, something she'd been working toward for a while. Mel had known Dani since college; Shannon, her girlfriend, was a few years younger, and they'd been together for a while now. She was blond, green-eyed, petite, and a small part Irish. Probably why she liked Guinness.

Not Mel. He was drinking some fruity beer that was so sweet, it shouldn't qualify as beer.

"You sure you have no plans to use me as a test subject in a science experiment?" he asked Adrian. "Maybe one that involves mixing various household cleaners together and lighting them with a match?"

"I think I saw someone do that on TikTok." Adrian stroked his chin. "Hmm. You want to participate in my experiments, Mel?"

"I'll be your lab assistant," Dani said.

Adrian pointed at her. "You're hired."

"Hey, I'm not agreeing to this," Mel said. "Just like I didn't agree to explain my jokes to my grandma. I noticed my grandma right after I said 'eating pussy.'"

Now that a few days had passed, he was able to laugh about it.

He certainly didn't want a repeat performance, but he could see the humor. Of course, it would have been funnier if it had happened to Adrian rather than to Mel.

He'd get back at his grandmother by . . . stealing her karaoke machine, perhaps.

"By the way," Dani said. "How was Toronto? I forgot to ask."

Right. Toronto. It seemed so long ago now.

"It was good," Mel said.

"Ryan Kwok's engagement party?"

"Bugged Ryan, bugged his dad. Also got knocked on the ground and someone fell on top of me, but so it goes."

Adrian frowned. "Did you get in a fight?"

"Yeah, man. It was rough. You should see the other guy!"

"Very funny," Dani said. "You wouldn't last two seconds in a fight, Mel."

"Only because I wouldn't want to risk anything happening to my pretty face."

"Some people find broken noses sexy," Shannon said, "but you need a good story. You can't just say, 'I lost a fight with a five-year-old.'"

"I did not lose a fight with a small child." Mel pretended his dignity had been hurt more than it had. To be honest, he probably could lose a fight with a five-year-old. It was good he hadn't tried to pursue his childhood dream of being a wrestler. "I think Vivian was about to kiss me, but then two other women walked down the hall. She panicked and pushed me away, the other women tripped . . . It went something like that."

"Vivian?" Dani said. "That name sounds familiar."

Mel stretched his arms over his head. "The woman I met in Toronto last year. The one who wanted me to fuck off when I said she should be an artist."

Before his comedy career had taken off, Mel had had a shitty job in marketing. With every day he'd spent at the office, he'd felt like he was losing more of his soul. The night he'd met Vivian, it had seemed critical that he stop her from ending up like he had, especially when there was obviously something else she could be doing. He truly had wanted to be encouraging, though he'd been a little rattled as he'd thought back to those years of his life. Perhaps that was why he'd been more judgmental than usual.

And Vivian was a stuck-up ice *queen*. She probably slept with her nose in the air.

The thought made him smile. It was easy to imagine her in prim, icy-blue pajamas with proper pockets and buttons, too good for the world even in her sleep.

Pity she was so hot.

She also had a lovely voice, something he was probably more attuned to than the average person. It was a little low, a little rough . . . and something else he couldn't explain.

"She came to one of my shows," Mel said with a shrug.

"Even though she thinks you're an asshole?" Dani asked.

"Yep."

"Maybe she secretly likes you."

"Well, of course she does." With his arms above his head, Mel shimmied to the right then to the left.

Everyone laughed, as intended.

"Hey. Sorry I'm late. I was at the restaurant." Pablo squeezed in next to Shannon and gave her a hug. "Congratulations."

Pablo's family owned a Puerto Rican restaurant in Brooklyn. He was actually an ex of Mel's. They'd dated four years ago—or was it five?—and had remained friends.

"Your hair," Mel said. "You forget it or something?"

Pablo ran his hand over his head. He'd been talking about shaving it for a while, and he finally had. "What do you think?"

"It looks nice, man." Mel could admit that Pablo looked nice today without it stirring up any feelings. Unlike when he admitted to himself that Vivian had looked nice at his show. That had stirred up feelings of annoyance.

With Pablo's arrival, everyone else forgot about Vivian and conversation moved on to other topics, but at four in the morning, Mel was thinking about her again.

He'd tried to sleep at one thirty, but two and a half hours later, sleep still eluded him—not a rare occurrence in his life—and so he was in the living room, listening to the recording of the jokes he'd performed on Tuesday night. The pacing was all wrong in the speed-dating story, and the line he thought was the funniest had barely gotten a chuckle.

It had taken him years to get good at stand-up. Open mics, classes, workshops . . . it had taken a while to figure out his persona, to really understand who he was onstage, what it was that people responded to about him. Making it seem easy, like he was just telling a funny story off the top of his head, was part of the skill.

Ten years of this, and he'd still managed to screw up on Tuesday night.

But nothing ever worked the first time. It was always about refining things, no matter where you were in your career. Knowing how to improve something, how to edit your jokes . . .

Yet he couldn't manage to completely reassure himself, and he couldn't figure out how the fuck he should edit any of this right now. True, it was four in the morning, and he'd been up for twenty-two hours and only slept five hours last night, but it shouldn't be hard to make this a little better.

What if he just wasn't funny anymore?

Yes, his friends had laughed tonight when he'd been telling stories and goofing off . . . but maybe they were just trying to be kind.

Would people still like him if he stopped being funny? What else did he have going for him? What would he do with his life?

Sometimes, Mel really fucking hated his brain. Shit was just a mess in there. It felt like he was having a four-way conversation with himself. How fun.

Not.

He put down his phone and his notebook. He needed to try to get some sleep again. It was nearing the longest day of the year, and there was something particularly depressing about not having fallen asleep by the time the sun came up.

He went to the bathroom and glared at the melatonin bottle. *You were supposed to help me sleep, damn you.*

Swearing at supplement bottles. That was always good.

Then he headed to his bedroom, turned on his white-noise machine, and hopped back into bed. And he thought about what would have happened if he and Vivian had kissed. He had to think about something, even if it might keep him up; he wasn't one of those lucky people who could just let his mind be blank.

Although Vivian was rather cold and stuck-up, he imagined their kiss as warm and wet and sloppy and *good*. There would be something thrilling about unraveling a person like her. Getting involved with her would be a mess, though—and it was a moot point anyway, since she clearly didn't want it.

And he just liked pissing her off and thought she was kind of hot. Nothing more. Besides, he thought lots of people were hot, though she did get under his skin in a way nobody else did.

Maybe because he felt a strange desire to save her from herself. From a lifetime of drudgery in a bank. The fact that she'd kept that job bugged the shit out of him, even if he didn't know exactly what she did.

It was just . . . Those pictures she'd done of *Just Another New York Sitcom*. There was something unique and compelling about her style, and it seemed like such a waste for her not to pursue it further.

Now he was pissed off, horny, exhausted, and self-loathing. Lots of great things to feel when you were wide awake at four in the morning.

Truly, it was a damn miracle when he finally managed to sleep.

Chapter 6

Lindsay walked out of the changeroom in a big white dress and nearly tripped.

Luckily, the saleslady was there to catch her.

Vivian had been skeptical when Lindsay's mom had insisted she try on this dress. Indeed, it was as poofy as expected.

But Vivian kept her thoughts to herself.

She felt rather uncomfortable in this situation. Sitting on plush seats with Lindsay's mom and Noreen, watching as Lindsay tried on wedding dresses. Vivian wasn't used to shopping with other people, let alone going to a bridal shop. She was afraid she'd say something horrible, and everyone would wonder what the hell was wrong with her.

The important thing was that Lindsay liked the dress and felt beautiful in it, so Vivian's plan was to take her cues from Lindsay's body language and maybe wait to share her opinions until other people had spoken.

Fortunately, Noreen's thoughts were similar to Vivian's.

"No," Noreen said. "It's too much, and you look like you're drowning in it."

"I agree," Vivian said simply.

"Really?" Lindsay's mom frowned. "I thought it was just the

sort of wedding dress you'd always wanted, Lindsay. That's why I suggested you try it on."

"It's the dress I wanted when I was six," Lindsay said. "I'm not six anymore."

Noreen snickered, and Lindsay's mom gave her a look.

It was all good-natured, though. The two of them were well acquainted.

Vivian tried to imagine this scene with her own mother and friends, but what friends would she bring, other than Lindsay? Would she bring her sister? Amanda would undoubtedly want to come if Vivian was trying on wedding dresses, and Vivian couldn't help tensing at the thought, even though she shouldn't.

She also couldn't help wondering what their mother would be like in a bridal shop. Quiet and disapproving? Happy that her oldest daughter was finally getting married? There would be no cheerful bickering, like there was here.

Lindsay twirled in front of the full-length mirror before going to try on the next dress, and Lindsay's mother turned to Vivian. "Noreen is married. Lindsay's getting married. What about you? You're a few years older than Lindsay, aren't you?"

"Uh, yeah."

But love meant giving, giving, giving. Vivian had always needed to give a lot to the people she cared for, without expecting much in return, and it was nice to be on her own. Better to keep people at arm's length.

"Maybe you'll meet a nice man at Lindsay's wedding," her mother said. "I'm sure Ryan has many handsome male friends."

What about non-male friends?

Most people didn't know about that, though. And Vivian wasn't interested in *any* relationship now.

"There's that guy." Lindsay's mom tapped her fingers on her

knee. "What's his name? Melvin Lee? You've met him before, haven't you?"

"Mom," Lindsay said, coming out to stand in front of the mirrors. "Mel and Vivian don't get along."

But Lindsay's mom was distracted from the conversation by Lindsay's lacy dress with a mermaid silhouette.

"Much sexier than the last one," Noreen said. "It's not bad, but I don't think it's *you*."

Lindsay nodded. "That's how I feel."

"It makes your shoulders look good," Vivian said, then wondered if that was a weird thing to say. But Lindsay did have nice shoulders, and she also had the figure to pull this dress off. It gave her nice cleavage, whereas Vivian was a bit too stick-like for such a dress.

"Do you have something that's more like a ballgown?" Lindsay's mom asked the saleslady. "Not quite like the first dress, but . . ."

There were, of course, countless options.

When Lindsay stepped out in the next dress, Vivian, despite her previous hesitancy in offering her opinion, immediately said, "I think that's the one."

It was partly because of Lindsay's expression. She looked radiant.

"I agree!" Noreen said. "You're stunning."

Lindsay's mom wiped away a tear. "I wish your father were here to walk you down the aisle. He'd be so proud of you, honey."

Noreen and Vivian headed to the front of the store so Lindsay could have a moment with her mother.

"She only tried on three dresses," Noreen said as they looked out the window. "I hope the bridesmaids' dress selection is this easy when we go next month."

"Me, too." There was a distressing amount of longing in Vivian's voice, which she didn't understand, but she knew it had nothing to do with bridesmaids' dresses.

Was it because some secret part of her wanted a wedding?

Or because she wanted a closer, loving relationship with her own mother?

. . . .

Ba helped himself to more scallops. "What were you up to this weekend, Vivian?"

"Wedding dress shopping with my roommate," Vivian said.

Her father nodded.

She was at a Chinese restaurant with her parents, sister, and brothers. Coincidentally, Vivian and her siblings were seated around the circular table in the order of their birth: Vivian, Andy, Stephen, then Amanda. It wasn't too busy in the restaurant—Ma liked eating early to avoid the crowds.

"Is this your friend who's marrying the movie star?" Stephen asked.

"Yes," Vivian replied.

"A *movie* star?" Amanda perked up. "Which one? Why didn't I hear about this before?"

"Ryan Kwok," Vivian said, then went right back to eating, purposely avoiding whatever looks her mother and sister were giving her.

"Ryan Kwok?"

"You don't need to shout, Amanda."

"How long have they been together?"

"A year or so."

"How old is she?" Ma asked.

"Thirty," Vivian replied.

"Hmm."

There was a world of disapproval in Ma's voice. Not disapproval of Lindsay, but of Vivian. The she's-younger-than-you-and-she's-getting-married-before-you sort. As the eldest daughter, Vivian was always subjected to the highest expectations.

"Best to find someone now," Ma said, "while you're pretty. Though you should stop wearing so much gray. Not flattering." She shook her head. "You will make such a good mother. You're very responsible and good with kids."

Whenever Vivian received compliments from her mother, it was always when she was being critiqued for something else. Frequently, like today, Ma criticized her for not meeting appropriate life milestones, like marriage and kids.

"You were always so patient with me," Amanda said.

Yeah, I was forced to grow up too soon.

"You know I don't want kids." This was something Vivian had avoided telling her family for the longest time, until she'd blurted it out in frustration last year. Though she still hadn't told them all the reasons why, and that wasn't going to change today.

"Who's going to take care of you when you're old?" Ma asked.

In Vivian's opinion, only having kids so they'd look after you in old age was a terrible reason to procreate, but she felt like she'd said enough for today.

"I still can't believe your friend's marrying Ryan Kwok," Amanda said. "Have you met him?"

"Many times," Vivian replied.

"He's very good-looking, don't you think? Or does he look ordinary in real life?"

"No, he's good-looking, and he's friendly. Unlike . . ."

"Unlike who?" Amanda pressed.

"Never mind."

Vivian felt a bit like a sulky teenager today. She glanced at Andy, who got to enjoy his food in peace. How lucky.

"I need some new clothes for the fall," Amanda said. "You

want to go shopping, Vivian? Not next weekend, but the one after?"

Ma sniffed. "Ah, I highly doubt you need *more* clothes."

But criticism from Ma always seemed to roll right off Amanda.

"So?" Amanda said to Vivian. "What do you think? You can pick where we go."

Vivian felt bad for all the times she'd refused to hang out with Amanda, but she couldn't seem to help the resentment she felt for her little sister, even if Vivian's lack of childhood hadn't been Amanda's fault. She opened her mouth to say yes for once, but then she remembered. "I can't. I have wedding stuff to do that weekend, including bridesmaids' dresses. Lindsay usually works both days of the weekend, but she's taking Saturday and Sunday off, and Ryan also has friends coming to Toronto to sort out tuxes and other things."

"That's okay," Amanda said brightly, though Vivian detected disappointment behind her sister's peppy voice. "Some other time."

Luckily, the conversation turned to other subjects for the rest of dinner. Vivian didn't talk much and did her best to push aside her guilt over being a bad sister.

When she got home, she changed into pajamas and took out her tablet. She pulled up her latest drawing of *Only the Best*—she was nearly finished with the picture of Dean Kobayashi and the Black cowboy that many fans were shipping him with, Vivian included—but after five minutes of staring at it, she decided she wasn't in the mood.

This was the great thing about drawing just for fun: she didn't have to force herself to do anything. Her ability to pay for her next meal wasn't dependent on quickly producing art and always looking for commissions.

She imagined snarling that at Melvin Lee.

After putting away her tablet, Vivian took out her hardback

spiral sketchbook, the sort she'd always wanted as a child but hadn't been allowed to have. She'd decorated it with a selection of vinyl stickers, some of which had cost more than stickers ought to cost, but she was an adult now. She could spend a few extra dollars on stickers if she wanted. Though she often drew on her tablet, occasionally she liked the feel of paper under her fingertips.

She finished off a whimsical sketch of hearts raining down from a tree. Nothing particularly unique, but whatever. The hearts were raining down because nothing ever lasted, she decided. It wasn't quite the cute image she'd had in mind when she'd started it, but that was okay. The wind was blowing the branches to the right—not a strong wind, but still enough to knock off the heart-shaped leaves.

She turned the page and let her mind wander, and she soon found herself drawing a face.

Wait a second. Why did that look like . . . ?

Vivian tossed her sketchbook on her desk in frustration. *I don't appreciate this, Mel.*

She didn't want to waste time thinking about him. Unfortunately, she'd have to see him again in a couple of weeks—in real life, not just in the pages of her sketchbook.

She told herself she wasn't looking forward to it.

Chapter 7

Mel was belting out Shania Twain's "That Don't Impress Me Much," which he was singing at his grandmother's request, when two small children barreled into him. Fortunately, the children in question were toddlers, and they were no match against his weight.

He crouched down and sang the last line of the song directly in front of his nieces' faces. They giggled.

"Unkie!" Ruby said.

"Unkie! Unkie!" Willow repeated.

"Unkie! Unkie!"

He was their only uncle, a position he took very seriously.

As soon as he lay down on the carpet, Ruby jumped on his stomach. Willow, meanwhile, grabbed his arm and attempted to twist it in an unnatural direction.

"Girls!" Mel's older sister, Chelsea, entered with a bag of supplies to keep the children entertained and clean for the next few hours.

This was Mel's childhood home in Queens. Joy lived here now while she worked on her PhD. Her room was probably full of drawings and textbooks about beetles.

Speaking of Joy . . .

She came downstairs a minute later, and Ruby immediately took the microphone out of Mel's hand and brought it over to Joy.

"Sing!" Ruby said. "Peas!"

Joy looked at the microphone. "You've got to be fucking kidding me."

Chelsea glared at her.

"Right." Joy rolled her eyes. "You've got to be frigging kidding me."

"You must sing," Po Po said decisively. "You have not sung in weeks. It's good for you to express what's in your heart."

Joy made a face. "My heart is shriveled and black and full of insects."

Ruby and Willow burst into laughter, even though they likely had no idea what Joy was talking about.

"Sing! Sing! Sing!" they shouted.

"There are so many great options," Mel said. "Classics like 'Quit Playing Games (With My Heart)'—I remember you loved the Backstreet Boys."

"When I was six. And that was only because Chelsea liked them and I was going through an inexplicable phase where I wanted to be just like her."

"No," Po Po said. "It's Shania Twain Day."

"Wasn't it Shania Twain Day last week?" Joy muttered.

"Wah, why are you complaining? You can sing 'You're Still the One.'"

"Nothing romantic," Joy said.

"What's the fun in that?"

"I don't know why you think singing is fun. That's the biggest problem with living at home. Every day, it's like, 'Sing this song, I want to laugh at you.'"

"Are you trying to imitate me?" Po Po asked. "You have my

voice all wrong. And I don't want to laugh at you . . . Okay, maybe I want to laugh at you a little. But you should want to make me happy. I'm your po po."

"Amfabig!" Ruby exclaimed.

"What did she say?" Mel asked Chelsea.

The twins had started talking six months ago, and according to Chelsea, they knew dozens of words. However, Mel couldn't understand most of what they said, though Chelsea always could. This would be a good subject for a joke: how parents could understand the gibberish that little kids spoke, even if it was incomprehensible to everyone else.

"Ruby says Joy should sing 'Party for Two,'" Chelsea interpreted.

Po Po nodded. "Yes, this is a sensible choice."

"Sensible?" Joy shouted. "Chelsea, I'm quite sure that's not what Ruby wants."

"Then tell me what she said," Chelsea shot back. "You don't know, do you?"

"She thinks it's bath time."

At the word "bath," Ruby started crying.

"Come here, baby," Chelsea said, sitting down on the floor. "I know, Auntie Joy said a bad word, but she'll make it up to you by singing a song, okay?"

"Sing, sing!" Willow said.

"Now you gotta sing." Mel slapped his younger sister on the shoulder. "You made Ruby cry. Sing, sing, sing!" He motioned for the girls to join in the chant, and they did. Yeah, he was a terrible influence.

"Fine," Joy muttered.

Joy actually had a much nicer singing voice than Mel, even though he was the one who'd sung onstage before. (Briefly. As part of a joke.) She glared at the microphone as she started the world's most unenergetic rendition of "That Don't Impress Me Much."

"Mel's version was much better," Po Po said.

"Thank you." Mel stood up and executed a bow.

"You need to learn to sing with enthusiasm. I'll give you a demonstration."

"No," Joy said. "I've heard enough demonstrations of your enthusiastic singing over the past year. Actually, over the past week. I cannot believe I'm actually living in the same house as a karaoke machine."

"Shh," Mel said. "You're hurting its feelings." He stroked the top of the karaoke machine as if it were a puppy.

Mom came into the living room with a bowl of his favorite rice cracker snack mix. The girls hugged her legs, less boisterous than they were with Mel.

"By the way," Po Po said, "I hear Felix is dating someone new."

"Okay," Mel said.

"You don't care?"

"No."

Po Po frowned. "I lied. He's not dating anyone. I was just hoping to make you jealous and take action."

"I've barely thought of him in the past two months."

"Except you were talking about speed dating in your show! I thought it was a sign you like one of them—I am a brilliant matchmaker, after all. If not Felix, is it Aubrey?"

Mel sighed. "I'm seeing someone, actually. His name is Nicky."

"Ah, why do you sound so depressed? You have a boyfriend. It's good news. What is . . ."

Time to take defensive action.

Mel felt a moment of guilt—she was his grandmother, after all—but then he reminded himself that she'd trapped him into speed dating in a limo. Plus, she'd come to the comedy club unannounced and thrown off his performance.

He headed to the kitchen and came back with a container of

leftovers, as well as a collection of Ziploc bags and a pair of kitchen scissors.

"What on earth are you doing?" Mom asked.

"I've been seeing Nicky for all of three weeks," Mel said. "You do not get to ask questions about him—"

"Then why did you tell us about your boyfriend?"

"So nobody sets me up on more dates!" In fact, Nicky didn't even exist; Mel had invented Nicky simply to avoid further match-making.

"This is no fair," Po Po said.

"If you ask me questions," Mel said, "I will throw out these leftovers, and I will cut up these Ziploc bags! Yes, that's right. The bags you lovingly washed after they were used."

Po Po gasped. "You would not dare waste food and plastic bags!"

"Yes, I would." Mel put down everything except the scissors and a single bag. He held the scissors above the bag, poised to cut into it. "Go ahead, ask a question about Nicky."

"Can I ask a question instead?" Chelsea inquired.

"You can, but if it's about my dating life, I'll do exactly the same thing as if Po Po asked, and when she starts crying about her ruined Ziploc bags, it'll all be your fault."

"This seems a bit extreme," Mom said. "When will we be allowed to ask questions?"

"Oh, I don't know," Mel said airily. "Maybe after Nicky and I elope."

"Elope?" Po Po screeched. "Deprive your poor grandmother of the chance to see you get married? You must really like this man."

In truth, Mel had never gotten anywhere close to marriage, despite being in his mid-thirties, and it wasn't because he was against the institution. Nor was it because he hadn't had lots of relationships. This was quite a contrast to Ryan, who hadn't dated much then proposed to the first woman he'd been with for more than three months.

What's wrong with me?

Lots of people liked Mel. Lots of people would date him. And yet . . .

"Uh, Mel?" Joy sounded slightly disturbed by his brooding silence, and he wasn't used to that. She was his little sister, after all. She tended to be more focused on pissing him off.

"Look, Po Po," he said. "If you don't want me to elope, then don't try to interfere in my love life. No more blind dates. And while we're at it, please don't show up at the club again and ask me to explain dirty jokes to you afterward."

"Wait, what?" Mom said. "When did this happen?"

"Several weeks ago. It was a Tuesday."

Mom glared at her mother. "You told me you were going to your friend's for karaoke!"

"Did I?" Po Po said, her tone milder than usual. "I don't remember."

"Yes, you do. You went all the way to Manhattan? Who was driving you?"

"My friend's daughter. She's a very good driver, don't worry. She didn't drink."

"Why did you lie to me?" Mom asked.

"What dirty jokes didn't you understand?" Joy asked.

"Aiyah!" Po Po said. "You're all making my head hurt."

Joy patted Po Po's hand. "Aren't you glad I told you he might perform?"

"You're the one who told her?" Mom asked.

"Why so many questions?" Po Po groaned. "You're supposed to be asking Mel questions instead."

"If you ask questions, I cut the Ziploc bags," he said.

Willow jumped up and made a grab for the scissors, and he held them above his head. Ruby, meanwhile, made a lunge at the karaoke machine, and Chelsea held her back.

"You know," Mom said, "there was much less of a racket when Mel was singing 'That Don't Impress Me Much.' Maybe we should go back to karaoke."

Mel gestured to Joy. "You should sing again. With about ten times the enthusiasm."

"Very funny," Joy muttered.

"Just you wait." Po Po shook her finger. "When you're eighty-five, you will be tired of wearing black all the time and studying beetles. I was like you when I was younger—"

"You really weren't," Mom said.

"—but now, I'm different."

"Well, you have changed, that much is true. Imagine if I'd tried to sneak out of the house to watch comedy when I was a teenager. You would have lost it."

"Wah, are you comparing me to a teenager? You want to find me *parking* with some boy? Smoking a joint?"

Po Po was a riot sometimes—as long as all her attention wasn't on Mel.

Mom turned to him. "You'll be on the road next week, right?"

"Yep. Got a bunch of shows in Chicago before I head to Toronto."

"Are you telling that joke?" Po Po asked. "That one about eating p—"

He cringed. "Po Po!"

It was one thing to tell dirty jokes in front of strangers, but his mother and grandmother were a different matter.

Especially his grandmother.

She could get under his skin in, well, the way he could get under other people's skin. Vivian, for example, seemed to find him intensely annoying.

He'd probably see her next weekend. He doubted she'd be at the tux fitting, and it was just supposed to be him, Ryan, Lindsay, and the maid of honor at the cake tasting.

But he seemed to recall some mention of a get-together with the entire wedding party . . .

Chapter 8

Vivian put on her headphones, so as not to disturb Lindsay, and started the video.

"Some people," Mel said on-screen, "are terrified of explaining same-sex relationships to their kids. They think it involves talking about sex, when really, all you have to say is, 'Some kids, like little Timmy, have two daddies instead of a mommy and a daddy. And no, that's not why little Timmy tried to stick a caterpillar up his nose, I don't know why he did that . . . No, don't you try that now . . . I said *no*!'

"I don't have kids, but I can think of dozens of things that would be much more difficult to explain to children. Death, for example. Institutional racism. Gerrymandering. Saying same-sex relationships are too hard to explain . . . that's just a terrible excuse."

There was a knock on Vivian's bedroom door. Quickly, she took off her headphones and closed all the tabs in her browser, not just the video. She felt like she'd been caught doing something illicit, when really, she'd just been watching a video of a man she professed to hate, even though she'd sworn not to watch such videos again. Nothing all that bad, but she still didn't want Lindsay to know.

"Come in," Vivian said.

"Hey!" Lindsay entered. "Sorry, was I interrupting something?"

"No, no, nothing at all!" Vivian sounded exactly like a guilty person.

Lindsay's eyebrows drew down, but she didn't comment on Vivian's obvious lie. "Are you free tomorrow morning?"

"Are we looking at dresses in the morning instead of the afternoon?"

"No, that's still on schedule. But Noreen was supposed to do cake tasting in the morning with me, Ryan, and Mel . . . and it's just not possible for us both to be away from the bakery all day tomorrow. There are some orders that really need to be placed, as well as—"

"You want me to go cake tasting?"

"I'm sure the three of us could manage if you can't come, but it'll be fun! We'll try all different sorts of cake. Lemon chiffon, mocha . . ."

Vivian had asked Lindsay previously why she wasn't having the cake done at her own bakery, but apparently Kensington Bake Shop didn't do wedding cakes and even if they did, it would be simpler this way—one less thing for Noreen and Lindsay to worry about.

"All right." Vivian doubted she'd be of much assistance— Lindsay ran a bakery, after all, and surely hers and Ryan's opinions were the most important—but wanted to support her friend. "I'll go."

"Excellent!" Lindsay skipped away, closing the door behind her.

After glancing around as though she were about to execute a crime, Vivian put on her headphones and started the video again.

As usual, Mel was wearing a floral dress shirt, though in this performance at a comedy festival, he had a blazer on top. His hair was a little longer in the video than it had been the last time she'd seen him, and she thought it suited him. And he always looked like he had such a good time when he was onstage, whereas Vivian would probably be shaking in the corner.

You're going to see him tomorrow.

She told her excitement to fuck the hell off.

"The thing about being bi," Mel said, "is that many people simply do not believe you unless you're literally banging both men and women every night. One day I show up with a boyfriend, and this guy named Chad—no reason I picked this name, none whatsoever, definitely not a real person—says, 'Congrats, bro. I'm proud of you for finally realizing you're gay.' When I'm like, 'No, man, I'm not gay,' he shoots me this dumb wink in return." Mel winked in an exaggerated fashion. "And he says, 'Yeah, sure you're not.' Then, six months later, I show up with a girlfriend, and Chad's like, 'So you're straight now?' And I'm like, 'I told you I was bi! Why don't you believe me?' But for some reason, Chad can't wrap his head around the simple concept, just like he can't wrap his head around the idea that doing a keg stand when you're forty isn't very smart. And like certain other people don't understand how someone can be both Asian *and* queer—'That's too many! You can only pick one!'" He then segued into a joke about Venn diagrams.

There were some comedians who seemed to glory in being mean, who made a point of being as politically incorrect as possible, who enjoyed racial stereotypes, who would think Vivian was a special snowflake . . . And those very same people would be extremely butthurt if you made jokes about them.

Melvin Lee, on the other hand, made her feel seen. In some ways, he was nothing like her and his experiences were very different from hers, but still, she felt like she was seeing herself represented.

If only he wasn't completely unbearable in real life.

· · · · · · ·

It was a hot, muggy day in Toronto. Ryan had said it was thirty-five degrees, and Mel had been confused before remembering that Ryan was talking in Celsius. No fucking way was Mel doing that conversion in his head, so he'd pulled out his phone. Ninety-five Fahrenheit. And the air was barely moving.

At least the wedding would be in the winter.

"I have sweat dripping all down my body," Mel complained to Ryan as they stood outside the bakery. "I thought they were two minutes away."

"That's what I said exactly *thirty seconds* ago," his friend replied. "Come on, we just got out of an air-conditioned car."

Sure enough, less than two minutes later, Lindsay and Vivian arrived. Vivian didn't appear to be affected by the heat. She was wearing wide-legged pants and a sleeveless pale blue shirt.

"Ryan." She smiled at the groom-to-be. "Melvin."

Apparently, Mel didn't deserve a smile.

"Shall we?" Lindsay said perkily, ignoring the frosty reception Mel had received.

The bakery was blessedly cool. They were led to a room on the second floor, and the baker set down some water glasses plus a platter with eight different types of cakes, each of them labeled. She then gave a more detailed explanation of each cake, and Mel tried his best to listen, he really did, but it was hard when he just wanted to *taste* the cake, and half the descriptions were lost on him. They probably meant something to Lindsay, though; she was listening avidly, and Ryan was holding her hand under the table.

Mel was also distracted by Vivian, who looked good, as always. He was particularly distracted by the tiny bow on her shirt. It was somewhat asymmetrical—an oversight on her part, or deliberate?

At last, the baker left them alone, which was for the best. Not that Mel would be afraid of speaking his mind in her presence, but it was better this way. He wasn't sure if the cakes were supposed to be tried in a particular order, but he reached for the chocolate truffle, and everyone followed his lead.

"This is really good." Mel nodded his approval. "Definitely get this one."

"We've got seven more to try," Ryan said. "Or do you not want to eat any more cake?"

"Ha. Very funny."

Next was the vanilla bean.

Vivian chewed thoughtfully. To Mel's annoyance, there was something weirdly compelling about her restraint.

"I really like this one," she said to Lindsay.

"It's a good vanilla cake, isn't it?" Lindsay smiled. "I had it at a wedding before—my friend Eunice used this place for her wedding cake—but I wanted to get other people's opinions on it. Though I suspect I'll end up going for a different flavor."

"Whatever you want, sweetie," Ryan said.

"Hey, don't leave the decision all to me. That's too much pressure."

"You're the baking expert, and you've made all the decisions about the cake so far."

"Which decisions have you already made?" Vivian asked.

Lindsay counted them off on her fingers. "I chose the bakery and which flavors we'd try today. I want a three-tier cake with two different flavors. No fondant on the outside, just buttercream. Possibly a semi-naked cake—"

"Semi-naked?" Mel wasn't willing to let that one go by without a comment. He elbowed Ryan. "Like some of your photos on Instagram?"

But Ryan wasn't paying attention. He was focused only on Lindsay, who was sitting across from him. They were making eyes at each other, and it seemed like semi-naked cakes were an inside joke between them?

Mel put a hand to his mouth and leaned forward. "Psst. Vivian. We can probably finish the rest of the cakes before they notice they're not the only two people in the room."

"I can hear you, Mel," Ryan said. "You might think you're whispering—"

"But they can hear me in Edmonton?"

"Why Edmonton?"

"I was trying to make it Canadian."

Vivian chuckled, and Mel wanted to continue making her laugh. However, Lindsay and Ryan were trying the next cake, and Mel wasn't going to miss out on that.

This cake, however, was fruitcake.

"Fruitcake is a thing people serve at weddings?" Mel asked.

"In some places, yes," Lindsay said. "It's what my dad's family usually has. I don't think I want fruitcake, but I figured we'd try it."

They tried the chocolate raspberry next. It was an excellent cake that gave the chocolate truffle a solid run for its money. After the chocolate raspberry, there was mocha, followed by a greenish cake. Matcha.

"But not matcha tiramisu," Lindsay said.

Unlike "semi-naked cakes," Mel knew the story behind this one. Ryan and Lindsay had met when he'd knocked over two dozen matcha tiramisu donuts in her bakery.

"Which do you like best?" Mel asked Vivian, as Ryan fed matcha cake to Lindsay.

"The vanilla," she said. "Though the fruitcake wasn't bad, either."

He frowned. "Not a big fan of chocolate?"

"I don't dislike it, but the others are better." She wiped away a tiny bit of buttercream at the corner of her mouth.

"Wow, I can't believe I'm saying this to someone," Mel said, "but you have terrible taste in cake. Vanilla and fruitcake over chocolate truffle?"

He'd meant for it to sound lighthearted, the way he'd tease his sisters or Ryan. But Vivian tensed, and he felt like he'd just insulted her career again. They'd agreed to avoid each other when possible and be civil at times like today, when they had to interact, yet Mel seemed to be doing a shitty job of it.

The baker appeared, carrying a tray with a teapot and four cups. "How are you liking the cakes? Any questions?" She blushed as she looked at Ryan.

"They're all very good," Ryan said with a smile. "I wish I had a cake tasting every day."

"Well, you could." Mel punched him lightly on the shoulder. "But I've heard a rumor that it's hard to maintain rock-hard abs when you're eating tons of cake. I mean, it might be worth trying, just telling you what I've heard."

Lindsay poured the tea after the baker had left. "What are your thoughts so far?"

"The chocolate ones are particularly good," Mel said. It wasn't a dig at Vivian—in his opinion, the chocolate ones were the best, and most people liked chocolate—but he winked at her anyway. "I'd skip the fruitcake, and the matcha was okay, but not as good as the others."

Lindsay nodded at him. "Yeah, I figured we'd get a chocolate one. Ryan probably likes the mocha . . ."

Ryan smiled and shrugged. "Guilty."

"But I'd go for either chocolate raspberry or chocolate truffle. Then, for the other cake . . . Well, we still have a couple more to try."

"Or you could make the cake, Ryan," Mel suggested. "Show off some of your *Baking Fail* skills. I would love to see you try to make a semi-naked wedding cake."

"I'm sure you would," Ryan said. "You always enjoy it when I make an ass of myself."

Next was the lemon chiffon, and Mel had always liked lemon in desserts.

Lastly, the lemon blackcurrant, which seemed to be the same cake as the previous one, but with a different filling and frosting.

"This one's my favorite." Vivian picked up another forkful of lemon blackcurrant cake.

"I'm glad you like it better than the vanilla," Mel said.

She gave him a pointed look.

He wanted to amuse her. She'd come to his shows, and she'd remembered words he'd said more than a year ago. But she sat there elegantly as she ate her cake, not laughing as much as he'd like.

"Elegant" wasn't a word anyone had ever used to describe Mel. Why, right now he was wearing cargo shorts and a short-sleeved buttoned shirt, which was white with blue and purple flowers. It wasn't quite as loud as much of his wardrobe . . . which wasn't saying much, to be fair.

"I really like the lemon blackcurrant, too," Mel said. "Though fruitcake and matcha would be a winning combination, don't you think?"

Lindsay laughed.

"Do you having a wedding planner?" he asked.

"Yeah," she said, "but I told her that I'd figure out the cake on my own. I thought she'd get in the way today."

"I think the lemon blackcurrant is better than the lemon chiffon," Ryan said. "If that's what you want, I support it."

"And the blackcurrant buttercream is a great color," Mel said. "I spilled a little, but it's no big deal because it matches my shirt."

Vivian smiled. Why did he care what she thought?

But it warmed his heart.

"Is that why you wear such busy shirts?" Ryan said. "So no one will notice if you eat like a toddler?"

"Nah, man. I wear them because I can pull them off! They enhance my natural beauty." Mel struck a pose.

Ryan took a picture of him. "I'm gonna post this on Twitter."

"Go ahead, I don't mind. But then I'll post the picture I took of you in your sleep."

"Were you watching me sleep last night?"

Mel replied with a faux innocent look. Although he really was innocent—of course he hadn't taken pictures of his friend sleeping. That would be weird.

The baker returned with a booklet of fully decorated wedding cakes, and she and Lindsay—with occasional input from Ryan—spent the next twenty minutes discussing the exterior of the cake. Mel tried his best to listen, and he gave an opinion or two when asked, but he kept looking at Vivian, who was obviously taking this more seriously than he was—or maybe she just took everything seriously, this woman who worked at a bank and always looked neat.

Ugh, why did she pique his curiosity? She shouldn't.

They left the bakery and returned to the sticky heat.

"All right," Lindsay said to Ryan when they stood on the sidewalk once more. "You and Mel go try on some tuxes, and we'll see you tonight."

Ryan leaned in to give her a quick kiss. "Sounds good, sweetheart."

"What will we do tonight?" Mel asked.

"Dinner, so everyone in the wedding party can meet each other properly," Lindsay replied. "Then karaoke."

Mel laughed, but out of the corner of his eye, he noticed Vivian frown.

Interesting.

Chapter 9

Ten people in a private room in a karaoke bar.

This was basically Vivian's version of hell.

She'd never understood the appeal of getting up in front of an audience and making a fool of herself, and this was even worse than regular karaoke. One of the people here, Juan Velázquez, literally had a career on Broadway. Mel and Ryan were also performers, and Ryan had a pretty good singing voice.

Having to sing in front of such people would be particularly embarrassing.

The other two groomsmen were Trevor, who was Lindsay's brother, and Vic, a childhood friend of Ryan's. Then there were the bridesmaids: Vivian, Noreen, Jenna, and Leah. Jenna was Ryan's sister; Leah was Lindsay's high school friend.

Everyone appeared to be having a great time, and everyone appeared happy to sing—except for Vivian. She might have been able to enjoy herself a little if she knew no one would force her up, but eventually, someone would notice that she hadn't sung and insist on fixing it.

It would likely be Mel, who was currently belting out "Total Eclipse of the Heart," his face twisted in an expression of comical anguish. He was loud, on tune (mostly), and sang with a large amount of theatrics. She wished she could laugh like everyone else, but she couldn't, not with the lump in her stomach and her heart beating far too fast. She should have faked a headache and left earlier.

In fact, she barely would have had to fake it. It had been a long day, beginning with Mel insulting her taste in cakes and then proceeding to the ordeal of the bridesmaids' dresses. They'd eventually decided on pink dresses that, while not exactly Vivian's style, weren't hideous, so she supposed she couldn't complain.

And now there was karaoke.

Juan sang "Black Velvet" with utter perfection, followed by Lindsay and Noreen doing "Wannabe" and Vic singing a K-pop song that Vivian had never heard before.

"How about a duet?" Mel said to Ryan and Lindsay. "'Don't Go Breaking My Heart'?"

Ryan and Lindsay looked at each other.

"All right," Ryan said.

He, of course, was a great performer, and Lindsay got into it, too, perhaps partly fueled by alcohol. Ryan shook his finger, and Lindsay pointed at him . . . and they looked like they were having a great time.

Vivian could not imagine enjoying such a thing.

Leah sang "I Will Survive," which Vivian suspected was a popular karaoke song. Not that she knew such things, as this certainly wasn't how she'd choose to spend her free time. Even if it was a bit surreal to be at a karaoke bar with the men who'd starred in one of her favorite TV shows, this situation was horrifying more than anything else.

Though as more songs were sung, Vivian started to relax. So many people were eager to sing. Perhaps they wouldn't notice that she was just sitting here, sipping her beer, rather than trying to find a song for herself.

But then Noreen pulled Vivian's wrist.

Oh shit.

"You should go next, Vivian!" Noreen exclaimed. "I haven't heard you sing yet."

"Yeah," Mel said. "You're up, Vivian. Any ideas?"

"Um . . ."

"No problem, I'll find something. 'I'm Too Sexy'? 'I Don't Know How to Love Him'?"

She felt like he was making fun of her.

"'I Wanna Dance with Somebody'?" Lindsay suggested.

Vivian really did not want to dance with somebody. Or sing. She didn't even enjoy singing in the shower when nobody was listening.

The terrified look in her eyes seemed to register with Lindsay, but Noreen didn't let up.

"Come on!" she said. "There's no way you can have a worse singing voice than me. Lindsay makes fun of me for it."

Yes, Noreen's singing skills were below average, but she'd seemed to enjoy herself—which could not be said of Vivian. No amount of alcohol would change that.

"We all have to sing!" Leah said. "Don't be a bad sport."

Ugh. Vivian refused to cave to peer pressure.

"Sing, sing, sing!" Noreen was rather drunk. Which was fortunate, or she might have succeeded at pulling Vivian out of her chair.

"You sound like my little nieces," Mel said, but strangely, he wasn't encouraging Vivian to sing anymore. "If she really doesn't want to go up, I'll sing 'I'm Too Sexy.' One of my favorite songs ever and extremely appropriate."

"I think Ryan should do that one," Juan said.

"Vivian!" Noreen said. "You have to sing."

Oh God. Oh God.

"How about Vivian and I do a duet?" Mel looked at Vivian and waggled his eyebrows. Then he leaned forward to whisper in her ear, and for a moment, the tension in her body over having to perform faded, replaced by tension caused by his proximity. "I know you don't want to sing. I'll do both parts."

She couldn't help smiling in thanks.

And she couldn't get over the strangeness of this situation. Mel wasn't making fun of her and telling her that he didn't understand her life choices.

"What are you two whispering about?" Leah asked.

Mel flashed Leah a grin, then returned to whispering to Vivian. "'Summer Nights' from *Grease*, okay? Unless you have a better idea."

Vivian shook her head. She had no ideas.

A microphone was thrust into her hand by the far-too-enthusiastic Noreen, and Vivian headed to the front of the small room. The music started, and okay, it was a little catchy, even if her blood was ice cold.

The first line was Mel's, and he sang it loudly.

The second line was hers, and she didn't start at the right time—she really had no musical talent—but Mel was serious about doing her part. He moved to her side and sang in a falsetto as she mouthed the words . . . and then she had to stop, not because she hated singing in public more than anything in the world, but because Mel was hamming it up so much.

He took a step away from her and did the man's lines, then it was back to the falsetto for her lines. And then they sang together. She tried to project her voice a tiny bit, so no one would accuse her of not singing, and it wasn't so bad.

Because everyone was focusing on Mel. Who was doing a weird walk, perhaps similar to what John Travolta had done in *Grease*? She wasn't sure; she'd seen the movie so long ago.

Vivian found herself looking at Mel strangely. He was doing this for her?

True, he loved being the center of attention, and this was no hardship for him. But he wasn't doing this because he hated the attention being on anyone but him. No, he'd understood she didn't want to sing and decided to help her out.

When the song ended, Vivian felt slightly disappointed, even though it meant she got to put down her microphone. Hopefully no one would demand a solo from her now.

"Okay, you're up, Ryan," Mel said. "You're the groom, so it's my duty, as the best man, to make sure you have as much fun as possible."

"I'm not sure that's exactly the job description."

"How about something with a nice country twang? Nah, not yet, I really want to hear you do 'I'm Too Sexy' with me."

"I think you should sit this one out. I can do it better by myself."

"Yeah, right," Mel said with faux disbelief.

Everyone laughed, and Vivian didn't feel nearly as tense as she had ten minutes ago. Nope, instead she found his ease, his confidence, and the way he could move his hips . . . far too sexy.

· · · · · · ·

At one in the morning, they were all at a soju cocktail bar just off Bloor Street. Most of the bridal party was spread across a few tables at the back of the room; Vivian was the only one sitting by herself at the bar, looking at her phone. It was nice to have a few minutes of peace with her gingery, citrusy soju drink.

Still, she kept sneaking glances at the nearby table where Ryan, Lindsay, and Mel were seated. She could make out bits of their conversation—Lindsay was discussing some of the wedding plans, including the menu—and Mel was offering what seemed to be reasonable advice. All good-natured, with a smile on his face, but he wasn't taking it as a joke. Vivian appreciated that he'd always been kind to Lindsay.

Tonight, he'd been kind to Vivian, too. It still boggled her mind.

Conversation turned to the bachelor and bachelorette parties, which would be held the same weekend in New York City, in part so Juan, with his busy schedule, could attend.

"Hey." Mel had squeezed onto the stool next to Vivian.

"Hi," she said.

"Are you coming to New York?"

"I am."

"Have you been before?"

"A bunch of times."

He nodded and had a sip of his drink. "You doing okay?"

"Why wouldn't I be? Is it so wrong to need a few minutes of peace after a day of wedding planning and karaoke?"

"No, no. Just making sure."

She shouldn't be so antagonistic. "Thank you for earlier. The, uh, duet."

"No biggie," he said with a shrug. "You looked petrified. No skin off my back if I get to act like a clown for another few minutes."

"But I bet you don't know what it's like. Not wanting to be in the spotlight."

"Well, what can I say . . ." He shot her a charming smile.

That made her swallow hard. He was acting more like how she'd hoped he would in real life, back before she'd met him for the first time. Friendly, kind, funny. It reminded her of how attractive she'd found him on *JANYS*.

"What's up?" He put his elbow on the bar and rested his cheek on his hand.

"I thought you would have pushed hard to see me embarrass myself."

"Not gonna lie, I did egg my sister on when she refused to sing 'That Don't Impress Me Much.' Eventually, she gave in. But that's different. It was just a few family members, and she didn't have an expression of utter terror on her face, like you did. She looked like she wanted to murder me, but that's a normal look for her."

"Is this the sister who likes bugs? Or did you invent an entomologist sister for your act?"

"Yes, that's Joy. She's very much real."

They were quiet for a moment. On the other side of the bar, the bartender was setting up soju bombs for another group.

"But this morning," Vivian said, turning back to Mel, "you insulted my taste in cake."

"I was trying to playfully tease you. I wasn't offended that you're not a chocoholic, just amused. That's the way I am, the way I show affection. By being a little annoying. I'm like the donkey in *Shrek*, though I've got the body of the ogre."

Vivian had been a teenager when *Shrek* had come out, but Amanda and Stephen had been little, and they'd wanted to watch it over and over on DVD. Like, every day. She'd seen the movie far too many times, and the whole thing annoyed her at this point.

"But if you don't like it," Mel said, "that's fine. I won't tease you again."

She felt bereft at his comment.

Suddenly, she wanted him to tease her again. Nobody else teased her. Vivian had few friends, and she wasn't close with her family. She tended to keep herself guarded and projected a cold, don't-fuck-with-me attitude.

"When we first met," she began, "and you insulted my career, was that teasing, too?"

He shook his head but didn't say anything more.

Okay. Maybe she'd just try to forget about that incident. It might be the best way to go forward with Mel so that they could get along for the rest of the wedding planning. Besides, he'd apologized for it the last time he was in Toronto.

Though one thing was still on her mind.

"The way you show affection," she repeated, very much aware of how his elbow was nearly touching hers. "Do you . . . like me?"

"Sure, why not?" he said easily. "I like a lot of people. You seem all right, even if we have wildly divergent views on cake and fashion."

She couldn't help snorting, and she hid her smile by sipping her drink.

"Maybe you intrigue me." He knocked back half his drink, as though that admission had cost him something. "But I know I've been mean at times, trying to annoy the shit out of you rather than playfully tease you. I don't entirely know why, but I'll stop. You can tease me, though."

"You can tease me a little as well. Like about the cake, now that I know how you meant it." She paused. "You do karaoke with your family?"

"Yeah, my grandma's obsessed with it. Your family's a little different?"

"You could say that."

In some ways, she had an advantage in this conversation. She knew a fair bit about Mel, but he didn't know much about her. However, even if he did have an entomologist sister, she was sure other things he'd said publicly, particularly during his stand-up, differed from the truth.

"How about I tell you a story," he said. "You can laugh at me. Actually, I'll keep telling you stories that'll let you have a laugh at my expense for as long as you like."

"That's really not necessary—"

"A while back, I was performing at a club in New York. Right when I said 'eating pussy,' I noticed my grandma in the audience with her elderly karaoke friends."

Vivian laughed, though she felt a bit bad about laughing, because God yes, that would have been mortifying.

But Mel was telling her this story and laughing along.

She wished she could be like him and not take shit quite so seriously. Wished she knew how to break tension, rather than causing it with uncomfortable silences. It was particularly uncomfortable now because certain thoughts were occupying her brain. Sexual ones. What would it be like if . . .

"Afterward," Mel said, "she wanted me to explain—"

"Okay, okay." Vivian held up a hand. "I get it."

"Your secondhand embarrassment is so strong that you can't bear to hear me finish?"

"Yeah."

"Well, there isn't much more to tell anyway. I cut her off."

"How do you just . . . laugh about it?"

"Let me tell you, I was not laughing right away, but my friend Dani was with me, and she found the whole thing freaking hilarious."

Vivian felt oddly envious of Dani for knowing Mel well.

"But basically . . ." Mel looked at the collection of bottles behind the bar. "Sometimes laughing at things is a survival technique, you know what I'm saying? If I didn't try to find the humor in them, I wouldn't be able to get out of bed in the morning."

She'd heard him say similar words onstage, yet as he spoke now, when it was just the two of them, she felt like she knew him in a different way than she ever had before. She understood what it was like for him, and there was an ache in her chest as she thought about what was behind his smile.

"Mel!" Juan called. "Got a question for you."

"Just a sec." Mel turned to Vivian. "You want my number? Just in case you, I dunno, need some advice about your NYC bachelorette plans? Since I'm an expert and all. Or you can ignore me if you like. No hard feelings."

When she handed over her phone, he entered his number, flashed her a grin, and headed over to slap Juan on the back. She admired the way he could be so easy with people.

Huh. Everything seemed a little topsy-turvy now, and not because of the alcohol.

It still felt freaking weird that she now had a positive memory of singing in public—though, to be fair, "singing" really stretched the definition of what she'd done—and it was thanks to Melvin Lee.

No one had ever done something like that for her before.

Chapter 10

VIVIAN (8:31 pm): Hi. It's Vivian.

> **MEL (11:08 pm):** Oh, hi! Sorry, I was onstage.

VIVIAN: I suppose that's a good excuse.

> **MEL:** 😆 glad you approve. I'm touring right now. Did a show in Denver tonight. Interviewed someone for my podcast this morning.

VIVIAN: How was the show?

> **MEL:** The audience LOVED me

VIVIAN: Of course they did.

> **MEL:** Was that sarcastic?

VIVIAN: No

VIVIAN: I have a question for you. I noticed there are a few places in NYC with mochi

donuts. I thought that would be a good
thing to do with Lindsay.

> MEL: Damn, I thought you were going to
> ask for my opinion on male strip clubs. I
> mean, comedy clubs. I know all about
> those.

VIVIAN: This is a bachelorette party for
Lindsay. Not for you.

> MEL: 😂

> MEL: I've never had mochi donuts before.
> How about I try all the options when I'm
> back in New York, then give you my
> opinion?

VIVIAN: That's really not necessary.

> MEL: When else will I get to do someone a
> huge favor by eating donuts?

VIVIAN: HUGE favor? That might be
overstating things.

> MEL: Exaggeration is my specialty. OK, tell
> me where these donut shops are . . .

. . . .

> MEL: I tried them all.

VIVIAN: Haven't you only been back in NYC
for 2 days? And you tried 3 donut shops?

> MEL: [sends picture]

MEL: Chocolate mochi donut from the first place. With the individual spheres, it looks like a teething ring, but I recommend it. A little denser and chewier than yeast donuts, but not in a bad way. They also had your favorite flavor.

VIVIAN: My favorite flavor?

MEL: Vanilla

MEL: To be clear, I'm just kindly teasing you.

VIVIAN: I know.

MEL: But I can always stop, so just tell me. Don't be shy.

MEL: [sends second picture]

MEL: That's a matcha donut from the second place. Not as good, in my opinion. Now for the last bakery . . .

MEL: [sends third picture]

VIVIAN: Um, are you sure that's food? It looks super shiny.

MEL: Like it was dipped in metal, yeah. Didn't taste metallic though.

MEL: [sends fourth picture]

MEL: I also tried their taro donut. It's a little sparkly on top, donut you think?

VIVIAN: I will not acknowledge your pun.

MEL: But you kinda did?

VIVIAN: How did it taste? Must have been
really good if you ate 2 donuts there.

MEL: I was with a friend. We split the
donuts.

MEL: It's a nice place. You could either
go for tea and donuts with Lindsay and her
friends, or just order a box to the hotel.

VIVIAN: Okay, thank you. We'll probably
plan for the last donut shop, since you
said they're good and they're very pretty.
Sparkles seem appropriate for a
bachelorette party.

MEL: Any other things you want me to try?
I'm really good at eating chocolate cake.
And pie. And dumplings . . .

VIVIAN: Actually, could you give me some
advice on dumplings?

VIVIAN: Lindsay has never been to NYC
before, and she'd like to spend some time
in Chinatown, I think. Dumplings would be
good.

MEL: I have been preparing for this moment
for years. But I don't think you have time
for all my thoughts on dumplings.

MEL: You free for the next five hours?

. . . .

MEL: I'm bored

VIVIAN: You want me to entertain you?

MEL: Actually, yes. I would enjoy that.

VIVIAN: Tough luck. I'm not in an
entertaining mood.

MEL: Neither am I. I'm all wiped out from
my performance last night.

VIVIAN: Where was this? Did it go well?

MEL: Yeah, I did a rousing rendition of I'm
Gonna Getcha Good! Shania Twain would
have been impressed. Also did Livin' on a
Prayer.

VIVIAN: Where did you perform these?

MEL: At my family's house. Just for my
grandma. She hasn't been well lately, so I
was trying to cheer her up.

VIVIAN: I hope she feels better soon.

. . . .

MEL: I recorded something for you

MEL: don't be alarmed

MEL: I'm sending you the link. It's not
searchable. Nobody can see it unless they
have the exact address.

After her morning spin class, Vivian had spent the rest of the day at home. She rarely had plans on a Saturday night. Occasionally, she and Lindsay did something, but Lindsay was seeing Ryan today. He'd been out of town for a few weeks, and this was his first day back in Toronto.

So Vivian had been working on *Only the Best* fan art—the season premiere of the show was next week—until she'd gotten this curious text from Mel.

They'd been texting on and off since karaoke last month. No deep conversations—it was mostly him giving her advice about New York. Not a big deal, but Vivian wasn't used to casually chatting with someone like this. Her siblings texted her when they wanted something. Lindsay might text to see if she felt like sushi after work, but no more than a few back-and-forths.

And Vivian certainly wasn't used to someone making videos for her.

She pulled up the video, not sure what to expect. Mel appeared on-screen, wearing a white dress shirt with fake paint splatters in a rainbow of colors.

"You know how some people have really bad taste in music or movies?" he said. "Like, they'll always suggest the movie that nobody else wants to see. Or if you're in the car with them and you have to listen to their music . . ." He grimaced. "You put your hand up to your ear, it's immediately covered in blood." He looked at his hand and his mouth dropped open in feigned shock. "Because the music is so bad it *literally* makes your eardrums bleed.

"Anyway, bad taste in movies or music. Bad taste in men. You might have a friend like that. But have you ever had a friend with bad taste in *cake*?"

A laugh escaped Vivian's lips.

Good thing Lindsay wasn't home. She would have asked why

Vivian was laughing like that . . . and Vivian wasn't interested in showing this video to anyone, not even her roommate.

"I have a friend," Mel said, "who has terrible taste in cake. Seriously. *Cake*. She likes vanilla cake and fruitcake." He made a face. "'But, Mel,' you say, 'both of those are good.' First of all, no, fruitcake is not good. It's fucking awful. Why are you spreading such lies? Second of all, vanilla cake is tolerable, but why pick vanilla when chocolate truffle is *right there*? Next time I see her, I'm going to buy a dry vanilla sheet cake from the discount grocery store and . . . I don't know. Get them to write something on the top. Or maybe just draw a giant dick in frosting because I'm mature like that."

He winked, and the video was over.

Vivian just sat there, staring at the screen, before releasing an undignified giggle. She had inside jokes with this man, the one she'd admired for years on-screen, both in his stand-up and on *JANYS*.

He made that just for me.

She was looking forward to her trip to New York next month. Nothing wrong with being excited about a trip to a city she loved, but she was most excited about seeing Mel, even with all that New York had to offer. Like mochi donuts.

Would there be vanilla cake, too?

· · · · · · · ·

Mel had finished half his beer and half his jerky by the time Dani arrived at Chu's. She wasn't late; he'd just happened to consume all that in five minutes, and his request for a drinking partner had been last minute.

Dani asked Mr. Chu for a beer. Then she sat next to Mel at the bar and covered his hand with hers.

There weren't many people he could call when he was down.

Most would expect him to crack jokes, or at the very least, fill the silence. But he'd known Dani for well over a decade.

"You want to talk about it?" she asked. "What happened?"

Mel sipped his drink. "I don't know. I guess it started when Ryan asked me a question about invitations? It got me thinking." Or spiraling, more like it. "Sometimes I feel as if I'm irreparably broken. I want what Ryan and Lindsay—and you and Shannon—have. It's not like I've sworn off love or some shit like that. Yet I'm thirty-four, and my relationships never last. Half the time I end them, half the time the other person ends them . . . but in all cases, it ends. Before I even get any hilarious meet-the-parents stories out of it."

"Maybe you just haven't met the right person yet. It's better to figure that out quickly rather than, I don't know, after three years of living together. Trust me."

"I guess." He sighed. "Or I've already broken up with the right person. I've been on so many fucking dates, after all. Not lately, though—I just haven't been interested."

Dani shrugged. "Look, I'm kind of shitty at inspirational talk."

Mel managed a chuckle. "I'm aware."

"But I don't think there's anything wrong with you."

Even though this was coming from one of his closest friends, he still wasn't convinced.

Mel had a few drinks with Dani. Not enough to get wasted, but enough to get tipsy. Then he walked her home and stumbled into his apartment. He eyed his bottle of rum, but more alcohol wouldn't ease the hollowness in his chest.

Instead, he decided to turn in early, ignoring the voice at the back of his head that said it was futile, there was no way he'd be able to sleep.

Sure enough, two hours later, he was still awake, and regrets were swirling through his brain. Regrets over little and not-so-little things. Recent and not-so-recent. He cringed as he thought of some of the things he'd said.

And nothing made him cringe like what he'd said to Vivian the first time they'd met. He'd been obsessing about that lately, which seemed like a sign that he *liked* her in that way, but he didn't.

Okay, maybe he did. Just a little. But it wasn't as if anything was going to happen. Besides, it would be silly to think it could be any different with her than it had been with the people he'd dated in the past.

He picked up his phone and scrolled through her Instagram. There was something about her art that was a little whimsical, which didn't come across when he'd met her in person. Nor in their texting, though she did joke around with him now.

Vivian seemed to have many layers of defenses, and he enjoyed peeling them back.

As he stared at the most recent picture, he couldn't help feeling jealous of Dean Kobayashi. She kept drawing pictures of him, and she no longer drew pictures of Mel in *JANYS*. Her Instagram was full of art of this other person, with his sexy stern gaze and cowboy hat.

It was clear she was super talented, and he couldn't bear the thought of her feeling the way he had more than a decade ago. He'd known he was lucky to get that marketing job, but sometimes, he'd go home and just cry. Or, worse, be unable to cry.

Vivian worked at a fucking *bank*, and she had no passion for her job. She was better than that. He didn't think he'd been entirely wrong in what he'd said, just in how he'd approached it with a woman who was a stranger at the time. He shouldn't have said anything then.

But things between them were good now, and he couldn't bring it up again, even in a much kinder way than before.

Nope, he'd just replay those words in his head, over and over.

After all, if it wasn't this, it would be something else that prevented him from sleeping. Trying to figure out a unique angle for a joke. Thinking of silly things to tweet. Going over the zillion ways he could have answered an interview question differently.

There was always something, no matter how tired he was. Maybe he should ask his psychiatrist about changing the dose of his meds. Hmm.

He tried to think of something positive he'd done lately.

At least you didn't read any comments on YouTube this week.

That was true.

And it's good you're not dating anyone now. They're better off without you, you dipshit.

Well, the situation in his brain was rapidly deteriorating.

Since he couldn't empty his mind, he did his best to turn his thoughts to Ryan's bachelor party instead.

Chapter 11

Mel looked at the seven other people crammed into the hotel room. "You ready to see the outfits you'll be wearing today?"

"You got us outfits?" Ryan said. "Of course you did."

"That's right. You'll be very stylish, I promise."

"Dear God. I'm probably going to be in some ugly orange shirt with purple flowers."

"Hey, don't insult the outfit I wore onstage yesterday." This earned Mel some chuckles. He reached into his duffel bag and pulled out a T-shirt. "What do you think?"

Ryan's mouth fell open. Mel was glad he could still shock his friend.

"Are you . . . Did you put my abs on a T-shirt?" Ryan asked.

"Not just your abs," Mel said cheerfully. He flipped the shirt around, which displayed Ryan's shirtless back. "It works from all angles."

"You had my body printed on a T-shirt."

"And I have a special version just for you." He pulled out another shirt, identical to the first, except it had "groom" written on the front.

"That font wouldn't have been cool even in nineteen ninety-five."

"Thank you for the compliment." Mel reached into the bag and pulled out more shirts. There were a few different sizes, and he tossed them around to the guys in the room. Juan would meet them later tonight, after his show, and Trevor hadn't come, so the only other groomsman here was Vic. He was currently talking to Ethan, another childhood friend of Ryan's, and Adrian Morales. Then there were Josh Oh, Dane Watson, and Albert Nguyen, who were all actors.

Mel didn't actually know Albert Nguyen. Neither did Ryan. Not well, anyway.

Albert Nguyen was an actor who'd bulked up for a superhero movie, which would be out in a few months, and that had caused many people to take notice of him and compare his abs to Ryan's. Jokes about the two of them had become a thing on Twitter, and Mel had made a "Should I invite Albert to Ryan's bachelor party?" tweet, which somehow snowballed. Albert had replied to the tweet, saying he'd be happy to come, and now, here they were.

"Why should I wear this when I could just go shirtless?" Ryan asked.

"Because you don't have the word 'groom' printed on your chest."

"This shirt is too small," Albert complained.

"No, man," Mel said, "you look great. Ridiculous, but great. All right, we've got a full day planned. Some poker, some karaoke. A bar with old-school pinball machines and video games. A comedy club, where I will spend at least a hundred percent of my set making fun of Ryan. You're free to drink, but remember, Ryan doesn't drink, and we're not going to force him. Instead, we'll start off with . . ." He gestured at a tray of disposable cups. "Three shots of espresso each, okay? If you don't want yours, I'll drink it."

"No," Ryan said. "You're not drinking extra espresso." He turned to everyone else. "Have you seen what this guy is like when he's hopped up on caffeine?"

"Please take all the pictures you can because tomorrow, I'm having photos printed—yes, that's a thing you can still do—and we're making a scrapbook." Mel held up a plastic container full of supplies. "I'm not kidding. I don't joke about scrapbooking. So, get Ryan to do as many embarrassing things as possible and take pictures. That's basically the idea. Now, I'm going to put a poll on Twitter, asking which song Ryan should sing first at karaoke. Any suggestions? Did I hear someone say 'Genie in a Bottle'?" He put a hand to his ear, then looked down at his phone, which was buzzing. "Ooh, our ride is here."

The ride in question was a familiar pink limo.

· · · · · · · ·

"Lindsay, stop looking at your phone," Noreen said.

"But check out the photo Ryan just sent me!" Lindsay thrust out her hand.

It was a picture of several shirtless men—no, wait, they weren't shirtless. They were simply wearing shirts printed with a picture of a man's chest. Ryan's chest?

"Yeah, yeah," Noreen said. "Your fiancé is hot. But tonight isn't about him. Now, let's all get washed up and changed, then we'll head out in, say, an hour?"

It was a relatively small bachelorette party: just Lindsay, Noreen, Vivian, and Leah.

Well, Vivian assumed this was a small bachelorette, not that she'd been to one before. But she'd occasionally seen groups of women at restaurants or bars, wearing matching T-shirts or, in one case, flower crowns.

The idea of matching outfits had quickly been ditched by Noreen, to Vivian's relief.

After showering—Vivian always felt gross after a flight—she changed into pumps, which were better for walking than some of her other shoes, plus gray pants and a pale pink top. It was late September, and the weather was beautiful in New York. Warm, but not oppressively hot, unlike the last time Vivian had visited the city.

"Okay!" Lindsay said brightly when they met up again. "Where to?"

They headed to Chinatown to eat dumplings, as planned. This was followed by mochi donuts. Lindsay exclaimed with delight and took forever with the menu, eventually settling on the slightly sparkly taro donut. Vivian ordered a yuzu one since sparkles weren't really her style.

When they were in a cab heading to the Rockefeller Center—stuck in traffic, which Vivian supposed was part of the New York experience—she texted Mel to tell him that he had good taste in mochi donuts.

He replied with a link to one of his tweets, a short video of Ryan singing Backstreet Boys. From the image frozen on-screen, it looked like Ryan was really putting his heart into it. However, after a surreptitious look around the cab, Vivian decided not to watch the video. She didn't want to deal with any questions from the other women about why Mel was texting her.

After Top of the Rock and a brief visit to Central Park, they went to a rooftop bar that Mel had recommended. It was full of comfy chairs with red cushions, sleek wooden tables, and pots of shrubs and flowers. They ordered a charcuterie platter and fancy cocktails. Vivian didn't understand all the ingredients in hers, but it was delicious.

The prices, however, were rather high, especially when she converted to Canadian dollars, but she reminded herself that this was okay. It wasn't like bachelorette parties were a regular expenditure for her.

Dusk fell, and there was something magical about being on a

rooftop patio in New York, surrounded by fairy lights. Vivian wasn't used to having a group of friends like this, and she was enjoying herself, even though Lindsay insisted on taking goofy pictures of them all.

Noreen had made reservations at an upscale sushi restaurant, so that was where they went next. She'd also done exhaustive research on exactly what they should order on the menu, and it was hard to imagine there could be anything better than what she'd selected.

Even though they'd had mochi donuts earlier, Lindsay wanted to stop somewhere for gelato after dinner. The place had almost fifty flavors, some quite normal—like vanilla and strawberry—and some more unusual. Like pink peppercorn.

Full of food, they headed to another bar, a crowded place known for unusual cocktails, such as ones that changed color. Lindsay got one with edible glitter, which, in Vivian's opinion, was a little over the top, but Lindsay seemed to enjoy it. Vivian preferred her own drink. It had rhubarb and strawberries, and it was a little smoky. Somehow, it really worked, though she couldn't explain why; rhubarb didn't seem like it belonged in a cocktail.

She took a picture and sent it to Mel, unable to help herself. Why did she want to tell him about everything?

"So, Lindsay," she said as she put her phone in her purse, "how do you like your New York bachelorette? Is it everything you thought it would be?"

"Yeah, it's great. Thank you for planning this." Lindsay shot a smile around the table.

"Speaking of planning," Leah said. "How's the wedding preparation going?"

Lindsay pretended to pull out her hair.

"I suppose it's not terrible," she said at last. "The big stuff is mostly taken care of, and nobody on Ryan's side of the family has strong opinions that they're demanding we follow. By the way, he wants to have door games on the morning of the wedding, so we'll have to figure stuff out for that. And I still have to get my cheong-sam made and . . ."

Noreen patted her back. "Don't worry about it now. Today, you're out with your friends, and we're going to stay up until four in the morning, drinking booze and consuming sugar."

"Just let me text Ryan and see how he's making out," Lindsay said.

As Lindsay picked up her phone, Vivian's phone beeped, and she checked her texts.

> We're not doing anything as sophisticated
> as drinking cocktails.

Mel had also sent her a picture, but she couldn't figure out what was going on. It looked like Ryan was in a sack of some kind?

> MEL: Potato sack races in Central Park.
>
> VIVIAN: Your idea?
>
> MEL: Of course

She snickered, and when she looked up, everyone was staring at her.

"Who are you texting?" Noreen asked. "Is it a guy?"

"It's just Mel," Vivian said. "He has them doing potato sack races. It'll probably be followed by three-legged races and a water balloon fight."

Lindsay raised her eyebrows. "You and Mel text each other?"

"To plan this weekend, that's all. Since he knows New York."

Yet they'd texted more than was necessary for planning.

"I thought you and Mel didn't like each other," Noreen said.

"We don't," Vivian said quickly, "but he's tolerable when we're texting."

"He totally stole the show at karaoke," Leah said. "You barely got to sing."

"I don't think Vivian's complaining about that." Lindsay gave Vivian a look.

Oh God. Lindsay was definitely suspicious. But she didn't linger on the topic.

"So," Lindsay said, "what's the plan now? We're meeting the guys at that bar near Grand Central at one, but there's still a few hours until then . . . Ooh! I forgot to tell you something."

"What is it?" Noreen asked.

"Irene Lai is going to meet us there."

Vivian kept her expression bland, but inside, she was freaking out, just a little. She was going to meet *another* famous person?

She couldn't help thinking back to last year, when she'd first met Mel and Ryan . . .

Chapter 12

By the time they got to the bar in Midtown, it was almost one thirty in the morning. In Toronto, it would have been nearly last call, but New York was different. Not that Vivian needed to drink much more anyway, though she'd heard good things about this place from Mel.

Something about this bar made her feel like she was stepping back in time. Like it could be the 1940s or '50s, and James Stewart, Humphrey Bogart, or Marilyn Monroe could be here—in black-and-white, of course.

Vivian liked the vibe, but she didn't wish she'd actually lived in those days. No, the twenty-first century was better for her.

She went to the bar and ordered a sidecar from the bartender. The bar wasn't packed, but it was a little busy. Lindsay immediately joined Ryan in a booth. They kissed as though they'd been away from each other for a long time, rather than twelve hours.

"Hey."

Mel suddenly appeared at Vivian's side, and she startled.

"Hi," she finally said.

He wasn't wearing the weird shirt with Ryan's shirtless body plastered on it—no, he was wearing a dark dress shirt with a design of white and pink flowers. He smiled at her, and in the slightly dim lighting of the bar, he looked . . .

She breathed in swiftly.

He looked really handsome.

He shot her a lopsided grin. "How was your evening?"

Embarrassingly, it took her a moment to find her voice. "Lots of food, lots of drinks. The dumplings and mochi donuts were excellent. Glad I took your advice."

"Of course you are. I always give great advice. Don't look so skeptical."

"Lindsay enjoyed herself."

"And you? Are you enjoying New York, not just the dumplings and donuts?"

"Yeah. I like big cities." Vivian couldn't imagine living somewhere that wasn't urban. She did appreciate natural scenery, but she still preferred cities when she traveled. Usually, she went on trips alone. She didn't have anyone to go with, and besides, she liked being in control of everything. She decided the itinerary. Where to walk, what food to eat. Her solo trips had certainly been better than the ones she'd gone on with Jared back in the day.

The bartender brought over her drink, and when Mel took a seat, Vivian sat beside him.

"How's your grandma?" she asked. "Is she doing better?"

"Yeah, she's more like herself again. Was afraid she'd throw out a hip when she sang 'Man! I Feel Like a Woman!' the other day, but she managed."

"She hasn't set you up on more blind dates?"

"No, I've been pretending to have a boyfriend to avoid such a fate. And I haven't gone on any dates of my own accord, either."

He shot her a look. A look that suffused her with awareness, a look that reminded her of the last time they'd seen each other in person, when he'd said she intrigued him.

A look that made her feel like *she* was the reason he wasn't interested in anyone else. A ridiculous thought, but not all feelings were rational.

If only.

"On the plus side," he said, "it means I haven't had any breakups in a while."

"You mentioned in one of your sets that you've never had a relationship longer than six months. Is that true, or just something you say onstage?"

"Yeah, I've had lots of short relationships. Nothing ever sticks." He had a gulp of his drink.

Vivian felt like she'd put him in a bad mood by talking about dating. She hadn't seen Mel in person that many times, but she wasn't used to seeing him like this—although maybe it was just the long day and the late hour.

She couldn't help remembering something he'd said at his show back in Toronto. *The problem with being a comedian is that people expect you to be funny.* And after karaoke, when he'd talked about laughter being a survival technique.

"I haven't had many relationships," she said. "My only breakup of note—"

"What about the ones that weren't of note?"

"There were a couple of breakups that happened after a few months. They didn't bother me near as much as the one a few years ago. I wish we hadn't been together for more than six months, and I wish we hadn't lived together."

"What happened?" he asked softly. "If you want to tell me."

"A bunch of things. He got pissed at me for nagging him to empty the dishwasher. Well, he called it nagging—I just asked him twice."

That elicited a chuckle as Mel spun his glass between his hands.

"And he thought I'd change my mind about wanting kids, even though I'd very clearly told him, many times, that I want to be child-free."

Mel didn't ask her why. Most people did. They felt like they were owed an explanation for something they considered unnatural in a woman.

But the fact that he didn't ask made her want to tell him.

"I'm the eldest daughter," Vivian said. "I spent my so-called childhood caring for my three younger siblings. I basically brought up the younger two myself, and I don't wish to do that again. My adulthood is just for me. But even if I hadn't had to raise my siblings, I don't think I'd want kids. I just don't have a strong maternal instinct."

"Where were your parents?"

"Working. Always working. I'm not close with them. My family . . . we don't tease each other like yours does."

He waggled his eyebrows. "Did you get a vanilla mochi donut today?"

"Stop insulting vanilla! Good vanilla is far from boring. But no, I got the yuzu donut."

"Now that's more like it. Was it good?"

"I already said your mochi donut advice was excellent. You just want to hear me sing your praises."

"What can I say?" Mel lifted a shoulder.

Very much the sort of thing she'd expect to come out of his mouth, but she didn't think he'd usually speak so quietly, with that hint of . . . she didn't know how to describe it in his voice.

"When we had gelato," she said, "I got blueberry cheesecake and pink peppercorn. The blueberry cheesecake was delicious, but the other . . . well, vanilla would've been better."

Vivian sipped her drink and looked around the bar. Ryan and

Lindsay had their heads bent together. Somebody else was nearly comatose on the table, his mouth partially open. Near him was a . . .

"What on earth is that? A giant . . . greeting card?"

"Yup," Mel said. "I got everyone to sign it. To wish Ryan well on his marriage. And by 'everyone,' I mean not just the people at the bachelor party, but dozens of strangers, too."

"Is that a unicorn on the card?"

Mel put a hand to his chest as though offended. "It's quite obviously a llamacorn."

"Mm-hmm. Sure it is. A fabulous llamacorn. Obviously."

"Vivian, are you being sarcastic with me?"

"No. I'm being completely serious," she said . . . with a completely serious face. "It's very fabulous."

"It's quite flashy. Not your style."

"Doesn't mean it isn't fabulous."

As Vivian was studying the card, Lindsay turned her way. It was hard to make out Lindsay's expression from this distance, but she seemed to be looking meaningfully at Vivian and Mel, perhaps raising her eyebrows.

Vivian decided to simply pretend no one existed except her and Mel. Yes. That was a perfectly reasonable thing to do, right?

She returned to what they'd been talking about earlier, since she hadn't finished what she'd intended to say. "Back to Jared."

"Jared? Your ex?" Mel asked.

"Yes. He . . ."

This was something she'd thought about telling Mel ever since the karaoke incident. Somehow, approaching it as related to her breakup felt safer.

"I also told him that I didn't think I was straight," she said. "Maybe my childhood obsession with Gillian Anderson should have clued me in, but I didn't start wondering until my thirties.

And after I binged *Just Another New York Sitcom*, I watched an interview you'd done. When you spoke about being an openly bi Asian person—and you seemed so comfortable with your identity—it made me feel represented in a different way than anything I'd seen before."

One of the things she'd later pondered was why it had taken a while for her to start questioning her sexuality—and whether it was in part because she'd been conditioned, when she was younger, to think of other people first and focus on what was expected of her. To push aside her own desires.

But once she realized she was bi, it felt like a bunch of things slotted into place. Made sense. However . . .

"I told Jared, and he thought I was just bullshitting, because I'd never kissed a woman. When I insisted I was bi, he was convinced I'd cheat on him."

Mel didn't say anything, and Vivian regretted her words. She was afraid of acting like a fool when she drank, which often made her even more guarded than usual, but today, she was oversharing. People probably said stuff like this to Mel all the time, and it was awkward, coming from a stranger.

But she wasn't a stranger, right?

She might as well finish her piece. "So, thank you for that," she said, hoping it didn't sound sarcastic. She really didn't mean it sarcastically. "I, uh, just wanted to tell you. I hope it wasn't weird."

Her cheeks were heating. It wasn't like her.

As she was wiping the condensation from her glass of water—because she felt the need to do something with her hands—Mel touched her wrist.

"No, it wasn't weird," he said softly.

"It totally was," she insisted. "I'm in a weird mood tonight. I'm not usually out at two in the morning with friends. In New York." She was suddenly close to tears. Usually, she was the master of herself, but not now. Unlike her family, Mel made her feel like her feelings mattered.

"Hey." He held out his arms, and she gave him a hug.

Hugging. Another thing she rarely did.

"I'm a mess." In front of Mel, who'd judged her in the past.

"Vivian." He unbuttoned his flowered shirt, revealing the totally bizarre T-shirt of Ryan's abs underneath. "I refereed a potato sack race between grown men. While wearing *this*."

But it's just who you are.

If she said that out loud, it might sound like an insult, but it wasn't. He embraced being messy and goofy in public, and she . . . didn't. In some ways, she was the opposite of him, but she was starting to realize how controlled parts of his public image were.

He moved the conversation to a different topic, and for that, she was grateful.

"Are you going back tomorrow?" he asked.

"Yeah. I wish I could have taken time off and stayed for a few days, but . . ." Vivian trailed off. Though she hadn't been paying much attention to her surroundings, it was hard not to notice the woman who'd just arrived.

Irene Lai was wearing a bright pink dress with a large bow, which would look ridiculous on most people, but on Irene Lai, it was hot. There was a large white man standing behind her—her bodyguard? It definitely wasn't Bennett Reed, her longtime boyfriend.

While Ryan's success had been relatively recent, Irene Lai was a little older and had acting credits dating back at least twenty years.

"Irene!" Mel called out.

Oh God.

Irene Lai was heading this way, and Vivian was half-drunk and hardly looking fresh. It had been a long day, and she didn't normally get so close to tears. In public.

"Hi, Mel." Irene Lai stopped in front of them.

"Looking sharp, as usual," he said.

Vivian was jealous of Irene Lai. Not because of her fame—Vivian would hate to be that famous—or her wardrobe, or her wealth, or her beauty. But because Mel was now looking at her.

"This is Vivian." Mel gestured to her. "Lindsay's friend."

"Nice to meet you," Irene said.

"Same." Vivian managed to squeak out the word as they shook hands.

"I should say hello to Ryan."

After accepting a drink from the bartender, Irene Lai made her way to the back, hips moving as though everyone was watching her. And it did seem like a bunch of people in the bar were doing so, though not as many as Vivian might have expected. Perhaps because New Yorkers were accustomed to celebrity sightings.

Vivian felt Mel's hand on her shoulder and realized she'd been staring. Shit. She jerked back and looked at the bottles behind the bar.

"Do you know Irene Lai well?" she asked Mel.

"Not well enough to set you up with her."

"Mel!"

"What? You were clearly admiring her."

"She has a boyfriend." Vivian could feel her face heating again. "Lots of people think she's attractive and—"

"I'm just teasing you."

"She's a movie star."

"Me, too. I voiced a penguin. The movie will be out for Christmas." He paused. "I was once told that you thought I was the most attractive star on *JANYS*?"

Well, this was definitely not a situation she'd ever expected to be in. It was horrifying, really. Like the day she'd met Mel and discovered he'd seen her fan art, she wished the earth would open up and swallow her whole. She'd had a decent enough run up here at the surface, hadn't she? Living underground, away from humanity, would be significantly less mortifying.

"Maybe I did," she said, trying to sound all cool and probably failing.

"And now?"

"Mel . . ." she said warningly.

He buttoned up his dress shirt and made a show of fixing his hair.

"Yes, I think you're cute."

"Mm-hmm," he said.

"What else do you want me to say?" She downed the rest of her drink and turned toward him. His skin was almost golden brown, darker than hers, and it seemed to glow in whatever magical lighting the bar used. She wanted to be enfolded in his arms again . . . and not for a friendly hug, like earlier.

Wait. Was he hitting on her?

Was *he* jealous? Because she'd been appreciating Irene Lai's good looks?

Vivian's head was spinning, and it had nothing to do with the sidecar. The way Mel was looking at her was different from the way anyone had looked at her in a long, long time. He reached out to tuck a lock of hair behind her ear. Never before had she been so aroused by such a touch.

She swallowed and ran her tongue over her lips—not a conscious movement, not one meant to turn him on, but his gaze immediately zeroed in on her mouth. He leaned forward on his barstool, stopping when his face was a few inches from hers, as if in question.

For a moment, she was completely still.

She wanted to kiss him, but how much of that was his comic

persona and his bubble bath–loving character on *JANYS*? The man she'd admired long before she'd met him?

Maybe if she didn't think she'd ever see him again, she could kiss him, just because, but they were in Lindsay and Ryan's wedding party together.

She pulled back and mumbled, "Sorry."

He chuckled. "It's all good."

She almost hated that he was laughing now. She wanted him to be serious again.

"I'm, uh . . ." she began. "I should go talk to Lindsay and Noreen."

She walked away without a backward glance.

. . . .

"What do you think of this picture?" Mel asked, shoving his phone in front of Ryan.

"It's hideous," Ryan replied.

"That's what makes it awesome! You're normally so photogenic, but here you look like you ate sushi that you found at the back of your fridge."

"What a lovely description."

"Thank you," Mel said cheerfully. "I do my best."

He was acting like himself, but he didn't feel like himself. His mind was still on Vivian, who was now sitting at the next table. She'd wanted that kiss, hadn't she?

He shook his head. There were so many people in the world, so many dating apps to try, but his brain had latched on to her. This woman who worked at a bank and whose favorite color was gray. Although bold looks, like Irene Lai's current outfit, were usually Mel's thing, for some reason, Vivian's more understated clothing really did it for him.

He doubted Vivian shared herself easily, yet she'd still told him what his work had meant to her, and it made his heart swell. Completely different from when he made a crowd of people laugh—that was a high, but it wasn't the same. Other people had told him things similar to what she'd said, but that wasn't the same, either.

For now, he'd push that to the back of his brain. His brain had a tendency to disobey him, but he'd try, at least.

"I also like this one." Mel pulled up the photo he'd taken of Ryan and Albert, shirtless, with #StarringRyanKwoksAbs and #StarringAlbertNguyensAbs written on their bodies in marker.

Ryan shook his head. "You're such a nut." There was less pep in his voice than usual. Probably had something to do with it being two thirty in the morning. "Are you putting this on Twitter?"

"I don't know, but it's definitely going in the scrapbook."

It wasn't much longer before they all headed back to the hotel—including Mel. He was staying at the hotel despite having his own place in Manhattan.

As he tried and failed to fall asleep that night, he didn't think about what sort of hijinks he could get up to tomorrow as the bachelor party drew to a close. No, he kept thinking of the kiss that hadn't happened.

And of the vanilla sheet cake that would arrive at Vivian's hotel room the next morning.

· · · · · · ·

There was a knock on Vivian's door.

Shit. Lindsay was early for brunch, and Vivian wasn't dressed yet. She threw on a shirt and walked to the door. "I'm not . . ."

Oops. It wasn't her friend but a member of the hotel staff.

"I was asked to deliver this," he said.

"Um, thanks." She took the box from his hand, thoroughly confused.

And then it hit her. Had Mel really . . . ?

She set down the box and opened it up.

Sure enough, a rectangular vanilla cake stared back at her. Not just any vanilla cake, but one decorated with a phallic-shaped cactus in bright green icing. There was a little pink blob at the top, which she was assumed was supposed to be a flower.

She laughed, then took a picture and sent it to Mel.

> MEL: Wow. It looks even better than I
> thought it would.

> MEL: And by better, I mean even more
> hideous. That green color looks like toxic
> waste.

> VIVIAN: Thank you for the gift.

> MEL: You shouldn't be thanking me. I
> bought you a cheap and ugly cake.

> VIVIAN: You know what I mean.

> MEL: Don't feel obligated to eat it.

> VIVIAN: I'll just cut myself a tiny piece.

> MEL: Cake at nine thirty in the morning?
> How scandalous!

> VIVIAN: Like you wouldn't eat cake at this
> time.

Before she tasted it, she touched her fingers to her lips and thought of last night, trying not to wish they'd kissed.

This weekend had certainly been different from her previous trips to New York.

Chapter 13

"I've heard the average person falls asleep in seven minutes." Mel took a step to the right, microphone in hand. It was mid-December, and he was at the club, trying out new material. "Sounds fake to me. Who are these freaks who fall asleep in *seven minutes*? Do their brains not keep them awake, worrying about how many emails are in their inbox? Or composing the perfect fifty-tweet reply to a troll on Twitter?"

He continued with a few more of the marvelous thoughts that prevented him from sleeping, briefly wondering what Vivian thought about as she tried to sleep.

Developing new material wasn't a fast process. Something would amuse him, and he'd write it down, then think of how to expand it. There was a lot of testing things out and refining them. Seeing how the audience responded. Some comics did most of their "writing" onstage, kept it in their head, but not Mel. He wrote shit down.

"To be fair," he said, "I've met some of these weirdos who get a good night's sleep—I've dated them. One woman could probably fall asleep on a bed of nails, and seven minutes would be *long* for her. I'd be lying next to her, seething in anger. 'How come she can sleep and I can't?'"

Mel pretended to throw a toddler-style tantrum, inspired by Willow's tantrum last week. Based on the audience's reaction, he needed to work on that bit.

"You know what I dream of? You know what, to me, sounds like the ultimate relationship?" He walked across the stage. "Synchronized insomnia. Wouldn't it be great to be awake at four in the morning, and instead of the other person snoring or farting in their sleep next to you, they were awake, too, also obsessing about their emails? Then you could, like, have sex or something, if you weren't too tired. Or just talk about that one joke that doesn't work, the punchline that just doesn't elicit the laugh you want . . . like, you know . . .

"I've tried a lot of stuff to help me sleep. Don't you dare suggest yoga or chamomile tea to me! I've heard it all before." He really had, and he described a bunch of his experiences. "I even bought a new mattress. Let me tell you, that was an expensive failed experiment. And I also tried getting new pillows on which to rest my beautiful head.

"Have you noticed that you can find anything on a pillow these days? Forget plain colors or polka dots. Why buy those when you can buy a pillow with a picture of a cute widdle baby seal on it? Better yet, a pillow that's shaped like a seal?

"Food pillows are all the rage now, too. Rather than going out for dim sum, you can get a larger-than-life siu mai pillow delivered straight to your front door. Rather than ordering some fried chicken, you can order a breaded chicken drumstick in pillow form—or a thigh, if you're a thigh guy. Seriously, it's amazing what we can do with technology these days."

Once again, his mind strayed to Vivian, wondering what she'd think about some of the weird pillows out there. Would she purse her pretty lips and try to look unamused before releasing a delicate chuckle? Or . . .

No, he wouldn't let himself be distracted from his set any further.

"Anyway, one of the times I was awake at four in the morning, I started wondering if anyone has tried to eat one of those pillows in the middle of the night. They're pretty lifelike, right? Sure, they might be a hundred times bigger than the actual thing, but when you're half-awake? It could happen." He pretended to eat a giant chicken drumstick pillow, then discover it was full of fluff—this got a pretty big laugh.

"I think you've really made it when you can find pillows with your face on them. Hasn't happened to me yet, but my friend Ryan Kwok? You know Ryan?" There were a few cheers. "Though he still hasn't reached the pinnacle of pillow achievement." Mel paused to build some anticipation. "Being on a *body pillow*."

· · · · · · ·

VIVIAN: Hey

MEL: How did you know I was awake?

VIVIAN: You retweeted images of dim sum plushies.

MEL: Oh. So I did.

VIVIAN: Are you on the West Coast? Is that why you're up?

MEL: No, good old EST.

VIVIAN: I agree with you.

MEL: Of course you do. I'm a genius.

VIVIAN: I didn't even tell you what I was referring to. But it's the recording you sent me. People who fall asleep in seven minutes or less are the worst. Jared was like that.

MEL: How dare he

VIVIAN: I wanted to punch him in the face when he'd been snoring for three hours and I hadn't had a wink of sleep yet.

MEL: Do you want to tell me more about your violent urges? Do you sometimes wish you could punch me in the face, when I'm just too damn fabulous?

VIVIAN: 😠

VIVIAN: Why do I talk to you. Why.

MEL: I don't think you'll like the answer.

VIVIAN: It's probably something to do with you being as fabulous as a llamacorn.

MEL: Maybe. You often awake at this time?

VIVIAN: No. I usually fall asleep within an hour. But every now and then, I barely sleep at all. Other nights, I sleep a few hours, then get up at three or four, wide awake. Like tonight.

VIVIAN: I liked your bit on pillows, btw. In the recording you sent me.

VIVIAN: I saw an avocado toast pillow the other day.

MEL: Very millennial 👁

MEL: We can't afford to save for retirement because we're buying avocado toast . . . in pillow form.

VIVIAN: I don't like avocados.

MEL: Neither do I.

MEL: Well, they're okay in California rolls.

VIVIAN: True

MEL: We should form a club.

VIVIAN: What would we talk about?

MEL: Hating avocados. Duh.

VIVIAN: I don't think we could discuss that for very long.

MEL: I can talk about anything for hours.

VIVIAN: But I can't.

MEL: That's okay. I'll do all the talking in our club.

VIVIAN: How about shrimp? I don't like shrimp.

MEL: 😮

MEL: You wound me. I'm not sure we can be friends anymore.

VIVIAN: We were friends?

MEL: I like to think so.

MEL: In fact, as your friend, I'm getting you
a Christmas present. What's your address?

VIVIAN: Should I be frightened?

MEL: No, it's a nice present, I promise.
Avocado and shrimp free, and it's better
than the cake I had sent to your hotel.

VIVIAN: Well, in that case . . .

Mel didn't return to bed when Vivian said she was going to try
to get a little sleep. He kept thinking about the fact that he'd just
experienced synchronized insomnia, even though they weren't dating and weren't even in the same country.

And it had been rather cool, yeah.

· · · · · · ·

VIVIAN: Thank you for the gift. It arrived
today. It goes nicely with the rest of my
throw pillows. Adds a nice pop of color.

MEL: What color are your other pillows?
Gray?

VIVIAN: . . . maybe 😳

VIVIAN: Some gray, some maroon. Solid
colors, of course.

VIVIAN: The pillow you gave me is nicer
than the one you got for Lindsay.

MEL: But a picture of Ryan, shirtless,
coming out of a watermelon? With sequins?

I couldn't resist buying it for her. I wonder who thought of that idea.

VIVIAN: You're sure it wasn't you? Did you design it?

MEL: Nah, my brain's not that weird.

VIVIAN: I'll take your word for it.

MEL: That was dripping with sarcasm, lol.

VIVIAN: Merry Christmas, if I don't talk to you tomorrow.

MEL: 🎅 🎄

Chapter 14

Andy was late, of course. Twenty minutes and counting.

Vivian shoved her hands in her pockets and stepped from side to side, trying to keep warm. To make the pickup process as quick as possible, her brother had told her to be outside. Not even right outside her building, but a block away, because that would be a more convenient pickup location.

At last, his car pulled up, and she hopped into the backseat with her bag of presents.

"Hi!" Amanda said, far too chipper for such a cold day, even if it was Christmas.

Vivian didn't ask the reason for the delay. She doubted it was traffic—she'd checked Google Maps while waiting on the sidewalk, and the roads looked not too bad—and if she asked, it would sound accusatory. Then one of her siblings would get pissed at her, and the entire drive would be tense.

"Did you have to work yesterday?" Amanda asked.

"Just until noon," Vivian said. "Now I'm off until the new year."

"We should go Boxing Day shopping!"

At some point, Vivian would agree to a shopping trip out of

guilt, but she wasn't in the mood, especially when the malls were so busy. She wanted a relaxing holiday.

Still, rather than a clear answer, she looked out the window and said, "Uh, we'll see."

With anyone else, Vivian wouldn't say "we'll see" when she really meant "no," but she'd said no to her sister so many times before—and not just recently, when it came to shopping. She felt like she'd used it all up.

No, you can't swim in the tank with the lobsters.

No, you can't take off your clothes in the middle of the frozen food aisle.

No, I can't re-form the banana slices into a whole banana.

She'd had no idea how to transition from her role as pseudo-parent in Amanda's life to grown-up sister, and the thought of spending more time together still brought up resentment. Plus, they had little in common. Amanda's extroverted peppiness was, well, nothing like Vivian.

They arrived at their childhood home in Scarborough half an hour later. Stephen was staying there now, home from med school at McMaster. He gave them all smiles and hugs when they entered with their gifts, as did Ba.

Ma, on the other hand, stood in the doorway to the living room with her arms crossed.

"Vivian," she said, "why are you wearing *that?*"

"What's wrong with my shirt?" Vivian asked defensively, then regretted it. It was best to stay quiet, and she was usually good at that.

Ma made a face that said, *I shouldn't have to tell you*, but Vivian had no idea what the problem was. Her soft brown sweater was good quality and perfectly respectable, and it felt amazing.

"It doesn't show enough skin," Ma said.

Wait. *What?*

"Why does Vivian need to show more skin?" Amanda asked.

"Ma, you make no sense. It's well below freezing outside, and if you want her to attract a guy, who's she going to meet at a family Christmas dinner?"

An awful thought occurred to Vivian. "Did you invite a date for me?"

"No, did you want me to?" Ma asked.

"Of course not."

"I'm just saying. You're getting old, and maybe your wardrobe is part of the problem. Conservative. Neutral colors. You could show more cleavage?"

Amanda started laughing. Ma shot her an indulgent look, then turned back to Vivian.

"My cleavage isn't very impressive," Vivian mumbled.

Ma glared at Vivian like her breast size was all her fault.

"You know what I would like for Christmas next year? A grand-child." Ba looked meaningfully at Vivian, then glanced at Andy before focusing on Vivian again.

Yeah, yeah, the expectations were all on the oldest daughter. As they'd always been. No matter how many times Vivian told them . . .

"I could have a baby!" Amanda said.

Ba looked alarmed. "You're still in school. Focus on that for now. But Vivian . . ."

Who said Christmas was a jolly holiday?

"Vivian, want to help me with the turkey?" Stephen asked, tugging her arm.

Stephen was the quiet but friendly one. He had an interest in culinary arts, and as a teenager, he'd asked to take over cooking the Christmas turkey, to which their parents had naturally responded, "Of course!" He'd experimented in the first few years, but now he'd more or less settled on the menu.

"What's new?" he asked as he checked the temperature of the turkey.

With Stephen, unlike with her parents, this didn't feel like a loaded question. Still, Vivian didn't say the first thing that came to mind, since that was, *Do you know who Melvin Lee is? He's a friend of my roommate's fiancé, and he sent me an* Only the Best *pillow* . . .

She loved the pillow, and she suspected it would be better than any Christmas gift she'd get today. Yes, it was just a pillow, but it had a picture of a hot cowboy next to his horse, and the show was awesome—the third season, which had just finished, had been her favorite yet. Plus, it was a present just for *her*, not a generic box of chocolates or hand cream.

Vivian hadn't thought she cared much about gifts . . . until now. There was something nice about getting a gift that was so personalized.

"Not much," she said to Stephen. "Work, Netflix. That sort of thing."

Stephen instructed her on what to do with the snow peas, and it was rather nice to not have to make decisions and figure out the logistics. She wasn't an amazing cook, but she could follow directions.

Stephen was the sibling she found easiest to be around. She didn't feel on edge like she did with everyone else in her family; she never feared what he would say next. It helped that he didn't expect them to be close, like Amanda did. Also, Vivian hadn't been quite as involved in his care as a small child as she had with her sister—she felt less resentment toward him.

They sat down to dinner at precisely eight o'clock. Turkey, bread stuffing, roasted potatoes with rosemary, snow peas, and squash.

For dessert, to Vivian's surprise, they had something Stephen had never made before. Something exotic.

Figgy pudding.

Ma peered at the pudding after Stephen set it in the center of the table. "It doesn't look very good. I've never heard of figgy pudding before."

"You know, like in 'We Wish You a Merry Christmas'?" Stephen said. "It's British."

"It's ready to eat?"

"No, first we cover it in brandy and light it on fire."

Ma just shook her head.

As it turned out, the figgy pudding was quite tasty. It was followed by Turtles chocolates as they opened presents.

From her parents, Vivian received a red sweater that was shockingly low-cut. Her mother seemed to be serious about this showing-more-skin-to-attract-a-suitor business—it was her mother who did the Christmas shopping every year, not her father. The sweater was accompanied by socks and nonperishable food items.

"OMG, these are so pretty!" Amanda exclaimed as she opened a small box, revealing the earrings that Vivian had bought her. "They're *just* my style. You have such excellent taste."

When Amanda gave Vivian a hug, Vivian found herself stiffening.

Why? She should be able to hug her sister, shouldn't she? Was she afraid that Amanda was leading into another question about Boxing Day shopping?

But Amanda didn't ask again.

At midnight, Andy dropped Vivian off at home. Vivian changed into her pajamas and wasted a little time on her phone, not feeling like going to bed yet. For some reason she wanted to talk to someone, which wasn't like her at all, and since it was Christmas, likely everyone had better things to do. Still, she checked to see if Mel had tweeted anything recently. If he had, she'd feel okay about bugging him . . . but he hadn't.

She tried not to feel disappointed.

. . . .

A strange thing happened every year at Christmas.

Mel missed his father.

He hadn't seen his father in almost twenty years. Joy didn't talk to Dad, either, and Chelsea—who'd been Daddy's girl when she was little—maintained minimal contact.

Dad had lost his shit when Mel came out, and ultimately, that had led to his parents' divorce—though Mom had assured him, more than once, that she doubted the marriage would have lasted anyway.

Dad was an asshole who didn't deserve to be missed, so Mel didn't miss him much. Except at Christmas.

His father had always made a big deal of the holiday. He'd buy lots of presents; he wasn't one of those men who left all the shopping to his wife. He'd dress up as Santa Claus and decorate the home with elaborate light displays. Not on the level of *National Lampoon's Christmas Vacation*, but still. Their home would look nicer than the others on the street.

It was hard, at times, to reconcile those two images of his father: the doting dad who'd loved the holidays, and the one who'd screamed at Mel that he was sick. Mel wouldn't say, precisely, that his father had ruined Christmas for him, but he enjoyed it less than he would otherwise. Because, paradoxically, of those happy memories.

Now his family sat by the tree, opening presents before dinner. Christmas music played in the background.

"Why don't you give this to Uncle Mel?" Curt—Chelsea's husband—said to Willow.

Willow took the small package wrapped in red paper and ran over to Mel. "Unkie!"

"Thank you," he said to her. She smiled and ran back to the tree.

The tag said it was from Po Po. He opened the gift to reveal three pairs of red boxers.

Again?

When he held them up, his sisters laughed. Ruby and Willow giggled, too, probably just because other people were laughing.

"You need some lucky red underwear," Po Po said.

"Why?" he asked.

"You haven't been lucky enough lately. You broke up with Nicky, yes?"

"I did." Mel hadn't felt like keeping that lie going any longer, so he'd faked a breakup.

"You need to meet someone nice. Hopefully these will help. You will run into a nice person at the bodega! Maybe spill hot coffee on them."

"So you're saying you want me to be clumsy."

"Aiyah! I'm just saying I don't want you to be alone. Fine for some people, but not you."

This conversation made Mel think of Vivian, which was silly. They'd merely gotten close to kissing. Once. Back in September. Though they did occasionally text at four in the morning when their insomnia synced up, and he'd been excited about buying her a pillow for Christmas.

Now he pictured buying her red underwear instead . . .

He pushed that out of his mind, pasted on a smile, and started singing along to the music in the background. *"Don we now our gay apparel . . . Girls, do you like my shirt?"* It was a busy design of snowflakes, bells, reindeer, wrapped gifts, Christmas trees, and other holiday imagery. "Do you know what this is?" He pointed at a snowman.

"Snowman!" Ruby shouted.

At least he was pretty sure that's what she'd said.

"Good job," he told her.

"Nice to see you've moved on from ugly Christmas sweaters," Joy said.

"I figure this is more my style. And it's not ugly."

"Maybe just a little."

"Says the woman who's wearing all black. You're supposed to be *'jol-ly.'* Mel sang the last word in a high-pitched voice. Then he went to the Christmas tree and pulled out one of his presents for the girls. "Ruby, Willow, you can open this together."

Last year, they hadn't quite understood how to unwrap presents, but this year, they were doing pretty well.

"Dashing through the snow . . . In a one-horse open sleigh . . . O'er the fields we go . . ."

He stopped singing once they'd torn through the paper. There were two boxes, and Joy laughed when she saw them.

Mel opened the first box for the girls. "See? It's a little drum set." He tapped the drumsticks on one of the drums.

Ruby took a drumstick and banged enthusiastically, not on any of the drums, but the cardboard box in which they'd come. Then she tried to hit Mel's head.

"No, no," he said. "My head is not a drum. It's like this." With his hands, he tapped the drum in time to the song. *"Jingle bells, jingle bells, jingle all the way . . ."*

Willow grabbed the other drumstick and banged along with him.

"Good job," he said. "Now, in this box . . ." He took out a rainbow-colored xylophone and played a few notes of "Jingle Bells." "It's got a cord so you can pull it to any room in the house."

"Leech!" Ruby said.

Mel wasn't sure what she was talking about.

"Yes, it's like a doggy's leash," Chelsea said. "Can you girls say thank you to Uncle Mel?"

"Tank you!" they said in unison. Ruby gave him a hug. Willow immediately went back to banging on the drum.

Curt raised an eyebrow at Mel, and Chelsea laughed.

"Remember that toy you got them last year, Mel?" she asked.

"Oh, yeah," Mel said. "It made lots of different noises and sung tons of annoying songs. The girls loved it."

"I took the batteries out one day, after I'd heard the same song for half an hour straight. They started crying, though that was a better noise than the annoying song. But at two in the morning, I heard that sound again! Curt thinks I hallucinated, but I swear I didn't."

"Musical instruments are very good for children," Po Po said. "It teaches them many skills, no? Maybe they will grow up to be great pianists."

Willow started hitting the cardboard box with both drumsticks. "Yeah, yeah, yeah!"

"I'm sure that's exactly what's happening," Joy said.

"Wah, you need to be more positive. Maybe I should get *you* lucky red underwear."

Joy looked appalled at the thought of wearing red under her black clothes.

"Then you could have a meet-cute, like Mel," Po Po said. "I don't know, maybe you spill a jar of beetles all over a nice man at school."

Mel shuddered. "Sounds like a dream come true."

They opened the rest of the presents, then Mom got up.

"Mel, could you lend me a hand?" she asked.

He followed her into the kitchen. She started getting stuff out of the fridge but didn't give him anything to do.

"You okay?" She turned to him.

"Of course. Didn't you see me singing out there in my Christmas shirt?" He gestured to his chest. "I got a good deal on this one."

She gave him a look.

Mel wouldn't crack under a mere look from most people, but his mother was a different story. Still, it took maybe a minute of intense staring on her part.

Okay, it took five seconds.

"I miss Dad at Christmas," he said. "I shouldn't because . . . you know. But Christmas was fun with him. He was over the top at times." *Like me.*

His mother nodded.

"Anyway," he said, "what do you need help with? Lumpy gravy is my specialty."

She squeezed his shoulder. "I'm proud of you, even if he isn't," she said. "How about you help yourself to the eggnog?"

"You know I hate that stuff."

"Mel!" Po Po called from the other room.

He went to the doorway of the kitchen so he could see his po po, sitting in the armchair, as well as Ruby running around with the xylophone and screaming "Good doggy!" or similar.

"Yes?" he said.

"You get me some eggnog, okay?" Po Po patted her stomach. "I lost weight when I was sick, and eggnog has lots of calories, yes? Maybe add rum to it?"

"Not much, or you'll fall asleep before dinner."

"Ah, fine, fine. Act like you know better than me, even though I've been alive more than fifty years longer than you. I have much wisdom, you know? And after I drink eggnog, I will use wisdom—"

"To sing 'That Don't Impress Me Much'?"

"How did you know? But after that, we will sing something else. Maybe from that movie with Olivia Newton-John? I like her."

Mom stomped out of the kitchen. "Did you know," she said to Mel, "your grandma wouldn't even let me go to see *Grease* when it came out? I was in high school. She was so strict back then! Not saying I didn't watch it anyway, but . . ."

Po Po clucked her tongue. "Ah, you were a bad kid! You're grounded!"

"Very funny."

Mel laughed more than he normally would and tried to erase his father from his mind.

. . . .

MEL: You awake?

VIVIAN: Yeah

VIVIAN: How was your Christmas? You saw your family?

MEL: It was pretty decent. The usual, more or less.

MEL: My grandma wanted to sing Summer Nights together, and it made me think of you.

He regretted the text as soon as he sent it. It seemed like . . . too much.

But texting Vivian late at night on Christmas, when they'd just talked to each other yesterday, and sending her a pillow—with the face of another person—were probably already too much.

And now he was jealous of a fucking pillow because it was in the same apartment as her.

Hmm.

> VIVIAN: I bet your grandma sang louder
> than me.

MEL: She sure did.

> VIVIAN: I feel bad that I didn't get you
> anything for Christmas. Maybe I'll give you
> something when you come to Toronto next
> month.

MEL: You don't need to.

> VIVIAN: I'll even tell you what it is.

MEL: . . . it's been three minutes, and you
still haven't told me.

> VIVIAN: I was building suspense. Like when
> you take a really long pause onstage. I'm
> going to get you . . .

MEL: I can't bear it any longer.

> VIVIAN: A plain gray dress shirt.

MEL: 😄

MEL: You wound me.

MEL: Who would ever wear something as
hideous as a plain gray shirt?

She didn't reply for a few minutes, and he wondered if he'd
gone too far. If she felt like her fashion sense was under attack, or
if she would take it as light teasing, as he'd intended.

She would, right? After all, she'd been teasing him with the gray-dress-shirt business.

Still, his anxiety ratcheted up a notch.

MEL: Not saying you don't look sexy in gray, but . . .

Shit! His finger slipped. He hadn't intended to actually send that. She did look sexy in her conservative outfits, but he didn't want her to know he thought so.

VIVIAN: What if the shirt had a floral design in different shades of gray? Would that be acceptable to you?

She hadn't taken that opportunity to flirt with him via text, which was . . . a disappointment? A relief? Both at the same time? Even if she wasn't flirting, the fact that they could playfully text about nothing in particular was nice.

His father popped into his head again, but without any of the emotion that had previously accompanied such thoughts.

He considered texting her about his father. She must have some idea of what had happened there—he'd probably talked about it in his set when she, Lindsay, and Ryan had come to see him perform in Toronto more than a year and a half ago. Anyone who had some familiarity with his stand-up knew that story.

He didn't tell it when he performed anymore. He felt like he'd outgrown it, even though his personal history hadn't changed and it wasn't like he saw it in a different light. He'd just prefer to talk about other things.

Vivian didn't mention anything about Christmas with her family, and he didn't ask. They chatted for a little longer before she decided to get some sleep.

Mel didn't bother trying to sleep yet. His brain was wired.

He had a few busy weeks ahead of him, culminating in Ryan's wedding, after which he'd have a bit of a break. Lots of things to worry about, in other words, but even when there wasn't much to worry about, his brain still found a way. It was remarkably skilled at that.

And today, he couldn't help obsessing over that text he'd accidentally sent Vivian, the one about her looking sexy in gray . . .

Chapter 15

"I was born in the year of the rabbit. I know, I know, it's very appropriate. I'm small, fluffy, and cute." Mel turned around and shook his ass. "That was me showing off my cottontail, in case you couldn't tell. But you could obviously tell, because it was a spot-on impression of a wild bunny. Yes, wild bunnies enjoy shaking their asses. They're wild, man."

He took a few steps across the stage as people laughed, and he found himself searching the audience for Vivian, even though he knew she wouldn't be here tonight—she had to do something with her family. But he was in Toronto, and he couldn't seem to stop looking for her.

Would she enjoy watching him shake his ass?

"I always knew I was born in the year of the rabbit, but I didn't know much else about the Chinese zodiac. In fact, there were lots of things I didn't know about being Chinese. My parents both grew up in the US, and my grandparents came to the US not all that long after the Exclusion Act was lifted. You know, that wonderful piece of legislation that banned people like me from coming to America.

"Anyway, for the Lunar New Year several years ago, I got a week's worth of red underwear from my grandmother. Now, I don't know about you, but I find getting underwear as a gift from my grandma . . . kind of weird. Just a teensy-teensy bit." He held his thumb and forefinger close together. "Underwear isn't the sort of gift you're supposed to get from your family when you're an adult, you know what I'm saying? It's like condoms or cigarettes—though you shouldn't be getting those for children, either. Obviously.

"So apparently when your zodiac sign comes around again, every twelve years, it's bad luck. My grandma was shocked I didn't know this. And I was like, 'Well, if you didn't tell me, how was I supposed to know?' The red underwear was to ward off bad luck, and she wanted me to wear it every single day. Just to make sure no bad luck snuck in through some green boxers, you know? She assumed I did laundry every week—but haha, joke's on her, I was too fucking depressed to do that much laundry."

He could joke about it now . . . but yes, his mental health had been in a bad state then.

"That was the year I started doing stand-up, so it was an important year, though I can't say it was a lucky year. My red underwear—which I religiously wore at each open mic, just in case—did not prevent me from bombing. Over and over and over.

"My younger sister is quite a bit younger than me, and she was born in the year of the dog. Kinda cute, isn't it? She's a dog and I'm a rabbit. My older sister, on the other hand, is an ox. Not quite as cute, in my opinion."

What about Vivian? Which year was she born in?

There was a lot that he didn't know about her.

"However, dogs aren't always cute. I used to live next to a lady who had a dog that was literally Satan's spawn. It must have escaped from the depths of hell—there's no other explanation. It was part chihuahua, and I don't know if you've ever had the misfortune of encountering a chihuahua before, but these are some bad-tempered, anxious motherfuckers. I understand the anxiety, I really do, but . . ."

He got down on his hands and knees and pretended to be a dog. This always elicited a good laugh because people enjoyed watching him make an utter fool of himself.

As he stood up, he noted a person at the table near the back. From the haircut and the way she laughed, she looked like Vivian, but then she tilted her head, and Mel could tell it wasn't her.

He felt unreasonably disappointed.

But he didn't let it show on his face. He continued with his set, talking about this dog—Jayne with a *y*—who'd barked up a storm and tried to nip him, a cute widdle bunny rabbit. Her owner had said that Jayne hated Asian men, and he'd been tempted to bark back at the racist dog before the woman had claimed it was just a joke—a joke!—and the dog actually hated all men.

"One more thing I forgot to tell you," Mel said. "That day I met Jayne for the first time, guess what I was wearing? My lucky red underwear, that's right. I hate to think what Jayne would have done if I'd been wearing blue boxers with a cat pattern . . . You've been a great audience! Good night!"

After his show, he felt a bit buzzed, as he always did; the high he got from making people laugh never got old. But all he kept thinking about were the two times he'd seen Vivian after his shows. The first time, when he'd insulted her life choices, and the second time, when they'd shared a snippy conversation.

Things were different now.

They texted.

They'd almost kissed.

He'd sent her a present for Christmas.

One of Mel's best friends was getting married in a couple of days, and sure, he was looking forward to the wedding—he did enjoy weddings—but Vivian was on his mind more than anything else.

Tomorrow, he'd see her for the first time in months. At the rehearsal.

. . . .

Mel stood with Ryan, Juan, and Mr. Kwok in front of the church in Scarborough. Ryan wasn't religious, but his mother would have wanted him to get married in a church, so this was where they were holding the ceremony.

"I saw you tweeted a photo of the repairs you made to your deck," Mel said to Ryan's father. "Maybe you could give me some lessons so I don't take out an eye the next time I try to put together furniture."

Mel wasn't really focusing on the conversation, though; he was looking out at the parking lot, waiting for Vivian to show up. Ryan was doing the same, except he was eager for the appearance of his bride-to-be, of course. Vivian and Lindsay would be arriving together with Lindsay's mother and her boyfriend.

At last, a blue sedan pulled up to a parking spot near the front of the church, and Lindsay and Vivian stepped out. Curiously, Mel's heart was beating . . . well, nearly as fast as it had when Jayne had tried to bite him.

"Hi." Vivian looked around, but her gaze lingered on Mel.

"Hi," he said.

"Okay, the bride is here!" Em, the wedding planner, clapped her hands. "Let's get this rehearsal started."

They took off their coats inside the church. Vivian was wearing a black jumpsuit, an outfit that Mel figured would look utterly ridiculous on most people—himself included—but she pulled it off, and she walked smoothly in her black stilettos.

They didn't start with the procession, but with everyone standing at the altar, bride and bridesmaids on the left, groom and groomsmen on the right. The wedding planner spent a bit of time adjusting their positions—whatever would be optimal for pictures tomorrow, Mel assumed. There was a photographer present at the rehearsal, too.

Then they went through each step of the ceremony, though the minister didn't say every line. When it was time for the rings, Mel made a show of patting his pockets with a look of horror on his face.

"Mel!" Ryan said sharply, which wasn't like him.

Mel immediately produced two Ring Pops, and Vivian chuckled.

Well, other people laughed, too, but he only cared about her.

The photographer got a close-up of the bride and groom wearing their large, colorful rings, rather than the platinum bands they'd get at the actual ceremony. Hopefully she also got a shot of Mr. Kwok's comical look of disapproval.

After going through the ceremony, they practiced walking out of the church. As the best man, Mel was paired with Noreen, and Vivian and Juan were next.

Finally, they practiced the procession. Mel wouldn't have to walk down the aisle; he, Ryan, and the groomsmen would enter from the side at the start of the ceremony. The bridesmaids were coached on how fast to walk and how much space to leave between them. The wedding planner told Vivian that she didn't need to walk like she was in a rush.

Then Lindsay entered on her mother's arm, and when Mel saw Ryan's glowing smile, he slapped his friend on the back.

They practiced the hand-off, and Em said, "We'll do it all one more time."

"Aiyah, is that really necessary?" Mr. Kwok asked. "I'm hungry."

"Our reservation isn't for another half hour," Ryan said, "and the restaurant is right around the corner."

So they did the whole thing again, and this time, Mel didn't hand over any Ring Pops. And when they practiced the procession for the second time, and Vivian walked slowly down the aisle, having listened to Em's advice, Mel felt . . .

Well, hungry. Like Mr. Kwok, he could definitely use some food.

But he also felt an odd thrill at seeing Vivian in that kickass jumpsuit and stilettos. She was dressed completely differently from the other bridesmaids, though tomorrow, they'd all be wearing the same thing. He liked that she stood out. Liked that she looked serious and managed only a slight smile when Em said, "You're allowed to smile, you know."

As she got closer and closer to him, he felt a tense anticipation, as though it were his wedding and she were the bride.

What on earth . . . ?

Yes, he thought she was sexy.

Yes, they seemed to get along now.

Yes, he wanted to kiss her.

But thinking about that sort of thing, even at a wedding rehearsal, seemed a little much.

Could anyone else feel this tension?

He was tempted to break it by making a silly joke, but he didn't think that would be appreciated. This wasn't the time. Instead, he gave Vivian the slightest of nods and pretended he was feeling completely normal inside, even though he never, ever felt normal.

You might think a grown man who barked like an angry, racist chihuahua onstage would feel normal sometimes, but you'd be wrong.

· · · · · · ·

Mel was wearing a dark gray suit, and Vivian was shocked he owned such a thing. She wanted to tease him about it, like she'd teased him about the gray dress shirt. She recalled what he'd texted her that night: *Not saying you don't look sexy in gray, but . . .* Her cheeks felt warm, and she tried not to focus on how good he looked today.

She didn't get a chance to speak to him at the church, though, since her group was the last to arrive and the rehearsal started immediately after that. Then they were in different vehicles on the short drive to the restaurant. She thought they might be seated at the same table, as it looked like Ryan and Lindsay would share a table with their families and everyone else would be at the other table, until Ryan said, "Hey, Mel, why don't you sit next to my dad?"

Vivian felt a disturbing level of disappointment. Really, it was just one dinner, and she'd get to talk to him at the wedding tomorrow.

Ryan's dad appeared equally disappointed—for completely different reasons.

"No way," Mr. Kwok said. "He will steal my phone and upload all sorts of garbage to Twitter."

Mel held up his hands. "I swear I won't! I only do such things to Ryan."

"Thank you," Ryan said, deadpan. "I feel very special."

"As you should."

"I still don't trust you," Mr. Kwok grumbled. "You will sit at the other table."

Vivian suddenly developed a strange affection for this grumpy old man.

"Very well." Mel pulled out the chair next to Vivian.

"No, absolutely not," Ryan said. "You two aren't sitting beside each other." He sent a stern look in Mel's direction.

Vivian deflated but didn't protest out loud. Lindsay, however, stood on her toes and whispered something in Ryan's ear. He nodded.

"All right," Ryan said to Mel, "but if there are any shenanigans—"

"Don't worry, there won't be," Mel said cheerfully.

Ryan looked skeptical but didn't object further.

Vivian couldn't help wondering . . . what exactly did Lindsay know? Did she suspect that Vivian texted Mel on a somewhat regular basis, and that Mel was the one who'd sent the *Only the Best* pillow? It had arrived separately from the sequined Ryan-coming-out-of-a-watermelon pillow, and Vivian had just mumbled that hers was from a friend.

She now felt extremely exposed, but on the plus side, she was sitting next to Mel.

"You're wearing gray," she said. "No flowered suit?"

"I'm saving it for tomorrow, of course." He winked.

She might seem cool and collected, but after many months of text-only conversations, she was actually talking to him in person, and it was . . .

Oh God.

She wanted to curl up against him and feel his arms around her. She wanted to kiss him.

It was different from the attraction she'd felt toward him previously, when she'd only known him from afar.

As the food was brought out by stern-faced, inobtrusive servers, Mel talked to the whole table, kept the conversation going among people who didn't know each other. Vivian admired his skill. It wasn't something she could do, but she wasn't surprised he was good at it.

She was glad he didn't pay her special attention—she didn't want to cause any raised eyebrows—but at the same time, she craved more, and she was annoyed with herself for that. Even if they could exchange friendly banter now, he was still the guy who'd insulted her career. They lived in different countries, and she didn't want a relationship, and he was her opposite.

And yet . . .

At nine thirty, the rehearsal dinner was over. She'd have an early start to her day tomorrow, as the hair and makeup artists were coming over at six.

"See you in the morning!" Noreen said brightly, waving, when they started to split up in the parking lot. "Ryan, you should be *very worried* about the door games we have planned for when you come to pick her up."

Before Vivian stepped into Lindsay's mom's car, Mel gave her a strange look, which she couldn't decipher, but it still made her shiver.

"You cold?" Lindsay asked.

"No—I mean, yes. I'm cold."

Lindsay looked at her oddly, perhaps because in lying, Vivian had made her voice unusually chipper, and she hadn't sounded like herself.

Tomorrow would certainly be interesting.

But her focus wouldn't be on Mel, shouldn't be on Mel; it would be on making sure Lindsay had a wonderful day.

Chapter 16

At eight o'clock in the morning, there was a knock on the door. Leah and Jenna, ready in their bridesmaids' dresses, hurried to open it, but Noreen and Vivian remained with Lindsay in her room, where she was in the middle of having her hair done.

"Are you nervous?" Noreen asked.

"Why would I be nervous?" Lindsay said. "He's the one who has to jump through all the hoops to see me. I just sit here and get prettied up."

"You're not having any doubts?" Vivian inquired.

Noreen gave her a look, but Vivian had wanted to check, just to be sure.

"Of course not," Lindsay said. "I'm very sure I want to marry Ryan." She grinned, giddy with excitement. "But I'm sad I don't get to watch him do all the tasks you have planned."

"You'll see the video later," Noreen said. "Now, Vivian, let's go."

They headed to the door and stood behind Leah and Jenna. The groom—ready to prove his devotion to his bride—and his four groomsmen were on the other side of the threshold.

Vivian's eyes were drawn to Mel in his tux, and she couldn't help feeling annoyed with him. Why did he have to look so damn handsome? If it were just the two of them, she'd make a joke about his plain white shirt, but they were surrounded by people.

"Lindsay is getting ready," Noreen said, "but we won't let you enter until you pay us ninety-nine dollars." She put her hands on her hips and turned to Ryan. "You may have starred in an action movie and done most of the stunts yourself, but trust me, we'll be able to prevent you from getting through."

"Come on, pay up," Jenna said. "Ninety-nine dollars."

"Why ninety-nine and not eighty-eight?" Trevor asked.

"It means eternity." She held out her hand and wiggled her fingers.

Juan fished a few red envelopes out of his jacket and handed them over.

Jenna made a show of slowly counting the money. "Very well. Come in. Ryan, you can take a seat at the table."

It was crowded in the apartment with the groomsmen, bridesmaids, videographer, photographer, and wedding planner.

"Now, remember," Em said, "you have one hour. We need to be in the limos at nine."

When they reached the kitchen, Jenna revealed a giant lobster bib and tied it around Ryan's neck. "We don't want you to get anything on your tux during your next task. You need to consume the four flavors of life. Something sweet, sour, bitter, and spicy."

Noreen placed the first item on the table. "This is sweet."

He peered at the shot glass. "What is it?"

"Maple syrup sprinkled with brown sugar."

Ryan took a large sip and started coughing, dribbling some of the syrup on his lobster bib. He finished it in smaller sips as Vivian placed a lime on a cutting board. She cut it into four wedges. "Now you have to eat the whole lime."

Ryan gamely did so, making faces the whole time. Vivian couldn't tell if he was playing it up a little.

"Bitter." Noreen put another shot glass on the table. "A concoction from an herbalist in Chinatown. I don't know the details."

He winced as he drank it.

"Wow, looks tasty," Mel said.

"Yeah?" Vivian said. "We've got some extra."

He gave her a look, and she couldn't help being aware of his nearness. She stepped back and almost took out Trevor.

"Lastly . . ." Leah placed a plate on the table. On the plate was an upside-down bowl.

Jenna removed the bowl to reveal a jalapeño. "We would have gotten you Thai chilis, but I didn't think you could handle them. Here's some milk in case you need it."

As it turned out, he did.

"What's next?" Ryan started to get out of the chair, but Noreen stopped him.

"We have something extra for you," she said, setting another plate with an upside-down bowl on the table.

When she revealed the item under the bowl, everyone laughed. It was a mini matcha tiramisu donut, like the sort Lindsay and Noreen sold at Kensington Bake Shop.

"I know you think tiramisu needs espresso," Noreen said, "but—"

"After everything else you had me eat and drink? I'm pretty happy with this." Ryan polished off the donut. "Do I get to see my bride now?" he asked, though he clearly knew that wasn't happening anytime soon.

Jenna took off his lobster bib—that had definitely been a good idea.

"Nope!" Noreen said. "It's seaweed time. Don't worry, you all get to participate in this one." She looked at the groomsmen.

Vic groaned. Juan, on the other hand, obviously had no idea what he was in for.

Leah held up a piece of seaweed, about two inches wide. "You have to stand in a line and pass the piece of seaweed along using only your mouths. Ryan, you're in the middle."

Juan started and passed it to Vic—somehow, Juan made it look easy. Vic, on the other hand, struggled to keep the seaweed on his mouth as he turned to Ryan, and the seaweed fell on the floor.

"That's okay," Noreen said. "We have lots of nori." She held up another piece, but this one was noticeably smaller than the previous one.

"Each time we fail, it gets smaller?" Mel asked.

"That's right!" she said cheerfully.

This time, Vic managed to successfully pass the seaweed to Ryan, who bent down and tilted his head in Mel's direction.

Vivian was certain that her thoughts were markedly different from those of the other bridesmaids. She couldn't help wishing she were in Ryan's place, passing the seaweed to Mel. Wanting to participate in this ridiculous game, in front of a whole bunch of spectators—that wasn't like her at all.

Well, she'd prefer to kiss him in private. But passing seaweed with their mouths in public would at least be something, his body close to hers.

She was more than a little irritated with her brain.

Mel tipped his head up and moved his mouth close to Trevor's, and when Trevor received the seaweed, he lifted it up in triumph.

"Now," Noreen said, "we have a little activity with ping-pong balls and tissue boxes."

Five empty tissue boxes had been tied to rope, and the bridesmaids needed to tie them to each man's waist. Vivian found herself heading toward Mel, then realized what she was doing, but it was too late. She was already standing in front of him.

She knelt on the floor and tied the rope so the box was just above his ass. Mel waggled his eyebrows at her, as though saying, *I like you in this position*, and when she shot daggers with her eyes—something at which she was very skilled—he laughed.

"Turn around," she said without a smile. Once he'd turned, she stuck three ping-pong balls in the opening of the empty tissue box.

"The way this works," Jenna explained, "is that you have to get all the balls out of your tissue boxes without using your hands."

No one told the men to do it one person at a time, but for some reason, they decided that was how it should work. Juan went first. He put his hands on his knees, and after a few seconds of twerking, all three balls had popped out of the box and everyone clapped. He kept twerking for just a little longer.

"Yeah, go Juan!" Mel said, clapping louder than anyone else.

Juan blew him a kiss as he stepped aside.

Vivian was glad she didn't have to do this one, but more than half these men were performers, so this wasn't a big deal for them.

Vic, however, was an accountant, not an actor. He looked slightly uncomfortable when it was his turn, but with a few jerks of his hips, he managed to get two balls out. The last one, however, stayed firmly in the box, no matter how much he moved.

"You've got to be kidding me," he muttered, after failing to get the ball out yet again.

Then he jerked his ass back with a distinct lack of enthusiasm . . . and the ball somehow came out of the box.

Next, it was Trevor's turn. "Could I get some music?" he asked.

There were a few seconds of silence before Juan began a dramatic rendition of an NSYNC song that Vivian vaguely remembered from her childhood, Ryan and Mel soon joining in. Trevor broke down in laughter before a series of awkward movements got the first ball out of the box. The next one was a little faster, and as the last of the three balls exited the box, Vivian found herself swallowing hard.

Mel's turn was next. She'd get to see him move his ass.

Mel danced around as though he was having a grand old time, but didn't try that hard to get the balls out. He did the cancan for a few seconds before effortlessly moving on to the Macarena. When he jumped and made a quarter turn, one of the balls came out of the box, and Mel put a hand to his wide-open mouth in a comical expression of surprise.

Vivian chuckled in spite of herself. She could never do that in front of a crowd. But dammit, she didn't want to laugh and find him sexy at the same time.

She definitely did, though. As he held his arms in the air and unselfconsciously gyrated his hips, she thought about what it would be like if they were alone, and he pressed up against her and moved like that . . .

Mel eventually got the ping-pong balls out of his tissue box, and lastly, it was Ryan's turn. He shook his ass up and down, and the first ball came out immediately, the second soon following.

Mel started a round of applause. "Let's go, Ryan, let's go."

Soon everyone had joined in . . . and the ping-pong ball came out of the box.

Ryan glanced at the closed door to Lindsay's room. "Is it time to see my bride?"

"Not yet," Noreen replied.

"Remember," Em said, "twenty-five minutes."

"A lot can happen in twenty-five minutes," Vivian said ominously. "All right, now it's push-up time."

"You knew you'd have to do push-ups, didn't you, Ryan?" Noreen said. "Now get on the floor—"

"Wait," Vivian interrupted. Mel's smirk was pissing her off, especially because she found it sexy—that pissed her off more than anything. "I think they should *all* do ten push-ups, and then Ryan gets to do another twenty by himself. One-handed, of course," she added, as if this were only sensible.

"I'll start the music." Jenna turned on ABBA. Vivian wasn't very familiar with ABBA but had heard this song when they were planning the door games: "Take a Chance on Me."

"You should all sing along," Vivian said.

"Hey, why are you looking at me?" Mel asked.

"I wasn't looking at you," she retorted.

She hadn't been, had she?

He shrugged with an infuriating smile, as though he knew he was right and wasn't bothered by whatever she said, which just pissed her off more.

"Try not to kill each other on my wedding day," Ryan said. "Save it for when we're on our honeymoon." He took off his jacket and rolled up his sleeves. "Come on, guys."

There was barely space for five men on the floor, even with the coffee table moved to the side, but somehow, they managed.

"One," Jenna said as they guys did their push-ups. "Come on, I don't hear any singing!"

Though Juan was the Broadway star, Mel sang louder than anyone else, and even if he was looking at the floor, it felt as if he was singing to Vivian.

But she did not want to take a chance on anyone. Nope, she was happily single.

After ten push-ups, Jenna said, "Okay, everyone can get up except Ryan. Ryan, ten more with your left hand, followed by ten with your right hand."

The song ended and "Knowing Me, Knowing You" was next.

"This song is inappropriate," Ryan muttered. "It's a breakup song."

He returned to singing and doing his one-armed push-ups, switching to his right hand after ten. Vivian knew he spent a lot of time at the gym to maintain his body, and this didn't seem at all difficult for him.

When he stood up, Jenna slapped him on the back. "That was very amusing."

"I'm glad you were entertained," he said to his sister.

Vivian forced herself to keep her attention on them so she didn't look at Mel.

"Now, for your last task," Noreen said. "This is for Ryan only. Since we don't have a karaoke machine, here's a fake mic from the dollar store." She handed him a bright green plastic "mic" and held up her phone. "You're going to sing along to this song. The whole thing."

Mel rubbed his hands together. "I can't wait to see what they'll have you do. Maybe a passionate version of 'Old MacDonald Had a Farm.'"

The music started, and a bunch of people laughed.

"Is that 'Truly Madly Deeply'?" Vic groaned.

"That's right," Noreen said. "Classic slow-dance song from middle school."

"Yeah, I remember," Ryan said.

"Ryan! Why are you talking? You're supposed to be singing."

Standing in front of the door to Lindsay's bedroom, Ryan started singing along, and he made a dramatic spectacle of it with over-the-top facial expressions.

The song was one of many that Vivian found cheesy beyond belief. Still, she envied Lindsay, who was having a famous man in a tux sing to her before they got married later today.

Vivian did not want this. She did not. Yet, as she watched Ryan, she kept imagining it was Mel singing to her instead.

What if she had to sing for Mel?

But he knew how she felt about singing. He'd seen the anxiety in her eyes. He would never expect her to sing for him in public.

And reminding herself of how he'd distracted everyone from her at karaoke . . . that just made her desire him even more.

When the song came to an end, the door to the bedroom opened slowly, revealing Lindsay in her red dress, her hair in a fancy updo. She was smiling with a glow that would be impossible to fake, and there were tears in her eyes. The makeup artist looked like she wanted to remind Lindsay not to ruin her makeup before nine in the morning, but everyone stayed quiet.

"Wow," Ryan said quietly, his demeanor completely different from how it had been half a minute ago. He appeared to have forgotten every other word in the English language, even if he'd spoken easily in interviews on major networks.

Lindsay threw her arms around him, and he held her close for a long time, whispering something in her ear that made her chuckle.

Vivian, despite her shitty experience with relationships, felt envious once more. She even found herself choking up. She refused to show that in her expression, though, even if it wouldn't be out of place for a wedding—she hated the attention it drew.

But Mel was looking at her as if he knew exactly what was going on in her mind, and he winked.

Damn him.

Stupid, infuriating, *thoughtful* man.

Chapter 17

Vivian stood in the vestibule of the church. Lindsay and Ryan's wedding guests were seated just beyond the wooden door in front of her. It was the first time she'd ever been in this position in a wedding as the organ music began.

Following the door games, the bridal party had taken two limos to Ryan's father's house—Ryan's childhood home—for the tea ceremony. This was attended by the families as well. A light lunch was provided, and then Lindsay changed into her white wedding dress. Ryan and the groomsmen had headed to the church while she finished getting ready, and Vivian, Leah, Jenna, and Noreen had accompanied Lindsay.

"You ready?" Noreen asked Lindsay.

Lindsay nodded eagerly, and her mother smiled.

Jenna touched her future sister-in-law's shoulder before adjusting the strap of her own dress and patting her updo, which was held together with a generous amount of hairspray. All of the bridesmaids had updos except Vivian, whose hair was too short. They wore one-shoulder pink dresses, the skirt ending below the knees.

"Go ahead," Em said to Jenna.

Jenna began walking down the aisle. Leah followed when Em

gave her the signal, and then it was Vivian's turn. She gripped her bouquet of roses and headed slowly down the aisle as the music played. The pews and altar were decorated with an exquisite array of flowers.

Vivian tried not to look too serious and uncomfortable as everyone watched her, but at least discomfort was a familiar feeling. She kept her eyes straight ahead and carefully avoided meeting Mel's gaze. She took her place at the front of the church, and Noreen soon followed.

And then everyone stood as Lindsay entered on her mother's arm, her expression luminous, just as it had been earlier.

Vivian focused on Lindsay, pleased her friend was so happy, and stubbornly pushed aside any musings on whether she could one day have the same thing. She briefly looked at Ryan, who was smiling at Lindsay as though he would have happily eaten a hundred times as many disgusting foods and sung hours of sappy songs if he could marry her.

"Welcome, family and friends," the minister began. "We are gathered here today to join Ryan and Lindsay in holy matrimony . . ."

The ceremony proceeded as it had in rehearsal; it was similar to the few weddings Vivian had attended in the past. The minister gave a short welcome message, and then there was a reading and a hymn. Ryan and Lindsay exchanged their vows.

Vivian had never been particularly moved by a wedding ceremony before, but for some reason, this one was different. Maybe in part because she was up at the altar and the bride was someone she knew well . . . and she'd watched Lindsay and Ryan's relationship develop from the beginning. When Lindsay said "I do" while staring into Ryan's eyes, an unfamiliar warmth suffused Vivian, and she shifted in her heels.

She couldn't help glancing at Mel as he handed over the wedding bands. No Ring Pops this time, but real rings, which the couple would wear from now on. Then the necessary papers were signed by Lindsay and Ryan, with Mel and Noreen as the witnesses.

Sun shone through the stained-glass windows on the cold January afternoon as the minister said, "I now pronounce you man and wife. You may kiss the bride."

Ryan dipped Lindsay low—a move that Vivian had seen them practicing a lot yesterday—before kissing her.

As she walked back down the aisle, Juan at her side, Vivian couldn't hold back a small smile. That had gone well.

But Mel and Noreen were walking in front of them, and as Vivian stared at his back, her feelings got a little more complicated.

• • • • • • •

Mel had been to many weddings before. He'd been a groomsman a few times. But this was the first time he'd been in the receiving line, exchanging a quick greeting with all of the guests after the ceremony.

Normally, the receiving line would probably be outside, but as it was winter in Canada, he stood with Ryan, Lindsay, Ryan's father, Lindsay's mother, and Noreen just inside the front doors to the church. It would likely take a good half hour, and he didn't mind, except every so often, his eyes searched for Vivian of their own accord. She was standing in the corner, talking to Leah.

No, he needed to direct his attention to the movie star in front of him, who was, as last time, unaccompanied by her musician boyfriend.

"Irene," he said. "So nice to see you at a wedding with no runaway penguins." A reference to *That Kind of Wedding*, which she'd starred in with Ryan. "And nobody got injured at the tea ceremony, either."

She laughed delicately. "Still time for things to go wrong, but with any luck, they won't."

"It's my job to make sure nothing goes wrong," he said. "Well, it's more the wedding planner's job, but I'll do my best. Though perhaps I should send back the goat that's scheduled to arrive at eight o'clock. Hmm." He put a finger to his chin.

Irene headed down the line and hugged Ryan. As she walked away, Mel thought she seemed a little sad, despite her flawless look, but he didn't have time to contemplate that.

At last, all the guests had headed to the parking lot, and only close family and the wedding party remained.

"All right," the photographer said. "Just a few more pictures here, then I'll head out with the happy couple for some more intimate shots."

"I might as well come, too," Mr. Kwok said. He looked rather stiff in his suit.

The photographer shook her head. "The parents usually make the couple feel self-conscious. It would be better if it was just us."

"He takes off his shirt for the whole world. I don't think he'll be bothered."

"Dad," Ryan said.

"Ah, fine. I can go home before the reception."

"Party at your house!" Mel said. "Sounds good to me." He slapped Ryan's father on the back. "Thanks for inviting us. I'm from out of town, so . . ."

Mel was just goofing off. Obviously, Mr. Kwok didn't want people over again, nor was that how Mel wanted to spend the next few hours—he was really hoping to spend time with just Vivian—but Ryan's dad was fun to annoy, and he looked alarmed at the suggestion.

"I'm kidding, I'm kidding!" Mel said, and Mr. Kwok released a skeptical grunt.

One by one, the group broke apart, starting with Lindsay and

Ryan walking to one of the limos with the photographer and her assistant.

Mel was pleased that Vivian didn't head off with any other group.

"So," he said, walking over to her with a smile when they were alone. "You want to hang out? I noticed you sending dirty looks my way, both this morning and after the ceremony, which must mean you desperately want to hang out with me so I can bug you even further."

"Someone's c-confident," she said.

"Are you shivering?" He took off his tux jacket and draped it over her shoulders. It was ill-fitting, as they weren't the same size, but she pulled it around her tightly. "I'll get our coats."

"I'm hungry, too."

"Since you know this city better than me, maybe you can think of a place to go. Or if you don't have any ideas, I'm sure I can find something on my phone."

Ten minutes later, they were in the back of an Uber.

. . . .

Vivian had to admit it to herself: she liked Mel, and she was charmed by the silly, annoying things he did. She also liked his easy manner with the Uber driver, who'd recognized him; the two of them were currently engaged in conversation, which gave Vivian more time to stew in her thoughts.

She did not want a relationship. She did not want to have feelings for anyone.

But she was starting to have tiny feelings for him, and now she was wearing his tux jacket and they were going out to eat together.

They pulled up to a café in a Chinese plaza. Vivian thanked the driver and disembarked with difficulty; her stilettoes were not made for this weather. Inside, they got a table, and she quickly decided on coffee and French toast from the long menu. She didn't need a full meal, but she needed something to eat.

Mel chuckled. "I can't believe they have poutine."

"I don't suggest you order it," Vivian said. "I doubt it's very good here. Besides, do you really want to have fries and gravy before a ten-course banquet?"

"Don't worry, I wasn't thinking of it." He ended up ordering yuanyang and a pineapple bun with butter.

She made a face.

"What?" he said. "You don't like coffee with tea? Too chaotic for you?"

Well, yes. But also . . . "It's still weird seeing you in person. You're much easier to handle via text message."

He barked out a laugh. It was nice to hear him laugh when they were alone, after all the commotion of the morning and early afternoon.

Then his expression turned more serious, and he leaned forward. "Is that because you're overwhelmed by my animal magnetism now?"

She snorted, even though, yes, she found him very magnetic. Her face burned.

Why was this happening to her? This was not *supposed* to happen. She kept herself apart from people. She guarded her heart. She was cold, even more so now than before.

But something seemed to have cracked open inside her.

"You're far too confident," she said.

"You know I'm not," he returned. "Not really. I'm a mess who can't sleep and is constantly trying to distract people from his insecurities."

"Don't say things like that."

"Why not?"

She shook her head. *It's too intimate.*

"Easier to do that via text?" he asked.

"Mm-hmm."

Their drinks arrived in chipped mugs, and Mel shot the server a smile.

"You do look nice today," she said once the server had left. "I'd rather be wearing a tux than a sleeveless dress in the middle of January. Lindsay would have been fine with it, too, but I don't know. It would draw extra attention to me."

"If you got married," he said, "would you wear a wedding dress?"

"Oh God, no. Wedding dresses are just too much. A white suit, I guess. I feel . . . sexiest in suits." She dipped her head, feeling a little weird about calling herself "sexy."

But Mel didn't seem bothered. In fact, he looked like he was picturing it in his mind.

"I like heels and makeup," she said, "but not dresses."

Their food arrived, and Vivian eagerly dug into her Hong Kong–style French toast with condensed milk on top. Now that she was warm, halfway through her coffee, and had some food in her stomach, she started to relax.

Today was an odd day—that must be why it was bringing up so many strange emotions. She felt affection toward Mel because of the wedding, and because he looked good in that tux. That was all.

It was one day. She could manage. She wouldn't obsess over her feelings; she'd simply enjoy hanging out with him as a friend.

And then the weekend would be over and normal life would resume.

Chapter 18

Vivian's mood seemed to have gone up and down earlier, but now Mel thought she appeared poised and efficient.

They were working at the welcome table. Only Vivian was supposed to be on duty for this half hour block, but he'd decided to keep her company. She greeted everyone, had them sign their names in the guest book, put their envelopes into a big red box—or their gifts on the gift table, for the few who hadn't brought money. She also pointed out the schedule and seating chart.

Mel was just dicking around and talking to people, but he suspected she liked it this way; she'd probably prefer having tasks to do rather than making small talk.

His gaze kept turning to her, like she was a damn magnet. He was obsessing over her toned arms when Ryan's cousin, Alan, approached the table. Mel noted the way Alan was studying Vivian, and a surge of annoyance went through him.

She's mine, dammit. Did she eat French toast with you or me this afternoon, hmm?

He didn't say that out loud, of course. Instead, he slapped Alan on the back, maybe a little harder than he usually would. "Hey, good to see you again, man. Just in Toronto for the weekend?"

After Alan, Ryan's father arrived.

"Mr. Kwok!" Mel said with an enthusiasm that made the older man wince. "What did you do this afternoon? Have a little party without me at your house?" Mr. Kwok did not deign to respond and spoke with Vivian instead, which made Mel laugh. "We still haven't set a time for you to come on my podcast."

"I don't think I'd enjoy being on your podcast."

"Why not?"

"Because you'd act like *this* the whole time." But Mr. Kwok shot Mel a small smile.

Mel hoped he'd have a couple of minutes to talk to Vivian before anyone else arrived, but then Lindsay and Ryan made their way through the front doors.

One thing that was a little different from the other weddings Mel had attended: the security. There were a bunch of large security guards in a few different places—they looked rather like the Secret Service.

"Hi, Ryan!" Mel said. "Have a good picture session? Get any shirtless photos outside in the Canadian winter?"

Ryan responded by placing a finger to his lips. "Shh."

Lindsay leaned toward Vivian. "I need some help. Can you come with me to the washroom?"

Vivian nodded and followed Lindsay down the hall.

"What did you do to your bride?" Mel asked Ryan.

"She thinks her makeup's smudged. I told her that it looks perfect and she's beautiful, and she said I was too biased to provide a helpful opinion."

"Well, she does have a point."

Little Ezra toddled up in an adorable pair of pants, dress shirt, and bow tie. He clutched Ryan's leg with one arm, and with the other, he securely held on to a stuffed toy. Some kind of green monster?

"Can you say congratulations to your uncle, Ezra?" Ryan's sister asked.

"Congrabbies!" Ezra said with a big grin.

Ryan picked him up, and the photographer snapped a picture. However, it wasn't exactly a happy picture as Ezra had scrunched up his face.

"Yeah, I know the feeling," Mel said. "Ryan makes me cry, too."

"He's not crying because of me," Ryan said. "Mel, pick up his monster."

Oh. The green monster had fallen on the ground. Mel put it back in Ezra's hands, and Ezra's face immediately lit up. The photographer snapped another picture.

After that, Mel supervised the welcome table alone for a few minutes. He kept looking down the hall, waiting for Vivian to return.

At long last, he glimpsed her and Lindsay. Vivian was strutting down the hall with her chin tipped up. He loved the commanding way she walked, like she wouldn't let the world get to her. He might have called her an ice queen before, but now he didn't see her as icy. Queenlike, perhaps, but not icy. Though she was a little cool, he liked her composure. At the same time, he liked when it cracked and she showed some him vulnerability. He wanted to strip her down completely and have her body wrapped around his.

He swallowed hard.

"Mel?" she said as she approached him. "Is something wrong?"

She was standing slightly closer to him than usual, and he couldn't manage to speak for several seconds, which was most unlike him.

"Um, no," he said at last.

Just thinking about how desperately I want to take you back to my hotel room tonight, that's all, no biggie.

With every minute, he wanted her more . . . and he thought she wanted him, too. Maybe?

He was doing a fine job of admiring Vivian's bare shoulder when an ear-piercing wail overwhelmed every other sound. A moment later, Jenna emerged from the room where everyone had gathered for cocktails, Ezra in her arms.

"Monsta!" Ezra screamed.

"It's okay, baby," Jenna said. "Daddy's looking for your monster."

"Monsta!"

Mel suddenly felt like finding a stuffed monster and stopping a child's screaming was an important part of his best man duties, and if he didn't do this correctly, he'd be failing Ryan, and all sorts of additional catastrophes would befall them. Like runaway penguins and such. He was good at catastrophizing.

"I'll help look," he said. "Where did you last see your monster?"

Ezra frowned as though this were a completely ridiculous and irrelevant question.

Despite the lack of assistance provided by the monster's owner, Mel went into the cocktail room and started searching. At last, he located the monster under one of the high-top tables.

"Guess who I found?" Mel asked as he approached Jenna and Ezra.

Ezra turned his tear-stained face away from his mother's chest. "Monsta!" He reached out with his hands.

"Thank you," Jenna said. "Can you say that, Ezra?"

"Monsta!" Ezra stuck the monster's foot in his mouth.

"Uh, he was on the floor," Mel said, not that it would put a damper on Ezra's enthusiasm.

Jenna and Ezra returned to the reception, and Vivian smiled at Mel.

"You know me," Mel said. "I'm an expert at finding monsters."

She didn't open her mouth, but her close-lipped smile broadened, and he couldn't help the fact that it went straight to his groin.

"Hey, you two!" Noreen said. "I'm here to take over welcome table duties."

He offered his arm to Vivian. "Let's go have some food and drinks, shall we?"

Noreen shot him a curious I-thought-you-hated-each-other look, but Mel ignored it as he and Vivian entered the crowd.

They were soon separated, however, as various people demanded their attention, but for the next forty-five minutes, his eyes kept finding hers across the room, and he couldn't help the way it made his face tingle.

Although it was a cold winter's day, it was warm in here with all the people. Deciding he needed a little space, Mel walked down the hall toward the bathrooms. And who should he see outside the ladies' room but . . .

"Déjà vu." He smiled as he stopped in front of Vivian. She was leaning against the wall, her phone in her hand.

"Déjà vu?" she said.

"Like the engagement party. When I impressed you with my terrible French accent and you pushed me onto the floor."

"An accident. I didn't mean for you to fall, even if I called you 'infuriating' that day." Her lips twitched.

He put his hand on the wall behind her and looked up—she had a few inches on him in those heels. "You remember the exact word you used. Interesting. That was more than half a year ago."

"And your point is?"

"I think you know what my point is." He leaned a little closer, and when she licked her lips, that was nearly the end of him. But he kept himself from pressing against her, kept his lips from meeting hers.

"Yeah," she said quietly, "I know."

"Whatcha going to do about it?"

"Are you this infuriating with everyone, or just with me?"

"I think you're particularly susceptible to my charms."

She snorted.

"Maybe I tease you extra," he said, "because I really like you. I wanna do things to you."

"*Things.* Such as forcing me to admit that chocolate cake is the best?"

He laughed. She was certainly more playful with him than she used to be.

"Nah," he said. "I want to feed you cake. Watch you lick quality vanilla buttercream from my fingers. I'd keep the triple chocolate fudge cake for myself."

"Do you only want me to lick it off . . . your fingers?" She spoke in a whisper, and the breathy quality in her voice made his pants tight.

Oh hell.

"No," he said with a seriousness he rarely managed.

Her lips parted, and she leaned toward him.

It was going to happen. She was going to kiss him . . .

· · · · · · ·

Unlike at the engagement party, when Vivian pushed Mel out of the way, this time she pushed him lightly. Just enough so she could sneak by and escape back to the reception.

She'd vowed to ignore her feelings for him, and she'd been doing an okay job of it. Not a great job, but enough so that she wasn't miserable. They'd been friendly as they worked the welcome table together, and she'd only occasionally thought about how good his generous ass looked in those pants.

Okay, more than occasionally, but still. She'd been managing.

Yet just now, he'd been flirting with her. Making comments about getting physical. And God, she wanted it, and he could tell.

This could not happen. It was not what she was looking for.

But she'd gotten so, so close to kissing him. Closer than ever before, including that time in New York, and it had taken every scrap of her willpower to run away. Maybe that wasn't the most mature response, but it had been all she could manage.

Thank God dinner was about to start. No more mingling.

Except when she arrived at her table, she discovered she was seated next to Mel, and unlike last night, it didn't make her happy.

"Did you switch the seating cards?" she asked him.

"Who, me? No. Besides, I'm emceeing. I won't be here half the time."

And then that ridiculous man *winked* at her.

There was no head table at the reception; Ryan and Lindsay were at a circular table, front center, with their close family members. Lindsay had changed back into her red qipao after arriving at the reception in her white dress.

As the waiters walked out with the first course, Mel went up to the microphone on the small stage. "Hi, everyone. I'm Mel, and I'll be your emcee for the evening. I'm Ryan's best man, and we first met several years ago when we shared an apartment in Brooklyn with Juan and a capybara named Dumpling."

There was some laughter at the reference to *JANYS*.

"We'll have a bunch of fun games and speeches for you tonight, but for now, sit back and enjoy your first course. For those of you who haven't been to a Chinese wedding reception like this before, it's the first of many, *many* courses."

Even though he wasn't next to her anymore, seeing Mel talk onstage wasn't helping matters because Vivian was still looking at him and admiring him.

He returned to the table as the server dished out the first course—roast pig and jellyfish—onto ten small plates.

Vivian picked up her chopsticks. She was hungry, but she

could barely swallow. Still, she did her best to remain poised on the outside, and she didn't think anyone noticed that something was up.

Until Mel whispered, "You okay?"

"I'm fine," she said curtly. *Just fighting this annoying attraction to you. Which I will not tell you about, because then you'll smirk.*

"All right." There was something in his tone that suggested he knew she was lying—damn him—but he didn't mention it. "What course are you looking forward to the most?"

"The lobster. Lindsay really likes the deep-fried crab claws. I think their table is getting an extra plate of those."

"That's the next course, isn't it?"

"Yeah."

"Did you hear there's a snowstorm coming?" Noreen asked the table.

"Oh shit," Juan said. "I'm supposed to fly out tomorrow morning."

"I don't think it's arriving that soon. You should be fine."

"The dangers of having a wedding in January."

"Though they did get some nice shots when it was lightly snowing earlier."

Vivian finished her first course, and soon the plates were cleared and the second course started coming out. The server brought a large dish to their table, then placed one crab claw on each small plate. Vivian reached for hers but didn't start eating yet—these suckers usually retained heat, and she didn't want to burn herself.

"Monsta!" Ezra shrieked from the next table. He leapt out of his mother's lap and ran toward the toy he'd thrown on the floor.

Unfortunately, he ran right into the path of a server. The man tripped but managed to stop himself—and the platter—from falling to the floor.

The crab claws, however, weren't so lucky.

Yet even as Vivian registered that the deep-fried balls of crab were flying off the platter and heading in her direction, she was rooted to her seat.

A moment later, three of them landed in her lap, and the rest landed on the floor.

"Shit!" she exclaimed, jumping up.

All three crab claws fell onto the floor.

"Shit!" said a gleeful, high-pitched voice.

Possibly Ezra.

Normally, small children swearing amused Vivian—unless those small children were her siblings and she was the teenager in charge of keeping them in line.

But she was focused on all those ruined crab claws. She couldn't just leave food down there, even if the staff wouldn't expect her to pick it up, so she grabbed a napkin and knelt on the floor. She only saw a single crab claw. The rest had probably rolled underneath the table, so she lifted up the bottom of the tablecloth and stuck her head underneath. She felt around and came up with one crab claw, which she put in the napkin.

Just then, someone bumped the table, and a moment later, they brushed against her.

She didn't have to look—not that she could see very well here anyway—to know it was Mel under the table with her. His right side pressed against her left, and even though there were two hundred people in this room, including a bunch eating at the table above them, it felt like they were in their own little world. His warmth seeped into her skin.

Still, she was determined not to be distracted from her task. She felt around and came upon another deep-fried crab claw. Wait, it wasn't quite—

"That's my knee."

Vivian was momentarily embarrassed . . . but they were under the table. No one could see exactly what was happening.

And maybe that was why she slid her hand up his thigh and leaned in. Whatever happened under the table wasn't *real*.

She planted a kiss on his lips.

Chapter 19

It had just been one solid kiss. Nothing lingering; no longer than a second. Vivian didn't know what it would have been like if Mel had kissed her back; she just knew what his lips felt like against hers.

Then she realized what she was doing, with her ass sticking out from under the table. She quickly found one more ruined deep-fried crab claw and stood up.

It wasn't long before the servers replaced the fallen food. Next, Noreen gave a speech, followed by Lindsay and Ryan playing the shoe game. They sat on back-to-back chairs, and they each carried one of Lindsay's shoes and one of Ryan's shoes.

"Who talks more in their sleep?" Mel asked.

Both Ryan and Lindsay held up Lindsay's shoe.

"Who plans fancier dates?"

This time, they both picked Ryan.

"Who snores louder?"

They both picked Ryan.

"Who's better at fixing things around the house?"

They both picked Lindsay.

"You know, it's more amusing if you don't always have the same answer," Mel said. "Next question. Who's more likely to take off their shirt in public? . . . Seriously? Who wrote these?"

There was some laughter.

"Pretty sure you did?" Ryan said as he held up his shoe. Lindsay held up his as well.

"Who's clumsier?"

They both chose Ryan.

"Who's more likely to steal the blankets in the night, leaving the other person shivering and helpless?"

Lindsay chose Ryan, and Ryan chose Lindsay. When everyone laughed, they looked at each other and smiled.

There were a few more rounds, and after a break for the happy couple to eat some food, Mel was back at the microphone for another game. He held up an egg, and a bunch of people groaned. "This is a raw egg. The game, for those of you who don't know, is called the egg roll. Lindsay, come up here, and I'll blindfold you." He shook the red scarf in his other hand. After tying it over her eyes, he had her kneel in front of Ryan on the stage, then passed her the egg.

"This isn't a raw egg," she said. "It's boiled."

"You didn't need to tell everyone that," Mel said in a stage whisper. "They're supposed to think there's a real chance of Ryan getting raw egg on his . . . legs." He turned to the audience. "Lindsay will roll the egg from the inside of Ryan's right ankle to the inside of his left ankle. As in, all the way up his right leg and down his left leg. Remember, she's blindfolded, and that's definitely not a hard-boiled egg, and Ryan's pants are definitely tighter than they need to be."

Lindsay started rolling the egg, to numerous chuckles, and unfortunately, this scene got Vivian's imagination going. Mel was also standing onstage, and she imagined doing the same thing to him. Rolling that egg higher and higher, not being able to see him, but being able to touch, like when she'd touched his thigh under the table . . .

And Mel was acting like his normal self, like nothing had happened, damn him!

But if she were rolling the egg, she'd make sure he couldn't have that relaxed facial expression. She'd let her hands linger, until she heard his sharp intake of breath . . .

Flustered, Vivian hurried out of the room, abandoning her plate of abalone and sea cucumber. She leaned against the wall in the hallway and took a deep breath.

A couple of minutes later, Mel joined her.

"Lindsay was successful with the egg," he said. "In case you were wondering."

"I. Uh. Yeah."

He put his hands on the wall, by her shoulders. "You kissed me."

"Do you have to talk about this?"

"Yes."

"It was only a brief kiss," she said.

"But you still did it, and you want to do it again, don't you?"

She closed her eyes and covered her face with her hands. When she peeked out from between her fingers, Mel's face was very close to hers. He wasn't touching her, and she was sure he'd step back if she asked him to, but . . .

God, she yearned to reach out and touch him.

It's just one night.

She'd been focusing on the fact that she didn't want a relationship, but why did it have to be a relationship? Why couldn't she just have tonight?

Perhaps if she slept with him, it would get him out of her system. True, some of her feelings weren't exactly physical, but the physical and the emotional were always tangled up for her; she couldn't cleanly separate such things the way that some people could.

And maybe sleeping with him would get rid of both.

The idea of a one-night stand didn't normally appeal to her. Usually people had them with someone they didn't know well, right? Vivian couldn't imagine sleeping with a stranger.

But she knew Mel. He lived in New York—it wasn't like a relationship could work between them even if she wanted it. They could have tonight, then continue to be friends who occasionally texted each other at odd times and sent each other odd presents. Nothing more.

She wasn't certain about this plan yet, but for now, she'd give herself a taste. More than that kiss under the table.

She gripped his ass and pulled him close. He squeaked in surprise, but then his hands were on her face, his fingertips brushing her temples, and when she kissed him this time, she didn't pull back a moment later.

This time, she *really* kissed him.

And he didn't disappoint with his warm, clever mouth.

It was rough at first, his lips moving urgently against hers. Like they were in a battle for who could kiss the other the most fiercely, and she relished every second of it.

"Yeah, you like that, don't you?" he said.

She didn't give him the opportunity to say more—and perhaps that was why he'd done it. To make her kiss him harder out of annoyance.

Then their kiss gentled and slowed, like a wave coming down from its peak, a natural undulation. She pulled him firmly against her and gasped when she felt his erection. The ache inside her grew.

He stepped back and raised an eyebrow.

"Stop it." She tried to kiss him again, but he held her chin and kept his face a few inches from hers. She rolled her hips against him, desperate for pressure between her legs, and released a frustrated growl.

"God, I love how hot you are for me."

She growled again.

After a few more seconds of pissing her off, his mouth met hers, and he kissed her before muttering a curse.

"I have a job to do," he said, "and you don't want to miss the lobster, do you? But later, will you come back to my hotel room?"

She breathed rapidly in the silence.

"Maybe?" she said.

"Okay, just let me know." He sounded more casual than he must feel.

And I'm the one who did that to him.

They returned to the reception and ate many more courses. Fish. Lobster. E-fu noodles and fried rice. Lindsay's mom and Ryan's dad each spoke briefly, and Mel gave a speech, too.

But Vivian was only half paying attention to his words because she was thinking about that kiss. She felt like everyone must know she'd made out with Mel in the hallway, like there must be a neon sign above her head, but nobody said anything.

After the noodles and rice, the cake was brought out. Two tiers of lemon blackcurrant and one tier of chocolate raspberry, slathered in buttercream. Not that you could tell the flavors from looking at it, but Vivian knew what had been chosen.

Lindsay and Ryan cut the cake and fed each other a little piece. Then the cake was whisked away to be cut up, and sweet red bean soup with lotus seeds was served.

Once everyone had finished their soup, the tables were cleared to the side so the married couple could have their first dance as husband and wife. Other people soon joined in the dancing, but Vivian stayed seated. Not just because she was trying to hide her dress, which was stained with oil from the crab claws; she'd never been much of a dancer.

"Vivian!" Noreen sat down beside her. "What's happening between you and Mel?"

Vivian blanched. What had Noreen noticed?

"I switched the seating cards so you'd sit next to each other!" Noreen clapped her hands. "Then you disappeared together."

"I was . . . cleaning off my dress," Vivian stammered.

Lindsay walked off the dance floor and joined them. "What's going on?"

"Vivian and Mel," Noreen said.

"I was wondering!"

Vivian hung her head. She didn't want her friends talking about her love life.

Though it wasn't exactly her *love* life. If anything more happened with Mel, it would just be sex.

"It's like Ryan's movie," Noreen said. "Where the best man and the maid of honor get together. Except I'm the maid of honor and I'm married, so it couldn't be me, but you're a bridesmaid. It's almost the same."

"But it would only be . . ." Vivian swallowed. "A hookup."

"You never know."

"Is that what you want, Vivian?" Lindsay asked. "Nothing more than a hookup?"

Vivian nodded.

Lindsay looked suspicious, like she thought Vivian was lying to herself, but she simply said, "Are you worried about regretting it?"

"I don't have any experience with this sort of thing," Vivian said.

"I had several one-night stands in the years before I met Ryan, and I don't regret any of them. Of course, everyone is different, but I think you should go for it. Have some fun. Certainly not what I expected when I asked you to be my bridesmaid and warned you that he'd be in the wedding party, but . . ."

Yes, Vivian would have some fun tonight. She wouldn't hold herself back from what she wanted: Mel stripping off her clothes, his mouth on other parts of her body.

Noreen and Lindsay headed back to the dance floor, but Vivian stayed where she was.

And then Ryan's cousin approached her.

· · · · · · ·

Mel had figured he'd dance a handful of songs then drag Vivian up for a slow song, or he could sit with her if she didn't want to dance. But a slow song would be nice. They'd be close together, and not in the hallway this time. Maybe she'd have an answer for him.

Except now Alan was talking to Vivian. He held out his hand, like he was trying to get Vivian to dance with him. Vivian's face was impassive—her ice-queen persona. She used it to keep people at a distance and protect herself, and Mel couldn't blame her. It made sense, given what he knew about her now.

But she wasn't always like that with Mel, not anymore, and it made him feel special.

When Alan didn't appear put off by her lack of interest, Mel walked up to them and reached for Vivian's hand. Just as a slow song started, coincidentally.

"You promised me this dance, didn't you?" he said smoothly, whisking her away before Alan could protest. She clasped her hands around his neck; he put his on her hips. "Before you say anything, yes, I'm sure you could have handled it yourself, but I know you want to dance with me anyway—"

"The arrogance of you," she muttered.

"Only because you already kissed me."

They swayed with the music for a while. Well, he did more swaying than she did. It felt just as good to have her in his arms as he'd known it would, perhaps even better.

"What's this song?" Vivian asked.

"It's by Air Supply. From the early eighties, I think. Before our time." He pretended he was holding a microphone and mouthed the lyrics.

She pushed his hand back to her hip, and he swallowed hard. She liked when he touched her, and that was certainly intoxicating.

"So, uh, what do you think about my question?" he said. "The one I asked you in the hallway." He tried to sound as casual as possible.

"Maybe I'll leave you in suspense for another hour or three."

"That sounds like a yes to me."

She narrowed her eyes, but she also ran her palm over his back, and he shivered.

God, he wanted her.

When the song ended, she led him off the dance floor.

"Are we heading toward the cake?" he asked, still attempting to sound cool and collected and probably failing. "Good idea. Too bad there's no vanilla for you."

They reached the cake table, and he immediately grabbed a plate of the chocolate raspberry. She selected the lemon blackcurrant.

"Mmm," he said after his first bite. "So much chocolatey goodness. You're missing out."

She rolled her eyes. "Mine's better."

"You really think so? Why don't you feed me some?"

He doubted she'd do it, but Vivian surprised him by picking up a forkful of the lemon cake and holding it to his lips.

"Not enough blackcurrant buttercream on that one," he said. "Don't you want me to have the full experience?"

She rolled her eyes again, but she swiped up some more buttercream with her fork. "Eat it and stop complaining."

He obeyed her, then made a show of licking his lips and releasing an over-the-top sigh.

His theatrics had quite an effect on her: she abandoned her half-eaten slice of cake and dragged him into the hallway. He couldn't help grinning, even if she was separating him from his chocolate.

She pushed him against the wall, dipped her head, and kissed him, the length of her body against his. He palmed her ass through the thin fabric of her bridesmaid's dress. Her lips and tongue were demanding, and he was happy to give her whatever she needed as she plundered his mouth. He desperately hoped she'd want more from him later.

When she pulled back, he whispered, "Is that a yes?"

She didn't say anything snarky.

She simply said, much to his satisfaction, "It is."

Then she went right back to kissing him, seemingly unworried about anyone else who might be in the hallway.

Which was pretty damn great for his ego.

But he said, "I think I should stay a little longer." Though it was almost midnight, dinner had ended less than an hour ago—it took a long time when there were so many courses. He should at the very least make sure Ryan didn't need anything else from him, even if he really wanted to whisk Vivian away right now.

"Okay," she said briskly. "Half an hour, we meet at the coat check?"

"Sounds good to me."

He couldn't wait to have his hands and mouth all over her.

All over her.

Chapter 20

Usually, Vivian was more nervous when she was with someone for the first time. More self-conscious. Afraid she wouldn't live up to expectations . . . and the other person wouldn't, either.

But tonight, she wasn't worried. She simply *wanted*.

And she was going to take what she wanted.

At the appointed hour, she and Mel took the shuttle that had been arranged for out-of-town wedding guests to the nearby hotel. He'd checked in yesterday, and so they went right up to his room.

As soon as they were inside, they kicked off their shoes—it was nice to be out of her heels—and then they were kissing each other against the wall.

Unlike earlier, there was no danger of someone interrupting them.

It was just him and her in a hotel room.

She surprised herself by releasing a giggle. She didn't normally laugh like that; in fact, she wasn't the sort of person who usually laughed much at all, but Mel . . .

She couldn't believe it. She was going to have a hot night with someone at a hotel. It was most unlike her.

When she tugged off his jacket, she nearly dropped it on the floor, but it was a rental, so she hung it in the closet. Then she made quick work of his tie before unbuttoning his shirt. She shoved the two sides of it apart and put her hands on his chest.

It had been so, so long since she'd touched someone like this, and all of a sudden, her body ached for him even more.

But Mel had gone still, as though he were . . . shy?

"Is something wrong?" she asked, pausing in her hurry to get him undressed.

"No, no," he said. "I'm just . . . are you sure you want to do this with me?"

"Earlier, you were cocky."

"You know that's a bit of an act. And you're so . . ." He gestured at her body.

She dropped his shirt on the floor. She wasn't sure what to say, so she tried to show him, running her hands all over his skin, loving that there was so much of him to touch. They were exactly the same height, so she could look him right in the eye and it was easy to kiss.

"I know what I want," she said at last, feeling like she needed to verbally answer his question. "I promise."

She unbuckled his belt, dropped his pants, reached into his boxers, and wrapped her fingers around his heavy cock. *Oh my.* As she stroked him, she pressed her lips to his neck and kissed the sensitive skin there. He smelled soapy, though there was a faint taste of salt on his skin.

With her thumb, she spread pre-cum over the tip of his erection. She lifted the skirt of her dress and ground herself against his thick thigh.

"Oh fuck," he muttered, a hand on his face. "Oh fuck . . . I can feel . . . how wet you are."

The next thing she knew, he'd lifted her in his arms. He walked across the room and deposited her on the bed, and then he was on top of her, kissing her wildly. He pulled her dress over her head and tossed it aside, and her sensible, strapless beige bra soon followed.

Her breasts were smaller than a handful, but she didn't worry about what he thought of them as he slid his hands up and down her body. She squirmed and enjoyed the pressure of him on top of her, pushing her into the mattress.

When his hand slipped into her underwear, they both groaned.

Sure, she touched herself on occasion, but she wasn't used to having someone else touching her there, and she'd missed this—

She gasped in surprise as he pulled her down the bed by her knees. Her legs dangled off the end, and he knelt on the floor and removed her boy shorts. Beige to match her bra. He buried his head between her legs, and when his tongue ran over her slit then circled her clit, she clutched the sheets.

Yes. This.

This had always been her favorite part. The one thing guaranteed to make her come.

She didn't even know what he was doing with his tongue now; she just knew it felt so good, and she wanted more, more, more . . .

God, he really was incredible at this.

She writhed on the bed, feeling like she was *meant* to be pleasured by him. Somehow, he knew how to make her skin feel as if it were shooting sparks, how to make her brain unable to form semi-coherent thoughts.

It was beautiful.

His fingers and tongue worked in tandem, and her orgasm caught her off guard. She couldn't even muffle her scream. Not that she was super loud, but it wasn't like her to emit more than a shuddered breath.

He crawled up her body, a self-satisfied grin on his face, and she was glad to see that smile. She didn't fire back with a saucy retort; her mind was flat out of those.

"Should I get a condom?" he asked. "Or, we don't have to do that tonight. We could take our time with—"

"Yes," she said. "Get one."

She'd totally forgotten about condoms; they weren't something she carried with her because she'd never had spontaneous sex before.

She missed his weight on top of her as he headed to the washroom. A moment later, he was back. He placed three packets on the bedside table, and she did nothing more than raise an eyebrow before she shoved down his boxers. Then she grabbed one of the packets, tore it open, and rolled the condom on.

Her heart beating quickly in anticipation, she grasped the base of his cock and slowly lowered herself onto him, groaning as he filled her. She rested her palms on the bed and tipped her head back.

Oh yes.

She stayed there for a few seconds, enjoying the fullness of him inside her, before she leaned forward and looked down at him as she started to move. She grabbed his upper arm with one hand.

"Fuck, that's good," he said. "Ride me."

As she bounced up and down, she felt sexy in an unfamiliar way. She didn't know how to describe it, couldn't think straight now, but there was a power that she hadn't experienced before in her sexual encounters.

He licked his thumb and touched her clit, and she shoved his hand away. Many people liked that during penetration, but she never had. Since she didn't want to do any talking right now, instead of explaining, she bent down and kissed him. Reveled in the pleasure coursing through her body from his cock, his mouth, his hands. His skin against hers.

Yes, just like that.

He cupped her ass. "I'm not going to last . . . I'm . . ."

With a jerk of his hips, he cried out.

After he'd disposed of the condom, he returned to bed and pulled her against him. She rested her cheek on his chest, one arm slung over his belly, his soft curves around her harsher lines. It was a nice feeling. Her brain felt like the jellyfish that had been served at the reception.

And then he said, "How can I make you come when I'm inside you?"

She lifted her head. "You can't," she said quietly, surprising herself by her honesty. "I can't come from penetration—I like it, but I can't finish like that. Nor can I come from you touching my clit with your fingers. I have to . . . oral sex or a vibrator. Those are the options."

She was thirty-four now, and she knew how her body worked. In the past, men had insisted on trying, fucking her until she was dry and in pain, and she'd felt like she was supposed to enjoy it. And she didn't actually enjoy clitoral stimulation when she was being penetrated like that—it was just too intense.

"Well, in that case . . ." Mel rolled her onto her back and buried his face between her legs.

It took a little longer this time, but damn, he was amazing with his tongue, and soon a powerful orgasm overtook her.

Then she returned to snuggling up against him.

"Mmm," she said, not feeling the need for any further words.

· · · · · · · ·

Mel felt privileged to see Vivian like this.

A faint smiled touched her lips as she lay curled against him. She looked relaxed; he'd never seen her like this before. She didn't seem to be asleep, just resting, but they weren't exchanging words. They didn't seem necessary, not right now.

He felt relaxed, too. He'd experienced a moment of unease when she'd started undressing him, but he hadn't completely hidden those feelings from her, as he'd usually do when intimate with someone.

Vivian shifted her head on the pillow, and he admired the sharp, elegant lines of her face, the slight curve of her naked hips and breasts, the shape of her arm muscles. She seemed quite comfortable in bed with him, and it was rather incredible.

If he said something stupid and funny, would he ruin it?

Good thing he wasn't in the mood to make jokes.

Her eyes fluttered open. She smiled at him as she walked her fingers down his chest. "I hadn't done that in a long, long time, and I don't think I've had my fill yet."

She slid down the bed, and when her hand was an inch from his cock, she raised her eyebrows. He nodded, and she began stroking him again. It hadn't been half an hour yet, and he wasn't a teenager anymore, but he quickly hardened for her. Her tongue peeked out of her mouth . . . Oh God, she was going to . . .

She licked the underside of his cock, and he arched his back and gripped the sheets. She was licking him like she was consuming the world's finest vanilla buttercream. Then she sucked all of him into her mouth, as though she had no gag reflex, and he bit back a growl, afraid he'd wake the entire damn hotel. Even just the sight of her, bent over him and squirming slightly . . .

"Jesus," he said, "I'm going to . . ."

She released him from her mouth and stroked him as she held her body above his. He spent on his stomach.

They lay in silence for a minute before she said, "How about we have a shower? It's been a long day, and you probably started sweating when you did push-ups at eight in the morning."

"Did you enjoy watching me do them?"

"I enjoy watching you do lots of things."

He wiped himself off with a tissue and headed to the bathroom. She joined him as he was adjusting the temperature of the water, and when she stepped under the spray, he admired the rivulets of water running down her body.

As soon as he was in there with her, they were kissing again, and his hand found its way between her legs. She released a little moan when he slid his fingers through her folds.

"I want you to say my name." He usually didn't care, but for some reason, he needed it from her. He knelt down in the tub and gave her one long lick.

"*Mel.*"

He smiled as she gripped his hair until it hurt. She held his head against her, the water raining down on them, and he sped up his pace.

"Yeah, that's hot," he said.

"Shut up and keep licking me."

He chuckled against her and licked her with long, luxurious strokes before circling her clit with his tongue. She tasted so good. She came against his face, making a series of incoherent sounds, as though she couldn't even remember his name.

Once she regained her balance, she soaped him up. He did the same to her, and the water washed the suds down the drain.

After they'd dried off, they returned to bed and didn't make a move to get dressed. They lay on their sides facing each other. She had a drowsy, contented look on her face. Her eyes drifted shut, and a few minutes later, her breathing changed. He watched her breathe softly for a minute or two before turning out the lights.

But more than an hour later, he was still awake, because of course he was. His ability to sleep had little to do with how tired he felt.

Feeling weird about being naked now, he got up and pulled some underwear and a T-shirt out of his suitcase. He put those on and, not knowing what else to do, returned to bed. At home, he'd go to the living room, but he didn't have a suite at the hotel, just one room.

He turned on the bedside lamp at the lowest setting, then looked over to make sure it hadn't disturbed Vivian. He was glad they weren't insomnia buddies tonight, even if it might be nice to have her company.

There was a sudden ache in his chest. Watching her come apart had been one of the greatest fucking things he'd ever experienced, but tomorrow, he'd return to New York, and she'd stay here. Now that the wedding was over, who knew when he'd see her again.

But there was no reason things had to end tomorrow, right? He'd had long-distance relationships before, and though they hadn't lasted long, that was true of all his relationships. Yes, she lived in another country, but Toronto and New York were a short flight apart, and he traveled regularly anyway. It was closer than Houston—that was his last long-distance relationship. A while ago now.

Whenever he looked at her, he just knew he really, really didn't want this to be over, and it wasn't simply a physical thing between them, was it? He eagerly reached for his phone whenever he got a text, hoping it was from her. He wanted to hear from her more than anyone else.

It didn't seem to be one-sided, either. He must mean something to Vivian for her to have acted the way she had. She didn't let people in easily, yet here he was.

Okay. He couldn't do anything about this now, so he ought to stop thinking about it—ha! As if his brain would obey.

But tomorrow morning, he'd tell her that he wanted to keep

seeing her, that he wanted to figure out how to make this work when they returned to their regular lives.

Even though he didn't have the greatest track record with relationships, as he gazed at those lips that had parted in ecstasy for him . . .

He couldn't help feeling hopeful.

Chapter 21

I had a one-night stand.

That was Vivian's first thought when she opened her eyes the next morning, and she couldn't help smiling. She'd never done something quite like that before, and it had felt *good*.

However, as she rolled over and looked at the man beside her, her smile disappeared.

Mel was on his side, facing her. He was so handsome in his sleep. One of his arms was slung across the bed, like he'd been reaching for her, and Vivian scooted backward, until her ass was nearly hanging off the mattress.

Sharing a bed with someone . . . it was just so intimate.

That was the problem with one-night stands, a problem she hadn't thought about last night as he'd fucked her and licked her in the shower. What the hell did you do the next day?

Mel would smile and crack a joke and send her off with a kiss. He wouldn't be awkward and weird about it, like she was now.

Oh God. Maybe this had been a terrible idea. Maybe she *should* feel guilty.

Except she'd taken so much pleasure in last night. She couldn't remember when she'd last orgasmed so many times. And although she usually kept herself a bit apart from the world, she still craved human contact on occasion.

Vivian was the eldest daughter, the responsible one who was always supposed to think of other people's needs first, who'd learned early in life not to show emotions because her feelings didn't matter.

But for quite a while now, she'd been living life on her own terms.

She'd enjoyed last night, and she wouldn't feel guilty, even if this wasn't what responsible eldest daughters did. She should be married with a couple of kids by now, not having a one-night stand with a comedian.

Whatever.

Yet even though she didn't regret it, that didn't change the situation. The sun was coming up; a new day was beginning. Facing Mel in the light of morning would be different.

Thank God he lived in another country and she wouldn't have to see him again.

But who would tease her like he did? Who would rescue her from karaoke? She might never kiss him again, never wrap her arms around him . . .

Why was she so sentimental? They'd had one good night together, and they no longer wanted to kill each other. That was all.

Perhaps the problem was simply that she wasn't used to one-night stands, and her brain and body didn't know what to make of this.

She shouldn't read too much into it.

No, the most important thing was to leave before he woke up. Before she'd have to stammer and try to make small talk.

Her chest still hurt at the thought of not seeing him again in person, but the idea of actually talking to him this morning was worse.

Mel stretched out his arm farther, nearly grazing her—oh God, she was still naked.

In her hurry to get away, she toppled onto the floor, and all she could do was worry that the noise had woken him up.

She peeked over the edge of the bed. Thankfully, he was still sleeping.

She tiptoed to the washroom and looked in the mirror. Her hair was a mess because she'd climbed into bed when it was still wet, and some of it was sticking up. She could hear her mom telling her that she'd get sick from sleeping with wet hair, but she shoved that voice aside. She needed to get out of here.

Vivian found a mini bottle of mouthwash—that was the best she could do for now. Then she put on her clothes from yesterday, including the bridesmaid dress with the oil stain.

Once she was dressed, she pulled back the curtain and glanced outside. It was snowing. Best to get home quickly. She'd get an Uber to Kennedy, then take the subway to the place that was just her home now, not hers and Lindsay's.

After dropping the edge of the curtain, she intended to head out immediately, but instead, she spent a few minutes staring at Mel, peacefully sleeping in bed. Had he fallen asleep right away, like her? Or had he still been awake at four in the morning?

What would he think when he woke up and she was gone?

She studied his light brown skin. His inky hair. The soft features of his face, even softer in his sleep. The bulk of him, covered in a pile of blankets.

Pain surged through her as she strode to the door, head held high.

It had been a good night, but now it was time to return to her regularly scheduled life.

. . . .

There was something wrong.

Mel was used to waking up alone in bed, but he wasn't supposed to be alone this morning; Vivian was supposed to be next to him. They were supposed to talk about starting a relationship. He'd rehearsed the words in his head before falling asleep.

He sat up. She wasn't standing by the window, or elsewhere in the room. He jumped up and ran to the bathroom—no, she wasn't there, either.

There were no clothes. No notes. No texts.

No hints that she'd been here at all.

How could she do this to him? He wasn't just some random guy she'd met at the wedding. Even if she didn't have feelings for him like the ones he had for her, weren't they friends? Hadn't he sent her a pillow of her favorite TV show?

Mel rarely felt angry like this, but . . . dammit.

He started to text her, then stopped himself. What was the point? She'd made herself clear. He'd just have to accept it.

His frustration turned inward, at his inability to have a fucking relationship that lasted. At the fact that he'd apparently fallen for the wrong person. At . . .

No, he wouldn't let himself mope. He had a plane to catch this afternoon.

He checked in for his flight. Everything seemed to be in order, but when he looked outside, he started to worry, and by the time he arrived at the island airport, his flight had been canceled. Nothing else would be leaving that day because of the storm.

Well, shit.

Normally, he'd call Ryan and ask to crash with him, but he wasn't going to disturb Ryan the day after his wedding. Mel could get a hotel room.

Or . . .

Vivian Liao was supposed to be his friend, wasn't she? Maybe she'd let him stay with her, and he could get some answers.

Despite the heaviness inside him, a mischievous grin spread across his face.

Chapter 22

Vivian was curled up on the couch with her tablet and a mug of tea when someone knocked on her door. She ignored it, but a minute later, they knocked again.

She stomped to the door to tell this person that they had the wrong unit, but when she threw open the door, the person on the other side wasn't a stranger.

No, it was Mel, snowflakes covering his jacket and toque.

"Surprised to see me?" he asked. "Thought you could sneak out and get rid of me?"

She scrubbed a hand over her face, her irritation building. "Why are you here? How did you know where I live?"

"Well, you did give me your address so I could ship you a Christmas present. Plus, I was here yesterday for the door games. I did push-ups over there." He pointed toward the living room.

Right. So much had happened lately. Hard to believe that was only yesterday.

"Then my flight was canceled, owing to the storm," he said cheerfully. "I don't know many people in Toronto, so I figured since we're such good friends who text each other in the middle of the night, I could stay with you." He held out his arms and flashed her a smile that made her skin prickle, much to her annoyance. "A kind lady held the door open for me downstairs, so I didn't even have to buzz."

Vivian just stared at him, and his smile faltered.

"Okay," he said softly. "But just tell me—"

"Fine. You can stay." Yes, there were hotels nearby, but it seemed mean to kick him out in a storm when his flight had been canceled.

"Excellent." He stepped inside with his suitcase and removed his snowy boots. "How shall we spend the rest of the day? Snuggling for warmth?" He waggled his eyebrows.

Dear God. This guy was impossible.

"My heat is working just fine," she said primly, "and I have lots of blankets."

"You sure liked cuddling with me last night."

She tried to wipe the look of shock off her face.

He seemed amused, but then his expression turned serious. "Do you regret last night?"

"No. I had fun."

"Me, too. But when I woke up this morning, you were gone. Care to explain?"

He stepped into her personal space. She took a step back; he didn't follow.

"We had a one-night stand," she said, swallowing. "Maybe it's not difficult for you to deal with the morning after, but I couldn't face the awkwardness."

"A one-night stand. Is that all it was to you?"

"Y-yes."

"It was more than that to me."

He stepped closer to her again, and this time, she didn't retreat. In fact, when he cupped her cheek, she leaned toward him. She couldn't help staring at his lips. He'd licked her all over yesterday, and she'd come against his mouth. More than once.

Today, he wore corduroy pants and a flower-patterned dress shirt, just peeking out under a navy sweater. She wanted to take them all off. Wanted to be toasty and warm inside with him as the snow raged outside. She didn't want to yearn for such things, but she did.

His lips were so, so close to hers . . .

She finally retreated.

"You want more?" she asked.

"I do."

"When did you decide that?"

"It's been a long time coming."

She shook her head. "Maybe I . . . don't feel that way about you." It was a little hard to say those words. Just a little. Because perhaps she did care about him. However . . . "I'm not interested in a relationship right now. I don't have a good history with relationships."

"Neither do I, as you know."

"But you've never been hurt quite like I have, right? So to me, you seem lucky."

He nodded and didn't refute her point.

When he was serious and didn't crack jokes . . . sometimes, that slayed her more than anything.

"If all your relationships have been short-lived," she couldn't help saying, "is that how you see it going with me, too?" Even if she'd wanted to start something, why try if it was doomed to fail quickly?

"I can't help thinking you're different," he said with a smile.

"Mm-hmm. Because of the synchronized insomnia?"

"I just really like you."

"Even though I prefer plain vanilla cake over chocolate?" she asked.

"I can overlook that."

"How magnanimous of you. And what about all the gray in my wardrobe?"

"You can spend more time naked."

"Yeah, very magnanimous."

"Look," he said. "I'm nothing like your ex. The reasons you two broke up . . . they're not going to be a problem."

"You don't want kids?"

"It's never been of particular importance to me." He paused. "And I believe you when you say you don't want them."

I believe you.

Those were powerful words.

God, was it too much to talk about kids when you hadn't even gone on a first date? Except, in your mid-thirties, it seemed important to be up-front about such things.

And Mel wouldn't have a problem with her sexuality, nor would he be terrified of anything that was the tiniest bit feminine, unlike Jared.

Why was she thinking about that? Those things didn't matter when she didn't want a relationship. When he lived in a different fucking country.

And then she reminded herself of the biggest problem.

He didn't understand her life. He'd ripped apart her choices the day they'd met, and they'd danced around it during the past few months. Sure, he might be thoughtful at times, and he might respect some of the decisions she'd made—but not all of them.

"No," she said firmly. "I'm not interested in a relationship with you. End of discussion. You can stay here until you find a flight, but that's all, and you're sleeping on the couch."

"We did such a good job of sharing a bed last night. Why don't we turn it into a two-night stand?"

"No, that will just complicate matters."

"What should we do until bedtime? Bake cookies together?"

She glared at him.

"What?" he said. "We need to do something to fill the time, and you've already rejected sex and snuggling."

"We can have instant noodles for dinner," she said crisply. "Then, I will give you the Wi-Fi password and you may entertain yourself. I assume you can manage not to make too much noise."

"I don't know. You're just so much fun to annoy."

She released what was probably the biggest sigh of her life. "Let me show you the choices for noodles. There are three different types." She hadn't planned to eat quite yet—it was only six—but she didn't know what else to do.

Once their noodles were ready, they sat across from each other at the small kitchen table. They shared a little conversation as they ate, but not much. She feared talking, convinced he'd have an annoying retort for everything she'd say.

But silence wasn't great, either. She was very much aware of his fingers on his chopsticks, fingers that had been inside her. His tongue, as he licked his lips . . .

She hoped the storm wouldn't last long and he'd be out of here tomorrow morning.

After dinner, she led him to the living room and got out an extra blanket. "I'll be in my room if you need anything," she said. "Help yourself to tea, coffee, food, whatever."

She headed to her bedroom before he could respond.

• • • • • • •

Mel was bored.

After staring out the window at the swirling snow, he switched to staring at the throw pillow that he'd bought Vivian. Dean Kobayashi's brooding face, partially shadowed by a cowboy hat, stared back at him.

Ugh. He half wished he hadn't gotten this for her. It was weird. But once he returned to New York, he might never see the pillow—or her—again.

He tried not to be too distressed by the thought, but he didn't like the way things were between them now. He'd hoped that last night could be the start of something, yet now he was out here on the couch, and she was in her bedroom. Possibly she'd changed into gray pajamas that would be fun to remove . . .

No. He shouldn't think like that. She'd made herself clear.

He wondered what he could have said differently, though maybe this was just the way it had to be. Not everything was his fault, even if he had a tendency to blame himself.

Hmm. A shower sounded nice, and it might clear his head. He headed to Vivian's room and knocked on her door.

"Come in," she said.

She was sitting in bed, her legs out in front of her, wearing gray pajamas with pink trim. That made him smile—he couldn't help it. In her hand was a sketchbook.

He'd meant to just ask for a towel, but now he was distracted. "What are you drawing?"

She shrugged and held it up. Tentatively, he stepped into the room and took a look. Flowers of some sort.

When he sat down on the bed, on top of the purple duvet, she shot him a glare but didn't ask him to leave. If she had, he would have left.

"May I?" He held a hand toward her sketchbook.

She hesitated. "All right."

He took the hardback sketchbook. On the cover were several vinyl stickers; one was an *Only the Best* sticker.

There was a random assortment of things on the pages. Some food, some nature, some fantastical imaginings. Most of them in pencil, a couple in black pen; there were small flashes of color—from colored pencils—here and there. A few drawings were unfinished.

All of them were really good. Like the first time he'd seen her artwork—before he'd even met her—he was impressed with her skill.

"The fan art I saw before," he said, "you did that on a tablet, right?"

She nodded.

He'd been flipping the pages at a slow pace, but then he came to one that made him stop. A grin spread over his face, and he looked up at Vivian, who'd paled.

She grabbed the sketchbook out of his hands. "You weren't supposed to see that."

"As the subject of that drawing, I disagree."

She rolled her eyes.

"Come on," he said. "Let me look."

"Fine. But only because you'd annoy the hell out of me until I gave you what you want."

"You know me well."

She handed back the sketchbook. In the drawing, he was sporting a big smile; it was a pretty good likeness. There was a date in the bottom corner. Last year.

"Why'd you draw this?" he asked. "Was it before or after I saved your ass at karaoke?"

"Before."

"But you didn't like me then. I pissed the shit out of you."

"You still piss the shit out of me."

He laughed. "Yeah, but it was different before."

They were quiet for a moment as they studied each other. Her hair was partially covering one of her eyes, and he itched to reach out and push it back. To see if those pajamas were as fleecy and soft as they looked.

He swallowed. She'd rejected him, but he still wished to find out everything he could about her.

"I was just doodling," she said, "and before I knew what I was doing, I'd doodled your face from memory. I'm surprised I was able to do that."

He flipped to another page. A side-profile self-portrait, capturing her sharp features.

"I think you've seen enough." She whisked the sketchbook out of his hands once more.

"Why don't you pursue art?" He should let it go, but for some reason, he couldn't.

"This again?"

"Your parents may have been told it wasn't a practical career choice, but—"

"You don't know how I was brought up. You don't get it."

"So, explain it to me."

She sighed. "Art is my hobby. It's just for *me*. Not everyone wants to make money from something they're good at. I can draw whatever I like, and I don't have to answer to customers. I don't have to hustle, always trying to find more commissions. That, to me, is freedom. The freedom I didn't have in my childhood. I have a decent career so I don't have to worry too much about money, luckily. I could find a better-paying job, but those jobs would be more time-consuming, more stressful. What I have now is a good balance. It's not like I hate my job and it's sucking the life out of me. I'm reasonably good at it, and I don't mind it."

"Oh," he said faintly.

"You want to tell me I'm wrong?"

"I guess I've never thought about it like that before. You see, after I graduated from college, I had a job in marketing. I hated it so, so much. It *did* feel like it was sucking the life out of me, though I knew it was better than lots of things I could be doing. But what

I really wanted was to make people laugh—and get paid for doing so. The night we met, even if I didn't know you, I couldn't stand the thought of you feeling like I had. So stuck and depressed—"

"But I'm not like you. Not in any way."

"Yeah." He chuckled. "You're not."

"I like my stable paycheck, which allows me to do whatever I want in my spare time."

"I get it now, I promise. I'm sorry I said all those things to you." It wasn't the life he'd want for himself, but not everyone in the world was like him.

He released a breath, and some of the tension between them evaporated. Tension that had been lingering for a long, long time.

Yet tension—of an entirely different sort—still remained. He was very conscious of the fact that he was sitting near her on a bed, and she was in pajamas. When she inhaled and exhaled, he was very conscious of that, too. This fascinating woman who was absolutely nothing like him.

She licked her lips and put her sketchbook on the bedside table.

"You're thinking about it, aren't you?" he said.

"Thinking about what?"

"Don't play innocent with me, Vivian." He prowled toward her on hands and knees. "You're thinking about my sexy animal magnetism."

"Yeah, sure I am." But her sarcastic tone wavered.

He crawled on top of her and dropped his mouth to hers.

Chapter 23

Vivian returned Mel's kiss. It was sweet, sweet relief to feel his mouth on hers again. He slipped his hand under her ass and molded her body against his. Even if she was all harsh angles, with him, she became a slightly different person. A little softer.

She kept kissing him. It felt right, even more so than last night, now that they'd talked about the one thing that had been lingering between them for well over a year. Mel had apologized to her before, yes, but he hadn't truly understood until tonight. And he hadn't doubled down on his incorrect assumptions; he could admit he was wrong.

He was gentle and heavy against her, and between his legs, he was very, very hard. When he undid the top button of her pajama shirt, she finally realized what was happening. Not that she hadn't known, but her brain had taken a backseat for a few minutes, and now it was functioning again.

"I don't think this would be a good idea," she said. "You want a relationship, and I . . ."

"Okay. I understand."

He stood up and padded to the door, but she couldn't bear watching him leave. He would sleep on the couch, even though it felt like he belonged in here, with her. Why was she so attached to him? She didn't want the same things as he did.

Or did she?

It wasn't smart or rational. She'd been burned badly in her last relationship, and she and Mel had hated each other at the beginning.

But they'd gotten past that.

"Come back," she said quietly, "and take off your pants. I don't want them to get my clean sheets all dirty."

"Have you changed your mind about something?"

"Let's try." She gestured between them. "For more than a night."

"Are you sure?"

"Yes." She was going entirely on instinct, which wasn't like her, but she would take what she wanted.

Mel didn't smirk; he shed his pants and joined her on the bed again. When he started unbuttoning her top, his gaze was laser-focused on each inch of skin he was revealing.

It was different from last night.

Yet just as good.

. . . .

Vivian's alarm went off at six thirty. Unlike yesterday morning, she was in her own bed.

But just like yesterday morning, Mel was in bed with her.

It wasn't a one-night stand, and her mouth curved upward. He half opened his eyes and mumbled something, possibly "It's so early," but it was hard to tell.

She had a shower, dried her hair, and put on a bathrobe. When she started making coffee, the smell seemed to rouse Mel. He entered the kitchen.

"That's why I came to your room last night," he said, pointing at her robe. "To ask for a towel so I could shower."

"Are you sure that's why you came to my room?" she asked. "Not to seduce me?"

He flashed her a grin. "I'm insulted. You never believe me."

"Well, you're full of shit sometimes." She meant it kindly, meant to tease him, though she wasn't sure if she pulled it off.

But he barked out a laugh, so she seemed to be doing okay.

As she moved about the kitchen, the familiar tasks of the morning felt somewhat odd with him watching her. She set out milk and a couple of types of cereal. "I hope this is okay for breakfast."

"Of course," he said, flashing another grin.

"You smile entirely too much," she muttered.

"Because I'm happy to be with you."

When she sat down next to him at the counter, he squeezed her hand.

His words hadn't been a joke.

"So. Uh," she said. "It's stopped snowing. You can try to book your flight."

"Can I stay until tomorrow, even if there's something available today? So we can spend some time together, and I'll avoid the rush of everyone trying to get out right after the storm. If it's okay with you."

"Yes, that would be nice." She pulled a set of keys out of her "junk" drawer—the junk drawer was quite neat, but it had miscellaneous odds and ends. "These were Lindsay's keys. Since she doesn't live here anymore, you can have them for the day. You can see the city in the snow, whatever you want. Just don't get into trouble while I'm at work."

"I make no promises."

She gave him a stern look. "Don't get into *too much* trouble."

"I think I can manage that. Maybe."

When she let out a long-suffering sigh, he laughed.

Vivian was out the door only five minutes later than usual, and she was more efficient than usual at the office. Not that she was normally *in*efficient, but she wanted to leave a little early, and she needed to get her work done.

At lunch, she received a text from Mel.

MEL: I got you a present

VIVIAN: Should I be worried?

MEL: Yeah, probably, since it just crawled under the fridge. I don't think it likes me, but I'm sure it'll like you.

VIVIAN: Because I'm so warm and cuddly.

MEL: You are!

MEL: That wasn't sarcasm, in case you couldn't tell. You're extremely cuddly when you're naked.

VIVIAN: I'm at work. Please annoy people on Twitter instead.

MEL: Thanks for the excellent advice. I will do as requested.

Her lips twitched. She tried to force them downward, but they wouldn't obey.

Vivian arrived home before six, curious to see what Mel had gotten her. And, more than anything, she was excited to see him. It was a strange feeling.

When she opened the door, he bounded over from the living room.

"How was work?" he asked with a deep bow, gesturing for her to hand over her coat.

"Not too bad," she said. "How was your day?"

He led her to the kitchen table, where there was a pot of tea. He poured them each a cup.

"I walked around Chinatown in the morning," he said. "Went to one of those knickknack stores selling postcards of Toronto that looked like they were from the eighties. I bought two, just because." He showed her a postcard of a streetcar on Queen Street and one of the CN Tower. "Then I went into another store and bought a couple of gifts for you."

"I thought there was just one gift."

"All in good time." He held up a finger. "Then made a giant snow dick in a random park, posted the picture on Twitter, and tagged Ryan's father."

"Mm-hmm."

"I ate some dumplings for lunch then came back here, where I decorated your bedroom."

"You decorated my bedroom?" she asked in alarm.

"Very temporary decorations, don't worry. I'll show them to you soon."

Vivian couldn't help wondering if this had all been a big mistake, but it was, undeniably, nice to come home to someone. To see Mel sitting across from her in a hoodie and jeans—no colorful shirts today.

Once they'd finished their tea, he led her to the closed door of her bedroom and opened it with a flourish. "Ta-da!"

Her room was a riot of rainbow streamers. In fact, she was so distracted by all the colors that it took her a moment to notice what was lying in the middle of the bed, with a pink ribbon around it.

She cautiously picked it up. It had to be close to a meter long. "Is this . . ."

"Why yes, it's a giant fried–chicken drumstick pillow. I thought of you when I saw it."

She did not ask for clarification. "This is what you lost under the fridge?"

"Oh, no. That's something else." He reached behind her pillow—her regular pillow, not the fried-chicken one—and pulled out two hedgehog plushies. One had a purple ribbon around its neck, and the other had a gray ribbon. They were both smiling, and unlike the chicken drumstick, they were actually kind of cute. "One for each of us."

"Let me guess. Mine is the one with the gray ribbon."

"Well, not exactly. The gray ribbon represents you, but I'm taking it back to New York. To remind me of you."

"A hedgehog reminds you of me?"

"It's spiky, with a soft underbelly and nice smile," he said, "The one with the purple ribbon will be my representative in your home. You can snuggle him when you miss me."

"You got us matching stuffed hedgehogs."

"Why yes, I did."

She just stared at him. It felt like he was already upending her life.

His smile faded. "Is it too much? I know that sometimes—okay, often—I'm a bit much . . ."

"No, no. The hedgehogs are cute." She rather enjoyed this ridiculousness, truth be told.

"Shall we go out for dinner? My treat. I was thinking pho, if you're into that? It would be nice on a cold day. Oh, and I booked my flight for tomorrow, early afternoon."

She couldn't help feeling a bit deflated. He would be gone soon. But she merely said, "Pho sounds good."

. . . .

When Vivian's alarm went off the next morning, Mel rolled over.

"Stay here for just a few minutes," he murmured.

And so she did. She could spare a few minutes.

He lay on his side and pulled her into his arms. For so long, she'd gone more or less without touching people, but it was comforting to feel someone's body against hers. To feel like she might not be totally alone, even if she prided herself on her independence.

Last night, they'd had pho at her favorite place, followed by Japanese cheesecake. Then they'd gone home, had sex, and watched a movie.

It had been fun. A break from her regular life.

She opened her eyes, and in the dim light of the room, she glimpsed the chicken drumstick pillow sitting on her desk. "Why did the fried-chicken pillow make you think of me?"

"Pillows in general have that effect, since I got you one for Christmas. And I imagined you wrinkling your nose in that cute way you do." He pulled away from her and imitated her expression of disgust. He failed miserably at it.

"I do not look like that," she said.

He pulled her close once more. "You kinda do."

His laugh warmed something inside her, as it always did, even when she pretended otherwise.

They had breakfast together again; it was starting to feel like a routine. Then she dressed in a gray pinstripe suit and a soft pink shirt, and he said she looked nice. She kissed him goodbye, telling him to leave the extra set of keys with the concierge, and also to text her when he arrived home in Manhattan.

At work, she couldn't concentrate as well as she had the previous day, and she dallied at the office longer than usual. It seemed weird to go back to her normal life after the weekend. After Lindsay's wedding and everything with Mel.

When she got home at seven, it was dark and empty. She tossed the two sets of keys in the little bowl by the front door. The sound echoed.

No Lindsay. She was married now and living with her new husband.

No Mel. He was back in New York.

She went to her bedroom and changed into a pair of yoga pants and a sweatshirt. On the bed, Mel had positioned the hedgehog so it looked like it was eating the drumstick.

She was about to head to the kitchen when her phone buzzed.

You had a wedding on the weekend, didn't you? Amanda asked. How was it?

Fine, Vivian replied.

Then she regretted her response. Her sister might find it terse and cold, and it was insufficient to capture everything that had happened, not that she wanted to tell Amanda most of it anyway.

She recalled her conversation with Mel on Sunday. The night they'd met, she'd briefly wondered if their conversation about her job had hit on some kind of sore point for him—and she'd been right about that after all. It had reminded him of a particular bad point in his life.

She breathed out slowly, trying to exhale her bitterness over her childhood. Her sister wasn't to blame for that.

It went well, Vivian typed. Nice ceremony, and I ate lots of good food.

Her phone buzzed as soon as she sent the text. Not Amanda, but Mel telling her that he'd arrived safely.

Are you home from work yet? he asked. I left you something on the kitchen table.

She scurried to the kitchen and flipped on the lights. There were two egg tarts in a plastic container on the table. She couldn't help smiling when she saw them.

Thank you 🖤

She mulled everything over as she helped herself to a tart. They were going to try to make this work, even though they were nothing alike.

Yeah, she liked Mel, even if he was a pain in her ass on occasion. Yeah, she had a good time with him. But it was easy to imagine things quickly going awry.

When they'd been cuddled up in bed this morning, she'd believed, but now, a stuffed hedgehog, a giant fried-chicken pillow, and one and a half egg tarts were the only evidence that he'd been here. He was in New York, in a life so different from her own. A life that involved going up on stage and having a Netflix special. He might not be as famous as Irene Lai, but still. She'd known this man—well, his onstage persona—for years before she'd met him. It was such an unlikely relationship.

How was this happening? And could it truly last?

Chapter 24

"Come on," Mel said to Joy, shaking the microphone in his little sister's direction. "Sing 'Barbie Girl.'" They were all gathered at the family house in Queens for the Lunar New Year, and "Barbie Girl" was, of course, the most appropriate song to sing.

"Absolutely not," Joy said.

"Fine, I'll sing it, then."

"Oh God. You're going to dance, and I don't think I can deal with that today."

"Well, I'm such a generous brother that I'm giving you a choice. You sing it, or I sing it."

"Maybe we could have a singing-free holiday for once?"

"That sounds like no fun to me," Po Po said from her place on the armchair. "I'm your elder! You should do what I want."

"Po Po, you can't pull that excuse five times day," Joy said. "And, Mel, if you must sing, can't it be a different song? Any other song?"

"Fine. If you won't let me sing 'Barbie Girl,' then . . ." He cleared his throat and began speaking in his David Attenborough voice. "The redheaded cockchafer can grow to a length of nine inches. It lives in Siberia and—"

"Stop it!" Joy covered her ears. She couldn't stand it when he recited incorrect facts about beetles. The redheaded cockchafer was found in Australia and certainly didn't grow to be nine inches long.

"By the way," he said, "I appreciated that picture of a beetle you sent me the other day, the one you claim looks just like me. The resemblance really was uncanny."

Before Joy could speak, the doorbell rang.

"Who's that?" Chelsea asked. "We're all here."

"Mel," Po Po said, "please answer the door."

"I'll get it." Joy stood up.

"No, Mel should answer it."

He approached the door warily, a sinking feeling in his gut. Sure enough, there was an unfamiliar white woman on the other side of the door.

"Happy New Year!" she said in a perky voice. "You must be Mel."

He simply stared at the stranger for a moment.

"Oh, sorry," she said. "It's . . . gong hei fat choy? Something like that? Is it really bad to say it in English?"

"Uh, I barely speak the language." He scrubbed a hand over his face. "Are you supposed to be my date for the evening? Did my grandma set this up?"

"Of course." Po Po shuffled into the entryway. "I need to up my game. You keep getting older!" She shook her finger in his direction. "Let me help with your love life. I am a great matchmaker—I made a good match for Chelsea, didn't I?"

"Po Po, stop surprising me with dates. And quit using your 'Best Po Po NYC' Twitter account to try to find matches for me online. It's just weird."

"Why should I stop?" She crossed her arms. "You're already seeing someone?"

"In fact, yes! Yes, I am."

She shook her finger again. "You're just lying to get out of this date."

"I'm not. I have a girlfriend. Her name is Vivian, and she lives in Toronto."

"Very suspicious. I think you made up this girlfriend in Canada. Or maybe she's real, but you lied about where she lives so I won't call her and invite her over."

"You'll have to excuse them." Chelsea came to the door and held out her hand to the mystery woman. "I'm Chelsea. And you are . . . ?"

"Melanie."

"See, isn't it funny?" Po Po said. "Mel and Mel. You have the same nickname."

"Please," Mel said. "I'm begging you. No more surprise dates."

"But if they weren't surprises, you wouldn't agree."

"That's exactly the point."

"Hmph. Doesn't sound like a good plan to me."

Melanie's eyes moved back and forth between them. "Should I leave?"

"No," Po Po said. "You stay. We'll have this matter sorted out soon." She held out her hand. "Mel, give me your phone."

Mom emerged from the kitchen. "What's this hullabaloo?"

"Hullabaloo?" Po Po frowned. "Is this English? Sounds like a fake word to me."

Mel threw up his arms in exasperation. "You think everything's fake!"

"So show me your phone. Show me Vivian's number."

"Fine." He unlocked his phone and pulled up her contact info. "You see?"

"Is this area code for Canada?" Po Po asked, grabbing the phone. "Joy? Do you know?"

"Why don't you call it and ask Vivian?" Joy replied with a smirk.

It was unfortunate that Po Po was holding the phone, not Joy. Mel could tackle his little sister to retrieve it, but he couldn't tackle his elderly grandmother.

Po Po pressed the call button. "Hi. This is Vivian?"

Oh God. It was really happening.

"I'm Mel's grandmother," Po Po said into his phone. "Has he told you about me? Very nice things? Did he say I have a fantastic singing voice?" She clucked her tongue. "Wah. Okay. He claims you live in Toronto and you're in a relationship with him. This is true?" Her eyebrows rose. "He isn't just paying you to say that? . . . I see. You will come to New York soon to visit him? Maybe next weekend so I can meet you . . . Since you're Canadian, have you met Shania Twain? Is Timmins near Toronto?"

"Okay, that's enough." Mel pulled the phone out of his grandmother's hands. "Vivian, I'm sorry about that. My grandma arranged a surprise date for our New Year's celebration, and I protested and said I was already seeing someone. She thought I was lying about having a girlfriend in Canada." Interestingly, Po Po hadn't been suspicious about his relationship with Nicky last year—and that had actually been fake.

"That's all right," Vivian said on the other end of the phone. "Have fun with your family tonight. Text me later."

When the call ended, he turned to Melanie. "I apologize. My grandmother invited you without consulting me. You're welcome to stay—I'm sure there's more than enough food."

"No, that's okay," Melanie said. "I'll head out now."

"Sorry for the misunderstanding."

She left, and Mel closed the door behind her.

"How did you meet Melanie?" he asked Po Po. "On Twitter?"

Joy snickered.

"Just you wait, Joy," Mel said. "She's gonna do this to you next."

Po Po hobbled back into the living room. "Melanie is my friend's granddaughter's husband's sister? Cousin? Something like that. I forget details." She shook her head. "Cannot believe you didn't tell me about your girlfriend. You embarrassed me."

"I'm sorry. But Vivian and I haven't been together long."

"As soon as you start dating someone, you should call up your po po and tell her!"

"Yeah, Mel," Joy said.

He glared at his sister. "Should I sing 'Barbie Girl' and do *all* my dance moves? Or share more fun facts about redheaded cockchafers?"

She stuck out her tongue.

"Tell us more about Vivian," Mom said.

"She works at a bank," Mel said, "and she was Lindsay's roommate."

"Who's Lindsay again?"

"Ryan's wife."

"Oh, did you meet Vivian at their wedding?"

"I first met her over a year ago, actually. Can we stop the interrogation and eat dinner?"

Unfortunately, it took over twenty minutes before he got his wish.

· · · · · · ·

When Mel got home, it was a little late for a weeknight, but he still texted Vivian after changing into his pajamas and collapsing into bed.

> MEL: Hey, you awake?
>
> MEL: I'm really sorry. My grandma grabbed
> the phone out of my hands and called you.

> VIVIAN: Seems like you're getting a taste of your own medicine 😄

MEL: You're supposed to be on my side.

> VIVIAN: Give me her number. Maybe we'll have a chat tomorrow.

MEL: I thought you hated talking on the phone.

> VIVIAN: Good point

Mel picked up his stuffed hedgehog, tied a red ribbon next to the gray ribbon, and put a red envelope in front of her. Since he was unmarried, his mom and grandma still gave him red envelopes, as well as telling him that he should change this situation by next year. He snapped a picture of the hedgehog and sent it to Vivian.

MEL: VeeVee wishes you a happy new year!

> VIVIAN: You named the hedgehog VeeVee?

MEL: Yeah, after you.

> VIVIAN: I'm not sure I like the name.

MEL: She purrs when I call her that, so I think she approves. I snuggle her because you're not here, and we have conversations late into the night.

> VIVIAN: That sounds normal.

MEL: How's Mellie doing?

> VIVIAN: Is that what my stuffed hedgehog is called? Really?

MEL: Shh! Don't insult his feelings.

> VIVIAN: He's fine. He sleeps and eats. You
> know, regular hedgehog stuff. Did you
> know hedgehogs sometimes cannibalize
> their young?

MEL: how shocking

MEL: VeeVee would never. She's such a
sweet little hedgehog. She's really come
into her own lately and developed a
personality.

> VIVIAN: Of course she has.

MEL: I miss you 💋

He and Vivian texted every day now. In some ways their conversations weren't all that different from before the wedding, except he told her that he missed her and sent her kisses. She didn't do the same, but he wouldn't read into that too much. It didn't really seem like her thing.

Okay, fine, a few times—maybe more than a few times—he'd obsessed over it, but his brain obsessed over lots of weird things.

MEL: how's Pete

> VIVIAN: Who's Pete?

MEL: You don't know who Pete is? 😮

MEL: Your fried chicken, of course.
Doesn't he look just like a Pete to you?

> VIVIAN: The two of us are having a cuddle
> party.

MEL: Welp, I'm jealous of a fried chicken
pillow. I think that's a first?

> VIVIAN: You're much more attractive, don't
> worry.

MEL: My ego just grew three sizes.

> VIVIAN: Uh-oh

MEL: 😄

After talking to Vivian for a few more minutes, Mel said good-bye and put down his phone with a smile. He wished he could pull her into his arms right now and press kisses up and down her body.

When he'd first met her, he'd certainly never expected her to make him feel warm and squishy like this. Silly conversations just seemed extra meaningful with her. He really needed to make sure this worked out and they didn't split up in three months.

He had a feeling it would hurt more than his usual breakups.

Chapter 25

Vivian's family had waited until the weekend to celebrate New Year's.

After a late lunch at a restaurant, they were now back at her childhood home in Scarborough. Vivian, Stephen, Amanda, Ma, and Ba. Andy had claimed he was busy, and Ma and Ba weren't happy about that, but they'd given him much less grief about not coming than they would have given Vivian.

And now, as they sat around the kitchen table with tea and pastries, they were giving Vivian grief about something else.

"You should be dating," Ma said. "You keep saying you don't want kids—and yes, I hear you, but the right man will change your mind. You need to find him before you're too old to get pregnant."

Oh God, not this again.

There was no point in arguing. Vivian had done it all before.

"In fact," Ba said, "my colleague has a son . . ."

Shit.

Apparently, her parents were now getting into matchmaking, like Mel's grandmother. Vivian wanted to scream.

"I already have a boyfriend," she said. At least that should stop any matchmaking, though it would just change the tone of some of the other comments.

"You do?" Amanda sounded a little too surprised for Vivian's liking. "Are you sure it's not a fake boyfriend to get out of this? Seems awful convenient when you haven't had a boyfriend in a while."

"Maybe I just don't tell you about the men I date. His name is Mel."

"What does he do?" Ma asked.

"He's a comedian."

This was met with a lot of raised eyebrows.

"Is this . . . how do you say it?" Ma said. "Code word for unemployed? You should have higher standards, Vivian. Your father's colleague's son—"

"He really is a comedian! He makes a living from it."

"What's his full name?" Amanda asked. "Maybe we've heard of him."

"Melvin Lee."

"I saw his stand-up special on Netflix," Stephen said. "He's pretty good."

Ma looked at Stephen. "He is a *legitimate* comedian?"

"He's been in movies and TV shows, too." Stephen pulled out his phone. "Let me find a clip on YouTube."

Vivian considered snatching the phone out of her brother's hands, lest her parents see Mel make a joke about "eating pussy." But she was afraid that grabbing his phone would make everyone more curious.

"Here's one about Chinese New Year," Stephen said.

Well, she supposed it could be worse than a joke about red underwear. Ma seemed a little skeptical when Mel shook his imaginary cottontail, but she did chuckle.

"How did you meet him?" Amanda asked.

Vivian sipped her tea. "He was Ryan Kwok's best man."

"I still can't believe your roommate married a movie star."

"Even I know who Ryan Kwok is," Ma said. "I think you should

230 • Jackie Lau

have gone for him instead. He got an Oscar nomination. He did not win"—she clucked her tongue—"but . . ."

"Maybe I could be your roommate now," Amanda said. "My lease ends in a few months. I wonder which famous people I'd meet?"

"Yes, that's a good idea." Ma nodded. "Close to the university. Very convenient."

Vivian was getting a headache.

It was a bit tough to afford the place on her own, but she hadn't been proactive about finding a roommate. When Mel visited, she'd prefer not to have a roommate, especially one who was related to her.

"Uh, I have a couple of people who are interested," she lied.

"Don't you want to help your sister?" Ma asked.

"Are you expecting her to live with me rent-free, too?"

"Well—"

"No," Amanda interjected. "I would pay you rent. Though I'm not sure I could afford market rent for that place . . . But don't you think it would be fun? Living together as grown-ups?"

Vivian barely managed not to recoil at the idea. Even if she were closer to her sister, she couldn't imagine it. Amanda would be in her face all the time, probably demanding all sorts of favors, and Ma and Ba would visit regularly. Vivian wouldn't feel like she had any privacy.

And she couldn't help remembering how she'd been forced to share a room with Amanda from the time Amanda was six months old. Vivian hadn't even been in high school, and she'd needed to look after a baby in the middle of the night.

"You should think about your family," Ma said. "If Amanda lives there, she won't have to commute. More time for studying."

"And meeting movie stars!" Amanda chimed in.

This was going downhill fast.

"Before I forget," Ba said to Vivian, "the washing machine isn't working. You fixed it last time. Can you take a look?"

"And I have an appointment on Wednesday," Ma said. "You're taking the day off to go with me, remember?"

"This is the first I'm hearing about it," Vivian said. Which was true. She wouldn't have forgotten. "I need more notice to take a day off."

"Call in sick and—"

"Why are you encouraging me to call in sick when I'm not sick?"

"—you can tell me more about your *boyfriend* in the car."

Everyone started talking at once, and Vivian just wanted to put her head in her hands and snuggle up with a fried-chicken pillow. Aka Pete.

. . . .

Vivian stayed up late that night so she could talk to Mel after his show, as they'd planned earlier. But when he messaged her at midnight, she started feeling guilty. Maybe he'd be out having a good time with friends if it weren't for her. She didn't want him to rearrange his life so he could message her.

They'd started using a messaging app so she wouldn't have to pay for a package with unlimited texting to the US. Smartphone plans were so expensive in Canada. Ugh.

MEL: Hey

VIVIAN: How was the show?

MEL: I was hilarious, of course. How was lunch with your family?

VIVIAN: It was okay.

MEL: Are you wearing those fleecy gray pajamas now? Rawr

Her jaw tensed, even though she wouldn't usually be bothered

232 • Jackie Lau

if he changed the topic and flirted. She leaned back in bed and stared at the screen for a while, not sure how to respond.

Then her phone indicated that she had a video call. From Mel, of course.

She smiled when she saw his face on the screen. It wasn't the most flattering view, but it was still his face. His dark eyes, with faint crinkles at the corners.

"You didn't reply," he said. "I just wondered . . . is everything all right? If you don't like 'what are you wearing?' questions, we don't have to do that."

"You asked how my lunch was. I said 'okay.' And you just . . . moved on."

Now that she'd said it out loud, she felt ridiculous because she normally hated when people pressed her for more information. Especially since she'd said "okay," not "terrible."

"Oh." He ran a hand over his face. "I took that to mean that it hadn't gone great, but when you didn't immediately add something else, I thought you didn't want to tell me more. So I didn't press you. I want to respect your boundaries. But it sounds like you'd prefer to talk about it."

She wasn't entirely sure what she wanted, but she started speaking. "My parents were trying to set me up with someone, so I told them about you. When I said you were a comedian, they thought it was a fancy way of saying you were unemployed, but my brother had heard of you, and he brought up a video on YouTube. Then they talked about Amanda living with me—which I don't want—and me accompanying my mom to an appointment, which she claims I knew about, but I didn't. Me fixing the washing machine . . ." She looked away from the screen for a moment. "In my family, I'm the one who does things for other people."

That's the only reason they love me.

She couldn't say those words out loud, but that was how it felt to her. She was loved because she could get shit done.

With Jared, it had been similar. She'd been in charge of managing their lives, keeping the household running smoothly, keeping everything clean.

"Why are you dating me?" she blurted out. "What do you get out of it? I don't do things for you. We don't live in the same city, so it's not like I'm providing you with regular sex. I'm not entertaining."

"I find you very entertaining." Mel spoke with a low, husky voice.

She just laughed.

"What?" he said. "You're fun to tease. We have a nice vibe together."

"Vibe. Right." She glanced at Mellie the hedgehog. "I wish you were here now."

"Me, too. One more month, okay?"

"God, I'm being needy." And she was never needy. It wasn't like her.

"Nah. Well, maybe a little, but you're allowed to be. You're always the one satisfying other people's needs. Even when you were a kid, you didn't know what it was like to have other people look after you and reassure you, so you're not used to it."

She hadn't thought about it that way. As an adult, she'd focused on doing the things she wanted to do, which she hadn't had the opportunity for when she was younger. But she hadn't thought much about the nurturing she'd missed.

Still, she couldn't help feeling guilty.

"In the future," he said, "if you ever say something's just okay, I'll ask you about it rather than moving on."

"I shouldn't expect you to pick up on hints. I can just tell you what I want to talk about."

"It's cool. I wanna figure you out."

Vivian was mystified. This seemed . . . too easy? They'd bickered before, but they weren't bickering now. He wasn't complaining about anything she'd done, wasn't asking for anything more from her. Could having a boyfriend really be like this?

Still, she'd make a point of not being too needy in the future. Remaining independent.

"What are you doing tomorrow?" he asked.

This time, she was grateful for the change in topic.

"Spin class in the morning," she said. "I should go grocery shopping, too. Better than doing it Monday after work. Other than that? Watch some stuff, probably." She yawned.

"You tired? We can talk tomorrow." He kissed his fingertips then held his hand toward the screen, a gesture that she found particularly sweet for some reason. "Good night?"

"Good night."

Vivian ended the call and set her phone to silent.

She fell asleep with Mellie in her arms.

· · · · · · ·

Vivian slept well on Saturday night, but Sunday night was a different matter. After a couple of hours of sleep, she was wide awake at two in the morning. She tossed and turned for a while, then went to the living room with her phone and sat on the couch. When her phone chimed several minutes later, she almost dropped it in surprise.

> MEL: Hey. Noticed you were online. Can't sleep?

> VIVIAN: Nah

> MEL: We're insomnia twinsies again. We should get matching shirts ☺

VIVIAN: Don't you dare.

MEL: Are you afraid they'd be too colorful?

VIVIAN: I bet you'd get some hideous design.

VIVIAN: Plus, I don't want to wear matching anything.

MEL: Aww

MEL: What are you up to?

VIVIAN: Looking at pictures of Helen Alvarez in a suit.

Vivian regretted those words as soon as she'd sent them. It was strange to talk about that with someone she was dating, wasn't it? But there had been some shots of Helen Alvarez out and about in London—London, England, not London, Ontario—and she looked hot. Which had led Vivian to do an image search of Helen Alvarez in suits.

VIVIAN: Sorry, that was weird.

MEL: It's not weird. You're allowed to think other people are attractive.

MEL: I mean, I assume that's why you were looking at pictures of her, but maybe you had some other reason.

VIVIAN: No, you're correct. Just admiring pictures of her and feeling very queer.

MEL: Nothing wrong with that.

Vivian liked people of all genders in suits. And hats. In the right circumstances, she had a bit of a thing for fedoras and cowboy hats in particular. She liked long hair, too. But there was a wide range of things she found attractive on women. For men, she'd long been drawn to big, goofy, cuddly guys—opposites attract, she supposed. Though Mel was the only guy like that she'd ever dated.

And although he was the same gender as the people she'd dated back when she'd assumed she was straight, it was different with him, and she felt like she could explore her sexuality.

MEL: Did you see the miniseries Helen
Alvarez was in last year? The one about
the investigative journalist?

VIVIAN: No

MEL: It's really good. You should watch it.

VIVIAN: I watched a few episodes of *JANYS*
today.

MEL: Aww, you really miss me.

VIVIAN: What were you doing before you
texted me?

MEL: Buying ugly flower shirts online.

VIVIAN: Um

MEL: Just kidding. I was annoyed that I got
mixed up with Ryan in an article again.
Also obsessing over a joke I can't get right.

MEL: I don't make a lot of sense at this
hour. Don't expect much of me, aside
from my insecurities.

VIVIAN: Are you insecure about me liking
those pictures of Helen Alvarez and you're
just not saying anything?

MEL: Haha, no. Insecure about my ability to
function like a normal person in the world.

VIVIAN: Nobody's normal

MEL: So I've been told

VIVIAN: I mean, I like vanilla cake better
than chocolate cake. I'm told that's abnormal.

MEL: 😄

Vivian went to bed not long after that and slept for a solid three hours.

Later that morning, during a coffee break at work, she pulled up the website for the mochi donuts place she'd gone to in New York. She ordered a box of four donuts to be sent to Mel's home. Four different flavors, including a chocolate one. Not because it was something she had to do, not because anyone expected it of her, but just because she felt like it.

It seemed like an indulgence. Getting donuts delivered to someone in another city.

Whatever. She could afford it.

All afternoon, she could barely concentrate, because she was eager for him to receive her present and message her—she knew he'd do that right away.

What the hell was wrong with her? She'd done something *cute*. Not as horrifying as matching shirts, but still.

MEL: Thank you. You're such a sweetheart
🍩💋

VIVIAN: Don't use that word with me, young man

MEL: Shut up, you like it. You're a ball of mush.

MEL: But seriously, I appreciate it. I only slept for like an hour last night, so it was just the sugar kick I needed.

VIVIAN: If I were there, I'd do other things 😌

MEL: Oh? Tell me what you'd do.

VIVIAN: They might involve a very large chicken drumstick pillow . . .

VIVIAN: I'm just saying. It's a possibility.

Chapter 26

"I would make a terrible parent." Mel was testing out new material at the club, and he'd carefully studied the audience, looking for his grandmother.

Po Po wasn't here, thank God. He was going to curse even more than usual tonight.

"Like, really, just a fucking terrible parent. I fucking swear all the time, and my kid would have the worst potty mouth. Their first sentence would probably be something like, 'Oh, for fuck's sake!'"

"And the thing is, I would laugh. I would laugh so fucking hard if we were out in public. Like, let's say I was debating between oatmeal and Froot Loops in the cereal aisle, and my cute little toddler blurted out, 'Oh, for fuck's sake!' I would be unable to control myself.

"I think you're supposed to be embarrassed if your little kid swears. It doesn't reflect well on the parents, does it? Little kids copy the things they hear, so people would assume they heard it from you." Mel went on to talk about how little kids had great comic timing. He did a quick act-out where he imitated a grandmother saying grace before Christmas dinner. She was interrupted by a toddler in a high chair shouting, "Fuck this shit!"

He kept his annoyed-toddler expression on his face as the audience's laughter grew for a few seconds, moving on when it finally started to die down.

Oh yeah. He was on *fire* tonight.

"If my kid is anything like me," he said, "they'd probably be addicted to people's laughter, and if they heard Daddy laughing whenever they said 'fuck,' they'd keep saying it over and over again. And I'd just keep laughing. I wouldn't be embarrassed. I'd be like, 'That's my girl! The one in the purple tutu, rainbow striped socks, PAW Patrol T-shirt, and dinosaur headband. She's got my sense of fashion, too." He gestured to his shirt.

After speaking about how he'd be such a pushover when it came to treats, he segued into a section on recipes and cooking. "I think having to work around a kid's likes and dislikes when cooking would be a pain in the ass. And I say this as someone who likes cooking. Now, I hate cooking every day—what horrible person decided we need to eat multiple meals a day?—but cooking on occasion is fun. I don't have an entire shelf of cookbooks like my mom does. No, instead I have this great thing called . . ." He drew out the pause to build suspense. "The internet. Have you heard of it before? Maybe?"

He walked across the stage, thoroughly enjoying himself up here. The energy of the audience . . . yeah, it was good. "Anyway, it's amazing. You can find recipes for anything, with a thousand words of backstory about how the author's great-grandma used to make this recipe back in Narnia, and how it always reminds the author of warm summer barbecues, where kids would bully the boy with a cool Care Bears knapsack, creepy uncles would get drunk, and one lonely toddler in the middle of it all would shout, 'Oh fuck!'"

God, he really did love the sound of a laughing crowd.

"Then there's the actual recipe. Some recipes, I swear, people make them up just to piss others off. I saw one the other day for potato chip salad." He ranted for a while about that. "But the best part of looking for recipes on the internet is the reviews section. Many are just fucking useless. Some people make so many adjustments to the recipe, then give it a low review. 'One star. Worst potato salad ever.' Well, maybe that's because you added raisins and crushed all-dressed chips, you dingleberry! Did you put in a chopped-up Snickers bar, too?

"The other day, I came across a review for a spicy garlic tofu recipe. They substituted chicken for the tofu because they didn't like tofu and apparently didn't want to choose from the ten bajillion chicken recipes on the internet. Then they didn't add the chili peppers because they didn't like spicy food. And you know what they added instead of garlic?" He paused and raised an eyebrow. "Raisins. They're bad enough in cookies and potato salad, but in non-spicy garlic tofu without the tofu . . . As my imaginary toddler with her cool purple tutu and dinosaur headband would say, 'Oh, for fuck's sake.'"

That callback got a pretty good laugh.

Comedy was a lot about how you said it, not just what you said. Someone else could say the same words as him, and it would be completely different. Although Mel ranted a bit on stage, it was always jovial, always with a smile on his face, whereas other people would speak with slightly unhinged anger.

Still, he tried not to tell jokes that lots of other people could make, even if they'd do it differently from him. He wanted his sets to feel unique, like they came from *him*, nobody else.

He wondered which parts Vivian would have liked. He'd started writing the bit about being a parent before anything had happened with her . . . and then she'd told him that she didn't want kids. Which was totally cool. He hadn't given much thought to having them, except when writing jokes.

An hour later, Adrian Morales went onstage. "The other day, I decided to do something important. When you're a grown-up, there are lots of un-fun things that are apparently necessary. Paying bills, renewing your driver's license, going to work, putting on clean underwear, eating something other than ice cream and hot dogs . . . These are important. So they tell me.

"Anyway, I decided to do another very important thing: testing the limits of my lactose intolerance. For science."

. . . .

The next day, when Mel showed up at Chu's, he was in a bit of a bad mood—and not because he'd drunk four milkshakes in an hour, like Adrian supposedly had. Last night had been good, but today? Not so much.

Mel occasionally went to open mics, the ones he used to frequent when he was starting out, just to watch. Occasionally, he saw someone with lots of promise.

Not tonight. The comics had included two white men who just talked about how much they hated their wives, plus an Asian guy whose entire persona was pretending to be Black.

Which was . . . A Choice.

Luckily, nobody was onstage for too long at these.

And now, Mel was sitting at a table with Dani, Shannon, and Pablo. He helped himself to some marinated tofu—actual tofu, not chicken that had been substituted for tofu—and prepared to reveal his news.

"I started seeing someone a few weeks ago," he said, pretending to be all nonchalant. But in truth, he felt a little giddy as he remembered the mochi donuts she'd sent him the other day.

"Oh, yeah?" Dani said. "What's their name?"

"Vivian."

"The woman you kept complaining about and called an ice queen? That Vivian?"

"Yeah, that Vivian." Mel kind of enjoyed it when his friends gave him shit.

"This happened when you were at Ryan Kwok's wedding in Toronto, I assume? Why am I only hearing about it now?"

"Because I haven't seen you since then. You've been busy."

"We've exchanged lots of texts!"

"Maybe I wanted to see your expression when I told you. And no, a video call isn't the same."

"How did it happen?" Shannon inquired.

"Have you liked her for a long time, even while you were complaining about her?" Dani asked.

"There's a slight possibility you're correct," Mel said. "Then there was an accident with deep-fried crab claws, and we kissed under the table. You know, the way all good relationships start."

Dani gave him a friendly shove. "When can we meet her?"

"She lives in Toronto."

"Oh. Right."

"But I'll get her here sometime in the next few months."

He froze after saying those words. He wanted so badly to still be with her in a few months. However . . .

When Dani and Shannon headed out, Mel asked Pablo to stay for one more drink.

"Got a question for you," Mel said. "Why'd you break up with me?"

Pablo raised his eyebrows. "That was a long time ago."

"I know, but indulge me. I'm going all *High Fidelity*."

"Talking to all your exes to find out why your relationships failed?"

"Not *all* my exes. There's a bunch of them." Mel paused. "If you're not comfortable, you don't need to answer."

"Well . . ." Pablo drummed his fingers on the table. "You liked me, but you weren't invested in the relationship, and you had trouble . . . really opening up? I don't know. I've seen you behave

244 • Jackie Lau

similarly with other people. Like you're afraid the person you're dating will discover you're just three anxious penguins in a trench coat—"

Mel couldn't help laughing.

"—and so you hide behind jokes. Because you're afraid of feeling vulnerable, maybe some shit with your father . . . I'm not sure. You're more open with your friends, I think."

"Pretty sure Vivian already knows I'm three anxious penguins in a trench coat."

"Maybe she's different? You really want to make it work with her, it seems."

"Yeah, I do." Mel considered Pablo's words. "I don't feel the need to always joke around with her. I mean, I still do it a lot, because she's fun to annoy—"

"And that's how you show someone you like them. I know."

"—but not all the time. Maybe it helps that she didn't like me at the beginning. Well, she did, before she met me. But the first time we met, I was a jerk." He looked down. "How do I make sure it lasts?"

"There are never any guarantees," Pablo said.

"True. I freak out about that on a regular basis. And she's in Toronto . . . I've had a bunch of long-distance relationships over the years, but now I'm thinking they sound like something you do in college, not when you're old enough that your grandmother is desperate to marry you off and regularly arranges dates for you."

"I don't know, man."

"Helpful." Mel smiled and gave his friend a light punch.

That night, he couldn't sleep again, so after listening to an old Margaret Cho album, he scrolled through review sections on various recipes online. How could he do a better job of making fun of these? *I swear, one day, I'll read a review of an eggplant Parmesan recipe, and the reviewer will be like, "Instead of cooking the eggplant, I just shoved it up my ass. Three stars, could have used some lube. But that wasn't in the recipe."*

Was that funny? Terrible?

Or maybe I'll see this review on a nut-free baking website: "I added cashews, macadamia nuts, and Brazil nuts. Too nutty. Two out of four stars." Or I'll come across a reviewer who changed a quintuple chocolate cake into a vanilla cake . . .

Vanilla cake. That made him think of Vivian.

And Valentine's Day was very soon. He needed to send her something.

· · · · · · ·

I just got the cake. I love it. Thank you.

Mel smiled at the message from Vivian.

A minute later, she sent a few pictures, and he was pleased to see that the cake looked even better than he'd expected. It wasn't a crappy cake from the grocery store this time. No, he'd put in a custom request for a small vanilla cake at the bakery where they'd done the cake tasting. He'd explained that he wanted "a few shades of gray in a sophisticated, artful presentation" and attached some pictures he'd found on Pinterest. He hadn't really known what he was talking about, but the bakery had pulled it off. On the sides, the buttercream graded from dark gray to light gray, and there were buttercream flowers on the top.

MEL: How does it taste?

VIVIAN: Haven't tried it yet. Just going to
admire it for a while and take a few dozen
pictures. It's almost too pretty to eat.

MEL: I wish I could eat it with you.

VIVIAN: I bet you'll eat lots of good things
when you visit me in a few weeks.

VIVIAN: I didn't mean that in a dirty way.

VIVIAN: But, fine, take it that way if you like.

Mel imagined watching Vivian slide a forkful of vanilla cake into her mouth—he'd never had fantasies about vanilla cake before, but things were different now. He imagined her delicately chewing the cake, her tongue peeking out of her mouth to lick a stray crumb. He'd put a bit of buttercream on her collarbone, which he'd then have to lick off. Maybe she'd roll her eyes at his antics, but she'd release a breathy moan and press herself against him . . .

His dick hardened.

A few more weeks until he saw her again . . . and what would that be like? Would it be weird? Would it be just like last time?

Although things seemed to be going well, relationships were more than just buying fancy gray cakes for Valentine's Day.

Yeah, he really was three anxious penguins in a trench coat.

Chapter 27

Vivian was curled up on her couch, watching Mel's comedy special.

"You know how all East Asian people look the same?" he said on-screen. "Like how Bruce Lee looks like Yo-Yo Ma, who looks like George Takei?" He pointed at someone in the audience. "You know what I'm talking about. You're Asian, and you think all Asian people look the same, don't you? No? Oh, you're nodding at the fact that white people think we all look the same. Which doesn't make sense to me. Like, have you *seen* white people?"

She'd watched this many times before. She'd also seen him do some of this material live, like the night she'd first met him.

But now she was dating this guy.

She'd taken dozens of pictures of the cake he'd sent her. He'd also mailed her a hedgehog card and deep-fried crab claw stickers—yes, apparently those existed. She'd stuck two of the stickers on the front of her sketchbook. Though Vivian had never been the sappy lovesick girl before, she sure felt like one now.

After glancing at a picture of the cake on her phone—she should really stop doing that so often—she looked back at the TV. How many people were in the audience at that theater? It was hard to tell, but he was commanding their attention, just one man on an empty stage. Talking conversationally, though she knew countless hours of work had gone into this. Even if it seemed spontaneous, it wasn't.

There was something sexy about the way he drew everyone's focus, making people laugh as he casually strolled across the stage.

After a wide shot of the audience, there was a close-up of his face. She'd always thought he was cute. She imagined unbuttoning his shirt and throwing it on the ground, his crooked grin before he dipped his head between her legs . . .

Well. Maybe it was time to get out her vibrator.

· · · · · · · ·

Vivian wasn't used to this feeling of anticipation.

She'd buzzed Mel up a minute ago. He'd be here any moment.

She tugged at her collar. She'd left on the gray suit and cream shirt she'd worn to work today, because she thought she looked nice in this outfit.

Despite her excitement, she felt a bit of trepidation. Some part of her expected everything to be completely different now, as though the small amount of time they'd spent together last month was an aberration, even if they spoke to each other regularly.

He knocked on the door, and her heart hammered as she opened it.

It was weird . . . for about two seconds.

"Hey." He hurriedly shed his boots and winter clothes, then wrapped his arms around her, as though he were desperate for physical contact after their time apart. "I missed you."

"I missed you, too."

His lips were on hers, his hand in her hair as he hauled her close. It was such a relief to touch him again, but at the same time, it was the exact opposite; her body was ready for more, more, more. When he pressed her against the door, she was caught between the hard door at her back and something softer in front of her.

"Too much clothing," he complained, divesting her of her suit jacket and the shirt underneath. As soon as he tossed her bra aside, he swirled his tongue over her nipple. Then he undid the button on her pants and slid his hand inside her underwear.

She was equally impatient to get to him; she unzipped his jeans and circled her hand around his hardening length as he hissed out a breath.

Nothing pretty or romantic. Just desperation.

They kissed each other sloppily and stroked each other, until he pulled away to slip off her pants and kneel on the floor. He licked her through her underwear, making it even wetter, before pulling those down as well and running his tongue over her slit.

His tongue and his mouth were like magic. Whatever he did, it felt amazing, like it was exactly what she needed. She let out a harsh breath and tipped her head back as pleasure radiated through her, and then she slapped a hand over her mouth, muffling her cry of ecstasy.

He stood up, and normally, she'd say something about that cocky grin, but not now; he deserved to be cocky. He picked her up with some difficulty—perhaps owing to the fact that his pants had fallen to mid-thigh—and headed to her bedroom, where he set her down on the bed.

He crawled on top of her. "I want you to do something for me."

She couldn't help tensing. "Yes?"

"Show me your vibrator."

"I don't need it now. You're here."

"I am." He flashed her a grin. "But I thought it would be fun if I used it on you."

To her, vibrators were secret masturbatory instruments that

nobody else ever, ever saw. At least, nobody had ever seen hers. Thank God there hadn't been any embarrassing incidents.

But maybe . . .

"We don't have to—" he began.

"No, I want to." She reached into her night table drawer and pulled out her small egg-shaped vibrator. "I actually . . . umm. I used it the other day. When I was thinking about you."

"Did you? That's hot."

"Don't turn it up to the highest speed. I don't like that."

"And I wanna know exactly what you like."

But rather than using the vibrator, he took it from her hands and placed it next to him on the duvet. He kissed her neck, her cheek, her mouth as he slipped his hand between her legs again. He pushed one finger inside, then a second; she squirmed against his hand, tasting herself on his lips as he kissed her.

There was a problem, however. He was still partially dressed, his pants and shirt undone but not removed. She struggled to take off his clothing and throw it on the floor, but at last his warm skin was against hers.

And then he picked up the vibrator and pressed it to her clit. She was so sensitive that she could feel it all the way down to the soles of her feet, and a moment later, he swallowed her scream with a kiss.

The vibrator was too much for her now. Too. Much. Since her brain couldn't form sentences, she grabbed his wrist and moved it away from her body. He dropped the toy, but it was still buzzing in the sheets, so she reached out and turned it off, his kisses slowing her down.

"I am obsessed," he said solemnly, "with watching you come apart like that."

The weight of him pushed her into the mattress, and she ran her hands down his bare back and ass.

She hadn't had sex until she was twenty-three because even though she'd wanted to, there had been something terrifying about the idea. Taking off her clothes in someone else's presence—it felt like sharing more than her body. Letting her physical instincts, her sexual urges guide her. It was hard for her not to be in her head, and even now, there was a little of that, but much less so than usual.

She reached down and took his cock in her hand.

"God, I missed you." His words came out very differently than they had by the door.

She stroked up and down, her gaze on his face. Cataloging the expressions he made. His noises. What made him squeeze his eyes shut.

His responses made her crave him even more.

"I want to be in you," he said.

She grabbed a condom and rolled it on. As soon as she settled onto her back, he slid all the way inside her, and she felt like she was being split in two. A very welcome intrusion.

"You okay?" he asked softly.

"Yeah."

He started thrusting. Slowly. Shallowly. Gradually increasing his speed and depth. She bent her legs and spread them wider, taking him again and again and again.

How could she find such bliss with just his body and hers? Being with him like this . . . it was simply incredible.

She arched against him, and he came inside her with a growl.

Afterward, she rested her head on his shoulder as she absently ran her hand through the sprinkling of hair on his chest. She still wanted to touch him all over, but without the urgency of before. Eventually, however, she shifted to the edge of the bed.

"Guess I should cook you something for dinner," she said.

"You don't need to make anything fancy—"

"I have something planned, don't worry."

At first, he tried to help as she bustled about the kitchen, but she refused to let him. This was her place, and he was her guest. After ten minutes, he finally gave up, took a seat at the counter, and just kept her company.

Once they'd finished eating the stir-fry, she brought out the blueberry cheesecake she'd made the previous day—Lindsay had given her the recipe.

"This is really good," he said before his last bite. "Thank you. But if you ever just feel like . . . I don't know, picking up some fried chicken for dinner, that's okay with me, too. It doesn't need to be a big production when I come over. I'm easy."

"Easy, you say."

"Yeah." He pulled her up with him, wrapping his arms around her waist. "Easy."

"Wait!" she said when his mouth was about to touch hers. "We have to do dishes. I always clean up right afterward."

"Surely you can make an exception for me, just for an hour. I'll do them later."

He pulled her shirt over her head and carried her to bed once more, and because his mouth was magic, he somehow made her forget about the dishes for *two* hours. And then he insisted on doing all the cleaning, and she was so lethargic that she let him.

She hoped the rest of the weekend would be just as good, but today seemed like a hard act to follow.

Chapter 28

Mel stared at his phone. It was strange to receive a text from Ryan when they were in the same city, only a few miles apart. He'd be perfectly happy to tell Ryan that he was in Toronto and dating Vivian, except he didn't know what Vivian wanted, and she was asleep.

But when he looked down at her, her eyes fluttered open, as if she knew he'd been looking at her. She was gorgeously drowsy.

"Morning," he said.

"You been awake for long?"

He loved hearing her voice first thing in the morning, when it was sleepy and unpolished, unlike the voice she usually used to speak to the world.

"Only about fifteen minutes," he said. "Sleep well?"

"Pretty well, but I'm still a bit tired."

"I must have worn you out yesterday. I tend to have that effect on people."

She chuckled. "How about you? You sleep okay?"

"Yeah. No four-in-the-morning insomnia." He rolled on top of her and was about to kiss her, but she turned her mouth away.

"Morning breath," she said. "Let me use mouthwash first."

"You don't need to."

Her stern glare made him laugh. She walked to the bathroom naked, and he certainly wasn't complaining about the view.

He took his turn in the bathroom after her. If she used mouthwash, he ought to do her the courtesy of using it, too. Then he returned to bed and set to work making her feel very, very good.

He held her close afterward, and they stayed in contented silence for a few minutes before he said, "Ryan texted me. They're back from New Zealand."

"Yeah? I haven't talked to Lindsay yet."

"Does she know about us?"

"No," Vivian said. "I mean, we did sort of talk about it at the wedding, when I was thinking of hooking up with you, but that's all."

"Would you mind if I told Ryan?"

"No, it's okay. Go ahead."

"If you're not sure," he said, "I don't have to . . ."

"Mel! It's fine. I wouldn't have said that if I didn't mean it."

"That's true. You tend not to be full of shit when you speak. Unlike me."

> MEL: I'm actually in Toronto right now.
>
> RYAN: Why?
>
> MEL: To see Vivian.

Mel couldn't help grinning as he imagined his friend's expression. He pulled Vivian against him so she could see the screen of his phone.

A moment later, his phone indicated an incoming video call from Ryan.

> RYAN: Why didn't you answer
>
> MEL: Because I'm not decent

RYAN: You're never decent

RYAN: But seriously? I thought she hated
you. Lindsay mentioned something once,
but I was skeptical.

MEL: I won her over with my animal
magnetism, of course.

RYAN: You want to hang out while you're
in Toronto? We could all have brunch.
Lindsay isn't working until Tuesday, and
I'm free until I fly to LA on Wednesday.

RYAN: If you like brunch.

MEL: Are you really suggesting I might not
like pancakes?

He turned to Vivian. "What do you think? If you don't want to,
that's okay. Maybe you have other plans for me?" He waggled his
eyebrows.

"I have no idea what you're talking about."

He gave her a gentle shove.

"Brunch sounds good," she said.

· · · · · · · ·

"Oh my God!" Lindsay launched herself at Vivian. "You and Mel
are really dating?"

Vivian awkwardly patted her friend's back, unsure how to handle her friend's enthusiasm. Brunch had seemed like a good idea
earlier, but she really was tired—and not the kind of tired that
came from having lots of good sex in the past twenty-four hours.

She appreciated that Mel had asked whether she wanted to tell their friends about their relationship, and whether she wanted to have brunch. He hadn't made those decisions without her. She hadn't been quite sure how to tell Lindsay, so this made it easier, actually.

Except the thought of conversation just made her exhausted right now.

Fortunately, she never needed to worry about carrying a conversation when Mel was around. They sat beside each other, and he kept his hand on her thigh . . . until he moved it to steal Ryan's phone.

Ryan rolled his eyes. "Are you going to call my dad again?"

"Good idea," Mel said. "I'll call him after I set up a Twitter poll from your account: 'Which would you rather see Ryan wear? Option A: Unicorn onesie. Option B: Inflatable T-Rex costume. Option C: Sexy Santa.'"

"Would you buy me the winning outfit?"

"Of course." Mel turned to Lindsay. "Which would you prefer?"

"You're putting me on the spot," she said. "It's a tough choice."

"I know, I know. Very tough. That's why I need a poll." He looked at Vivian. "Which would you like *me* to wear?"

Vivian's brain felt like it was stuffed with straw, and this question seemed too difficult. "Um . . . you could pull all of them off?"

Mel laughed. "Well, obviously."

"Sexy Santa, I guess. If I have to choose."

"I'll remember that for Christmas."

Lindsay leaned across the table. "Vivian? You okay?" she asked quietly.

"Yeah. Of course."

But Vivian's coffee was strangely unappetizing, and when her pancakes with vanilla cream were put in front of her, she picked at them listlessly.

Mel put a hand on her shoulder. "You don't look so good."

"I'm fine," she said automatically, even though she really didn't feel fine.

She poured more maple syrup on her pancakes and tried to focus on getting food into her mouth. Focusing on the conversation around her was too difficult. She could only do one thing at a time . . . and why was the room spinning . . .

She bolted to the washroom, afraid she was going to throw up.

It turned out to be a false alarm, but she braced herself on the counter and closed her eyes. Sweat beaded on her forehead, but she couldn't bring herself to care.

An indeterminate amount of time later, Lindsay entered the women's washroom.

"I think I'm sick," Vivian said.

"Yeah, you look like you need to be in bed. I'll tell Mel to bring you home, okay?"

Vivian wanted to protest—she didn't want to ruin brunch—but it was too much effort, so she accepted Lindsay's assistance in returning to the table. Accepted Mel putting down some money for them, bustling her into a cab, and helping her into the elevator at her building.

As soon as she was home, she ran to the washroom and threw up in the toilet.

After splashing water on her face and rinsing her mouth, she went to the bedroom and put on her pajamas, yet despite their warm fleeciness, they weren't enough. Her teeth were chattering, but she was also sweating. She had a headache, and she was so, so tired . . .

"Here." Mel handed her a hoodie. His hoodie, not hers, and it was big and comforting.

She climbed into bed, and he lay on his side next to her.

"You should stay away from me," she said. "I don't want to get you sick."

"Don't worry about me. I almost never get sick. I'm healthy as an ox."

"I thought you were . . . Year of the Rabbit. Like me." She pulled the blankets up higher. "You don't need to look after me. I feel guilty for getting sick when you're visiting."

"You can't control these things. I'm glad I'm here to look after you."

She made a face. Or tried to. Her facial muscles didn't feel normal. "I can look after myself."

"I know, but—"

"You flew all the way to Toronto. Go out and see the city. Hang out with Ryan."

"I came here for *you*."

"That's too much pressure," she mumbled.

"Sorry. I didn't mean for it to feel like pressure."

He stroked her sweaty hair back from her face, and she stiffened. She hated that he was seeing her like this. She couldn't remember the last time she'd been this sick; before today, she hadn't thrown up in at least a decade.

When he left the room, she breathed a sigh of relief.

And then she fell asleep.

. . . .

It was a dreamless, uncomfortable sleep, and Vivian woke up a bunch of times. One time, she was too hot and took off the hoodie. Another time, she was too cold and put it back on.

At some point in the afternoon, she got up to use the bathroom. Mel wasn't around.

Good.

He was out enjoying the city. She should have recommended some places to go, though her brain seemed to have forgotten every neighborhood, restaurant, and bar in Toronto.

She stumbled back into bed, her legs like jelly, and was half-asleep when her phone buzzed. Seeing Andy's name made her feel even more exhausted. He only texted her when he needed something, and she was barely capable of staying awake right now. He'd have to wait until tomorrow.

She didn't read the message, just put her phone on silent and fell asleep again.

The next time she awoke, it was darker in the room. The sun had started to set. She still didn't feel great, but she shuffled into the kitchen and was momentarily disoriented.

Why was someone in her kitchen? Why did it smell so good in here?

Was that a chicken carcass on a plate?

"You're awake." Mel led her to a chair and put a glass of water in her hand. "You need to stay hydrated. Are you hungry?" He gestured to the fruit bowl.

She frowned. There had been only one apple this morning, but now there were clementines and kiwis and other things. She picked up a kiwi.

He whisked it out of her hand. "Let me slice it for you."

"I'm capable of doing it myself."

"Just sit there and drink your water. It's fine."

He removed the skin of the kiwi with a paring knife and cut it into five disks. She couldn't remember the last time she'd eaten a kiwi, but usually she just cut it in half and scooped out the flesh with a spoon.

He set the plate in front of her. "Do you want me to feed them to you?"

"I can do it myself."

"Are you sure?"

"Why are you so bossy?"

After finishing the kiwi and glass of water, she stood up to rinse off her plate and put it in the dishwasher. While she was up, she looked at what was happening on the stove. Chicken broth? There was a package of wontons on the counter as well as some bok choy.

Mel led her to the bathroom. "Let's check your temperature."

"I don't have a thermometer," she said.

"You do now."

"You didn't need to—"

"Open your mouth."

Sighing, she did as requested. She didn't have the energy to argue further.

He read the display. "A hundred and one point two."

The numbers swam in her head, not making sense, even though numbers usually made sense to her—she had a degree in financial math, after all. That was a really big number . . . Fahrenheit?

"Not too bad," he said. "If you're uncomfortable, you can take a painkiller to help bring it down, but you don't need—"

"Why do you know this stuff? You said you never get sick."

"Well, there's this thing called Google. It's pretty new. Maybe you haven't heard of it."

She was so tired that she couldn't even roll her eyes.

"You were out earlier," she said. "Where did you go? Did you have fun?"

He frowned. "I went to the pharmacy and grocery store."

When they returned to the kitchen, she saw a plastic bag on the table. "You went to the expensive one."

"Don't worry, I didn't buy all that much."

"Yes, you did." She gestured around as she took a seat.

"Do you have any other symptoms?"

"Um, my throat hurts a little."

He pulled out some ginger lozenges. "Here. Suck on one of these while I make wonton soup. Drink more water, too."

She could feel her blood pressure rising. "Stop bossing me around!"

"I'm not trying to boss you around." He knelt in front of her. "I'm trying to look after you. Can you let me do that? It's no hardship, I promise."

To Vivian's great mortification, she burst into tears. They burned her already hot cheeks. When Mel wrapped his arms around her, she pushed him away.

"I got your germs this morning and last night," he said. "No sense worrying about it now." But he stepped back and handed her a tissue box. When she shoved it away, he chuckled.

"Stop it," she said.

"My God, you're a terrible patient."

"I'm not a patient. You're not my doctor."

"You can't stand feeling useless, can you?"

"I'm not useless!"

"But you're used to feeling *useful* all the time. You don't know how to let someone take care of you for a day or two."

He wasn't wrong; she found the idea terrifying. She hated being like this around someone else. She wished he'd leave so she could sleep and drink water in peace.

"I bet you looked after your siblings when they were sick," he said gently, "but who looked after you when you were ill?"

"I stayed home from school alone and took care of myself."

"Starting when you were how old?"

"I don't know. Seven or eight? My parents couldn't just take time off because their daughter was sick."

He looked slightly horrified but kept his mouth shut. Smart of him.

She pulled her phone out of her pajama pocket. She didn't read Andy's message, but she had a text from Lindsay. Vivian assured her friend that she was okay and cursed herself for letting Mel tell

262 • Jackie Lau

Ryan and Lindsay about their relationship. It made everything feel complicated, and she was already so tired, and tears were streaming down her cheeks.

And so Vivian Liao did something she never, ever did.

She gave up.

She let Mel make her a small bowl of wonton soup. She didn't think she could keep down a lot, and he didn't force her to eat much. She also let him clean up the kitchen.

"You want to watch something?" he asked after dinner. "Or go back to bed?"

"Watch something." Though having to choose a TV show or movie was rather overwhelming.

"I've never seen *Only the Best*. Want to watch the first episode with me?"

"You've never seen it?" She managed only the mildest outrage.

"I've been meaning to, but I haven't gotten around to it yet."

"Well, that's a travesty. We should change that."

He sat on the couch, and she lay down with her head in his lap, his hands absently running through her greasy, messy, sweaty hair. He'd put a glass of water, two lozenges, and a tissue box on the coffee table.

Her eyes opened and closed throughout the show. It was hard to focus, so it was good he'd picked something she'd seen a bunch of times.

That was probably part of the reason he'd chosen it.

There were a few funny moments in the episode, and whenever Mel laughed, his stomach moved against her head, which made her smile a tiny bit.

Yeah, she was starting to relax.

Maybe letting someone look after her a little—just a little—wasn't so bad after all.

• • • • • • •

When Vivian woke up on Sunday morning and still didn't feel well, she was pissed.

Goddammit. Why did her sickness have to coincide with Mel's visit?

There was ibuprofen and water on her bedside table, and that caused a warm—but not feverish—sensation in her chest. Unfortunately, the warmth soon faded and she was pissed off again.

She sat up in bed and swallowed a painkiller and half the glass of water. It was already eleven o'clock, and Mel wasn't in bed.

Wait. How did she get to bed?

Last she remembered, she'd fallen asleep on the couch during *Only the Best*. He must have carried her. Or she'd walked and her memory was malfunctioning, just like the rest of her brain and body.

"Hey. You're up." Mel appeared in the doorway. "How are you feeling?"

"Not great. My head really hurts, though I think my fever has come down."

"That's good. You want anything to eat?"

"Toast." She stood up to head to the kitchen, then realized he wanted to get it for her.

She went to the washroom, and when she entered the kitchen, there was a piece of toast on a plate. Jam, butter, and peanut butter were on the counter next to it.

Mel held out her phone. "The screen flashed a bunch of times. I think you have messages. Don't worry, I didn't read them."

Amanda had been blowing up Vivian's phone this morning, apparently.

Andy said he can't get in touch with you.

Are you okay??

You never sleep past 10.

I'm worried about you, please answer me.

Oh jeez. Vivian started typing as she spoke to Mel. "It's my sister. She was concerned when I didn't reply. I've explained that I'm ill."

"Does this mean your entire family is about to descend on you with soup and jook?"

"I . . ." Was he joking? She couldn't tell. "Is that what your family would do?"

"My sisters would tell my mother, who would definitely come over within the hour, and my grandmother would try to come as well . . . This is all conjecture, though, because I never get sick aside from the very rare cold."

Right. Lucky him.

"But I've seen what happens when my sisters are sick," he said, "and if I was sick, it would be particularly concerning. They might all come over."

That sounded annoying, but perhaps a little nice, too?

"Maybe Amanda will tell my mother," Vivian said, "and she'll give me a call. A short lecture on what to eat, but that's it. Like I told you, when I was sick as a kid, I was on my own."

"Well, I'm here." He grinned then executed a deep bow. "At your service."

After she ate her toast and showered, they spent several hours curled up on the couch, finishing the first season of *Only the Best*. A day of watching TV, not doing chores, and avoiding Andy's text. It wasn't something she was used to.

Mel was flying out on Tuesday morning, and she hoped she'd

feel better tomorrow—Monday—so she could go to the office, and then they'd go out in the evening.

But Monday morning, she still wasn't feeling well enough to go to work, though she was certainly improving. So once again, they spent a lazy day at home.

And once again, she felt guilty. He'd come all this way, only for her to be no fun at all.

Vivian was under no illusions: she wasn't a terribly fun person even at the best of times, let alone when she was sick. She'd planned a bunch of things for the weekend, things she thought he'd enjoy, and those plans had been for nothing.

She hated not following her plans.

Early in the afternoon, Mel went to get some takeout, and Vivian started her laundry. When he returned and served her food, he placed an envelope under her fork.

She raised an eyebrow and opened the envelope. It was a "Get Well Soon" card with a puppy wagging its tail and holding a bunch of flowers in its mouth. She'd never received a "Get Well Soon" card before, and she felt a bit weepy again, but she managed to hold back her tears.

But that night, she cried into the pillow as Mel snored lightly beside her. He hadn't complained one bit about taking care of her, but she still felt like a burden.

And Vivian hated being a burden.

He was right about her need to feel useful. How could their relationship survive when she wasn't providing him with anything and it was so inconvenient to see each other? Although this relationship wasn't a mess like her previous one, she still regretted starting something with Mel when it seemed clear it couldn't last.

In the near darkness of the bedroom, she reached out and touched the card he'd given her. She appreciated it, but she was still uncomfortable with someone doing things for her.

Mel rolled over and wrapped his arms around her. "I can hear you."

"I'm not crying."

He laughed softly. "You deserve to have someone look after you, you know." He kept his arms around her.

Several minutes later, he seemed to be asleep again, but she was still awake.

Maybe she did deserve this on occasion, yet that didn't change the fact that their relationship couldn't last. She was already a weepy mess, and she hated it. She should pull back so that when the inevitable ending came, it wouldn't hurt quite as much.

After all, this was someone she'd deeply admired before she'd met him. Someone who'd made her feel seen, who'd made her realize who she was, even if they were different in many ways.

The ending was already going to be very, very difficult.

Chapter 29

MEL: I got the part!

VIVIAN: Congrats!!

MEL: Look at you, using two exclamation marks. Did you think I wouldn't notice?

MEL: It's just a small part. Only a few days of filming in Vancouver. Have you ever been to Vancouver?

VIVIAN: No, actually.

He nearly asked if she'd like to meet him there and have a little vacation, but he held himself back. It wasn't like planning to move in together, but suggesting they go on vacation together would be a big deal for him. Bigger than the offhand comment he'd made about the sexy Santa costume.

I'll remember that for Christmas. As if they'd still be together at the end of the year.

"Sexy Santa" hadn't won the Twitter poll he'd posted for Ryan. No, the unicorn onesie had been most popular, and someone had suggested that Ryan unzip it down to his hips and make it a sexy unicorn. That was probably why the inflatable T-Rex costume hadn't won: partial nudity wouldn't be quite so convenient in such a costume.

But if Mel had run the poll about himself, the results would have been different. T-Rex likely would have done better in that poll.

Mel wasn't universally known for being sexy. There weren't long threads of people thirsting over him on Twitter, for example, and if he tried to make his image "sexier," there would probably be some laughs.

And that wasn't the way he wanted to make people laugh.

It was okay. It really was. He might not be as well-known as Ryan, but he was reasonably successful at what he did. He'd accomplished more than his twenty-two-year-old depressed self had dared to dream.

Plus, some people did find him sexy. Vivian, for example. Last Friday, before she'd gotten sick, she'd been all over him.

She was fine now. She'd woken up on Tuesday morning feeling like her usual self, and she'd put on a navy suit and headed to work while he headed to the airport. Unlike many people, he'd never found suits particularly sexy before, but on her, it was a different matter. He liked the polished, buttoned-up look she showed the world.

She, however, seemed troubled that he'd seen her sick, and she kept apologizing profusely for last weekend. He suspected she didn't apologize like this often.

But maybe something else was up, too. He couldn't quite figure it out.

She also hadn't booked her flight to New York yet. The plan was for her to come at the end of March. They'd talked about it on Thursday, and she'd said she'd do it, but she hadn't.

And it was now Saturday.

Hmm. Vivian seemed like the sort of person who'd get shit done, rather than goof off on social media for half the day and eat instant noodles at eleven at night.

You know, unlike him.

But perhaps he hadn't thought this through. She might not have booked the ticket yet for financial reasons. Her mortgage was likely expensive.

> MEL: I'll send you the money to pay for the flight.

> VIVIAN: You don't need to do that.

> MEL: It's not a problem. I'd come to visit you, but I have a show on the Saturday.

> VIVIAN: I can't let you pay for the flight. I have the money. I'll do it.

> MEL: I just really want to see you again.

He scrubbed a hand over his face. He felt like he was doing something wrong and this relationship was already going south. Even though he didn't really hide with Vivian and she understood who he was. Even though he'd treated her well last weekend—and that hadn't been a chore. He just hated to see her sick.

It had taken her a while to let him do anything for her. The woman really wasn't used to letting someone look after her, which made him angry. The idea that someone would make soup when she was sick seemed beyond her comprehension.

He started a video call, and when Vivian's face appeared on-screen, he couldn't help smiling. Every sharp line, from the point of her nose to the angle of her asymmetrical haircut, was perfectly beautiful.

"Hey, sexy," he drawled.

She raised a finely shaped eyebrow. "Are you serious with that?"

He wagged his eyebrows in return. "You know I'm always serious."

She snort-laughed, her stern look fading. He liked the stern look when she was wearing a pressed pantsuit, but he also liked making her serious expression collapse into something lighter. Freer. It made him feel as if he could control the weather.

"Just don't call me that in public," she said.

"Okay, sugar bear."

She rolled her eyes with an affectionate look that said, *You're impossible.*

"You can be the one who calls me sugar bear instead," he suggested.

"Very funny."

He hesitated. "Do you not want to visit me later this month? Is something wrong, and that's why you haven't booked it yet?"

Three anxious penguins in a trench coat? Yeah, he definitely felt like that right now. Papering over his anxiety with jokes, even though he knew she could see through some of it. And that didn't alarm him. Not much.

He was more alarmed at what might be wrong.

"I'm fine," she said. "It's only been two days since we decided."

He wasn't reassured. "Vivian . . ."

"I'll book it tomorrow morning. I promise."

"All right. Do you want to meet my friends while you're here?"

"Will they like me?" There was more uncertainty and vulnerability in her voice than usual, which squeezed at his heart. He really was crazy about this woman.

"Of course," he said. "I'm not just saying that. They'll like you."

"Okay." She nodded. "I'll meet your friends."

They talked a little longer, and then Mel turned out the lights and climbed into bed.

Before he drifted off to sleep, he didn't think at all about the part he'd gotten—Mr. Shum, aka the cool English teacher who was also the lead singer in a country band of dubious talent. He just thought about Vivian coming to visit him, though he didn't want to focus on that too much until she'd booked the flight.

• • • • • • • •

The next morning, Vivian sent Mel her flight information, and he grinned.

Not long after, he headed to Queens to have lunch with Mom, Po Po, and Joy.

"Ah, Mel!" Po Po said when he arrived at the house. "Where is your girlfriend?"

"She's in Toronto, remember?"

"When do we get to meet her? Is she coming to visit you soon?"

"I haven't even gotten a chance to take off my shoes yet." He made a big show of slowly unlacing his shoes, as though moving through molasses.

Joy snickered.

Two minutes later, he finally entered the living room. He sat on the couch next to his sister. His grandmother was in the armchair. Mom stood in the doorway, holding a spatula.

"So," he said, crossing his arms behind his head, "you see the Rangers game last night?"

"You're being silly," Po Po said.

"What else is new?" he asked cheerfully.

"You still didn't answer the question. When is your girlfriend coming to visit?"

"In a few weeks."

"That's very nice. You can invite her here."

"I don't know. We haven't been together that long."

272 • Jackie Lau

"But I have a good feeling about this one," Po Po said. "She will last."

That made him feel warm and fuzzy inside, but he shouldn't give too much credence to his grandmother's "good feelings." After all, she'd had a good feeling about speed dating in the pink limo.

And the lottery ticket she'd bought for Chinese New Year.

And . . .

"Call her on your fancy phone with the video, yes?" Po Po said. "I'll talk to her and plead my case. She won't be able to say no to my face."

"I'll ask her later," he said, but he pulled out his phone just to check that he didn't have any messages.

"Joy." Po Po turned to her youngest grandchild.

Joy sprang into action. She jumped on Mel and grabbed his phone.

"Vivian, Vivian, Vivian," she said as she looked through his contacts.

"Give that to me." But his annoyance would only fuel Joy.

"Here we go. It's ringing."

A moment later, Vivian answered.

"Hi, Vivian!" Joy said, in a voice that was unnaturally cheerful for her. "I'm Mel's little sister. Our grandmother wants to ask you a question, okay?" She walked over to the armchair and held the phone in front of Po Po's face.

"Ah. You're very pretty," Po Po said. "You're coming to New York soon, I hear? You will visit me? Mel is very eager for you to meet us all."

"She's lying!" Mel shouted. "I'm afraid of subjecting you to them."

"You see, it is my dying wish."

Even Joy didn't go along with that one. "Cut it out, Po Po. You're not dying."

"How do you know? Am very old."

"I think you watch too many dramas." Joy turned the phone toward herself. "Vivian, please come to visit us. We'll tell you all sorts of embarrassing stories about Mel."

"You know I tell half of those stories myself," he said. "Onstage. She's heard them."

"Okay," Vivian said. "I'll come to visit you all."

"You can change your mind later!" Mel called out. "I know you're under extraordinary pressure right now."

From the doorway, his mother chuckled.

"Joy, turn it back to me, please," Po Po said, and Joy did as instructed. "Vivian, we'll sing Shania Twain songs together. I look forward to this."

That was enough. Mel grabbed his phone back. "You don't need to sing any songs, I promise you. We'll talk later, okay?" He ended the call.

To be honest, he did like the idea of Vivian meeting his family and becoming entangled in all parts of his life, even if that was rather frightening at the same time. But he didn't want her to do anything she didn't want to do.

He looked around the room with a glare. "Please don't scare her."

"I'm scary?" Po Po asked. "Am barely a hundred pounds. She could take me."

"Do not make her do karaoke. She doesn't like singing."

"Why not? Is so much fun!"

"I mean it. She won't appreciate it."

"Fine, fine. Will do what you say." Po Po let out an exaggerated sigh. "You're very serious about this one."

"Yes," Mel said, "I am."

Chapter 30

Vivian was nervous. Meeting new people was far from her favorite thing in the world, and this weekend in New York would involve lots of new people. But she was curious about Mel's friends—Dani, Shannon, and Pablo—and she did feel better with him by her side.

They were sitting in a Chinatown bar called Chu's, which Mel said he visited all the time. Indeed, the bartender seemed to know him well.

She had a small piece of five-spice jerky and sipped her drink, which had ginger, vodka, lime, and some other things. Her hands were shaking slightly.

He kissed her temple. "It'll be okay. You can bond over pissing me off."

Maybe she was particularly nervous because when she'd met her ex's friends, it hadn't gone well. When she'd failed to laugh at a misogynistic joke, they'd thought she was a stuck-up bitch with no sense of humor.

So far, her visit to New York had been good. She'd taken a day off so she could fly out on Thursday after work. By the time she took the train in from Newark and met Mel at Penn Station, she'd been pretty tired, but as soon as she saw him her spirits lifted, and she threw herself into his arms, somewhat alarmed at her enthusiasm. Then they'd gone back to his place and hadn't been able to keep their hands off each other.

Today, they'd walked around different parts of the city he liked and eaten lots of food before coming to Chu's.

Mel lifted his hand to wave at someone as the door opened. A moment later, two people came to sit at the opposite side of the table. The one across from Vivian was a butch East Asian woman with spiky hair. Her hand was clasped with that of a blond white woman.

Vivian started to relax.

"I'm Dani," said the Asian woman. "Vivian, right? I've heard a lot about you." She laughed, probably at the alarm on Vivian's face. "You called him an ass the first time you met. That's pretty cool."

"He *was* acting like an asshole."

"It's true," Mel said affably, "and she doesn't like to take shit from anyone."

"Nice blazer," Dani said.

"Oh. Thank you," Vivian replied.

"It's very much an I-don't-take-shit-from-anyone blazer."

The blond woman held out her hand. "I'm Shannon. Dani's girlfriend."

Vivian felt a rush of longing to have queer friends back home.

"How did you meet Mel?" she asked.

"We went to college together," Dani said.

"Yup," Mel said. "She was a much better student than I was."

"He spent too much time goofing off. Playing beer pong the night before a big exam and shit like that. I tried to be a good influence, but . . ."

"He's immune to good influences." Vivian cracked a smile. She was getting used to this teasing business.

Mel shot her a mock glare. "I bet you were a serious student who actually took notes."

"But of course."

A South Asian man walked up to their table. "Um, hey. Are you Melvin Lee?"

"Yeah, that's me." Mel talked to the guy for a few minutes with a grin on his face, made him laugh a couple of times.

Over the stranger's shoulder, Vivian noticed another guy watching the scene. When the first man walked away, the other sat down at the end of their table.

"I'm Pablo. You must be Vivian."

"Nice to meet you," she said.

"I hear you're dating this ass?" He spoke good-naturedly, giving Mel a friendly shove.

"So it seems."

Pablo laughed before turning to Mel. "Haven't seen you in a while. How was your visit to Toronto last month?"

"Pretty good."

Vivian gave Mel a look. "It was not. I was sick most of the time."

"That sucks," Dani said. "Did he do a good job of playing nurse?"

"He did."

His friends didn't seem surprised. They might give him shit, but they knew he was a kind, thoughtful person.

· · · · · · ·

When Vivian and Mel ambled back to his place at midnight, she was in a good mood.

"I liked your friends," she said.

"That's good. They liked you, too." He paused. "By the way, Pablo is my ex. Just thought you should know in case it comes up at some point. There's nothing between us now, I promise."

It surprised her that the two of them had dated. There had

been no awkwardness. Then again, Mel wasn't really awkward with anyone.

"It was quite a while ago now, and it didn't last long," he said.

She nodded. She wasn't bothered by it at all, and she trusted Mel. She stumbled as she realized just how much she trusted him.

"You okay?" he asked.

"Yeah. I shouldn't have worn heels."

"We can get a cab."

"No, it's fine. It's not much farther, right?"

She'd wanted to feel fabulous tonight, hence the heels and the nice blazer. It was like armor for her, but it turned out that she hadn't needed armor.

"I wish I had friends like yours in Toronto," she said wistfully. "How do people make friends when they're out of school?"

"Hobbies? Maybe there are some nice people in your spin class."

"They aren't really my type."

"There might be some events you could go to."

"And stand quietly in the corner?"

He flashed her a grin. "Bring me. I'll get people talking."

She chuckled. Yeah, he was good at that, but he didn't seem to find it weird that she had trouble with it, and his presence had helped her feel more comfortable tonight.

In his apartment, she embraced him, and he immediately dropped her blazer on the floor.

"Hey!" she said.

But then he kissed her, and her outrage evaporated.

• • • • • • •

Meeting Mel's family made Vivian more nervous than meeting his friends, despite Mel's reassurances. Though the unexpected phone conversations with his grandmother had gone okay, she also found the fact that his grandma was so eager to meet her a little disconcerting.

Mel opened the door without knocking, and two little girls rushed toward them, circled their arms around Mel's legs, and started jumping up and down. They looked a bit like Amanda had at that age.

"Fudge, fudge, fudge!" the girls chanted.

"Fudge?" Mel said. "Did someone tell you that I was bringing fudge?"

The girls giggled.

"They don't know it's food," he explained to Vivian. "Auntie Joy has been trying not to say the F-word around them, so she says 'fudge' instead, and the girls have picked it up."

"Fudge sake!" said one girl.

"Fudge sake!" said the other.

Mel crouched down. "These are Ruby and Willow. Girls, this is Vivian."

They nodded solemnly, then started running around again.

Mel led Vivian into the living room and introduced her to the rest of his family. His sister Chelsea—the mother of the little girls—and her husband, Curt. His sister Joy, whom Vivian had spoken to briefly on the phone. His mother and his grandmother.

"Mel told us that we can't make you do karaoke," Joy said. "I think this means you definitely need to do it."

Vivian stiffened. Joy was probably joking, but Vivian couldn't tell. It was hard to know with someone she'd just met.

"No, no," Mel said, "she's not doing karaoke, end of discussion."

"Oh fudge!" shouted Ruby.

The twins were identical, but Vivian had memorized their outfits so she could keep them straight for today. Of course, that wouldn't help if she saw them again in the future.

"Please help yourself to some fruit." Mel's mom pointed at the tray on the coffee table. "Don't worry, you don't need to sing. We'll just interrogate you later."

"I'll sing for you," his grandmother said to Vivian. "Since you're a big Shania Twain fan . . ."

Vivian didn't bother correcting her.

"Which of her songs would you like?"

Oh dear.

Vivian thought back to the last time she'd heard a Shania Twain song. "'That Don't Impress Me Much'?"

"Mel, you set it up for me, okay?"

A minute later, his grandmother was singing. She wasn't as theatrical as Mel, though that wasn't saying a lot. She was still pretty animated, and she had a better voice than Vivian did, that was for sure.

"Ma!" Mel's mom said. "Don't move around so much. I don't want you to fall."

"Aiyah! You're interrupting me. Now we need to start the song over again, and I'll make even bigger dance moves."

Sure enough, the song was restarted.

Afterward, Vivian clapped, and his grandmother took a bow.

"So, Vivian," Mel's grandma said when she sat down. "Have you seen any moose? Or reindeer?"

Vivian was momentarily thrown by the shift in conversation. The questions must have something to do with her being Canadian. "Only at the zoo."

"What about beavers?"

"There were beavers in the park near where I grew up. They caused lots of damage."

Mel's grandmother nodded sagely, as though giving the matter careful thought. "Mel, please take me to Toronto to see beavers. Do they have nice karaoke bars in Toronto? We can visit those, too."

"Wow. He looks so enthusiastic." Joy pointed at Mel.

"Maybe you'll have your wedding in Canada," Mel's mom said with a little smirk. "We can all go then."

"Mom!" Mel protested.

"Ah, yes. Good idea!" his grandmother said. Then her face fell. "But I made detailed plans for your wedding in New York. Now they will go to waste."

"What kind of plans?" he asked. "How scared should I be? Do they involve being kidnapped in a limo?"

"I'm insulted you think I would do that again. I don't reuse my ideas."

Even if Mel's family talked about him getting married, it was different from Vivian's family. In her family, there was an underlying tension that didn't exist here, although maybe Vivian was the only one who felt that tension. Maybe nobody else in her family did, and an outsider would be unable to pick up on it.

All of a sudden, she felt an ache in her stomach, an ache that only increased as Joy teased Mel and he threatened to sing "Barbie Girl."

"Where's the washroom?" Vivian asked.

"Here, let me show you." Mel stood up and took her hand. When they reached the bathroom door, he pulled her inside. "You okay?"

Shit, she hadn't thought she was that transparent. Hopefully it was only Mel who noticed.

"I'm not close with my family, like you are with yours," she said. "It makes me . . . sad."

"You sure my family isn't scaring you off?"

"No, no." She paused. "My siblings would be too frightened to tease me the way Joy teases you. Well, 'frightened' isn't the right way of putting it, but . . ."

"Teasing doesn't have to be a part of every relationship. It's just the way I am, and you can see where I got it from."

"I know." She sighed. "But my family . . . I can't help feeling tense around them."

"I'm sorry," Mel said. "Take a few more minutes here if you need it, and when you come back, I'll sing 'Barbie Girl' for you, Joy be damned."

"Will I enjoy this performance?" Vivian asked.

"You like my moves, don't you?" He winked, gave her shoulder a lingering squeeze, and headed back to the living room.

Vivian looked at herself in the mirror for a long time. She was used to feeling composed. In control. Used to understanding her relationships to other people based on what she did for them and how useful she was. She was glad it was different with Mel, but she felt like she didn't understand the world anymore.

· · · · · · · ·

"Good morning, Vivian!"

She opened her eyes. There was a stuffed hedgehog, adorned with a gray ribbon, staring her in the face.

"We're so glad you're awake!" the hedgehog said in a slightly high-pitched voice.

"Fuck off," she muttered.

"We have an exciting day planned for you, and then you're going back to Canada to frolic with the moose and beavers. It makes VeeVee very sad." VeeVee was incapable of making facial expressions, but Mel pouted behind her. Even if he'd interrupted her sleep, it was nice to see him first thing in the morning.

"You told me to wake you up at eight thirty," he said in his normal voice. "It's eight thirty-five. Be thankful I kept VeeVee out of the bedroom for an extra five minutes."

VeeVee jumped up and down on his thigh. "We made coffee for you."

Mel headed to the kitchen, then returned with a tray containing two empty mugs and a French press. He poured the coffee and had a sip from his mug.

"Coffee isn't good for hedgehogs," he said, apparently feeling the need to explain why VeeVee wasn't partaking in the coffee. "It gives them the runs."

Vivian snorted.

"You want any food?" he asked. "I'm still full from tacos last night, but—"

"No, I'm good for now."

He picked up VeeVee and made her say, "Are you sure?"

"Okay, enough puppeteering for the day," Vivian said.

He put down the hedgehog. "VeeVee and I will have long conversations when you're gone."

"I'm sure you will."

He shot her a yeah-I-know-I'm-impossible grin, which was a very charming look for him, then planted a quick kiss on her cheek, his lips slightly warm from the coffee.

"I have a gift for you." Mel handed her a small box wrapped in colorful paper.

Vivian swallowed, suddenly anxious. It looked like jewelry, and she had a terrible track record with receiving jewelry from men.

"You didn't have to," she said.

Slowly, she unwrapped the paper. She didn't hurriedly rip it, which was what she suspected he'd do, and he chuckled at the care she took.

She opened the box, revealing a small geometric silver pendant on a chain.

"I . . . umm." He scratched the back of his head. "I thought it was your style, but if you don't like it, I can exchange it and get something else or—"

"No, no. It's perfect," she rushed to reassure him.

Because it really was.

It was the first time anyone had gotten her jewelry that she actually wanted to wear. She knew she was difficult to shop for. A lot of jewelry wasn't to her taste at all, but this was nice and understated.

"Okay," Mel said. "That's good."

It seemed like he didn't quite believe her, and she didn't mind soothing his insecurities, those insecurities he often hid behind bravado.

"I'm not bullshitting," she said. "I've had no qualms about telling you to fuck off in the past."

"That's true."

"Jared bought me a heart pendant with crystals."

He made a face. "I can't imagine you wearing heart-shaped jewelry."

"Exactly. But I felt obligated to wear it."

Mel took the necklace out of the jewelry case. "May I?"

She nodded. His fingers brushed her skin as he clasped it at the back of her neck, and she felt herself blushing.

"It goes nicely with your gray pajamas," he said.

She chugged the rest of her coffee, and then she kissed him.

After they had sex, she tried to help him clean the kitchen, but he wouldn't let her. He insisted on emptying and filling the dishwasher himself. Just like he had in Toronto when she'd been sick.

As Vivian took the train out to Newark that afternoon, she thought back to last night. She'd watched him do a show for the first time since last summer. There was a bit about how it was fun to pretend he didn't know English when dealing with someone annoying—and how his grandma, at one point, had fourteen and a half people who thought she didn't speak English. (Mel had speculated that she'd sawed someone in half in a magic trick gone wrong.)

Having now met his grandmother, it was particularly entertaining to hear him talk about her onstage.

Afterward, they'd had late-night tacos before getting on the subway, and she'd rested her head on his shoulder, enjoying the simple pleasure of knowing him in a way his audience didn't.

But their relationship still seemed like a holiday, not regular life. Was it really sustainable? Could she really keep just visiting him in New York every couple of months? It didn't feel like a relationship for someone in their mid-thirties, someone who was already settled with a full-time job and owned property.

Yet he'd already introduced her to his friends and family—and given her jewelry—so he seemed to be serious about her, even if she didn't provide him with much. It was perplexing.

Vivian touched the pendant just below her collarbone and sighed. She was supposed to be pulling back to protect herself, but she couldn't quite manage it, not with Melvin Lee. She just kept getting herself in deeper and deeper. Falling for him a little more each day.

Chapter 31

It wasn't like Vivian wished her family did karaoke like Mel's. After all, she absolutely hated singing, especially in front of people. But she couldn't help wishing her family was just . . . well, a little more like his, as she silently ate dinner in her childhood home. There were five of them tonight: Vivian, Ma, Ba, Andy, and Amanda. Stephen was at school in Hamilton.

"We really think it would be good for Amanda to live with you," Ba said.

"Don't you want to help your little sister?" Ma asked. "Housing is so expensive downtown near the university. Why should she spend so much time looking at apartments and finding roommates when you have a place right there?"

"Why can't she live in the same place again?" Vivian asked.

Ma clucked her tongue. "Landlord is terrible, didn't you know? And this way, you can look out for her."

Vivian shook her head. When she'd been Amanda's age, her parents never would have helped her find a place to live.

"Why not?" Ma asked. "You want your sister to live in a moldy basement?"

"Don't be dramatic. I'm sure she'll find something."

"It'll be so much fun!" Amanda said. "We'll have a schedule and alternate cooking dinner, and we'll go out on Friday nights." She turned to her mother. "Don't worry, we won't drink much and will be home by midnight."

Vivian sighed. She felt like the walls were closing in on her.

But she was an adult. She didn't need to listen when her family tried to tell her what to do. She wasn't dependent on them for anything.

"No," she said. "End of discussion. It's not happening."

"I don't understand why you have a problem with this," Ma said.

Vivian put down her chopsticks. "That's all I am to you. The responsible eldest daughter. That's all I ever was to you."

"Vivian—" Ba began.

But now that she'd started, she couldn't stop. "I always knew my job was to not cause any trouble. To grow up when I was still a child. To babysit after school, every single day, starting when I was eleven. To put the kids to bed. To teach them how to brush their teeth. How to use the toilet. How to read. I had to cook and clean more than is reasonable. I was the one running the household while you were both working all the time."

"You don't understand—"

"I wasn't allowed to complain about anything, even though all I wanted was to see friends and go to visual arts club once a week. Not much. You didn't care who *I* was, what *I* wanted, not even a little."

"Vivian," Ma said harshly, and even though she was an adult, Vivian still couldn't interrupt when her mother spoke to her like that. It felt wrong. "You think you're so special? I'm the oldest, too. I did everything you did."

"It wasn't a childhood."

"Maybe not. But this is the way it is."

"You didn't want things to be different for me?" Vivian asked. "Why should I suffer just because you did?"

"You don't know what it was like for *us*. We came here when you were a baby, and we had to make sure we succeeded. Lots of people to send money to back home. And . . ." Ma trailed off and shook her head.

Vivian had gaps in her knowledge of her parents' past and their extended families. There were some things they just never talked about, which wasn't unusual; Mel had mentioned something similar about his grandmother. Vivian felt for her parents, even if there was a lot she didn't know, but that didn't fix her childhood. The unfairness of it.

"We also wanted to make sure our children had a good start," Ma said. "We paid all your university tuition, so it was easier for you to save to buy your own condo."

"I didn't force you to do that. I would have preferred a smaller education fund if I got to have you around more. And maybe you shouldn't have had so many kids."

"You wish your brothers and sister were never born?" Ma demanded.

Amanda gasped.

"I wouldn't put it like that," Vivian said, "but I was a third parent. The most important parent, much of the time. I had to share a room with a baby and look after her in the night. How was that fair to me? And it was all *me*. Because I'm the girl. Andy's less than two years younger, but what did he have to do? Just mow the grass."

"Hey!" Andy said. "You have no idea what things were like for me."

He was wrong. She'd known exactly how different his life had been from hers; she'd been acutely aware of it.

"He didn't have to be responsible for anything," she said, "and I had to be responsible for *everything*."

"You were so good at it," Ba said.

"Because I didn't have a choice. But I'm thirty-four now. I don't depend on your money, and I don't need to look after Amanda."

"You wouldn't have to look after me!" Amanda protested.

"I just . . . I can't. Not anymore." The idea felt like a heavy, heavy weight. "I don't want to be a parent. I never wanted to be a parent."

"Are you saying you won't have children of your own?" Ma asked.

"Yes! How many times have I told you? Why won't you believe me? I know exactly what it's like to be a parent, and I know it's not what I want. To me, Amanda isn't my sister."

Amanda's lower lip trembled, like it did before she cried. Vivian had needed to console a crying Amanda countless times over the years.

"It wouldn't be like living with a sister," Vivian continued, swallowing. "It would be like being a parent again. It would remind me of the childhood I lost. If it had simply been an hour of babysitting a day and doing my own laundry, that would have been fine. But it was so, so much more . . ."

She wasn't used to speaking this much around her family; she was used to keeping it inside. But the idea of living with Amanda . . . something in her rebelled so strongly, and she couldn't help it.

She'd watched her younger siblings enjoy freedoms she'd never had. It had been particularly tough to see Amanda, the other daughter, get to do after-school activities and socialize with friends as a teenager.

Now Vivian did what she wanted with her time. She got to be herself . . . except when she visited family.

She clenched the table with both hands. "I can't be who you want me to be. The one who will swallow her own feelings and desires for everyone else." She nearly added, *I'm sorry*, but stopped herself.

She looked around the table. Ba was frowning, Ma and Andy looked angry, and Amanda looked hurt. Nobody said anything.

Vivian didn't see the point in staying, and she didn't have any appetite.

So she left. Nobody stopped her.

She took the bus to the subway station, then the subway back to her condo. She hesitated at the entrance to her building, not feeling like going home, so instead she walked to Kensington Market and entered a brewery that she'd been to with Lindsay a bunch of times. She ordered a Centaur Baltic Porter from the bartender, whose name she was pretty sure was Adam. He merely nodded as he set the beer in front of her, and nobody else talked to her, thank God. She wasn't in the mood.

As she sipped her beer, she tried not to think too much about how she'd finally talked back to her family . . . but then Amanda's hurt look flashed into her mind, and she felt horrible.

Amanda didn't deserve this. She wasn't to blame for Vivian's lack of childhood; she'd been an innocent little child herself, who'd taken her first steps under Vivian's supervision.

Amanda isn't my sister.

Her family had kept pushing the idea of them living together, and Vivian had snapped.

Perhaps she was an awful person. It wasn't like Vivian had any prospective roommates. Amanda would be done with grad school in a little over a year, so it wouldn't be for long, and it would be very convenient for her. Why couldn't she have done this one favor for Amanda?

But that didn't change Vivian's mind.

She had a healthy swallow of her porter, then took out her phone and started typing a message to Mel, but she didn't send it. He would listen to her, of course, yet there was a tiny fear in the back of her head that he would think less of her, even though he likely wouldn't. She felt safe with him, and he was the one who'd made her feel that she could be loved for some reason other than being useful. Which she was still having trouble believing, but the seed had been planted.

Was that the reason she'd lashed out tonight? Was Mel changing her?

He hadn't *said* he loved her, but they were on the way to those words, even if their relationship still didn't feel sustainable to her.

She downed more beer and continued to feel miserable. Her brain was a mess of thoughts clashing together, and she wasn't used to this. But even though her thoughts were jumbled, the image of her sister's expression was clear in her mind. It haunted her.

What kind of big sister was she?

"You want another?" asked a quiet voice.

Vivian looked down. She'd already finished her beer.

"Yes, please," she told Adam, and he brought her a pint.

This would be Vivian's last beer. Then she'd go home and . . . she didn't know what. Drawing would make her feel even guiltier, and wasn't that just what she needed?

Her phone buzzed, and she braced herself before taking a look.

But it wasn't anyone in her family. It was Mel, sending her a picture of VeeVee the hedgehog "drinking" a glass of wine.

VeeVee misses you, he said.

Suddenly, Vivian felt so undeserving of having someone who'd send her pictures of stuffed hedgehogs and buy her fried-chicken pillows and make her laugh. She nearly rested her head on the bar and started crying.

But, no.

Vivian Liao did not cry in public. Instead, she merely sipped her beer.

And then someone knocked into her and mumbled, "Sorry."

That voice . . . she knew that voice. Her spine straightened, her chin tilted up. Any tears that had been pooling in her eyes—those immediately fled.

"Jared," she said coolly. "Haven't seen you in a while."

"Vivian." He leaned heavily against the bar. Drunk. "Miss me?"

No, she hadn't. Not at all.

"Realize you made a mistake in throwing me away?"

She raised a single eyebrow.

"You were always a bit of a frigid bitch," he said.

On the inside, Vivian stiffened, but on the outside, she doubted anyone could see the difference.

Jared made a sound of protest, and she realized that Adam had come around the bar and was in the process of throwing her ex out.

"Don't harass the customers," Adam said.

She nodded at Adam once he'd returned to his position behind the bar. "Thank you."

He grunted in response and started drying some glasses.

Frigid bitch.

The words kept running through her head. Jared was an asshole who hadn't been worth her time, but then she'd thought of how Mel had initially seen her. He'd called her an ice queen—and he wasn't wrong.

Tears stung her eyes, and she couldn't help feeling worthless. Like a bad daughter and sister and girlfriend.

Oh God. She didn't appreciate all these stupid *feelings.*

It was better to keep the world at a distance. That life suited her. Her armor had started to crack lately, and now she was having a breakdown in a damn bar. She needed to pull herself together.

After she finished her second beer, she left a generous tip for Adam and walked home. Once she'd changed into her pajamas, she picked up her sketchbook and sat down in the middle of her bed, and for some reason, she started drawing a self-portrait, even though that wasn't something she'd done in a long time. She could see her face in the mirror above her dresser. Her severe, angular features.

An icy sort of beauty that wasn't ever supposed to melt, or it would make a big, big mess.

Chapter 32

> I don't know why anyone in the LGBTQ community supports @MelvinLeeHaha. How can he be part of it if he's dating a woman?

> Do you know what being bi means, you idiot? He's not magically straight because he's dating a woman right now.

> You've got seven numbers in your Twitter handle. You're clearly a troll.

Mel scrubbed a hand over his face and leaned back on the arm of his couch. He'd been trying to ignore some comments on YouTube, ones that were almost comically over the top, so he'd come to Twitter and found out he'd been tagged in . . . yeah.

He wouldn't respond. But how did they know he was dating someone? He hadn't talked about it, though he hadn't tried to hide it, either. Somebody must have seen them together in public.

This kind of comment was nothing new, though; he'd heard it all before. He shouldn't let it get to him, but he'd never managed to develop as thick of a skin as he wanted. And he also felt a bit tender after his dismal performance at the club the other night,

294 • Jackie Lau

when he'd been trying out new jokes. He'd gotten a few laughs, but not nearly enough.

This was just part of the business. No matter how much experience he had, he still needed to practice in front of an audience, figure out what worked, and edit his material. But sometimes, it made him feel like he was terrible at his job. An unfunny fraud.

Just then, there was a knock at the door. He got up and opened it. His sister Chelsea, who'd said she would stop by this afternoon when she was in the neighborhood.

"Hey," he said, trying to inject some pep into his voice. "Come in. What would you like? Coffee, tea, wine, sangria?"

"You made sangria?"

"Nah, but I could. I mean, aside from the lack of fruit in my apartment."

"Coffee?" she said with a smile, but then she sobered. "You okay? You look tired."

"Nah, I'm good, I'm good."

"What are you wearing?"

"Oh, this old thing?" Mel looked down. "Since I'm doing laundry right now, I put on one of the T-shirts I made for Ryan's bachelor party."

"So those are his abs, not yours."

"Exactly."

She didn't say much as he made their coffee, but he sensed she was working up to something. Like she'd stopped by not simply because she was nearby. There was a reason for this visit, which felt more serious than usual.

They sat down at his small table, and she had a sip of coffee.

"Dad wants to see you," she said.

And there it was.

Mel didn't miss his father a lot. Just at Christmas, and occasionally when he passed fathers with their children at the park. Not so much when he saw white fathers, but ones who looked like his.

"He's sorry," Chelsea said, "and he wants to tell you that in person."

Sorry. A single word felt painfully inadequate for the past eighteen years.

"Right." Mel swallowed.

"You don't owe him anything."

"Of course not. He's the one who abandoned *me*, when I was just a teenager."

"Don't worry, I told him that. You don't need to listen to him apologize, and you're not obligated to forgive him, but if you think it would help . . ."

He shook his head. It would just dredge up lots of stuff. Besides, it had taken *eighteen years* for Dad to get to this point, and Mel had trouble believing the man truly wanted to make amends. When he was younger, he would have jumped at this, but not now.

Eighteen goddamn years.

How would his life have been different if his father hadn't rejected him?

"That's okay," Chelsea said. "I get it." She couldn't completely understand, but Mel appreciated that she wasn't trying to force a happy family reconciliation. She squeezed his hand, and he gave her a slight smile and a nod.

When there was another knock at the door, he nearly jumped, but his sister didn't seem surprised. She opened the door and his nieces barreled toward him, Curt a few steps behind.

Chelsea must have planned this to cheer Mel up after her news about Dad.

"Fudge, fudge!" Willow shouted.

"She's noticed that people always laugh when she says it," Chelsea explained, "so she won't give it up."

Well, Mel knew what that was like.

Ruby lifted her pant leg to reveal a princess bandage on her shin. "Fall down," she said solemnly. "Ouchie."

"It was two weeks ago," Chelsea said. "It's completely healed now, but she likes the bandages. She cries if she doesn't have one."

"Makes perfect sense to me," Mel said. "I'd cry, too, if I didn't have a princess bandage."

If he just so happened to have princess bandages in his bathroom—which he did not—he'd put one on right now.

The girls distracted him, but an hour later they left, and he was all alone with his thoughts. And frankly, being alone with his brain was a terrible place to be.

His brain was fucking *messy*.

At times, he still yearned for his dad's approval, even though he shouldn't care about the man. He didn't *want* to see his father again, but some small part of him couldn't help it.

Maybe that was just the masochist in him. Ugh.

He went for a walk that evening. It was April now, and he didn't need a jacket. When a man gave him a weird look, he remembered he was still wearing the ridiculous bachelor party shirt. Oh well. Looking silly was nothing new to him.

The walk through the city calmed him a little, but just a little.

When he returned home, he took a picture of himself in the mirror and posted it on Twitter with the words, I've always had a good sense of fashion. People seemed to enjoy his photo, but that didn't make him feel better. He just lay back on his couch and rubbed his temples, and he messaged Vivian, but she didn't answer. Well, she probably had something better to do than lie around on the couch and take pictures of herself wearing other people's abs. She'd respond eventually.

Though with every minute that passed, he spiraled further.

What if someday she decided he was a ridiculous fool and wanted nothing more to do with him? What if he was already failing at being her boyfriend and she hadn't told him yet?

Maybe because they were approaching the three-month mark, he'd been worrying more about this lately.

Stop it, he told himself.

He made a note to call his therapist tomorrow to schedule an appointment. Then he reminded himself that it was okay to feel out of sorts after hearing about his father, and his father's rejection all those years ago didn't mean Vivian would reject him. Everyone was a bit flawed, and it wasn't like he was a zillion times more flawed than everyone else, even if he felt that way at times. He was still dedicated to making it work with her, and when he saw her next, he'd ask if she wanted to take a longer trip together at the end of the summer. It would be all right.

But at four in the morning, a voice crept into his head again, telling him that it wouldn't.

· · · · · · · ·

Mel looked across the table at Vivian and grinned.

She'd met him at the entrance to the airport, and he'd whirled her around and given her a kiss, delighted to see her again. Then they'd headed out for dinner at a Thai restaurant. They were sharing pad thai and panang chicken curry with rice, and they'd had mango salad to start.

After that one bad night, he'd been doing better for the past week, but in her presence, he finally felt like he could breathe again. It was unfortunate that he wouldn't be able to see her for at least six weeks after this—he'd be on the road for much of that time.

Today she was wearing a beige suit that might look boring on many people, but she made it sexy. Around her neck, she had a colorful (for Vivian) silk scarf, the necklace he'd given her peeking out from underneath it. She had studs in her ears, and he wanted to nibble on her earlobe and hear her half-hearted protests.

"Do you not like the food?" she asked, gesturing at his plate. She was nearly finished, and he'd only had a few bites.

"It's delicious." He leaned forward. "But I can think of something even more delicious."

She responded with the sexiest eye roll he'd ever seen. "You're impossible."

"I know," he said cheerfully.

God, he liked seeing her so sophisticated in public, knowing he'd get her completely disheveled and crying his name later. There was something particularly thrilling about that.

After dinner, they went to her condo, and as soon as they'd removed their shoes, he cupped her cheeks and kissed her properly. Sure, he'd kissed her at the airport, but that had been a quick kiss. Now he could do it the way he wanted. He could touch every inch of her body and do the things he'd been dreaming of in their time apart.

He shoved off her trench coat as he kissed her, pulling back just long enough to unwind the scarf from her neck. She worked on his buttons, tossing his shirt on the floor a moment later and putting her hands all over him, and even though they'd done this many times before, he felt slightly in awe that she wanted him like this. He pushed her against the door, and she rolled her hips against him; they both groaned.

God, he was so hard. Desperate to sink inside her slick heat, to be as close to her as possible. Nothing else would do. He craved *her*.

Fortunately, he'd planned for this. He dug a condom out of his pocket and held it up. When she nodded, he pulled out his cock and rolled the condom on, then bent her over the table near the entryway. As soon as he shoved down her pants and underwear, he slid into her. She cried out as she gripped the edge of the table with her long fingers, bending her knees a little to get the angle right; his own fingers pressed into her hips.

Oh fuck. Mel loved her responsiveness to him. He wanted this over and over again. Couldn't get enough of it.

He leaned down and kissed the side of her neck, and when she jerked, she knocked over the bowl where she kept her keys and a few other things. She stilled for a second as the keys skittered across the floor, like she was contemplating setting everything to rights, but then she pushed back against him even harder and allowed chaos into her life.

He pounded into her, his need for her so acute after the month they'd had apart. He'd fantasized about this every day, and now he was here, and she was squeezing his dick . . .

He came so hard that he forgot what words were.

But he definitely wasn't done pleasuring her.

When he lifted her up so she was sitting on the small table, she protested. "I'm not sure it'll hold my . . ."

One good, long lick between her legs put an end to that sentence.

He concentrated on her scent, her taste, every breathy moan and small movement of her body, and it wasn't long before she stiffened and cried out.

And then one leg of the table gave out, and she pitched forward on top of him.

He got his arms around her so her head didn't hit the floor. She was flushed and laughing, though she did give him a look, accompanied by, "I told you I was too heavy for that."

"Actually, I think you were too distracted to finish expressing that idea."

Naturally, she replied with another stern look, which he rather adored. In fact, he adored it so much that he had to take her to the bedroom and give her another orgasm.

Vivian insisted on cleaning up the front hall after that. Bringing all their clothes to the bedroom, putting away everything that had fallen on the floor. He slid her arms through the sleeves of his shirt, which she'd probably say was hideously colorful, and buttoned up only two buttons. Yep, he liked the look of her in his shirt, so different from what she usually wore. He'd fantasized about seeing her in his clothes back when they'd barely known each other, and now here they were. He wrapped his arms around her and pulled her into bed.

"My dad wants to see me." Mel hadn't thought the words before he spoke them; they just popped out of his mouth. Which wasn't unusual for him, but he rarely talked about this type of thing without thinking first. "He wants to apologize, that's what Chelsea says, but I still don't want to see him. Is that terrible of me?"

"No. Did your sister try to tell you otherwise?"

"She didn't, but still. I keep thinking about it." He ran a hand absently over her side.

"I'm sure that's natural."

"Honey," he said, "there's nothing natural about what goes on in my brain."

"He's your father, and he was around for most of your childhood. Even if you don't want him to have any kind of hold on you, it's not surprising that he does."

"I guess."

"And I like your brain." She patted his head.

Usually, he'd feel the need to make some kind of joke here, and he opened his mouth to do so but then closed it. She'd like him even if he wasn't constantly trying to make her laugh.

And he really liked making her laugh—it was one of his favorite things in the world—but it was nice, on occasion, not to feel like he had to joke around.

There was something vulnerable about being serious. Jokes were the way he'd gotten people to like him back in school. Without them, he was certain he would have been an outcast.

Vivian ran her hand through his hair and smiled at him, a little hesitantly, but he sensed that hesitancy wasn't related to what she thought about him.

He wanted to take away whatever was causing it.

"I missed you," he said.

"The fact that you fucked me right inside the door gave it away."

Now she was the one brushing things off with little jokes.

"Vivian, I mean it. It's not just—"

"I know," she said quietly. "I know."

He touched the pendant of her necklace.

"I wear it all the time," she told him. "Everyone says I'm hard to shop for, but you got something that was just my style." She spoke a little wonderingly, as though, even a month later, this was still a surprise.

He was pleased she liked it, but he wanted to make such things—someone giving her a thoughtful present or looking after her when she was sick—less extraordinary in her eyes.

In fact, he really, *really* wanted it.

Vivian opened her mouth as though she wanted to say something more, but then she closed it and just snuggled up closer to him.

It was perfect.

He had a few things to talk to her about, but those could wait until morning. He was used to his relationships not lasting, but he was starting to think those questions would go well.

Wouldn't they?

Chapter 33

Vivian was sitting at her desk, wearing just an oversized T-shirt and looking at stuff on her laptop, when she heard movement behind her. She turned.

"Morning." Mel sat up and ran a hand through his hair. The sheet slipped partway down his bare chest, drawing her attention. "Whatcha doing?"

"Looking at tables to replace the one we broke yesterday."

"Ah." He shot her a lopsided grin. "I'll pay for it, since it was my brilliant idea."

"Hmm." She put a finger to her lips. "I'll allow that."

"Come back to bed."

She didn't hesitate, slipping under the covers and running her foot along his calf. Then she snuggled up against his big chest, which she loved. It was so soft and comfy. Maybe she'd fall asleep again . . .

"I have a question," he said.

"Mmm. Let's hear it."

"What do you think about going on vacation together this summer? I'm kind of busy, but I have a week in August, if that works for you. Wherever you want to go. We could meet in Vancouver after I'm done filming, if you like, or somewhere else. I'd enjoy spending more than a weekend with you."

Vivian stiffened.

She enjoyed travel, as he knew. She enjoyed exploring cities—by herself.

When Mel had shown her around New York, that had gone well, but this felt different. She'd traveled a couple of times with Jared, and it had always gone poorly. Their biggest arguments had been on vacation.

So there was that. But also, August was a long way off. A few months felt like forever in a newish relationship. He seemed confident they'd be together then, but she certainly wasn't.

She thought of her fight with her family. She hadn't talked to them since, and she hadn't told Mel about it.

Amanda isn't my sister.

He would never say a thing like that.

Her family might not say they loved her, but she was sure they did . . . when she was useful. That was her role in her family. Her role with the people who cared about her. She got shit done.

She didn't know how to manage a relationship without that. Much as she'd cursed Jared for not doing his share of the chores, there was comfort in knowing she provided something tangible for him.

She didn't want that anymore, though.

And yet . . .

"What's up?" Mel asked. "Do you have plans for your vacation time already this year? If so, that's okay, I just thought—"

"You think we'll still be together in August?"

"Yeah. I'm sure of what I want."

He was smiling at her, but she could see some anxiety peeking through. Straining his expression. She wanted to wipe it off his face, but she couldn't.

"We live in different cities," she said. "Maybe we should talk about that. How can this work, long-term? I'm not uprooting my life for you."

"I never asked you to. Why would you think I'd do that?"

"You didn't approve of my life choices when we met—"

"Why are you saying this now?" He jerked away from her. "I know I was wrong. I was an asshole. But it's been almost two years—can't you believe I've changed?"

"Yes, I do." She sighed. He had changed, and she also understood how their first conversation had triggered bad memories. Still . . . "We have to fly, or drive more than eight hours, to see each other. Maybe we should just accept . . ." Her voice wobbled. "This can't last."

"We can figure something out."

"We're not university students. We have our own established lives and—"

"Vivian, I love you." He said it harshly.

The words didn't shock her. Because she'd *felt* them. Felt like he loved her. But hearing him say it out loud made her realize just how misplaced his feelings were.

"You don't believe me?" he asked when she remained silent. "Should I do all the door games to prove it to you? Eat chili peppers, sing sappy love songs—"

"I believe you, and I believe you'd do all those things for me. That's not the problem. We can't just will ourselves out of an impossible situation."

"It's not impossible. I don't see it that way."

How could he not see that they were on a doomed path and she didn't suit him at all?

But in time, she was sure he'd understand. This could only have ever been temporary. She didn't have more than that to offer him because she just wasn't that person anymore. She hadn't even wanted a relationship; he was the one who'd convinced her to give it a try.

If only she'd left it as a one-night stand. Instead, she'd let him through her armor. Slowly, but it was enough, and now the broken table was a sign of the mess she was in.

She hated messes.

It might start with a vacation, but he'd gradually want more and more from her. It wasn't like she'd been doing everything for Jared right from the beginning, after all; it had happened over time.

Mel would want her to give something up for him.

She'd already given up so much for her family. Years of her childhood that she could never get back, and they weren't even sorry for it.

Now she had to preserve her independence so she could keep living the life she wanted. She wouldn't let other people draw her into their complicated webs. She would only live for herself, as she'd vowed to do. Go after the things that *she* wanted.

But you want him.

Yeah, she'd enjoyed their time together, but anything more would be too much.

"I won't sacrifice myself again," she said. "I refuse to do it."

"What are you talking about?" Mel asked. "I'm not asking you to sacrifice anything."

"But you will. I don't see how it's possible otherwise, when you want a long-term relationship."

"I'm not like your family. I'm not like your ex. Why can't you see that by now?"

"Why do you think you're so special?" she shot back.

Vivian jumped up. She couldn't have this argument when she was in bed with him, and she couldn't have it when she wasn't fully dressed. She turned away from him while she took off her T-shirt and put on her bra, even though it was nothing he hadn't seen many, many times before. On top of her bra, she slid on a short-sleeved black turtleneck. Next, gray pants.

The room was strangely silent, aside from the sounds of her getting dressed. She turned around and looked at Mel, surprised he hadn't said anything.

"You're right," he said at last. "I'm not special."

His words broke something in her. Mel often came across as fairly confident, but it was an act. She knew those words would have hurt him. Shouldn't you at least be special to someone you'd been dating for three months?

She shoved those feelings down. They were getting in the way, and she had to extricate herself from this situation. Had to start building back the walls she'd foolishly allowed to crumble. Though part of her longed—

"No, dammit." He stalked toward her, wearing only his boxers. "You don't understand."

"Well, that's rich—"

"You think relationships only work one way. By you giving and giving and getting nothing in return. I understand why you believe that, and I'm sorry it happened that way." His face softened. "But it doesn't have to be like that with us. We'll figure out a way to make this work for both of us."

"For both of us?" She laughed ruefully.

"You still can't believe in me? At all?"

"You're the successful entertainer. I'm . . . nobody."

"Vivian—"

"I know what you're going to say." She held up a hand. "I'm not nobody. Fine. But no one knows who I am, and many people know who you are. I like my life, but I've had to fight for what I have, and I won't give it up. I won't live for someone else."

"For the last time." He'd never sounded angry like this before. She shut her eyes; she couldn't bear to look at him. "I don't expect you to live for someone else. To be something you're not."

"That's exactly what you expected the first time we met!"

"Why are you going back to that? I'm sorry. I mean it. I was wrong."

She started shaking.

She hated when her body disobeyed her. She usually had good control over it, but not lately. Tears had come to her eyes the other day. Now she was trembling, and he was wrapping his arms around her, and it felt so good . . .

Vivian allowed him to hold her for a moment. Relaxed into the bulk and softness of him. But when he brushed his lips over her cheek, she pushed him back.

She had a weakness for him, and she didn't like having a weakness. Didn't like anything that could prevent her from living life on her own terms.

"It doesn't matter," she said quietly. "It's over. I'm sorry. I just . . . I can't."

He normally had an expressive face, but now it was carefully blank.

"Okay," he said at last. "Okay."

Some ridiculous part of her wanted him to continue to argue, but it was a good thing that he didn't. The sigh she breathed out—it was one of relief, wasn't it?

He was quiet as he got dressed and packed his bag. There wasn't much to pack, since his visit was only supposed to be two nights anyway.

Unlike how he'd come into her life, he left without a word.

Vivian made herself some coffee and pretended nothing had ever disrupted her peaceful little life.

• • • • • • •

Mel wasn't sure how long he'd been standing on the corner with his suitcase. Maybe a minute. Maybe twenty. His brain didn't know how to process time right now.

Vivian had broken up with him. That was enough to try to process.

Once again, his relationships never seemed to last.

He'd desperately wanted this one to last, more so than usual. That was why he'd told her that he wanted to go on vacation together. That was why he'd tried to talk about the future.

She'd shut him down and refused to listen to his protests.

He was convinced there must be something he could have said, something that would have persuaded her and allayed her fears. But maybe not.

And now here he was.

He wanted to get the hell out of Toronto, but his flight was tomorrow evening. He could go to Billy Bishop Airport and try to get something earlier, but he wasn't sure he had the energy and patience for that. Frankly, he wasn't sure his brain was working well enough to figure it all out, and the idea of spending extra time in an airport wasn't something he relished.

Instead, he walked to Ryan's, and he only got lost twice on the way.

Ryan was home, thankfully, and buzzed him up. But as soon as Ryan opened the door to his condo, Mel realized his error.

Ryan didn't live alone anymore. No, he lived with Lindsay, Vivian's friend and former roommate. In fact, that was how Mel had met Vivian in the first place and why they'd needed to spend so much time together: Ryan and Lindsay's wedding.

Ha.

"What's up?" Ryan's voice was light, but he sounded concerned.

Right. Because Mel usually would have slapped his friend on the back and tried to steal his phone. "Where's Lindsay?"

"At work."

That was a relief. Mel didn't think he could deal with a happy couple right now, especially not the two of them.

"Vivian broke up with me. So, you know, I need somewhere to crash." He spoke as though it was no big deal and flashed Ryan a grin.

Ryan gestured him inside. "I'm sorry."

"Before you ask," Mel said, starting to feel a tiny bit like himself and actually able to string words together again, "I didn't do anything stupid. It's not like when you told Lindsay that you wanted to take a break. I asked Vivian to go on vacation with me this August, she flipped out, told me she wouldn't sacrifice her life for me, something like that. I objected, but she wouldn't listen. Anyway, it's over now. You got coffee? I haven't had any yet today. Or do you just have that disgusting green shit you drink for breakfast?" He made a face.

"I can make you coffee." Ryan stared at him for a moment. "You're not okay. I can tell."

"Yeah, yeah, I'm really not okay." Mel waved this away. "But let me pretend for a while, all right?"

Chapter 34

Vivian looked at the fried-chicken pillow in her left hand, then the pair of kitchen scissors in her right hand. She'd been holding them for ten minutes but still had yet to destroy the pillow.

Destruction was one of the ways she coped with breakups. It helped release her anger.

After Jared had moved out, she'd cut up his *Star Wars* apron. Though Jared had baked for her on occasion, he'd always been resistant to wearing an apron because they weren't manly enough—some silly excuse like that. Of course, he'd been quite a messy baker, and she'd been the one who did all the laundry.

Anyway, he'd finally agreed to wear the *Star Wars* apron, but he'd either forgotten it or purposely left it behind. She hadn't tried to give it back; she'd simply cut it up, along with the stupid lingerie he'd given her, the stuff that hadn't suited her at all. She'd also poured out the beer he'd left in the fridge. (She didn't consider it a waste of good beer—Jared had terrible taste in beer.)

Childish, but she'd taken a small amount of pleasure in destroying those things.

But for some reason, she couldn't stab the scissors in the pillow. Her hand refused to obey her brain, and the idea of doing it didn't give her any pleasure.

She'd instigated every single one of her breakups. All four of them. The previous three times, she'd had some righteous anger. A *lot* of anger with Jared in particular.

She didn't have any this time.

No, she just felt sad.

Instead of stabbing the fried-chicken pillow, she sighed and put it in the linen closet, next to the *Only the Best* pillow and Mellie the hedgehog—she hadn't been able to throw out or cut up those things, either.

When had she gotten so freaking sentimental? It was pathetic.

Her phone beeped. Another text message from Lindsay. Want to grab a drink when I finish work today? Or I could bring over some cupcakes?

Lindsay had been trying to meet up for the past two weeks, ever since Vivian had dumped Mel. Apparently, he'd shown up at Ryan and Lindsay's after leaving Vivian's.

She'd text Lindsay back soon, but she'd give some excuse for not being able to go out tonight, just as she'd done the past few times. She'd also been dodging calls from her father and texts from Amanda.

Yep, Vivian sure was social these days.

Every time she got a message and it wasn't from Mel, she couldn't help feeling disappointed. Not that she expected him to contact her. No, she was glad he wasn't messaging her. She was *glad.*

She was just accustomed to hearing from him on a regular basis, that was all.

But it had only been a three-month relationship. She'd dated Jared for much longer, and she didn't remember feeling this sad two weeks later. She'd just been angry at him, and angry at herself for staying in the relationship for so long and living with him.

She missed Mel. Missed the random stuff he used to send her and their conversations in the middle of the night. She wondered if the breakup had made his insomnia worse.

No.

She shouldn't worry about him so much. He'd manage.

But the way he'd just walked out without a word . . .

She needed a distraction. Something unrelated to *Only the Best* because she kept remembering the time she'd watched it with Mel. She'd also lost any interest in drawing the characters in it. She'd tried, but she couldn't muster any enthusiasm.

And *JANYS* was out of the question.

Yesterday, she'd watched a tragic movie about two women who'd fallen in love in Victorian England; today, she needed to do something that wouldn't make her quite so weepy. So, after vacuuming and mopping, she sat down in bed and started sketching a vase of flowers, but the end result was far from happy. The flowers had lost most of their petals, which were scattered on the surface of the table.

Next, she found herself drawing a capybara in a cluttered apartment.

Dammit.

The picture might not have any people in it, but it was a scene from *JANYS*. Annoyed with herself, she tore out the two pages and threw them in the trash.

Vivian was deciding what to do next when there was a knock at her front door. Swearing, she got up and flung open the door to reveal her former roommate. She should have known she couldn't avoid Lindsay forever.

"Hi!" Lindsay put a Kensington Bake Shop box on the table beside the door. "Huh. This is new."

"Uh, yeah," Vivian said. "The other table broke."

"How did it break?"

Vivian shot her a glare, but Lindsay didn't seem perturbed. She removed her shoes and carried the box to the kitchen, where she got out two plates.

Vivian peeked inside the box. Red velvet cupcakes, lemon meringue cupcakes, and Nanaimo bars.

"Don't tell me you have no appetite," Lindsay said.

Vivian was indeed a little hungry, seeing as she hadn't had much desire to cook lately. She picked up a lemon meringue cupcake.

Lindsay let Vivian eat half of it in silence before saying, "What happened with Mel?"

"Do you really need to sound so perky?" Vivian muttered.

"Well?"

"He must have told you something. Or told Ryan something, which was relayed to you."

"I want to hear it in your words."

"Tell me what you know first."

"Fine," Lindsay said. "I heard he wanted you to go on holidays together, and you freaked out and said you didn't want to make any sacrifices for him. Not much more than that."

"Was he angry at me?"

"No, he didn't sound angry. Just heartbroken and trying to cover it up."

Vivian hated the strange sensation in her chest. She held up a finger and finished her cupcake before relating the events of two weeks ago. Not the sex that had broken the table, nor what Mel had told her about his father, but what had happened the following morning.

Lindsay didn't eat any of the baked goods. She simply listened.

". . . and that was that," Vivian said. "Satisfied?"

"No," Lindsay said slowly. "Not at all. I think you have a

skewed view of relationships, and you could make it work with Mel if you wanted to."

"How? He lives there, I live here, and I'm not moving."

"See, that's what I'm talking about. You're assuming you have to live in the same city, in the same apartment, all the time. It doesn't have to be that way. Not everyone wants that. And you don't want kids—which he knows, right?"

Vivian nodded.

"That gives you more flexibility. There are people in long-term relationships who never live together. I like living with Ryan, but he's gone part of the time, and that's okay. Kensington Bake Shop is important to me, so I haven't given it up to follow him around. You can do the same. It sounds like Mel's perfectly open to that."

This conversation was a little weird, probably because Vivian wasn't used to having friends who were comfortable enough to tell her when she was being foolish.

"It's . . . hard for me to believe that," she said.

Lindsay patted her hand. "I know."

"It's hard for me to imagine he won't want me to keep giving until there's nothing left, and if I don't provide him with anything—"

"You're providing him with yourself. Your company."

Vivian stared at the refrigerator. "I still have trouble believing anyone could want me just for that."

"So you assume it can't last if you don't give up everything and, quite reasonably, you refuse to give up everything?"

"Yes. That's why I had no interest in a relationship. When I was young and naïve—"

"I can't imagine you truly being naïve."

Vivian shrugged. "I thought it could be different, but I kept being proven otherwise. You hear about women getting divorced and feeling free—that's how I felt. Some men are helpless without someone to do all the chores and run their lives for them."

"But he's not, is he?"

"No, but—"

"Stop it," Lindsay said. Vivian wasn't accustomed to hearing her speak so severely. "Stop with all the excuses. You're worried about something because of past experience, but he keeps showing you he's not like that."

"Why are you pushing so hard? Why do you want me to be with him so badly?"

"Because I'm your friend, and I don't want you to sabotage a good thing. When Ryan and I saw you for brunch—"

"The weekend I was sick."

"Yeah, that was unfortunate, but I could still tell you were happy together and cared for each other. At first, when I noticed there was something between you two, I wasn't quite sure what it meant, but after that brunch . . ."

When Vivian thought of long-term romantic relationships, she thought of unhealthy relationships between a man and a woman. That was what her brain jumped to. Always. She imagined passionate honeymoon periods followed by unhappy marriages. Wives "nagging" husbands who never pulled their own weight and thought looking after their own kids was "babysitting."

Her brain was seriously lacking in creativity, even though there were other options. In fact, she sought them out in the media she consumed, but she hadn't been able to imagine those possibilities happening to *her*, despite the fact that she wasn't straight and didn't want kids.

But maybe it could be different? With Mel?

"I'll think about it," Vivian said. "Really, I will."

Lindsay appeared satisfied with that answer for now. "You

want to go out for dinner so you don't have to cook? Sundubu jji-gae? Or lots of tasty shrimp rolls?"

Vivian had been wrong before; Mel wasn't the only person who teased her. Lindsay did on occasion, too—she knew Vivian hated shrimp.

Vivian swallowed. "Sundubu jjigae sounds good."

· · · · · · ·

A few days later, Vivian received a text from an unfamiliar number.

Hey, it's Dani Yoon. Mel's friend.

Did he tell you we broke up? Vivian asked.

Yes, I'm aware of that.

Vivian waited for Dani to accuse Vivian of breaking Mel's heart, but it didn't happen.

Dani just texted, It's too bad. You're cool, and I liked you two to-gether.

Vivian wasn't sure how to respond.

That's not why I contacted you, though, Dani continued. I have a friend in Toronto, and she's living with her parents but it's really not a good situation, and I want to get her out of there. You were living with Ryan Kwok's wife before, right? Do you have a spare room? Some-where she could stay for a few months until she finds something per-manent? She does have some money saved and could pay you a little rent . . .

Vivian stared at her phone for a long time. The text had acti-vated the part of her that dreaded just being the useful one, and yet . . .

I know it's weird, Dani added. Me texting you out of the blue. I just want to do everything I can to help her. Mel thought it would be okay for me to ask, but if not, it wouldn't be the first time he's been wrong.

Vivian considered Dani's words. The last time she'd gotten a roommate, it had gone well. She'd been skeptical at first, but she'd become friends with Lindsay.

Okay, Vivian replied. Give her my number.

Thanks so much. Her name is Tamara.

Chapter 35

"The problem with being a comedian," Mel said, "is that people expect you to be funny."

It was a pretty big problem right now, to be honest. All he wanted to do was curl up in a corner and cry himself to sleep. Though, realistically, he wouldn't sleep at all. His sleep had been shit lately, and he couldn't talk to Vivian in the middle of the night.

"If you're an actuary, people don't expect you to talk about actuarial shit in your free time, right? In fact, they really, *really* don't want you to. And if you're a plumber, nobody wants you to talk about literal shit and sewage at a party. I mean, I hope not . . ."

But as he continued his set, he started to feel a bit lighter. He liked that he was still able to make people laugh, and he'd done these jokes countless times before. He knew them like the back of his hand.

Sometimes, all you had was laughter.

He was lucky; he had more than that. But he really missed Vivian, dammit. And being up here was more effort than usual.

Still, this was what he wanted to do with his life, his dream back when he'd worked at that horrid desk job that felt like it was stealing his soul. He was always working at perfecting his craft. Always trying to get better. Occasionally dreaming of bigger shows.

But he was *here*, in this moment.

He kept on talking. Doing his thing. Doing some silly act-outs.

Then he got to the part about a Viking, a Samurai, and Shakespeare walking into a bar. This was the point when he'd seen Vivian at his show in Toronto last year.

He could never keep her out of his mind for long.

"You know what else this scene needs?" he said. "A Chinese grandmother. A Chinese grandmother walks into the bar, with her thirty-five-year-old bisexual comedian grandson—no idea who that could possibly be, I just made him up—and she senses an opportunity . . ."

A chill went through him.

Oh dear God. Now that he was single again, would Po Po try her hand at matchmaking?

• • • • • • •

There was a knocking sound inside Mel's head, but it couldn't be due to a hangover—he'd only had one drink last night. It must be related to his shitty sleep. He closed his eyes again, but the knocking continued.

Wait a second . . .

He stumbled to his door and threw it open.

"Surprise," Joy said in a bored voice.

"Where's your enthusiasm?" Po Po asked. "Try pretending he's a beetle!"

This was a dire situation. His mother, grandmother, and little sister were at his apartment on a Saturday morning. He was so not in the mood for their shenanigans. Crawling into a corner and crying definitely sounded more appealing. Maybe he should order that giant Pokémon plushie he talked about in his set.

"We're worried about you," Mom said.

"Last weekend," Po Po said, "you didn't have proper enthusiasm when singing 'That Don't Impress Me Much.'"

He sighed. "It's my karaoke performance that has you worried?"

"Aiyah! It's not just about karaoke. You aren't yourself. I can tell." Po Po tapped her head. "So we came to surprise you and take you for dim sum."

Dim sum. That sounded good, actually. Suspiciously good.

There had to be a catch.

"Are there going to be speed dates?" Mel asked. "Or a pink limo?"

"I don't know," Po Po said. "You'll just have to wait and see."

"Ma," his mother said. "Stop it. He's not in the mood for such jokes."

Po Po clucked her tongue. "Fine, fine. I will stop. I liked Vivian, and she was going to introduce me to beavers and moose and Shania Twain—"

"Um," Mel said.

"—so I'm not ready for you to date someone else yet, either. Maybe in two days."

"Po Po!"

"I'm still teasing."

Mom looked at Joy. "Take your grandma downstairs. Mel and I will join you in a few minutes."

Once it was just the two of them, Mom stepped inside. She put her hands on Mel's shoulders and studied him with a seriousness that he found rather disturbing.

"I hear your father wants to apologize to you," she said. "Is that part of the reason you've been down?"

Mel shook his head. "No, it's because of . . ." He made a vague gesture because he couldn't seem to say her name.

"Vivian," Mom said softly.

"She was the one who ended it. I was trying to make it work."

Mom didn't say anything, just gave him a hug.

His father wasn't part of his life, but he did have one parent who'd always been there.

"I really thought I could do it. I . . ." He lost his ability to form words.

"I know," Mom said. Like she truly believed him.

"Could you please make sure Po Po doesn't resurrect her Twitter account and attempt more matchmaking in the next few months? I don't think I could bear it."

"I'll try my best."

"She can turn her attention to Joy," he said. "Or . . . You know, it's interesting she never tries to set you up with anyone."

"Well, she sure made an effort forty years ago."

"But not recently. You're single, aren't you?"

Mom hesitated. "No."

"You're just saying that because you don't want—"

"No, I'm really seeing someone."

"How long?" he asked.

"I don't owe you details."

"I'll try saying that next time I'm . . ." He trailed off. It was too hard to think of next time, when it had only been three weeks since Vivian had broken up with him.

"That's different," Mom said. "I'm your mother."

"So does Po Po know about your active love life?"

"No."

"You're sneaking around!"

"I wouldn't call it sneaking around. I'm sixty-three. It's just . . ."

"Lying by omission?" he supplied. "I mean, you live together, so you must be taking some pains to hide it from her if she doesn't know."

Mom glared at him, and he couldn't help laughing.

"I'll tell you more eventually," she said.

"I'll hold you to it."

They went downstairs together and headed out for dim sum.

Mel still felt far from okay. There was a heaviness in his chest that he couldn't escape, almost like multiple hippos were sitting on him. It was hard to breathe, and he was so damn tired. He'd never truly been heartbroken before, and man, it sucked.

But as he looked around at his family, at his mother and grandmother—who both kept trying to put food on his plate—and his little sister, something in him eased slightly.

Shitty things had happened before, and he'd made it through.

Somehow, he'd do it again.

But, dammit, he really wished Vivian were here with them. Maybe he'd accidentally drop some chicken feet on the floor and they could kiss under the table, or maybe he'd buy her a siu mai pillow.

All sorts of weird and random things were fun when they were with her.

• • • • • • •

Vivian wasn't sure what to expect. None of her siblings had visited her place before, but Stephen had texted a few days ago saying that he and Amanda wanted to visit on Sunday afternoon, and Vivian had agreed.

When Stephen and Amanda entered, Amanda placed a Japanese cheesecake box on the new table by the door. Stephen looked like his usual self, but Amanda appeared oddly solemn.

Vivian made some tea for the three of them, and they sat down in her kitchen. The last time she'd had anyone here was when Lindsay had stopped by two weeks ago.

This was strange. It wasn't the way things worked in her family. She couldn't help feeling nervous, but she didn't show it, of course. Wouldn't let those nerves get through her armor. She wished Mel were here to say something that would break the tension . . .

Vivian pushed that thought aside. She could think about him later.

At first, she'd done her best to avoid thinking about him, but after Lindsay's visit, she'd been letting him into her mind, just a little. Daring to hope for something different from what she'd had in the past.

But now wasn't the time for that.

"I'm sorry!" Amanda burst out suddenly.

It took a moment to process her sister's unexpected words.

I'm sorry. Vivian felt something unfurl in her chest, and then the horrible things she'd said to Amanda rushed back to her.

"No, I'm sorry for hurting you." Vivian hadn't apologized until now; she'd been too wrapped up in her breakup. "I said I couldn't think of you as my sister."

"But I get it now," Amanda said. "I was so little when you left for university. I didn't remember all that you had to do for us—but Stephen did. I agree it was super unfair." She glanced at their brother before turning back to Vivian. "I understand how you could be resentful of me."

Just hearing her sister acknowledge the past . . . Vivian appreciated it.

"Thank you." She swallowed. "You know, it's not really about *you.*"

"I know. It's about what Ma and Ba made you do, but I get how difficult it would be for you to have a normal sisterly relationship with me after that. That's all I wanted when I kept inviting you to go shopping with me, and when I wanted to move in with you, I was just thinking about how fun it could be."

Vivian raised an eyebrow. "You honestly thought it would be fun? Living with *me*?"

Amanda laughed. "You're the one who's dating a comedian."

"Actually, I'm not. Not right now."

"Oh. I'm sorry." Amanda's voice fell. "We can go out together and meet other men?"

No reason to restrict myself to men, Vivian nearly blurted it out. She wouldn't say that, though. Not today.

"Or we can go out to eat, just us!" Amanda said. "I'm not sure what you like, but I want to learn. I don't want you looking after me; I just want to actually get to know you. As adults. Don't worry, I won't ask to live with you again. I've found a place that I think will work out. Fingers crossed!" She started serving the cheesecake.

When Vivian exhaled, some of her resentment left her body. She could now imagine living with Amanda without it being like her childhood all over again, but it would still be best to hang out with Amanda without actually living together. Less pressure. And Tamara would be moving in next week.

"Yes. I'd like that." Vivian turned to Stephen. "Did you come to Toronto just for this?"

He nodded, chewing his cheesecake. "It wasn't fair that you were basically a third parent, but just so you know, you did a good job. You were very patient with me, and I appreciate it."

Amanda nodded her agreement.

Vivian lifted up a forkful of cheesecake, but then her phone rang. Someone else was downstairs, wanting to be buzzed in? Huh?

She answered. "Hello?"

"Vivian, it's your father. Can you let me in?"

She did, then turned to her siblings. "Did you invite him?"

They shook their heads.

"I promise," Amanda said, "I had nothing to do with this. Is it just him?"

"I'm not sure."

Amanda's question was answered a few minutes later when there was a knock on the door. It was just Ba, holding a hat in his hand, an unfamiliar expression on his face.

"Ah, Vivian," he said. "I am very sorry . . . about everything."

She hadn't thought she'd ever hear those words from either of her parents. Too stunned to speak, she remained silent.

Still standing in the hallway, her father continued, "Though it was hard for us, yes, we shouldn't have expected so much of you. It was always about saving money, but we should have spent a little more to ensure you had a childhood. You were right. It was unfair that it was all on you, never Andy."

Vivian was acutely aware of Andy's absence now. Had Amanda and Stephen talked to him about this? If so, how had he responded?

She shook her head and focused on her father. There was a look of anguish on Ba's face, one she'd never seen before. She leaned forward and gave him a tentative hug, which he returned.

"Would you like to come in?" she asked. "Amanda and Stephen are here. They brought cheesecake."

"Oh. They are here?"

Her siblings hadn't been lying. It was apparently a coincidence that everyone had shown up at the same time.

Amanda cut their father some cheesecake and made more tea.

"Where's Ma?" Vivian had considered saying nothing, but she couldn't seem to let it go.

"I don't know," Ba said. "We had . . . a fight."

Vivian's parents had fought on occasion when she was a child, but not often. Her father was the sort who went along with things rather than getting into arguments.

"About me?" She frowned, and a flicker of guilt crept up her spine. "What—"

"Don't worry about it," he said. "That's not your job. I'm sure it will be worked out."

She was used to everything being her job.

"Okay," she said. "I won't worry."

This was a lie. She wouldn't be able to help worrying a little.

Vivian was accustomed to uncomfortable silences with her family, but it felt different this time: the tension of an unfamiliar situation. She supposed that was something.

After they finished the cheesecake, Amanda wanted to see the rest of Vivian's place, so Vivian gave her family the tour, though it wasn't a very long tour.

"Are you getting a roommate?" Ba asked as he glanced in the second bedroom.

"Yes," Vivian said. "She's coming next weekend."

They moved on to Vivian's bedroom and then to the main living area.

"Oh my God!" Amanda exclaimed, holding up the *Only the Best* throw pillow. "Where did you get this?"

"Uh, Mel got it for me." Vivian had kept it in the closet for a couple of weeks, but she'd taken it out the other day because, well, she liked the pillow. The chicken drumstick pillow was still packed away, though, which was good—she didn't feel like explaining that to her father.

"I love this show." Amanda traced her finger over the horse. "Do you watch it?"

"Yeah," Vivian murmured, "on occasion."

Well, that was understating it.

Amanda grinned, as though particularly pleased they had something in common, and Vivian smiled. Yes, she believed they'd figure out how to rebuild their relationship. The next season of *Only the Best* was starting in a few months—maybe they could watch it together?

As she looked at Amanda now, she thought of the toddler Amanda had once been. So cute, but an unstoppable whirl of motion who'd constantly caused trouble for Vivian. She hated that she had so many memories of frustration when it came to Amanda, but things could be better one day. Though she still had work to do on dealing with her bitterness over her childhood, she could now see a way forward.

· · · · · · · ·

Once her family had left, Vivian felt wiped out. She wasn't used to having company. She lay back on her couch, put her hand on her forehead, and took a few deep breaths.

Usually, her life was fairly steady, but she supposed it had started changing when Lindsay moved in, more than two years ago now. More than anything, though, it had started with the bachelor and bachelorette parties. Or maybe karaoke . . .

Lindsay was right: Vivian's creativity, when it came to certain parts of her life, needed work. She hadn't dreamed that things would ever be any different with her family, but she'd been wrong. And a long-term relationship didn't have to be similar to her past experiences. Mel was completely unlike the other people she'd dated, after all.

When she'd said she didn't want another relationship, in truth she just hadn't wanted the same *type* of relationship again. She shouldn't have to settle for that.

And she wouldn't.

It had never been a one-way relationship. No, with Mel, it went both ways. She looked after him when he needed it, but the reverse was also true. When she'd been sick, for example, but he'd looked after her in other ways, too. He wanted to know her; he didn't only want to know what she could do for him.

Maybe that was easier to believe now, after what her siblings had said. But though she and Mel were very different, he'd shown her again and again that he understood her, going back to when he'd sung both their parts in "Summer Nights."

Yet she'd still believed that he might expect her to give up her life for him.

It wasn't so much because of their argument the first time they'd met, but because she wasn't able to see past her previous experiences, even as he gave her the perfect necklace and had silly, meaningful conversations with her in the middle of the night. Even as he treated her like no one else ever had.

During Lindsay's visit, Vivian had begun to wonder if she'd made a mistake, but now it was clear. She was in love, in a way she'd never been in love before. Those feelings had been too scary for her to admit earlier, but she wouldn't run from them going forward.

She blew out a breath. Now that she knew what she wanted, she had to take action. She hoped he hadn't changed his mind. She pulled out her phone and checked flights to New York then texted Dani: I need your help.

By the time everything was arranged, it was almost bedtime. Vivian took Mellie out of her closet and snuggled up with him. "Are you ready to go on a trip?"

Oh dear. Was she really speaking to a stuffed hedgehog? What would happen next? Would she talk to a giant chicken drumstick?

Well, she supposed she could live with that, if everything worked out.

Chapter 36

It had been a few weeks since Vivian had dumped him, and Mel still wasn't in a great mood. He wished his heart would hurry up and heal already.

He sipped his drink and looked at Mr. Chu, who was mixing a drink behind the bar. Mr. Chu was usually stone-faced, but he'd sent Mel concerned looks the last two times Mel had been here, which was unsettling.

Dani, who was sitting beside him, was also behaving in an unsettling manner. Her disposition was disturbingly cheerful, like she was hoping that by acting very happy, it would lift his mood.

Instead of listening to her, he glared at his drink.

He'd actually slept last night, but the night before had been a disaster. At two in the morning, he'd been obsessing over something that had happened in middle school—yep, that must be healthy—and an hour later, he'd been once again obsessing over every detail of his last morning with Vivian.

"Are you okay?" Dani asked.

"No," he sulked.

She kept on chattering as though she hadn't heard him, which was unlike her. He felt like everything was off-kilter and he was the only one who'd noticed.

And then he saw something outside the dingy windows that struck fear in his heart.

Now, normally Mel liked the color pink. The shirt he was wearing, for example, had an eye-popping pattern of pink and purple flowers. But just outside was a bright pink limo, and he'd had bad experiences with those.

He groaned. It appeared Mom had failed to stop Po Po's matchmaking efforts.

"Dani," he said, pointing out the window, "have you been talking to my grandma?"

"Ooh, your ride's here." She put some money on the bar. "Let's go."

"I'm not in the mood. I don't want more speed dates."

"There won't be any speed dates, I promise."

Maybe Dani was telling the truth, but there was probably some other dating-related nightmare awaiting him in the limo. He downed the rest of his drink and let Dani drag him outside. Although he didn't want to do this, he couldn't avoid it forever. Best to get it over with.

Dani opened the door and shoved him inside the limo, and Mel was still trying to figure out what was going on when it pulled away from the curb. He didn't see Po Po anywhere. Instead, he saw lots of balloons in a rainbow of colors.

"Hey."

He nearly jumped as someone slid next to him. It certainly wasn't whom he'd expected to see with a colorful array of balloons, but she was a most welcome sight.

Vivian Liao.

"Uh. Hey." He scratched the back of his neck. "You're here."

Wow, Captain Obvious. Real smooth.

But it was hard for him to say something intelligent in this situation.

Vivian was wearing a gray pantsuit, a light blue shirt underneath, and a necklace—the one he'd bought her.

His lips curved upward and hope surged through him. The fact that she'd shown up in a limo with lots of balloons should have been enough of a sign, but it was the necklace, more than anything else, that told him what was coming.

She took his hands in hers. "I'm really sorry, Mel. I'm sure the last few weeks were horrible, and you were probably awake at four in the morning with no one to talk to. It sounds arrogant to say that I know you missed me, but . . . I know you did. Because you showed me, over and over, how much you care for me. I didn't know what to do with that; I still expected our relationship to be like all the other ones I've had. But I was wrong. It was silly of me to think you'd demand sacrifice and give me nothing back. I just had no imagination."

He couldn't help chuckling, and her lips twitched—she'd been serious until now.

"So, this is me telling you," she said, "that I love you, and I want to figure out how to make this work for us."

Mel was filled with pure joy.

Words temporarily deserted him, so he simply pulled her close and melded his mouth with hers. It had been a month, and that wasn't unusual for them; they were accustomed to kisses after absences, but not after breakups. It felt so good and right to kiss her again, to sweep his tongue into her mouth, as he'd first done the night of Ryan and Lindsay's wedding.

He leaned back with a smile. "Is there a chocolate cake somewhere? Did you put aside your love of vanilla and get me a chocolate cake covered in ten colors of buttercream?"

It seemed like she was trying to hide her look of horror, but she failed, and he laughed.

"I do like how you tease me," she said.

"Mmm. I know." He was about to kiss her again, but then her phone started ringing.

"Shit. It's a video call, and I suspect she'll call again if I don't pick up." Vivian held her phone in front of them, her cheek pressed against his, and answered.

His grandmother's face appeared on the screen. "Hi, Mel. Did you enjoy your surprise?"

"You knew about this?" he asked.

"Who do you think had the hookup for the pink limo?"

"You're talking as though you know a cocaine dealer or—"

"Speaking of cocaine—"

"Po Po!"

"I hear pot gummies are nice. Your mother has them sometimes, but she refuses to share. How do I buy them? Is it legal? I can't remember."

"I'm ending this call right now." He hung up and turned to Vivian. "How did you get my mom's number?" His grandma didn't have her own smartphone, and she'd called—or, most likely, someone else had done that for her—from his mother's phone.

"Dani," Vivian said.

"Right. I gave her your number."

"Yeah, her friend Tamara is moving into my condo today, but I asked Lindsay to help get her settled, since I had somewhere else to be."

"Now you can tell Amanda that she can't move in because you already have a roommate."

"Actually, I had a talk with her and Stephen, and things are better now."

Happy to hear that, he squeezed her hand.

"About how to make this work between us," Vivian began.

He started kissing her again.

"Hey!" she said with a sternness that he loved. "We still have some things to talk about."

"I really missed you. Missed kissing you." He kissed her temple. "Missed touching you." He ran his hand up her thigh, and she made a strangled sound. "But you're right. We should talk."

She folded her hands in her lap, probably because it was an effort for her not to touch him, which made him grin.

"I think . . . the way things were," she said. "It worked for me. Is that weird? I liked having my own life, and the weekends we saw each other were special. I'm not looking to live with a partner in the near future—though maybe one day—and things might be complicated because we're citizens of different countries. But would it be possible for you to spend a little more time in Toronto? Like, during the week, on occasion. I've spoken to Tamara . . ."

"I'd like that. It's not possible in the next month, but after that, absolutely."

"Okay. I'm always open to discussing it and figuring out what's best for both of us. That's more than worth it, if I get to be with you. I know you won't ask me to change who I am. I trust that. I didn't before, but I should have, and I'm sorry."

He ran a hand through her hair. She'd gotten it cut since the last time he'd seen her. "It's okay. I'm glad you're here now."

The limo pulled to a stop outside a hotel.

"You ready to go inside?" she asked. "Or should we drive around a bit longer?"

"You got a hotel room?" In the last several minutes, he'd developed a new appreciation for pink limos, but a bed would certainly be welcome. He lifted her into his lap.

"Just for one night," she said. "Like our first night together. I thought . . ." She trailed off as he slipped his fingers under her shirt. "Dammit, Mel, I forgot what I was going to say!"

"That's okay. You can tell me later." He pressed a kiss to her neck, and she moaned and shifted in his lap.

If they were going to make it to that bed, they better go now.

Up in their room on the tenth floor, he hauled her against him as soon as the door shut behind them. There was no table just inside the door to set her on, which was perhaps a good thing. After kissing by the entrance for a while, they made good use of the king bed.

Very good use.

Then she rested her head on his chest, and he lazily trailed his hand up and down her body, content to lie here in bed and hold her for as long as she wanted. The first time he'd met Vivian, so long ago now, he'd certainly never imagined they'd end up like this.

Naked.

In love.

With a giant cake in the corner of the room.

How had he missed the cake? He started laughing.

"You finally noticed it," Vivian said mildly. "I suppose I should be flattered you were so distracted by me that you failed to see the cake."

He walked over to the cart containing the two-tiered cake. He'd been right: she'd gotten a cake with many different colors of buttercream, and her look of horror earlier must have been because he'd somehow guessed this surprise. The buttercream had been artfully swirled to make a profusion of flowers, and it honestly looked like one of his shirts.

But he still didn't know if it was chocolate inside, so he picked up the knife on the cart and cut a piece from the top tier, followed by a piece from the bottom tier.

The top tier was vanilla.

The bottom tier was chocolate.

He laughed again. "You didn't want all chocolate? Too much sophistication for you?"

"Ha." She walked over to him.

He fed her a forkful of the vanilla cake. She fed him a bite of the chocolate cake, and he made a show of tipping his head back and groaning in pleasure.

Her eyes darkened.

Next, he swiped his finger through one of the blue buttercream flowers and slowly licked the buttercream off his finger. "Mmm."

"All right," she said. "Enough with the sexy cake eating."

In response, he ran his finger through some pink buttercream and rubbed it on her collarbone, then licked it off *very* slowly.

"Mel . . ." she admonished, but she looked at him with such exquisite fondness that he nearly forgot to breathe.

He was about to take her back to bed when he noticed something delightful on the nearby armchair: a pink throw pillow with her face on it.

"It's for you," she said. "I remember you saying something like, 'You know you've really made it when you can find pillows with your face on them.' I may not be famous, but I feel like I have it made right now. And so you know, there are companies that make personalized pillows. If you also want one with your own face, maybe on a baby seal's body, that could be arranged."

"No, this is better. I'll be able to see your face first thing every morning." He pulled Vivian into his arms. He couldn't wait to spend more time with her, and he figured he'd start by kissing her senseless.

All in all, it was an excellent afternoon, which certainly wasn't what he'd expected when a pink limo had shown up in front of the bar.

But sometimes past experiences didn't prepare you for the future possibilities unless you used your imagination.

Epilogue

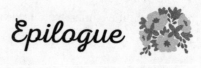

A YEAR LATER . . .

"I've achieved my ultimate goal in a relationship: synchronized insomnia." Mel held for laughs and looked out at the audience. "Yes, I'm serious, that was my ultimate goal! Someone who understands me?" He made a dismissive gesture. "Ha! That's child's play."

Well, he was exaggerating, but . . .

"At least I'm sleeping better these days—I can usually fall asleep in less than three hours. It's a big accomplishment, but let's be honest. It's thanks to drugs. Now, I'm not going to tell you whether those are my antidepressants or the sketchy gummies in an unsealed bag that my grandma got me."

The truth? It was the former.

"I used to have a big problem with envy in relationships. I'd keep dating people who'd fall asleep in less time than it takes Shania Twain to sing 'That Don't Impress Me Much,' and honestly, it did impress me. How the fuck could they fall asleep that quickly? Seriously, it's just not natural.

"Anyway, my girlfriend now, she's great." Yep, she really was. He'd once worried that he was incapable of having a relationship that lasted six months; he was happy to have been proven wrong.

It turned out he was well suited to long-term relationships—as long as he was with Vivian Liao.

"It usually takes her half an hour to fall asleep," he said into the microphone, "and that's respectable. It's not like I have to listen to her snoring the instant I turn out the light. And occasionally, it'll be three in the morning, and I'll be awake, either because I've been thinking of that time I farted in English class twenty years ago, or because I suddenly woke up from a bad dream about being eaten by ginormous redheaded cockchafers that escaped from my sister's lab. About half the time, my girlfriend will be awake, too, which I think is pretty remarkable. I'll text her if we're not in the same city, and we'll talk about stupid shit."

Like her terrible taste in cakes, but that was a detail Mel didn't say onstage. It was a detail just for them.

"Doesn't that sound awesome?" he said. "Having someone who will make you smile in the middle of the night, when you're an exhausted mess? I think it's even more awesome than my karaoke version of 'Summer Nights' from *Grease*." He paused. "I sing both parts, of course."

Before launching into his next bit about karaoke—which eventually led to a story about his grandmother—he glanced at the back corner of the club. It was hard to see with the bright lights, but he could just make out Vivian in her pinstripe suit.

Though he didn't say it out loud, he couldn't help thinking how very, very lucky he was.

• • • • • • •

Vivian buckled her seat belt before turning to the man sitting beside her.

"You know," Mel said, "this is the first flight we've been on together."

She tilted her head to the side. "Yeah, you're right."

She'd flown to meet him a bunch of times in the past year—both to New York and elsewhere—but she hadn't actually been on a plane with him before.

But last week, she'd flown out to Austin, Texas, at the end of his tour, and they'd had a mini-vacation. Now they were flying to Toronto, and he'd be staying with her for two weeks. Doing a couple of shows and trying to write some new material while she was at work.

It would be the longest they'd spent together, and the arrangement was working out well for her. She still enjoyed that every time she saw him, it was a big event, and they spoke and messaged each other every day when they were apart.

Tamara had moved in with her girlfriend last month, and Vivian wasn't planning to get a new roommate—Mel would stay with her more often and contribute to some of the expenses. But she'd liked living with Tamara, and they were good friends. Vivian had also become good friends with Shannon and Dani, who were getting married later this year and hoping to have kids soon.

When Vivian thought about the upcoming wedding, she couldn't help remembering Ryan and Lindsay's wedding and the subsequent snowstorm. That was how she and Mel had first hooked up, but now it was so much more than a hookup. Even though she'd been hesitant at first, she was very happy she'd taken a chance on him, and he'd helped her understand herself more than anyone else.

She no longer felt that people only wanted her because she was good at being responsible. They liked her for lots of reasons, and it wasn't just Mel who appreciated those reasons, though he was the most important person in her life. She'd also gotten to know her sister better in the past year, and they'd developed a bond that was very different from what it had been like in their childhood.

Sadly, things weren't as good with her mother or Andy, but at least Ma had stopped talking about Vivian having children one day.

"Hey," said a guy sitting across the aisle. "You're Melvin Lee, aren't you?"

"Yeah, man," Mel said, "that's me."

Mel talked to the stranger for a bit. Vivian admired how he could make people feel like they were friends within minutes.

She also felt honored that she got to know the other sides of him, beyond who he was onstage and how he interacted with the public. Like the side who'd give her cute presents and pamper her when she was sick. Fortunately, she hadn't had anything but a mild cold in the past year, and though he hadn't been visiting during it, he'd gotten soup delivered to her. She knew she could count on him when she needed him.

And he felt the same about her.

Perhaps they'd get married one day, but she didn't think about it much. She knew they'd stay together either way, and for now she was just enjoying her life as it was.

They watched the safety demonstration, and soon, they were speeding down the runway.

"Ready?" Mel asked, squeezing her hand.

"Ready." She smiled at him, ready for all the adventures they'd have together.

Acknowledgments

Writing a book (especially during a pandemic) involves lots of days alone in my apartment, sitting in front of the computer with mugs of tea and coffee and trying not to bang my head against the desk. But getting a book out into the world is far from a solitary activity.

I would like to thank:

My agent, Courtney Miller-Callihan.

My editor, Kristine Swartz, for all of her insights and helping me make this novel the very best that it could be. Thank you also to the rest of the team at Berkley, including Bridget, Daniela, Yazmine, and Mary. And Vi-An Nguyen for the incredible cover.

My fellow Berkley authors, Toronto Romance Writers, and all the author friends I've made over the years.

My husband, who has always been so incredibly supportive, and the rest of my family.

All of my readers. Sometimes, it's still hard to believe that I write books and people buy them. Thank you for making this possible.

Keep reading for an excerpt from Jackie Lau's

Donut Fall in Love

Available now!

When Ryan Kwok woke up on Tuesday morning, he discovered his abs had become a social media sensation.

It had started with a scathing review of his latest movie.

The best part of *That Kind of Wedding*? Ryan Kwok's abs. But the last thing Canada needs is another actor named Ryan.

It was his first leading role, and the critical response had been a bit of a mixed bag—okay, leaning toward negative—so this review wasn't exactly a surprise.

The review didn't appear in a major publication, but the author had started a thread on Twitter dedicated to his abs, cataloging their obvious beauty and many talents, complete with close-up shots from the trailer and his Instagram account. She appeared to be quite a fan of his abs, even if she liked nothing else about the rom-com.

And that thread? It had gone viral.

He'd had a spike in Instagram followers.

#StarringRyanKwoksAbs was trending.

People were discussing the roles his abs could play in movies, how they should appear in postapocalyptic and period pieces alike.

When he'd gone to bed at eleven last night, there hadn't been a whiff of this.

And now . . .

Well, he couldn't help but laugh.

"Good job, boys," he said, looking down at the body part that was now gaining international fame. If he was honest, they weren't quite as glorious as they'd been when *That Kind of Wedding* was filmed. In the past four months, he'd been following his diet and workout routine . . . mostly. But the past four months had been the worst of his life.

At least now the promotional tour was over. He'd struggled to fake a smile for late-night talk show hosts, given what was happening in his family and—

Oh, dear God.

Ryan's dad was going to see this, dammit.

Once upon a time, he'd assumed his father didn't pay attention. But a year ago, he'd caught his father looking at his Twitter account.

That was quite a shock, considering his father was anti-Twitter and all social media. In fact, Dad was anti a lot of things. He was also anti-stoner-movies, as Ryan had learned when he'd filmed *The Journey of the Baked Alaska*, though this hadn't surprised him one bit. And anti-sitcoms, which Ryan had known his whole life.

This hadn't changed when Ryan got his first break in *Just Another New York Sitcom* several years back.

Speaking of *Just Another New York Sitcom* . . .

He had a text from Melvin, one of his co-stars on the show.

Please convey my congratulations to your abs.

· · · · · · ·

Lindsay McLeod wasn't used to seeing abs in her Instagram feed. Mostly she saw pictures of Toronto. And food. Lots of food.

She gave the photo a few seconds of attention and idly wondered if the man in question would ever eat anything as delicious as her chocolate espresso donuts, or whether such indulgences were strictly off-limits for this Ryan Kwok guy.

Then she uploaded a photo of her latest creation.

New donut alert! Here for spring: matcha tiramisu donuts

A couple of hours later, Lindsay was piping buttercream onto some chocolate raspberry cupcakes when Raquel came into the kitchen.

"Your mother's here," Raquel said, gesturing to the front of the bakery.

Excellent timing for once.

Ever since Lindsay's mom had moved downtown five months ago, she'd been popping into Kensington Bake Shop—the bakery Lindsay ran with her best friend, Noreen—on a semi-regular basis, and she had an uncanny ability to arrive at the worst possible moments. Last time, it had been literally a minute after Noreen had spilled cherry jelly on the floor, on a day when they were running way behind because of a malfunctioning oven.

But today, even though Noreen was away on her honeymoon, everything was in order, more or less. Lindsay could spare five minutes to talk to her mother.

"Oh, I should probably mention," Raquel said. "Your mother's not alone."

Yes, sometimes Lindsay's mom brought one of her friends into the bakery. She was always bragging about Lindsay's donuts, cupcakes, and other creations, and she wanted to show them off to everyone she knew. Sometimes it was a little embarrassing, but it was all good.

"In fact," Raquel continued, "I'm pretty sure she's on a date."

Say what now?

Lindsay washed her hands, then headed to the front. As always, the simple elegance of the shop made her smile. She and Noreen had argued for ages over paint chips; Noreen had eventually won, and Lindsay had to agree her friend had been right. The light blue was perfect. On the walls were two watercolors: one of donuts and one of cupcakes. There were only four tables—all cream in color—with small glass vases, each containing a single flower. Space was expensive in downtown Toronto.

Lindsay's mom wasn't seated at one of the tables. No, her Asian mother and an unfamiliar middle-aged white man were peering at the display cases.

The appearance of the man gave Lindsay pause.

He looked, well, a bit like her dad.

Not enough that she thought she'd seen a ghost, but it was a little eerie. Though his build was similar, it was his haircut more than anything else. That terrible haircut her father had gotten every six weeks at the local barber?

She'd never thought she'd see it again, but here it was.

Oh, Mom.

"The orange cardamom is my favorite," Mom said to her companion. She pointed at the display case to the left of the cash register, which contained today's eight varieties of donuts. "The filling is custard with a hint of cardamom, and the orange cardamom glaze is delicious. And that candied slice of orange? Mmm."

"Hi, Mom," Lindsay said. "Maybe you should work here. Your sales pitches are great."

"Lindsay, this is Wade. Wade, this is my daughter, Lindsay."

Lindsay would have stuck out her hand, but she was behind the glass display case, and it would have been awkward.

"Hi," she said. "Nice to meet you."

"You're giving me a weird look," Mom said.

"No, I'm not."

"Wade and I just had our first date at that Italian restaurant on Baldwin, and since we were in the area . . ."

Bringing a man to meet your daughter on your very first date seemed a little much. Especially when the daughter in question had no idea you were dating.

In theory, Lindsay was fine with her mother going on dates— yes, this was something she'd thought about before. Her father had been gone for seven years. Her mother had an active social life, and it was surprising this hadn't happened sooner.

But theory was different from practice.

Now that Lindsay was confronted—unexpectedly, at that— with a man her mother was seeing, a man who was not her father, she was digging her fingernails into her hands so hard they'd surely leave marks. And her mother was acting as though this was all no big deal.

"The chocolate espresso is really good, too," Mom said to Wade. "It's filled with a chocolate espresso custard—I think they should include the filling on the labels, don't you think? Because you can't see it. So they should tell people. I do recommend getting a donut, and not something else, because that's their *thing*." She glanced at the cupcakes, cookies, and squares to the right of the cash register before turning back to the donuts. "Lindsay, the matcha tiramisu—is that new?"

"Yes, today is the first day we're selling it."

"And the filling?"

"Matcha mascarpone cream."

Mom turned back to her date, who looked overwhelmed by the

choices. "And I suggest getting a donut with a filling. The others aren't as exciting, aside from the one with cream cheese frosting, but they don't have it today."

Her mom was talking too much, which meant she was nervous. Lindsay managed a small smile.

Eventually, poor Wade decided on the orange cardamom and Mom decided to try the matcha tiramisu. Lindsay left them alone with their donuts and coffee as she headed to the back to finish those chocolate raspberry cupcakes, but the perfect swirls of pink buttercream, garnished with chocolate shavings and raspberries, didn't lift her spirits. Nor did the aroma of fresh donuts—Beth was taking some out of the deep fryer now.

Lindsay's mother was dating. Her best friend was now married after a whirlwind romance. Of course she didn't object to either of those, but she didn't want things to change quite so much so quickly.

Another thing that had changed recently: Lindsay's living situation. She and Noreen used to live in a cramped apartment within walking distance of Kensington Market. It had been chosen for its proximity to the bakery more than anything else, and they'd lived there together for nearly four years.

But now Noreen lived with her husband—or she would, once she got back from India—and Lindsay had moved into a building near Wellesley, with a roommate she didn't know at all.

At first she'd looked for a place to live by herself, but vacancies were low and prices were high in Toronto, so she'd started considering alternatives. This woman, Vivian Liao, was about her age. She owned a two-bedroom condo and was looking for a roommate.

Lindsay found the situation a little puzzling. Someone her age owning a *two*-bedroom condo in downtown Toronto? This woman must be making very good money at her job in finance.

Except she was renting out the second bedroom . . . so why hadn't she bought a one-bedroom place instead?

It clearly wasn't because Vivian wanted the companionship of a roommate. Vivian had been polite but not super friendly when Lindsay had toured the suite. Lindsay had figured that would change once she moved in, but no. Vivian wasn't a terrible roommate . . . she was just a little distant and kept to herself, and she often seemed to be busy.

Which was fine. And it was Vivian's place.

But Lindsay had hoped to be friends with her new roommate, though she supposed things didn't always work that way. She was just used to living with her best friend, and the idea that a living situation could be like this—well, it had never occurred to her.

And now that her best friend was out of the country for a month, she could use a friend. Someone to tell, however briefly, about the day's events. *My mom showed up at the bakery today with a date. Who looked disconcertingly like my father.*

Lindsay didn't need a deep talk about her feelings. She could have just half laughed about it with someone, you know?

Except Vivian didn't know much about her. They'd had a short conversation about their careers, but that was about all. Vivian didn't know anything about Lindsay's family.

When Lindsay got home that day—though the place didn't quite feel like home yet—Vivian popped out of her room, still immaculately dressed in one of the pantsuits she always wore to work, and said, "I'm heading out soon to run errands. Just wanted you to know you have mail." She nodded at the small table by the entrance.

Huh. Lindsay had yet to receive mail at this address.

It was a wedding invitation—one of her friends from university was getting married to her longtime boyfriend—and had been forwarded from her old apartment, the place that still felt like home to her. That old apartment had been furnished with IKEA furniture, including a wobbly coffee table they hadn't assembled properly and a large assortment of clashing throw pillows. The new apartment felt more grown-up, but nowhere near as cozy.

Lindsay brought the invitation into her room, then went to the kitchen and made herself a Havarti grilled cheese sandwich for dinner, as she'd done so many times before, in all the many places she'd lived. It had been her father's favorite.

As she thought of everything that had happened recently, everything that had changed, she couldn't help feeling like she was being left behind.

Photo by J. Mitchell

Jackie Lau decided she wanted to be a writer when she was in grade two, sometime between penning "The Heart That Got Lost" and "The Land of Shapes." She later studied engineering and worked as a geophysicist before turning to writing romance novels. She is now the author of over a dozen romantic comedies.

Jackie lives in Toronto with her husband, and despite living in Canada her whole life, she hates winter. When she's not writing, she enjoys gelato, gourmet donuts, cooking, hiking, and reading on the balcony when it's raining.

CONNECT ONLINE

JackieLauBooks.com
🐦 JackieLauBooks
📷 JackieLauBooks

Ready to find
your next great read?

Let us help.

Visit prh.com/nextread

Penguin
Random
House